G000154090

Kathryn Adams

Winter Wolves
in Grondère

An Alpine tale of peaks and predators

This is a work of fiction. Any resemblance of the characters in this publication to real persons, living or dead, other than those clearly in the public domain or who have specifically given their consent, is entirely coincidental.

Grondère is a fictional place and all the people, places and events mentioned in this publication relating thereto are also entirely fictional. Where inspiration has been drawn from real life, the author has, for the purposes of her story, twisted, fabricated, stretched and distorted to such an extent that no one should find in its description, anything close enough to the truth to offend them.

THE GRONDÈRE SERIES SO FAR
Death in Grondère
Summer Shadows in Grondère
Winter Wolves in Grondère

You can follow the Grondère series on
www.facebook.com/grondere/

Ski4All Wales is a genuine charity and you are warmly encouraged to get to know it better on www.ski4allwales.cymru and www.facebook.com/ski4allwales.

All rights reserved.
No part of this publication may be reproduced in any form without the specific permission of the publisher.

The moral right of the author has been asserted.
© Kathryn Adams 2021

Cover design: Kirstie Swinnerton

Thank yous

My thanks once again to Bethan Drinkall and the team at Ski4All Wales for allowing me to use their real names. Thank you to Lindsay Reuss for continuing to let me pillage her character to bring you Poppy, to Lee Hammond (and Jack) for inspiring the character(s) of Johnny (and Louie), to Tommy for inspiring the character of Tommy and to Chris Jones for kindly agreeing to let me do what I want with him and call him Humphrey.

I newly extend my thanks to Suzie Vaill for appearing as herself, to Jean-Marc Farquet, my local expert who appears here as a nature warden and mountain guide and would like me to point out that I promoted him without authorisation.

My gratitude also to Marcus Bratter, who continues to allow me to use him as the inspiration for Malcolm McDonaghue and his son Sebastian. Marcus's monthly articles on wine can be found in Verbier Life Magazine. www.verbierlife.com

Daniel Yeomans is a talented painter based in Switzerland and currently producing stunning landscapes and portraits of this beautiful country and the people who live here. He has also kindly agreed to appear as himself in this story. https://danieljamesyeomans.com

Whilst these wonderful people provided a starting point for my characters, no one should mistake the originals for the creations they inspired: once let loose on the page my characters tend to do their own thing

Character List

In rough alphabetical order according to first name or title.

Alain Dupertuis, Capitaine in the *Police judiciaire* responsible for murder investigations. Lucy Wilson's boyfriend.

Alessandra Rosset, Ruthless and ambitious head of the White Snowflake consortium.

Anne Dupertuis, Mother of Alain Dupertuis and ace curtain-twitcher.

Anya, Manager of La Grande Cour hotel.

Bethan Drinkall, Appears as herself, Chair of Ski4All Wales.

Carla Sturridge, Mother of Sebastian, currently in Swiss prison.

Charles Sidforth-Sykes, A bit of an old buffer.

Christophe Brouchoud, Farmer / Tommy's business partner.

Daniel Yeomans, Swiss-based British portrait and landscape artist.

Danny Morend, Ski god who died in an avalanche in *Death in Grondère.*

David Drinkall, Appears as himself, Ski4All Wales stalwart.

Eddie Johnson, Lucy's housemate, Émilie's boyfriend.

Émilie Morend, World Cup skier, Eddie's girlfriend, Danny's sister.

Genna Hobbs-Davison, Disappeared in mountain accident in 1970s.

Genna McDonaghue, Sister of Sebastian McDonaghue.

Gluey Hughey, Renowned gatecrasher with wood-carving talent.

Herr Schmutz, Bern detective.

Humphrey Watson, Grondère old-timer and mischief maker.

Jacques Aulnay, (Maître) Sebastian's lawyer and Anne Dupertuis' partner.

Jamie Corcoran, Gourmet chef, friend of Lucy.

Jean-Marc Farquet, Appears as himself, Verbier and Glacier Patrol legend. Also auxiliary nature warden.

Jemima Watson, Humphrey's cousin.

Jilly Ferguson, Detective Inspector with Scotland Yard, Blonnay's girlfriend.

Jo Inkin, Appears as herself, Ski4All Wales co-founder.

Jodie Scott, Lucy's ski buddy and Grondère's singing nightingale.

Johnny, Grondère's favourite ski bum. Has a famous dog called Louie.

Laeticia Braythwaite, British social climbing fraudster.

Lara Stanley, Businesswoman. Founder of the Grondère Diamond Ski Club.

Laurent Blonnay, (Inspecteur chef adjoint) Word and murder investigator (in that order).

Leo Onion, Tonita's half-brother, Ruby's brother.

Lina Lewandowska, Best friend of Maria Kowalski. Raclette entrepreneur.

Lionel Sturridge, Diamond Ski Club member, Carla's second ex-husband.

Louie, Johnny's famous Jack Russell with exceptional sniffing skills.

Lucy Wilson, Ski instructor / mid-mountain guide-in-training and trouble-magnet.

M. le Procureur, Head of Swiss investigation team.

Malcolm McDonaghue, Deceased father of Sebastian, Carla's first ex-husband.

Maria Kowalski, Former chambermaid at La Grande Cour.

Mia Martin, Appears as herself, Ski4All Wales instructor.

Milly Stanford, (parents Rupert and Caroline) New seasonnaire, ski instructor.

Poppy Smythe, Ski instructor and botanist known for her forthright opinions.

Prince Anwar, Friend of Sebastian and Tonita, witness to the murder in *Death in Grondère.*

Rory Gordon, Diamond Ski Club leader.

Ruby Onion, Tonita's half-sister, Leo's sister.

Rusty (Jordan) Russell, Bar and hotel owner.

Sally Collins, Co-manager of Le Cerf sous la Lune vineyard, Lucy's best friend and ski buddy. Dating Tommy Pike.

Sammy Vine, Local bar manager and entrepreneur.

Sandra Guérin, Co-manager of Le Cerf sous la Lune vineyard, winegrower and winemaker.

Sebastian McDonaghue, Viscount Lunstag, Lord Shilton, Owner of La Grande Cour hotel, Le Cerf sous la Lune vineyard and fiancé of Tonita Shalott.

Suzie Vaill, Real-life superwoman but for this book appears as a Diamond Ski Club leader.

Sylvie Jacquier, (Inspectrice) Murder investigator with firepower.

Tommy Pike, West Country lad with good heart. Lucy's housemate and friend. Dating Sally, works in ski shop but going into farming.

Tonita Shalott, Jewellery designer engaged to Sebastian, Lord Shilton.

Dedication

There are people who enter your life and who, despite your character defects, your worst errors of friendship and physical separation, will not shift. This book is dedicated to the 'ever fixed marks' of my life who have looked 'unshaken' on all my 'tempests' since our college days.

To Nicky Christie and Sarah Francis-Clarke.

Glossary

Some words or terms I leave in their original language because it reflects local usage. You will find a handy glossary of these terms at the back of the book.

Prologue

One beast and only one howls in the woods by night.
Angela Carter, *The Company of Wolves*

The sound was unmistakeable. Lucy shuddered. It could not be anything else: the howl of a wolf was not something she'd ever thought she would hear in Grondère. Sitting on the balcony, drinking her morning cup of tea and watching daybreak, she held her breath and listened attentively; the eerie sound came again, this time from further away. It seemed sad and lonely as if the creature were calling for company. Her housemates were still sleeping and she didn't want to wake them: she sat in complete quiet and stillness. After the initial shock, she wondered how she felt about sharing the forest and mountains that she loved with this returning predator. She was so used to hiking alone: would this prevent her from roaming the surrounding hills with the same sense of freedom?

Lucy knew there would also be concern among the farming community whose herds grazed in the mountain pastures over the summer. In other areas in Switzerland where wolves had returned there had been attacks on livestock and, inevitably, unauthorised shootings of wolves. She wondered how Tommy, her housemate, would feel about it. In the summer, his Herens cows and their calves would be up in the very hills from where the wolf had called. She did not hear it again but the sound had filled her with a deep swelling of nostalgia: it was as if the wolf call heralded the changes that were to come at the end of winter.

One

*And this winter, once again, I will climb up to the high
mountain ridges to meet my love, powder snow, and
continue the dance.*
Dolores LaChapelle, Deep Powder Snow

Lucy Wilson lived in the ski resort of Grondère in the
Swiss Alps where, in order to be in the mountains she
loved, she worked as a ski instructor in winter and was
training to become a mid-mountain guide in summer.

She was a pretty, young woman in her late twenties with
long, dark auburn hair, a sweet, heart-shaped face and
bright green eyes that missed nothing and delighted in
every small detail of the natural world around her. She was
of athletic type and was happiest outdoors in all weathers,
skiing in winter and hiking in summer with a penchant for
wild swimming in mountain lakes and rivers. She also
possessed the kindest and most gullible heart in Grondère
which is possibly why she seemed to attract attention, and
occasionally, unwanted attention.

Lucy shared a small, old chalet set on the heights above
the ski resort with Eddie, Tommy and Sally, Tommy's
girlfriend. The chalet was a bit remote and a long uphill
trek from the main part of the resort but it was still
accessible for their places of work in the centre. When the
ground was deep with snow the hike home became even
more challenging but this somehow made it all the more
worthwhile on finally reaching its cheery warmth.

Tommy and Eddie had lived in the chalet for five years
now; this was to be Lucy's second winter season sharing
with them and Sally's first but, for all of them, it was their
last season in the rickety wooden home they had grown to
love. Their time sharing a home together was drawing to a
close: they had been given notice by their landlord that the

chalet and all the surrounding land and adjoining properties had been purchased by the White Snowflake consortium which would be ripping the whole lot down to put up luxury chalets for wealthy investors.

It wasn't pleasant being forced out but the timing was right – their little group was beginning to disperse anyway. The following spring, Tommy and Sally would be moving down to the valley permanently: Tommy was entering into a farming partnership with his friend Christophe Brouchoud and Sally had recently obtained a full-time job running a vineyard. The young couple was having one final season in Grondère to enjoy the skiing before settling into their new home and new careers. When spring came, Eddie and Lucy would also have to move out and find alternative lodgings.

But it wasn't so much leaving the chalet Lucy minded: it was the change it represented. The look and feel of the little hamlet known as Le Hameau de la Colline would be lost forever. Lucy loved this secluded, low-key spot on the periphery of one of the busiest resorts in the Alps. It was essentially a collection of small wooden chalets built in the sixties, scattered randomly over the hillside, separated by large meadow gardens. As the centre of Grondère had grown over the previous fifty years and transformed into a busy hub with smart modern chalets, large apartment blocks, shops and businesses all crammed together, the hamlet had remained untouched and to her mind, unspoiled. In winter it was a secluded little world where, apart from the rare visit from a snowplough, the only sounds were provided by the elements; in summer it became a buzzing hub for bees, other wildlife and wild flowers. Hikers and bikers passed by, but the lack of passing space on the road and absence of parking places meant that the only cars that ventured up were those of the residents. Lucy loved her mountain home.

As she sat there, her melancholy thoughts, brought on by the sad howling of the wolf, also reminded her of the day the ill-fated Malcolm McDonaghue had given her a lift home in a snowstorm. He had commented on how he loved the area and told her that it reminded him of how all of Grondère had been when he first arrived in the seventies, just small chalets surrounded by fields. How ironic, she thought, that it should be a consortium he had founded that was now about to tear down one of the few remaining bastions of the old days.

But Malcolm himself was no longer around to see the Colline disappear: he had been murdered shortly after having told Lucy of his affection for the area. Malcolm's shares in the White Snowflake consortium were now in the hands of his former fiancée and Lucy's friend, Tonita Shalott. However, Lucy knew there was no point in telling Tonita how she felt: Lucy had her pride and she also knew that Tonita was no sentimentalist when it came to business. Anyway, despite being the majority shareholder in the consortium, Tonita was pretty much a sleeping partner. The White Snowflake group was now being run very competently but ruthlessly by the Swiss property magnate, Alessandra Rosset. White Snowflake already had one ongoing major development – a large modern complex was gradually taking shape on the site of the old school holiday camp site, with smart shops and apartments. The locals were looking forward to it providing lots of seasonal and permanent jobs: Tommy and Eddie had already spent the summer labouring on its foundations and laying utility pipes. The Colline would be the consortium's second project and Lucy dreaded seeing the bulldozers arrive to rip out the soul of the place.

She sighed: there was no point in dwelling on things she couldn't change. At least in summer she could move into her boyfriend Alain's chalet, which was even higher up the

4

mountain. The property speculators would never make it up that high. It was just a shame that it was too high to live in over winter.

The door opened and Tommy came out onto the balcony, bringing her, as he often did, her second cup of tea and joining her for a moment's peace there before the others awoke.

'Saturday! Big day,' he grinned.

'Big day,' she smiled back and his rosy cheeks and wide grin immediately cheered her up. His unruly brown hair fell over his eyes and he pushed it back, blinking at the bright sunlight now reflecting on the mountains all around them. Lucy decided not to mention the wolf yet; she didn't want to shift attention away from their special day.

'We'll have to wake the others soon, we have to be at the heliport by 8 o'clock,' she said, gratefully clasping the steaming mug of tea. She had been so lost in thought she hadn't realised how cold her hands were.

'Give them a little longer: once Sally's awake it'll be noisy. She was already raucous enough laying out all her kit last night.'

'I know what you mean,' Lucy smiled back. Sally's Australian ebullience would know no bounds on that particular Saturday. Lucy was so happy her best friend Sally had found love with her adored housemate, Tommy, but since Sally had moved into the chalet it could not be denied that the noise levels had gone up considerably.

It was mid-December and, thanks to heavy and steady snowfall throughout November and constant low temperatures, the ski season was already underway. The resort wasn't yet full of visitors but all the seasonnaires were there, ready to welcome the holidaymakers for the first peak in the season, Christmas and New Year. The fields around the chalet were covered with untouched snow, apart from a few tracks left by Lucy and her housemates where they had skied down to the resort.

'Just look at that view.'

Lucy looked across to the Massif du Cortey on the opposite side of the valley, dominated by the huge white mountain, le Grand Cortey and its glacier. The Grand Cortey and its surrounding smaller satellite peaks formed the daily backdrop to their view of Grondère. Too perilous for construction, it was free of any man-made structures and was the preserve of the heli-skier and the mountaineer. Every day it looked different to Lucy: it seemed to change shape and colour depending on the weather and the colours of the season. That morning it was completely covered in white: its frosted sheer cliffs and massive snowfields glowed under the bright morning sun. It looked ethereal but tinges of blue ice at the edges and on the ridges of the glacier, hinted at the mortal danger it held.

'Can you believe we're actually going there? Today?'

'No: for all the years I've lived here and looked across the other side of the valley, I can't believe I'm finally getting to go there.'

Tommy looked around nostalgically.

'I will so miss this place.'

'Me too, I was just thinking the same thing. At least you and Sally won't be here to see it all ripped down.'

'No, I'm glad about that.'

'I know, it's ridiculous to be emotionally attached to an old wooden shack.'

'No, it's not. I feel the same way, I have had such happy times here. But where we're moving to is beautiful too, in a different way. It's full of character and charm and surrounded by nature, just like this place, but on the valley floor.'

'I may become a regular visitor.'

'I hope you will.'

They sat in comfortable silence until loud and cheerful noises from inside told them that Sally was up: their peaceful start to the day was over. They grinned at one another and moved inside. Life was never dull with Sally around.

The helicopter rotor blades spun noisily and blew hard grains of snow into their faces as the friends scrambled aboard. Lucy was determined to enjoy the experience to the full this time, in contrast with her previous helicopter trips when, on both occasions, she had been fleeing for her life. This trip was purely for pleasure and promised the joy of skiing untracked powder far away from the busy slopes of the ski resort. It had snowed heavily two days earlier and Alain had reserved the date as soon as they had seen the forecast.

This heli-ski experience was the fulfilment of a promise Alain had made to Lucy when she had been evacuated to the top of the Lesteraarhorn in the Bernese Alps after having unwittingly witnessed a murder and been identified and stalked by its instigator – a promise to take her and all her friends on a heli-ski trip.

And so this time the mood was very different, Lucy had almost all of her dearest friends with her, Poppy, Tommy, Sally, Eddie, Émilie, Johnny and, of course, Alain. The only one missing was Jodie, her other ski buddy: Jodie was now studying voice in Lausanne and was singing in a concert that evening so had been unable to join them. With the guide, that made for a party of nine.

The helicopter only had room for half the party and so Alain, Lucy, Poppy and the guide were dropped off first on the flat top of the Petit Cortey. As they waited for the others, they had ample time for scoping the view. All around them, as far as the eye could see, rose dark, pointed peaks with the Grand Cortey standing central, like a giant meringue.

There was no sign of human intervention, no man-made structures and no sound except the wind.

'I feel very small,' Lucy said.

'Yes,' Poppy agreed. 'It's very different to the Lesteraarhorn. There the rocks were more exposed, and we were perched on top of it all, looking down on a 360° panorama of mountain peaks: it made you feel rather grand. Here we're embedded right in the centre of a giant white duvet like tiny bed bugs.'

They may have been used to admiring the Petit Cortey from Grondère, but though it was part of their everyday scenery, it was very different close up. What seemed like smooth surfaces from a distance were full of wind lips, curves, trenches, gullies and huge blocks of ice. The ice blocks, when seen close up, had thousands of layers of snow and ice, collected over decades, centuries even, and each layer was a different shade of white, grey or blue. It was amazing to see how so limited a colour palate could have so many variations.

'I see why we need a guide,' Lucy said. 'I could easily get lost amongst all this whiteness.'

Directly beneath them, jutting out from neatly windswept skirts of snow, dark jagged rocks framed long steep inclines with large flat expanses of fresh powder below. There was not a sign of a single crevasse, but they knew they were there.

For a quarter of an hour they admired the view and Poppy took countless photos. Alain fitted Lucy with a harness and camera on her chest so she could record the whole descent. The distinctive throbbing of helicopter rotors came closer and Poppy took shots from all angles as the second group landed and unloaded. They all gathered their kit, ducked to the ground and waited for the helicopter to take off again before giving their full attention to the guide's briefing. Lucy was thrilled but she was also nervous: she knew she was the weakest powder skier. It was also the first time she had ever skied with her boyfriend Alain and he, being Swiss, had skied since his earliest childhood.

Just my luck, she thought, the first time we ski together and he's going to see me in my least flattering discipline.

Lucy worked as a ski instructor during the winter but she was restricted to teaching beginners and intermediates on the slopes, she was not qualified to take clients off-piste. Alain was also nervous, he desperately wanted Lucy to be a good enough skier to make him want to ski with her when they got the chance, although how often that would be, with her working as a ski teacher and him as a detective with the *Police judiciaire* for the canton of Valais, he did not know.

The party did a final check of their avalanche detectors and then one by one set off down a gentle incline behind the guide, following at safe intervals and keeping within the areas he had indicated. As they set off, there were high fives and great whoops of joy: Alain saw that his gift was truly appreciated. Of his guests that day, Eddie and Émilie had been heli-skiing a few times, Poppy twice but quite a while back, but Johnny in his late sixties had thought this was an experience that had passed him by and so was demonstrably excited. As she bounced gently through the light powder Lucy forgot all her nervousness: it was heavenly. The powder was so light it flew into the air in front of her and sparkled in the sun's rays, forming mini rainbows. Alain watched on with pleasure as he saw that Lucy was a very neat little skier: she just lacked a bit of confidence in the powder but that would come with experience. The others flew down with a gusto and flair that defied the knowledge that they had not grown up in the mountains like Émilie, Alain and the guide.

The initial descent was a short one: after that they had a short traverse before skinning up a steep incline which gave them plenty of opportunities to practise the tricky direction-change technique of conversions. As the final part of the ascent became too steep they removed their skis, attached them to their backpacks and bootpacked up the final 50 metres. As they stomped through the deep snow, making sure of a good foothold with each step, Lucy admired how Poppy was making light work of it. Not many women of 70 could manage that. Most difficult was the last section: the wind-exposed ridge was bare of snow and the rocks and compacted ice made it difficult to get a foothold in ski boots. Without any attempt at elegance they all eventually scrambled up and were rewarded with breathtaking views of a pristine white snowfield below them.

'From here, it's 2,000 metres of pure downhill,' the guide told them. They looked at one another with huge grins. It was paradise for skiers and they felt very privileged to be there. There was a sense of nervous anticipation. Lucy had never seen such a wide expanse of untouched snow.

The first section of the slope was steep and, as they each set off, they kept a good distance apart with the guide leading the way. They made their own tracks but were careful to stay within the markers he had pointed out.

Playing the role of backmarker as he had promised the guide, Alain held back: it gave him a chance to observe the others and he was amused to see how each person's skiing style reflected their personality. Tommy skied with strength and confidence but his sense of fun and humour showed in his rocking movement. Johnny, an old ski bum who had learnt to ski powder when skis were long and thin, glided effortlessly on his wooden, handcrafted powder skis, but with a little bit of a swagger. Poppy's sense of determination and justice shone through her direct, strong attacking turns. Sally seemed to bounce deeper into the snow than anyone else; Alain could see she was doing it deliberately to immerse herself in the white element. This, he thought, was illustrative of her love of the finer things in life, such as wine. Eddie, probably the best skier of all the non-Swiss, still revealed the timidity that was a part of this gentle soul. He was so light on his skis, he seemed to ski over the powder, hardly touching it. Émilie, he noticed, not without a certain amount of patriotic pride, had raced down to the meeting point without him having a chance to watch her, but then, as she was part of the Swiss downhill racing team, he would not have expected anything less of her.

Alain waited until they had all collected together at the bottom of the first run before launching into his own effortless descent, not concerned in the least that they would all be analysing his technique and style as he had theirs. Lucy watched with pride as he put together elegant and seamless curves and left tidy, uniform tracks as you would expect of a Swiss policeman.

It was a huge wilderness and Lucy could feel the power of the silence – loud with emptiness. The guide led them through large gullies, and across vast expanses of untouched snow, stopping at reasonable intervals so that everyone could catch up and no one lost sight of the group. They repeated the process all the way down the mountain, always regrouping in line with alterations in the topography where it was natural for the skiers to change rhythm and speed. One section was a flat glacier and they were told to pick up speed and not take too many turns. Lucy had never skied so fast and in such a long straight line but she trusted the guide and let herself go. The snow was so soft and deep that she wondered if she would be able to stop without falling, but the slope began to rise slightly and she found she had just enough speed to make it onto the crest before coming to a natural halt.

'That was glorious,' she beamed.

'Pure joy!' Sally agreed, trying to push her blond locks back under her helmet. They had a habit of escaping her plaits when she was skiing.

Where they had halted they were in a wide gorge, surrounded by sheer, dark cliffs and their voices seemed to echo. The next section was steep and, having been protected from the wind, the powder was deeper. It was a chance to bounce down in beautiful little curves and trace patterns in the virgin snow. Tommy and Sally set off together and criss-crossed all the way down, leaving a corkscrew pattern.

'Aw, sweet,' Poppy said before she set off.

Lucy took a deep breath and dived into the slope. All the theory of powder skiing suddenly made sense, she grew in confidence and took up more speed that enabled her to turn more easily.

This is what it's about, she thought. This is the absolute high I have heard them all talk about. Something had suddenly clicked and she was able to let go, trust to her skis and fly. She realised that, whilst she had skied powder before, she had never 'powder skied': she had always held something back, trying to control her turns and avoid picking up speed. Suddenly she had had the confidence to let go, not overthink her technique and the reward was an incomparable floating sensation that lifted her soul.

The feeling of elation was universal, as they skied, and at each halt, there were more whoops and expressions of joy that ordinarily most of them would be embarrassed to express but, in this situation, it seemed the right behaviour.

'I know this is cheeky, Alain,' asked Sally at one stop when she and Alain were standing a little apart from the others, 'but I'm feeling a bit uncomfortable about this. Was it very, very expensive?'

Alain gave her a wily grin.

'Very,' he replied. 'But not as much as it would have cost if the owner of the helicopter company hadn't been a friend of mine.'

'Oh, good,' she laughed. 'I feel much better now. I was scared I would have to offer you a contribution out of politeness but now I won't bother.'

Alain felt his phone buzz in his chest pocket and he had a intuition that it was a call he could not ignore. He stopped and looked at the message and groaned.

'What is it?' asked Lucy.

'My heli-ski is over. Thank goodness I got one run in.'

He made a quick call and then had a chat with the guide.

They continued downwards: the scenery changed and the terrain too, from wide open snowfields surrounded by rocks and ice boulders, the passages narrowed into gullies and man-made paths and they found themselves skiing between bare sapling trees and eventually the forest. They could now see the valley floor below and the familiar hillside villages. As they approached the appointed pick-up point where their helicopter was already waiting to take them up again, a second helicopter was landing – the police helicopter with Alain's colleagues, Inspecteur chef adjoint Laurent Blonnay and Inspectrice Sylvie Jacquier inside.

'Enjoy yourselves,' Alain ordered, 'take it gently, I expect a full report tonight.'

They watched Alain climb into the helicopter and waved him off before the first group clambered back into the helicopter poor Alain had booked and paid for.

For their second run, the guide, having seen their capabilities, took them down a different and steeper incline and then another.

Eddie kept the rear and the guide kept Lucy close to him as he could tell she was the least confident. But as the day went on, Lucy, growing in confidence, was relaxing into her turns and trusting the spring in the powder.

Other groups were on the mountain too but their guide still managed to find fresh, untracked inclines where they could leave tidy tracks side by side in pristine powder.

At one point, Lucy realised that she was skiing alone behind the guide. She had noticed the others whispering and realised that they had generously offered her the privilege of making the first tracks and choosing her line through the powder. This is an act of great generosity for any skier, especially a good one, as, even when there is plenty of fresh snow, making those first tracks is one of the best experiences a skier can have. Lucy embraced the moment and bounced her turns with energy and let the feeling of complete elation invade every inch of her being.

'Is your soul full?' Tommy asked her when they stopped for a frugal picnic break.

'It is,' she grinned.

'You have improved so much,' Poppy complimented her. 'You are a different skier to the one who started this morning.'

The guide nodded in agreement. It was clear that Lucy had moved up a level that day.

'I won't be leaving you at home again on a powder day,' Sally told her.

'Wow, I finally made the grade! Praise indeed.' Lucy blushed, she knew something had changed and was genuinely happy to have it confirmed by her companions. As they continued, Lucy was able to ski the powder and appreciate the beauty of the scenery whilst bouncing round her turns. From the pure white silence of the upper heights to the steep valley sides interspersed with rocky boulders and gnarled larches, with the entangling bare twiggy branches of saplings increasingly sticking out and interrupting their path. As they skied down the final narrow path towards the village that marked the beginning of civilisation and the end of their second descent, it became increasingly tiring to make all the short turns needed to stay within the path's confines, made bumpy and icy by all the skiers that had already passed that way. As they reached the bus stop, they all agreed that their legs were too weak to do another turn, even Émilie.

They hopped into a little shuttle bus that looked after the heli-ski route and it took them to Pattier where they headed for the nearest bar and ordered beers and *röstis* all round, insisting, as was correct, on paying their guide's share.

'That was brilliant,' sighed Poppy. 'A once-in-a-lifetime. What a shame Alain missed the full day.'

They all agreed that it was a pity that the person who had financed the expedition hadn't got the full benefit. What they didn't know was that Alain's heli-skiing day had continued, but on the other side of the valley, in one of the off-piste sectors of Grondère.

Two

*The presence of evil was something to be first
recognised, then dealt with, survived, outwitted,
triumphed over.*

Toni Morrison, *Sula*

'So,' asked Alain, 'accident?'

He, Inspecteur chef adjoint Blonnay and Inspectrice
Sylvie Jacquier were looking at the twisted body lying at
the foot of the steep cliff to the side of Le Monstre. The
two slope security patrollers who had discovered the body
were beside them.

'So it would *appear*,' replied one of them, a woman in her
early thirties who had greeted Sylvie Jacquier warmly:
they had been at school in Grondère together.

'But you have doubts?'

They both nodded.

'There are a couple of things,' her colleague said. 'Firstly,
when we picked up his skis we noticed they've still got
skins on; to get to the point from where he fell, you would
normally have removed them. Secondly … it's good you
have your skis with you.'

The helicopter dropped them back at the summit of Mont
Froid, the departure point for the tricky descent down its
north face known as Le Monstre. Following carefully in
the tracks the same patrollers had made that morning they
all slid down the ridge to the cliff edge from where the
unfortunate skier must have fallen. They soon understood
why the patrollers were concerned: there were no tracks.

'The cable car was closed yesterday; the weather was still
poor and there was too much fresh snow to let the powder
hounds up. We didn't get time to bomb it until much later.
That means that anyone who came up here yesterday must
have skinned up. We took the first car up this morning to

begin our check and our boss radioed us to say he had spotted the body from the helicopter. We skied down to confirm the guy was dead, but there are no tracks other than ours, there hasn't been enough wind overnight to completely cover any tracks from yesterday, so how did he get there?'

'You think somebody deliberately covered the tracks?'

'Yes, in places it's too smooth, as if someone slid down, wiping out all tracks, all the way to the bottom. It just doesn't feel right.'

'Must have been a good skier,' Sylvie commented, 'there are some really technical passages down this face.'

'No cameras this side of the mountain, I suppose?' Blonnay asked.

'Nope, the cable car arrival station has one but it faces the other direction.'

The police officers looked at each other, concerned. Another murder in Grondère was exactly what the resort did not need. There would be a lot of pressure on them from the cable car company and the tourist office to conclude an accident: Alain decided that it might be in their interests to play along.

'Look,' he told the two patrollers. 'We're going to say publicly that we are initially treating this as an unfortunate accident. But we're going to investigate it as a possible murder. You happy with that? Can you keep it to yourselves?'

The pair nodded grimly. Alain knew they could be trusted. They all knew the negative impact an unexplained murder could have on a ski resort, especially at the beginning of the season.

———————————

'All the same,' asked the procureur when they returned to base, 'don't visitors have the right to know there's a killer loose on the slopes?'

'If this was some random murder I would agree with you, but I think this was a targeted murder, our victim knew his killer: he voluntarily skinned up Mont Froid with whoever it was.'

'Okay,' concluded the procureur, 'you can hush it up for now. If the murderer thinks he's fooled us it might put him or her off guard.'

'Or ...' hesitated Sylvie.

'Or encourage him or her to kill again. It's a risk,' Alain concurred through gritted teeth. 'But a calculated one we can reverse at a moment's notice.'

'Do you have a name yet?'

'Yes, the guy had his ski pass and insurance card with him, not that that'll do him any good now,' Blonnay answered. 'Our victim is Jordan Russell: his phone records indicate he was known as Rusty. He's a South African who has been resident here for four years, set up a hotel/restaurant business, even got his *patente*.'

'Nothing about who he had arranged to ski with?'

'Nothing. Ski pass check has come up with nothing. We think he was skiing with someone on a day pass, paid for in cash. Camera coverage is sketchy: we can't spot the victim anywhere.'

'Family? Acquaintances?'

'No family in Switzerland. Doesn't seem to have been in a relationship. Our initial information tells us he skied with many different people, some kind of ski club, but no mention of plans to ski yesterday on his phone. We will, of course, follow up on all of his contacts, mostly local expats ...'

'Oh dear,' Alain groaned.

'Why, oh dear?' his team looked at him puzzled and then it dawned on them.

'Mademoiselle Wilson and her friends may know him,' Blonnay guessed.

'You can count on it.'

As Alain and his team were opening their new case and waiting for the forensic squad to extricate the body and confirm the cause of death, Lucy and her friends were tucking into their late lunch with gusto and admiring the action videos Lucy had taken of them all.

'Aren't you two nature-lovers a bit ashamed of yourselves, having indulged in the environmental crime of heli-skiing?' Johnny baited Lucy and Poppy.

Lucy and Poppy looked a little embarrassed. It had been the subject of discussion between them.

'I have to acknowledge, Johnny,' Poppy replied, 'that it's a fair cop. I am guilty of eco-hypo.'

Eddie and the others gave her puzzled looks.

'Ecology-hypocrisy,' Poppy explained. 'I know that taking a gas-guzzling helicopter up the mountain just for the purpose of sliding down it for my own pleasure is an indulgence incompatible with my environmental principles but on the basis that this was the chance of a lifetime and that I could soon be dead, I made a deal with myself to offset my share of the trip.'

'Ah,' Johnny, having eaten his wholesome fill of melted cheese, bacon and potato, pushed back from the table to lean back into a more comfortable position and crossed his arms. 'So how are you going to do that?'

'I will not be using a car or taking an aeroplane for a year.'

'Christ!' he said. 'That's nigh on impossible. What if you have an emergency?'

'I'm not that extreme: I will make an exception for real emergencies but I truly am going to try and stick to it.'

Johnny nodded his head, 'Respect, Popps. And what about you, Lucy?'

Lucy shook her head.

'I have decided to live with the guilt and to try and make amends to the planet in other ways.'

'But you're already pretty environmentally conscientious, Lucy,' Sally commented. 'What more can you do?'

'I don't know,' she replied honestly. 'I thought I could spend a week's penance cleaning beaches of plastic or oil spills or something.'

'That's a good idea.'

Johnny was impressed but a little disappointed, he thought he had caught his friends out, but their consciences clearly had been bothering them.

What Lucy hadn't said was that her perspective was more complicated than she had admitted. For her a helicopter was not just a piece of machinery, it was a thing of great beauty. Whenever she heard the hum of one approaching, she stopped and searched the sky so she could admire it. That surge of power, the pure gymnastic capacity of the apparatus plus the emotional element of knowing that aboard was a team of skilled mountaineers and doctors on their way to save a life, including, on two occasions, her own, never failed to fill her with wonder. The truth was that Lucy simply loved helicopters and would always find it difficult to resist the chance to fly in one.

'What about you, Johnny?' Sally asked. 'No moral dilemma for you?'

'None at all,' he grinned. 'That was fucking awesome, I can die happy now and your Alain, Lucy, is a top bloke!'

Lucy smiled at the reflected compliment.

'Lucy, I'm going to show you a photo and I want you to treat it confidentially.'

'Okay, sounds intriguing,' Lucy smiled. She had had a lovely day in the powder despite Alain's absence and was now enjoying a soak in the bath in Alain's mum's flat with a glass of *Petite Arvine* in her hand. Anne had kindly disappeared, as she did most weekends, down to Savigny to stay with Jacques Aulnay, her companion.

Alain showed her the photo from Jordan Russell's ski pass.

'Oh, that's Rusty. Is that who was found dead at the foot of Le Monstre this morning? Oh no!'

She sat up and looked hard at Alain.

'So that's why you had to rush off. But they're saying it was an accident. Wasn't it?'

'We don't know,' he replied honestly. 'We just have to check it out to make sure. Did you know him well?'

'Well, not hugely. He was in my French class, always very friendly and sociable, but he stopped coming when he passed his *patente*. He was setting up a swanky bar and hotel, he promised to invite us all to the opening but it wasn't ready at the beginning of the season. Funny really.'

'Why funny?'

'Well, going to all that trouble and then not opening at the beginning of the season. It is a big building, there isn't just the bar, there's also a restaurant and he knocked all the walls down between the bedrooms to convert them into massive suites. Apparently, it's really high-spec with beautiful furnishings and jacuzzis on enclosed balconies. You'd think he needed to start recouping his investment. Not very good business planning, was it?'

'No, I guess not. Any idea why he wasn't ready?'

'I think he was ready, Tommy said he was being really finickity over the final touches. We all thought it was a bit odd. We were wondering if he had some other line of business, you know?'

'Drugs?'

'Yes. He was known to like other forms of powder in addition to snow.'

'That's useful, thanks.'

'You could ask Tommy, he might know a bit more about what the hold-up was. Sally introduced them a while back when Rusty was looking for someone to do a bit of building work on the side. He worked on the bar renovation.'

'Should you be telling me this?'

'I'm trusting that any information Tommy might be able to give you is more important than him earning a few bucks on the side.' She looked at him sternly.

'And I thought Tommy was the sensible one in your household.'

'Well I always told you that was just because you didn't know him well enough.'

'True.'

'Now, you're not going to get Tommy into trouble, are you?'

'No, of course not. I am grateful for your confidence in me. And I'm glad you didn't know Rusty well: that means I can continue to lead the investigation.'

'Good. Now skedaddle: my water's going cold.'

Lucy switched the hot tap on and slid under the surface.

While Lucy continued easing off her powder muscles Alain called Tommy and asked him about Rusty.

'I was asked not to say anything to anybody,' Tommy said, 'but as the poor guy's dead and you're the police, I guess I can break my promise. I did a lot on the renovation of the bar but I guess the bit that interests you is that he asked me

22

to work on my own to enclose a really elaborate safe in concrete and build a concealed wall panel in front of it.'

'We didn't find a safe.'

'Ah ha!' Tommy replied with a smug satisfaction in his voice. 'Worked then!'

Alain grinned to himself.

'It did. And now, because you did such a good job, you've just forfeited your Saturday night.'

'I'll be back in an hour, keep an eye on the supper,' Alain called to Lucy as he ran out to Rusty's bar and boutique hotel to meet Tommy and Inspectrice Sylvie Jacquier.

Lucy laughed her agreement, thinking it was the least she could do after a day's heli-skiing at his expense when the poor soul had only got one run in himself.

Tommy and Sylvie Jacquier were waiting outside the sealed bar and restaurant when Alain arrived. Sylvie unlocked the premises.

'Someone's been here,' Sylvie said. 'I can't explain it but I'm pretty sure things have shifted around a bit.'

Sylvie had overseen the initial search of the building which had indicated someone had been there before them, but they had no way of being sure. This time she had a point of comparison: she consulted the photos on her phone.

'Yes, definitely, look, the bottles have all moved slightly on the shelves and all the cupboard contents have also changed position. A neat turnover but not perfect.'

'Well, whoever it is didn't find what he was looking for the first time, I wonder if he (or she) fared any better the second. Let's hope your secret work fooled our murderer as well as us,' Alain said grimly to Tommy.

Tommy led them into the bar of the restaurant, he removed the row of bottles from in front of the large mirror in the centre of the bar then climbed the ladder propped up against the bar, removed the few bottles sitting on the high shelf, which he then slid out.

Behind the shelf was nothing but a blank white wall. Tommy pressed a panel which popped out and then he pulled a small lever behind it but nothing happened Then he clambered down the ladder, moved it and repeated the same procedure on the other side. He then clicked a concealed button behind the heavy gilt frame of the huge mirror in the middle of the bar. The entire wall swung out to reveal another blank concrete wall. Tommy then clicked on something in the concrete panel and lifted it out to reveal a high-tech safe.

'I can't help you with the next bit,' Tommy said.

Alain whistled in admiration, Sylvie's mouth was open in astonishment: the police search had tried but failed to move the mirror and concluded that it was plastered firmly to the wall, which of course, it was.

'Good, isn't it?' Tommy grinned.

'Yes, could anyone else know about this?'

'No one. Rusty swore me to secrecy and said he would know if I'd told anyone because he hadn't.'

'Good, then keep it that way. Our murderer hasn't found what he wanted and so he may come back, and next time, we'll have a camera on him. Remember, Tommy, no one, not even Sally or Lucy: Rusty has already lost his life for whatever secrets this safe holds.'

'Okay.' Tommy looked a little abashed.

Sylvie called Blonnay and told him to bring back-up and a safe-breaking team with him while Alain called the head of the local municipal police, Adjudant Corthay, for immediate protection. Adjudant Corthay was always a bit nervous when Capitaine Dupertuis contacted him: it was never a social call. But, as he was engaged in his least favourite task, dealing with a group of noisy drunks leaving The Pub, he was happy to take his team and support the *Police judiciaire*. He arrived in a matter of minutes.

'Off you go,' Sylvie urged Alain when she spotted him looking at his watch. 'This could take a long time. I'm safe with Adjudant Corthay and his team, Blonnay will be here soon. I didn't have anything special to do this evening and Lucy has already had her day disrupted enough.'

'Thanks,' he smiled. 'I owe you.'

He ran back to the flat just in time to prevent Lucy burning the chicken to a crisp.

It was 3 o'clock in the morning when the locksmiths finally managed to crack the safe. They stepped back to let Sylvie and Blonnay remove its contents. Blonnay whistled as Sylvie emptied hundreds of diamonds onto a bar mat.

Adjudant Corthay grimaced.

'There must be millions' worth there.'

Sylvie nodded, 'No wonder he wasn't in a hurry to open his restaurant, it was clearly just a front. We'd better get them somewhere else quickly.'

'Bern?' suggested Blonnay.

They had recently worked with the *Kriminalpolizei* in Bern on another case and it seemed to make sense to get the diamonds out of Valais. Blonnay woke Herr Schmutz, their Swiss-German colleague, and agreed that Blonnay and Inspectrice Jacquier would drive to Bern immediately with the diamonds where Herr Schmutz would arrange for them to be placed in a safe in the National Bank of Switzerland. The diamonds were carefully counted and photographed and the pair set off with another car for escort.

'Isn't this all a bit extreme?' asked one of the younger officers. 'Couldn't it wait till morning?'

'Somebody killed for these and I'm not risking any of our officers,' Blonnay replied, 'Besides, if I don't get them out of temptation's way, someone might feel inclined to help themselves to one or two, including me,' he winked at the young man as he hopped into his car.

It was mid-morning before they were back in Savigny where Capitaine Dupertuis and the procureur were waiting for a full report.

'So now we are sure it was murder,' said the procureur.

'Yes, someone had definitely searched the bar and the safe contents give us the motive.'

'No prints or DNA from the bar.'

'Forensics are still working on it but we're not expecting them to turn up much, it looks like whoever it was, covered his or her tracks pretty carefully.'

'Well as long as our murderer doesn't work out the *Police judiciaire* have got hold of the diamonds, he may come back for another search. Keep the place sealed for now or he'll realise.'

'Will do.'

'How did you find out about the safe?'

'Uhm, a local informant,' Alain mumbled.

The procureur caught Blonnay grinning at Sylvie.

'I see, well just make sure that your "local informant" doesn't inform anyone else.'

'I can assure you of that, M. le Procureur,' Alain promised.

'Does that mean we go public that it's murder?' asked Sylvie.

'Not yet,' the procureur smiled wryly. 'We'll just get our spokesperson to make a bland statement that we are still investigating and haven't ruled out any eventuality. Hopefully our murderer has business elsewhere and will return to wherever he or she came from.'

'If our murderer isn't a local, that is,' sighed Alain.

The procureur looked at him scornfully.

'Don't be ridiculous, Capitaine Dupertuis!'

'Sorry,' agreed Alain. 'Of course not.'

'New word for you, Blonnay,' Alain volunteered as the pair stood in front of the coffee machine.

Blonnay was a linguist, with a passion for the English language that verged on obsession and, since the murder of Malcolm McDonaghue, when their investigation had brought him into contact with numerous members of the English-speaking community in Grondère and consequently a constant stream of new and obscure vocabulary, he had kept a small notebook in which he wrote down the wonderful words that came his way. This notebook was filling up nicely, especially as he now, like Alain, had an English girlfriend, whom he had met when investigations in their previous case had taken him to the United Kingdom.

He looked at Alain expectantly.

'As I left home yesterday evening, I was told to skedaddle. I'm assuming, from the context, that it means "scram".'

'That's a glorious word,' Blonnay said with genuine gratitude in his voice. 'How do you think it's spelt?'

'Ah, that I leave you to investigate. I wouldn't want to spoil your fun.'

Blonnay grinned, Alain was right: Blonnay loved nothing more than to dip into a dictionary and thoroughly research new vocabulary.

'Skedaddle or skidaddle?' Blonnay wondered out loud. 'Ah, found it "ske", although in our case maybe it should be "Ski-daddle"?'

Alain smiled and left him to his musings which, he correctly suspected, would form one of the topics of conversation that evening when Blonnay had his daily video chat with his girlfriend, Jilly.

Three

*Yes'm, old friends is best, 'lest you can catch a new one
that's fit to make an old one out of.*
Sarah Orne Jewett, The Country of the Pointed Firs

For Lucy and her friends, their favourite venue for meeting up after work was the Pub Mont Grondère. December was a quiet month, and it was a great time to catch up with old friends and get to know the new faces in resort before they got lost amid the crowds of visitors.

Lucy was mostly occupied in refresher training during December and, on her way to The Pub, after an intensive day of skiing on one leg and jumping round turns, a new instructor from her ski school asked if she could tag along. 'Sure,' Lucy replied, remembering how nervous she'd been in her first season and how Sally and Jodie and welcomed her into their circle of friends. 'I'm sorry, I can't remember your name.'

'Milly,' answered the young woman. 'Milly Stanford.'

They exchanged the usual niceties on the way to The Pub and Lucy was struck at how young Milly seemed even though she must only have been five or six years younger. A ski season, she thought, will make her grow up fast. You have to learn to stand on your own two feet pretty quickly. Johnny, Grondère's coolest ski bum, was already in position at his favourite corner of the bar, with Louie, his Jack Russell, sitting on his shoulder drinking Guinness out of a shot glass, always a crowd-puller. Lucy introduced Milly.

'That is soooo cool,' Milly said, admiring Louie's drinking prowess.

Louie, in his turn, gave her a discerning look, dismissed her as being of little interest and harrumphed to be set down on the floor as he had finished his Guinness ration, he knew he wouldn't be getting any more that evening and balancing on Johnny's shoulder was comfortable for a short while only.

Poppy, Lucy's great friend and sharer of adventures, arrived: Milly was awestruck, she was having a beer with three Grondère legends. Wow! she thought to herself.

Unaware that their reputations carried such weight, the three bantered on as usual without much regard to the shy newcomer. Other friends turned up and Milly, enthralled to be surrounded by all these seasoned seasonnaires, seemed happy to just listen in. At the end of Happy Hour, people started drifting home and Milly eventually realised she was beginning to wear out her welcome.

'She's very young, isn't she?' Sally said, after Milly had reluctantly said goodbye and left. 'Why did she tag onto you? There are lots of people her own age in here.'

'I think she's got a crush on Lucy,' smiled Poppy.

'Two murder cases and her boobs on display all over Switzerland and beyond,' teased Johnny, 'Our Lucy is fast acquiring celebrity status. And you too, with all your various entanglements with murderers: the poor child looked completely awestruck.'

'Don't be ridiculous, Johnny,' Poppy gave him a playful tap.

'Still, I hope she does make some friends of her own age and doesn't get too clingy,' smiled Lucy.

'Quite! One Gluey Hughey is enough for Grondère,' Sally said emphatically.

'I haven't seen Hughey yet this season,' Lucy commented to Sally as they meandered up the hill to their distant chalet.

Gluey Hughey was an earnest young man who tended to tag along with whoever would let him, especially if free drinks were involved, and who could prove quite difficult to shake off if you weren't experienced. It was accepted in

Grondère that if you were holding any kind of a party, you could always count on at least one guest turning up – Gluey Hughey. He never needed an invitation and he never seemed to consider it necessary to have one, but nobody knew much else about him. Lucy had ceased minding Hughey's freeloading ways, in fact she even had a bit of a soft spot for him and, it would seem, he for her: at her birthday party in the summer, she had become the only person in Grondère ever known to have received a birthday present from Hughey.

'It's a surprise he didn't latch on to our heli-trip,' joked Sally.

'Now you mention it, yes. How did we get away with that one?'

Lucy and Sally chuckled happily as they plodded uphill. Sally had given up her job in the clothes section of a ski shop since she had landed her dream job running the administrative side of a vineyard further down the Rhône Valley for Sebastian McDonaghue. Sebastian was also the new owner of La Grande Cour, Grondère's only five-star hotel. Much of her work Sally could do from home and she was planning to make the most of her flexible working hours to enjoy her last winter in Grondère. She linked arms with Lucy.

'I'm determined to get lots of good skiing in this winter before Tommy and I move down to the valley. I've got no Jodie anymore, so I hope you don't get too many clients.'

'I don't think you're going to be in luck there,' Lucy said. 'My boss Melanie tells me I'm booked solid over the holidays; I'm starting to get return clients and she says people have been asking for me by name.'

'Ah, it's that celebrity status Johnny was talking about, you're a victim of your own notoriety!'

'I have no idea, but I hope after the holidays it'll calm down and we can get some ski time together. I love teaching but I also want to get out on the hill with you as much as I can, while I have you for this last winter.'

'You make it sound so sad and final. We won't be far away, we may even have *more* time to ski once we're weekenders.'

'I hope so, but where will you stay? With the little chalet due for destruction, I don't even know where I'm going to be living.'

'You'll find something: maybe you could share with that Milly girl,' Sally teased.

'I don't think so, my days of burning the candle at both ends are over and hers are just beginning. Plus, she looks like she's into make-up, jewellery and fashion and, as you know, I'm not very up on all that stuff.'

'Yes, sadly no conversation with you on those subjects is ever very rewarding,' Sally gave a mock sigh. 'Hopefully she'll make some nice friends of her own age.'

'I'm sure she will, look how I found you and Jodie. But, when you think about it, there are three decades between us and Poppy, and the age difference doesn't seem to matter.'

'True, but then Poppy isn't like anyone else, the normal rules don't apply to her. Hey and what about Mardi Gras? I hope we can do that again this year.'

'Oh yes, let's. I had a great idea for costumes when I was hiking with Poppy in the summer. I had this vision of you as a eucalyptus tree, me a beech and Jodie a weeping willow.'

'Ohmigod, love it but … ambitious or what? We'll have to start work now.'

And the gleeful pair made their plans all the way to the chalet and Tommy's lasagne.

Lucy didn't have to wait long to catch up with Gluey Hughey. A few evenings later there was a book launch in The Pub. Someone from Lucy's ski school had written a book on freeriding and, as usual, when there were free drinks and nibbles to be had, Hughey was already ensconced in a convenient corner, helping himself to the meats and pastries. He waved shyly at her and she went over to say hello.

Not a great conversationalist, any discussion with Hughey tended to be one-sided and after ten minutes of talking about herself, Lucy was beginning to flag. Sammy came over to rescue her.

'Come and sort Jamie out for me, Lucy,' Sammy demanded. 'He's convinced you're hiding gory details about Grondère's latest mystery from him.'

Lucy allowed herself to be led away with a smile.

'Thanks,' she whispered.

'You must be the only person in Grondère who voluntarily goes over and chats to Gluey Hughey,' Sammy shook his head. 'I can't always be there to rescue you from your own stupidity.'

Lucy was happy to have some time to chat to Sammy before the high season began: Sammy Vine ran an upmarket bar and, once the tourists arrived, Lucy and her friends would have to go there if they wanted to see him. His close friend, Jamie Corcoran, a highly qualified chef, also worked there. As it turned out, the pair had more information about Grondère's latest mystery than she did and Sammy had set his sights on Rusty's vacant bar and boutique hotel.

'The place is beautifully decorated,' Jamie said. 'That mirror centrepiece behind the bar is goooorgeous!'

'Tommy will be happy to hear that, he did a bit of work on that. I haven't seen it: Rusty promised to invite us to the opening, but nothing ever came of that.'

'No, and won't now,' Jamie added.

'If I get the lease, I will invite you, Lucy,' Sammy said. 'I'm just desperate to have it. It's a great location and all the work's already been done. It's just a question of ordering stock and hiring staff. But the competition's tough.'

'Really?' Lucy wondered who on earth could have enough money to step in to an expensive lease at such short notice.

'Yes, apparently I'm in competition with some London-based chain and that Alessandra Rosset who runs the White Snowflake group.'

'That is interesting,' she replied.

'Yes. You might like to mention that to a friendly policeman of yours.'

'I don't see how that could change anything.'

'Well, I'm sort of hoping she'll turn out to be the murderer and that she got rid of Rusty because she wanted his bar and that, with her out of the way in prison, I'll get the lease,' Sammy grinned unashamedly.

'That is outrageous!' Jamie exclaimed, pretending to be shocked.

'You are both outrageous,' Lucy laughed. 'But who said anything about murder? Alain told me they hadn't concluded anything yet.'

'Oh come on, Lucy,' Sammy teased. 'You don't really believe that! No one else in Grondère does. Shifty late-night police visits, 24-hour-a-day surveillance and reinforced security? Give me a break.'

Lucy looked at them, stunned.

Jamie nodded in agreement with Sammy.

'It's okay giving out that sort of story to reassure the tourists but everyone in town knows that there's something dodgy about Rusty's death.'

Alain looked grim as Lucy revealed to him that evening that the whole of Grondère was treating Rusty's death as murder.

'It proves how impossible it is to keep this town in the dark about anything.'

What Alain didn't say was that there was no point in the police keeping the place under surveillance any longer. If everyone in Grondère knew that the police had an eye on the place, then so did the killer.

'It seems that I'm the only person in town who hadn't worked it out. I feel like a real dope.'

'Don't,' he smiled. 'I have to keep certain things from you to avoid putting you in an awkward position with your friends: it means I did a good job.'

'Well, bully for you,' she grunted, 'I certainly didn't have to lie to anyone, how can I be such an innocent after all that's happened over the last year?'

'Because you always want to believe the best of people, and that's not a weakness.' He hugged her and she snuggled into his chest and sighed.

'As long as you really believe that, I can cope with the fact that the whole town knows that the only person around who doesn't know when a murder has happened is the investigating officer's girlfriend!'

'Trust me, that's a good thing!'

'I am not sure,' Lucy admitted to local nature warden, and mountain guide, Jean-Marc when they briefly crossed in the street one day, 'how I feel about wolves.'

'No,' he said, non-committally, 'it is a difficult one.'

'Have you ever seen one when you're out on the mountain?'

'Twice. Once, in winter, many years ago, I followed the tracks of one and saw it a long way off in the distance. It was climbing a steep face of deep snow and I could not believe how fast it was travelling.'

'And the second time?'

'Again, from a distance, but more recently, on top of the Petit Cortey.'

'You are kidding!'

'No, I was guiding a group who were all pretty excited to spot it, but the helicopter scared it off. It scarpered pretty quickly into a rocky outcrop.'

'So, they are here.'

'Ah yes, they're here all right.'

'And now we have one in Grondère.'

He looked at her, surprised.

'How do you know that?'

'I've heard it.'

'Ah.'

Lucy realised he was being very guarded about what he said. He must be used to it: the topic of wolves was an emotive one.

'If I'm totally honest, putting aside the environmental arguments, it's my safety I'm thinking about. Would wolves ever attack? A hiker like me on the hill for example?'

'I do not know. Centuries ago wolves learnt to be wary of man but now they seem to have realised that man has changed his attitude. Who knows how things will develop. I doubt a lone wolf would attack an adult human but who is to say what a pack would do if faced with a small child? They definitely have attacked domestic pets on farms in Italy and Eastern Europe. Unprotected livestock now, that is another matter, alone or in a pack.'

'You haven't really helped much.'

'No. I can tell you one thing though.'

'Yes?'

'I don't care what the experts say. Wolves prefer the cover of darkness or thick fog – wolf weather, I call it. That's when they attack. Here, in any case, I have only ever had to deal with dead or wounded livestock early in the mornings and usually after a foggy night.'

'Aren't you scared? You're up in the mountains all the time on your own.'

He grinned at her naïvety.

'I am armed. And not with rubber bullets.'

She smiled back.

'I suppose that's reassuring for you but the rest of us don't have that back-up.'

'No, but then in 50 years of roaming these mountains I have never needed it, and if I did, I'd have a lot of explaining to do: most of these creatures have trackers on them. I think you are worrying unnecessarily.'

'Let's hope so.'

'Too many fairy tales, Mademoiselle Lucy. All those stories of *Peter and the Wolf* and *Little Red Riding Hood* have got to you.'

She laughed, 'I'm sure you're right!'

And with that they went their different ways, both continuing to think very different thoughts.

He was thinking about how often Lucy roamed the hills and how, although she had never seen a wolf she had most certainly been seen by one or more.

She was wondering how much he hadn't told her.

Four

Tell me, what is it you plan to do
With your one wild and precious life?
                                        Mary Oliver

A few evenings later, in The Pub, after work, the friends all gathered for a drink before heading home. Johnny was holding court in his usual corner with Poppy keeping him straight, also as usual. Lucy found herself talking to a live wire called Suzie. Initially she was worried that Suzie was another nosey-parker who was going to quiz her about the latest murder but Suzie had heard about Lucy's heli-skiing trip and wanted to quiz her about that. Lucy was more than happy to talk lengthily about her day on the Petit Cortey. Suzie was in Grondère for the season but was checking in coats at a nightclub so she could get in as much skiing as possible.

'Usually I come as a ski leader with the Grondère Diamond Ski Club,' she said, 'but they only let you do two-week stints and I wanted to be here for the whole season. I still ski with them but I also get to do my own thing.'

'What on earth is the Grondère Diamond Ski Club?' asked Lucy who had never come across this term before.

'Don't you know?' Suzie looked at her, surprised. 'It's a club of people, mostly from the home counties, who ski here a lot; most of them have chalets here. The members are all ski-mad and, when they're here, they want to ski with other ski-mad people who are the same level as them. It's mostly a social arrangement, you get to meet some lovely people. Come and join us one day.'

'But I'm not a member! And I'm certainly not home counties!' Lucy's northern accent confirmed the truth of this statement.

'They won't mind if you're with me.'

'Okay, I will,' promised Lucy: Suzie seemed fun, and Lucy was also curious to find out more about this exclusive ski club. 'It's a good time as I won't have much teaching work until the holidays start.'

'I admire you teaching,' Suzie told her. 'You must have the patience of a saint.'

'I enjoy it,' Lucy replied. 'I love introducing people to the sport I love, watching them improve and get the bug.'

'I can relate to that,' Suzie allowed. 'But it doesn't change the fact that you have the patience for it and I do not. I'm too selfish, I just like to ski for myself.'

'That's not selfish, just honest. I admire you for being so committed to your sport. You really get up to be on the first lift every day? That's true dedication, I don't have that.'

'I know this sounds a bit odd but I promised myself from an early age that I wouldn't live an ordinary life. It's not an easy route and certainly not a comfortable one but I try to stick to it.'

Suzie continued to explain that she worked as a management consultant but that she refused to spend her life working just to amass money when she could be outside. She'd rather do sporadic contract work and then pick up odd jobs to fill in the gaps than be tied to an office. As a result, she'd skied all over the world, volunteered in disaster zones, spent the summers crewing on yachts, climbing mountains and seizing any other adventure life offered her.

Lucy looked at her amazed, she had never met anyone like Suzie before. Maybe this Diamond Ski Club was full of Suzies.

After Suzie and she had exchanged numbers, Suzie moved on to chat to other friends and Lucy looked over at Poppy, floored.

'I feel totally inadequate now.'

'I have to agree that Suzie is quite out of the ordinary. Reminds me of Genna Hobbs-Davison.'

Genna had been Poppy's friend when she was young: she had, with a little assistance from the same person who had murdered Malcolm McDonaghue, fallen to her death in a mountaineering accident.

'Really?'

'Yes, Genna was the same type of live wire, but Genna had money, Suzie has to work for her life of adventure.'

'Amazing, isn't she?'

'But there's no need to feel inferior, you're just as special as her, but in a different way. And Suzie would be the last person to want to have that effect on anyone. Especially you: it looks like she's taken a liking to you.'

'Thank you, Poppy, you always find the right words. So how come I've never heard of this Grondère Diamond Ski Club before?'

'You don't really fall into their sphere, they tend to be high-income, high-energy types and they like to keep it exclusive.'

'Ooh, I take that right back about finding the right words: thanks for all the compliments. But, from what she told me, Suzie isn't high-income.'

'No, but she's high-energy and, like the other chap who comes out as a ski leader, Rory, she has mountain knowledge and expertise. They are the *paid help*, you see. She's also very discreet and they like to keep their secrets safe.'

'I can do discreet.'

'I'm sure you can, but you're going out with a policeman which immediately makes you a "no-go" associate. Why all these questions? Feeling left out? Do you want to join?'

'Not at all, I am just astounded to discover that such things exist.'

'Actually, it was founded by an old acquaintance of yours,' Johnny winked.

'Of mine?'

'Carla Sturridge set it up with some friends, yonks ago. They realised that a lot of Ski Club of Great Britain members were looking for a more *exclusive* group of ready-made ski chums to ski with. So they created the Grondère Diamond Ski Club, charged an extortionate membership fee to keep out the riff-raff, creamed a bit off the top and used their contact base to set up a network of exclusive arrangements with local businesses. It was popular from day one although Carla dropped out of the organisation years ago.'

'So who runs it?'

'Oh, some old cronies of Carla's who don't live here anymore but I think it's so well-established that it pretty much runs itself.'

'Well, I'm staggered. There's a whole world out there I had no idea even existed.'

'My parents used to ski with that crowd,' Milly suddenly interjected. She had arrived to hear the end of the conversation.

'Really,' Poppy asked, curious to know if she knew Milly's parents. A brief namecheck confirmed that she did remember them, but not well.

'Farming folk, aren't they?'

'Yes, arable and a bit of livestock. But they always made sure we got a ski break. I learned to ski here: that's why I came here for my ski season,' Milly explained. 'Plus loads of Mum's old cronies are here and so she felt happier about me doing a season, knowing I could call on them if I got into trouble. Ridiculous, but I didn't mind as I wanted to come to Grondère anyway.'

'Goodness,' Poppy raised her eyebrows. 'The Grondère Diamond Ski Club is the last place it would occur to me to seek safety or moral guidance.'

'I know what you mean,' Milly laughed. 'But they're just a bunch of harmless old hippies and drunks really.'

Poppy nodded sceptically, she didn't want to contradict Milly or undermine her naïve image of her parents' friends but she could have shared some tales of debauchery that would have shocked both Milly and Lucy. She decided to just issue a cautionary warning.

'Mind,' she said. 'Watch out for that ski club lot all the same.'

'Why?' Lucy looked at her askance.

'Sometimes they can be a little over-enthusiastic and ebullient on the mountain: don't be led astray,' she said cryptically.

Lucy raised her eyebrows questioningly, but she knew when Poppy had concluded a speech.

One Saturday afternoon in late December, everything in Grondère ground to a halt. In the village the locals crammed into the bars, whilst up on the mountain, ski teachers in training fought for space around the tiny screens in the canteens and restaurants. Nobody was going to miss the local girl's first World Cup descent in Europe. She had come close to a podium position in the first race of the season in Canada and hopes were high: Grondère had not had a local champion for decades.

Tommy and Sally were watching in Golden Mountain, the ski shop where Tommy was working his final winter. The event was taking place in Val d'Isère and Eddie had made the short trip across the border into France to support his girlfriend. He would be somewhere in the stands, with

Émilie's parents, underneath the large red and white starred flag of Valais that the members of Émilie's growing fan club had taken with them.

Lucy and Poppy, as friends of Émilie Morend, were allowed front row seats in the big canteen at Cauettes. Milly squeezed in beside them just as Émilie left the gate. The canteen almost shook with cheers and stamping feet as the television cameras scanned the Swiss spectators in the stands with their Valais cowbells and Swiss flags going crazy.

Early season tourists from mountain-less countries, unused to seeing a crowd gather around a screen for anything other than football and rugby games, wondered what could be the cause of such excitement. They watched on in amazement, as the normally taciturn Grondèrians screamed their girl down the slope to a majestic third place.

'Her first World Cup podium!' Poppy shouted. 'Attagirl!'

There was great hubbub, back-slapping and the wine flowed while the crowd stayed in place for the prize-giving.

'Look!' Lucy said, 'there's Eddie!'

Eddie was shown full screen as he and Émilie enjoyed a celebratory embrace across the barrier while she waited in the enclosure for the ceremony.

'Isn't that lovely? Danny would have been so proud.'

Danny, Émilie's brother and Eddie's best friend, had died the previous winter in an avalanche. Lucy knew that, as Émilie stood on that third step, she would be wishing her big brother was there to share the moment.

Poppy looked at her and knew where her young friend's thoughts were leading – to melancholy.

'There'll be no more training today, our instructor is half-cut, look at him. How about we ski down and celebrate in The Pub?'

Lucy smiled. She knew it was a deliberate ploy and she appreciated the deflection from sad thoughts. It was a time for joy.

'Race you!'

They raced to the ski rack laughing and clicked on their skis as quickly as they could, Milly tagging on behind. Poppy had some hard snow frozen into her bindings and so that slowed her down a bit as she tapped her pole hard against the ski to remove the ice. But Lucy and Milly's headstart didn't give them much of an advantage: Poppy had been taking the path down to resort for forty years and knew the racing line by heart. Poppy soon whizzed past Milly and snuck past Lucy on one of the final bends, sticking her bum and her tongue out as she did so.

They were still laughing as they arrived in The Pub where Émilie's victory had everyone in party mood.

'Our girl done good,' Johnny raised his beer glass in greeting. Louie, sitting carefully out of the way of clumsy ski boots under Johnny's bar stool, barked his own greeting. He didn't want any of these over-excited humans standing on his tail.

'Your round, Milly,' said Poppy, 'you were last!'

'Looks like I need to speed up or it could be an expensive season,' Milly grinned as she turned to the barman who was already preparing their standard order.

The year end was rapidly approaching. Each day, as different countries released their children from school for the holidays, waves of cars with registration plates from those nations, made their way steadily up the winding mountain road. The Swiss from the lowlands joined the increasingly long procession of overloaded cars which eventually ground to a standstill on the outskirts of the resort. Badly parked 4x4s blocked the traffic, their drivers, in their stress, not realising (or caring) what havoc they were causing, holding up the traffic as they collected their keys from their agent or their meat order from the butcher. The ski bus caught up in the gridlock honked at the visitors in vain as hot sweaty skiers regretted their decision not to walk the 300m back to their hotels. The butcher's well-dressed, well-groomed line of customers spilled out onto the pavement as the butcher, well versed in the requirements of each nationality, served up the best cuts of meat and the fattest turkeys available in Switzerland. His team smiled politely and spoke to all of the clients in their own languages (except the Swedish) whilst the butcher wandered up and down the line, on first name terms with many, performing a public relations exercise that would have outshone any MBA graduate.

Eddie worked for a rental company as an odd job/maintenance man and this was his busiest time of the year. From changing lightbulbs and replacing blown fuses to unblocking sinks and unlocking doors for clients who had locked themselves out, there was no end to the ingenuity of the temporary residents to keep him occupied. However, Eddie had a dilemma; Émilie was due to race in Andorra and he naturally wanted to be there.

'I'll do it,' said Sally.

'You're kidding, really?'

'Yes, I don't mind. Tommy's busy, Lucy's busy, the slopes are busy, I may as well be busy too. I can change fuses, light bulbs and unblock sinks. If it gets more complicated than that I can ask Tommy or call you.'

'Sally, you're a champ, I owe you big time.'

Eddie gave her a hug that squeezed all the breath from her. Sally pushed him away, laughing.

'Just go! And don't come back without a podium!'

Five

If there is anything worse than spending Christmas with your own family, it is spending Christmas with somebody else's family. Because ... you will also be completely baffled: 'Oh yes we always sing Little Donkey in eight-part harmony in the garden at midnight'.

Victoria Wood

Inspecteur chef adjoint Laurent Blonnay's idea of English Christmases was largely drawn from Dickens and the film, *Love Actually*. His Christmas Eve arrival at Gatwick Airport had certainly lived up to the latter, with his girlfriend Jilly leaping into his arms excitedly as he came through security. Now it was Dickens who came into his thoughts as they were sitting on a rather dingy train heading for Clapham Junction. As Jilly chattered away, giving him some family background, 'they're a bit wacky,' she was saying, he looked out of the window at the industrial dereliction that backed on to the weed-infested railway line and wondered where all the litter caught in the bare twigs and branches came from. As they got closer to London, the rear facades of the tall, red-bricked houses and their back gardens in varying degrees of upkeep fascinated him. The Victorian and Edwardian architecture of South London never failed to take him back in time and conjure up images of Sherlock Holmes and Oliver Twist.

At Clapham they fought with the hordes of commuters heading home, loaded with last-minute parcels and rolls of wrapping paper, to board another suburban train.

Blonnay wondered how people could be so disorganised and last-minute and yet, he had to admit to himself that it lent a sense of excitement and colour to the occasion.

'We'll go straight to Mum and Dad's and then head to my place after supper, if that's okay,' she told him, as they arrived at the closest station to Jilly's family home. 'If we go there first we'll lose an hour.'

Laurent had been to stay with Jilly before so he nodded knowingly: covering even the shortest distances in England's capital city could take a surprisingly long time. He had not, however, met her family before: this was a new and welcome sign of their deepening relationship.

Their arrival was boisterous, the dogs leapt on them as soon as the door was opened and Jilly's brothers eagerly crowded around them to get a look at the new man in their sister's life. Jack and Julian were large rugby-playing types, a fact borne out by them both wearing rugby shirts. Jilly's parents, Harry and Andrea Ferguson, were friendly but flustered, getting supper ready. Harry gratefully accepted the bottle of *abricotine* that Blonnay had brought with him and immediately started to debate with himself what he could mix it with.

'Dad takes the art of cocktail-mixing into the unknown,' Jilly teased, 'we have tasted some horrendous concoctions over the years.'

'Rubbish! I've never known you not finish one of my cocktails. Get the man a drink for goodness sake,' the chemistry teacher told his daughter as he retreated into a steamy kitchen.

A few minutes later, Blonnay, a beer in his hand, was being shown around the garden by the three siblings and three dogs.

When they returned inside Blonnay found himself hypnotised by the Christmas tree.

'Ghastly, isn't it?' Jilly laughed, seeing him looking at it. 'Mum doesn't believe in under-decorating at Christmas time.'

'Indeed,' he agreed, 'it is hard to see any greenery at all.'

47

'She would consider that to be a success, her Christmas kitsch knows no limits.'

'Do the English use "kitsch" too?'

'We do,' Andrea said firmly, bringing in the supper, 'and don't listen to her. If she had her way, we'd have all tasteful little crafty decorations and no tinsel.'

Jilly agreed, 'Some of those decorations we've had as long as I can remember.'

'That's right, and that's what makes them special, each little decoration holds a memory. Look, you made this one at school when you were ten.'

'Oh Mum, you have my permission to chuck it, it's so ugly.'

'Of course it's ugly, but I will always remember the look of pride on your face as you produced it and asked me to put it on the tree.'

The boys groaned.

'You boys lack romance!'

'We're hungry.'

'Three Js,' remarked Blonnay during supper. 'Was that deliberate?'

'Mum denies it,' Jack joked, 'but we reckon she was hoping we'd form a singing group called the Three Jays or the Singing Jays.'

'More like StingJays,' retorted Andrea.

'We're such a disappointment,' Jilly said. 'Mum wanted musicians and she got two engineers and an officer of the law.'

'That's not true,' Andrea denied, 'I am very proud of you all and you all sing beautifully!'

Harry agreed.

'You made sure of that! I hope Laurent, that you can cope with the racket they're going to make later.'

After supper they gathered round the piano for a carolling sing-song. Andrea was a piano teacher and they sang a few raucous carols before she turned to Blonnay and asked, 'Can you yodel?'

'Yes, of course, all Swiss people can yodel,' he replied with a wink.

'You're kidding!' Jilly looked at him incredulously.

'Okay, all Swiss people can't yodel.'

'But you can?'

'Yes, I was asked so many times by foreigners that I taught myself with tutorials on the internet and then I took some lessons to perfect the art.'

They all looked with disbelief at this geeky Swiss man, all except for Andrea who eyed him with glee.

'Can you do that Frank Ifield song, *She taught me to yodel*? He was my mum's favourite, Frank Ifield.'

'I can.'

'I do not believe this,' Jilly stood back with dread to watch from a distance, her bothers enjoying her discomfort.

After Blonnay's competent rendition of the old classic, Jilly looked at her family. Her brothers were grinning from ear to ear, her dad was clearly impressed and Andrea was smitten. Blonnay's total lack of inhibition and willingness to join in the silly family fun had won them over completely. They loved him from that instant!

Andrea wanted to go to midnight mass and so Julian took her in the car and made a little detour to drop Jilly and Blonnay off in Clapham.

Christmas Day with the Fergusons was also a lively affair: there was more heavy food, raucous carol singing, watching the Queen's speech and a walk through the local park. A light mist was floating around their legs as Blonnay and Jilly walked, arms linked, inhaling the damp perfume of rotten leaves, moss and fox pee, unique to London parks.

'Are those things legal?' Blonnay asked Jilly as they ambled slowly behind the others.

Harry had doctored the crackers with extra gunpowder to make a louder bang.

'Oh, I doubt it. He does it every year. It's quite common, I believe. The manufacturers make them pretty tame because of health and safety rules. Mum has to pretend she hasn't noticed that the box has gone missing so he can *surprise* us. But I won't be arresting him.'

'No, there are worse crimes.'

Jilly nodded, she was currently working on unravelling a major fraud, involving international money transfers through opaque tax havens. He, of course, had his murder investigation to return to. Their working lives took them into close contact with a side of life that was very far from the innocent Christmas fun of the moment – which was what made it so precious. It was also their working lives that had brought them together: Laurent's previous case had required a British counterpart and Jilly had been assigned as his contact whereupon the two detectives had quickly discovered they had more in common than just their profession.

'And how is your case going? Still no progress?'

'No. I have never had a case with zero suspects before. It is very perturbing.' Perturbing was a new word he was practising.

Blonnay and Jilly spent Boxing Day together, just the two of them, wandering around Covent Garden and going to a pantomime matinée. Jilly had initially scorned his request to go to a pantomime, but Blonnay's insistence, so curious was he about this strange tradition, had eventually won the day. He had first researched the pantomime when he had come across it in a previous murder investigation and had wanted to see one ever since. He watched enthralled as the public were encouraged to misbehave, shout and have things thrown at them. He joined in the *He's behind yous* and the *Oh no it isn'ts* as loudly as any of the children and Jilly, caught by his enthusiasm, did the same.

'Did it live up to your expectations?' she asked as they wandered around Covent Garden afterwards.

Blonnay loved musicals and his imagination had him seeing dancing chimney sweeps and dustbin men jigging around the cobbled streets.

'It was wonderful. No wonder the British are so raucous if they grow up being allowed to shout in the theatre.'

'I thought we had a reputation for being cold and reserved.'

'Not in Switzerland, we are also reserved as a people. Besides, the British have been misbehaving in my country for centuries.'

She thought of Byron, Shelley and then Hesse, Highsmith and Mann and smiled.

'Not just the British.'

'Oh no, not just the British. But you do seem to top the charts.'

He told her a bit more about the previous two murder cases he had been involved in where the British and Polish had competed for first place in the misbehaving stakes.

'But your current case hasn't got any British links, has it?'

'Not as far as we know, but I can't see them being left out of the action for long.'

Jilly just smiled tolerantly in response.

'I hope we've got it all resolved before you come out in February.'

'I hope I can get my current case resolved so I can come out for February. Either way, I'll see you in a couple of weeks for the wedding.'

'I am looking forward to being in Leicestershire again.'

As Blonnay sat on the train back down to Gatwick the next day, he reflected upon the differences between Christmas in the two countries. He compared the turkey dinner, crackers, silly jokes, puzzles and games with the more formal family meal he was used to, and reluctantly decided that, on the whole, the English version of Christmas was more fun. There was a noisy crowd of young Londoners on the train who were heading to Grondère for New Year. Ah, New Year, on the other hand he thought, Grondère was hard to beat for that!

On boarding his plane at Gatwick, Blonnay was delighted to find he was seated beside a familiar face. Charles Sidforth-Sykes was not quite so pleased to see Inspecteur chef adjoint Blonnay. The first time that Charles had met Blonnay had been the night Malcolm McDonaghue died and the last time had been when Blonnay had arrested him for suspected fraud and money laundering just a few months earlier. Despite being cleared of any criminal involvement in either affair, Charles had not covered himself in glory and the memories of that period were uncomfortable ones of which he would rather not have been reminded, especially during the festive season. The plane, however, was full: there was no escape and so Charles realised he would have to endure Blonnay's company for the one-and-a-half-hour flight to Geneva.
'Good to see you, Officer,' he lied.
Blonnay, on the other hand, was genuinely pleased to see Charles. Blonnay was a very pragmatic man who looked at facts and searched for the truth and never took any unpleasantness encountered in the process personally. As he never bore anyone ill-will, it would never have occurred to him that previous suspects, such as Charles, might hold it against him. But he had another, and more personal reason for appreciating Charles Sidforth-Sykes: Charles

was a goldmine of fabulously outdated, pompous and snobby vocabulary.

They exchanged niceties as they buckled in, with Blonnay explaining he had been visiting English friends for Christmas (carefully not mentioning his English girlfriend) and saying how much he had enjoyed Christmas in England.

Charles replied that he was pleased to hear that and, having ascertained the humble milieu of Blonnay's friends, launched into a description of his own Christmas with its vastly superior connections. It was everything Blonnay could have wished for.

'My sister is married to landed gentry, you know. We had Christmas at their country seat in Wiltshire.'

'Oh,' Blonnay asked, eager to encourage Charles's boastfulness. 'Is it a big estate?'

'Oh huge, you can hunt all day and never leave their land. The hunting and fishing are excellent to say nothing of the extensive gardens – landscaped by Capability Brown himself.'

'Ah yes, I have heard of him,' Blonnay smiled. 'The man who redesigned the English countryside.'

Charles nodded, surprised at Blonnay's knowledge, but he was also unsure if he had or had not detected a little facetiousness in the Swiss man's tone. But Blonnay's expression was all innocence and so he decided to dismiss the suspicion.

'The estate also has some very rare specimen trees brought back by plant-hunters from the farthest reaches of the planet on expeditions funded by my brother-in-law's ancestors.'

Blonnay was not sure how to respond to this piece of information so he decided to say 'ah' and look impressed. He refrained from asking if these were the same sort of people who had brought back grey squirrels, Dutch elm disease and the Colorado beetle from the farthest reaches of the planet.

'Of course, like most of the landed classes, they live in a constant state of genteel poverty.'

'Really?' asked Blonnay, this seeming an intriguing statement as the only British aristocrats he knew were Lord and the soon-to-be Lady Shilton and they seemed very wealthy.

'Ah yes, our upper classes were destroyed by death duties and socialists.'

'But the world is a fairer place, these days, is it not?'

Charles looked at Blonnay with condescension: I should have known he was a socialist, he thought to himself, but saying only in response, 'Yes, every Tom, Dick and Harry has a car and cable TV now and every Sharon can wear a tiara. But I think that a degree of romance has been lost: nobody knows their place anymore, there is no distinction of rank.'

It took all Blonnay's will power to resist reaching for his vocabulary notebook. He would just have to concentrate hard to memorise all these wonderful expressions until he could write them down.

'Forgive me,' Blonnay said, 'but I come from a country where we don't have ranks. I don't really know what you mean.'

'No,' Charles said, 'I don't suppose you do. The structure of Swiss society is pitifully homogenous and poor old Blighty is headed the same way. But at least we still have some strongholds, The Queen, the Royal Family, polo … there are still some bastions as yet unpolluted by the hoi polloi.'

'Hoi polloi!' Blonnay exclaimed. 'Can you say that in English?'

'Yes, it is English!'

Blonnay, who had studied Classics, knew that this was not the case.

'I think you'll find its origins are Greek. How fascinating that you use the article with it, it's like saying "the the masses".'

'Really,' said Charles, 'I didn't know you were a Classics scholar.' He didn't say how boring he thought this was. He would have preferred to talk about polo or cricket.

'Classical and modern languages,' Blonnay volunteered.

'Isn't that unusual for a police officer?'

'Perhaps: personally, I find it very helpful in my work. To understand someone's language and their use of language leads to a better understanding of the person, don't you think?'

Understanding people had never been a priority for Charles. If he had thought about it, had it been of greater importance to him, he might have made fewer errors in his choice of friends and business partners. But it was not in Charles's nature to consider himself lacking in any quarter and so he just shrugged.

'I hear you have a new body on your hands.'

'Indeed.' Blonnay replied. He loved the word 'indeed': it was his absolute favourite, it was so versatile and he was always happy to give it an airing. But Charles was to regret his flippant reference to this troubling case, for Blonnay was not one to miss an opportunity to dig for information.

'Did you know Jordan Russell, M. Sidforth-Sykes?'

Charles was clearly flustered by the question; he had carelessly opened the door to an informal interrogation.

'I knew him, yes, everyone knew Rusty, but not well.'

'Any background information you could supply would be most appreciated.'

Blonnay looked at Charles directly, he was not going to let the man off that lightly.

'He was a very outgoing, friendly chap. Member of the same ski club as me.'

'Your ski club?'

'Yes, the Grondère Diamond Ski Club. It's a good way to meet people to ski with and, in a club, you can ensure those people are of your own social standing.'

'Ah yes, no hoi polloi.'

'Exactly. Although now you mention it, it is strange that Rusty was accepted into my ski club, as he wasn't really a good fit.'

'You mean he was hoi polloi?'

Charles scowled; he could detect socialist undertones again.

'I suppose so. I only skied a few times with him but I don't remember ever really having an in-depth conversation with him about anything other than skiing. He was a good skier and pleasant enough chap to have a beer with, but he was a bit brash, not the sort of person you'd spend any serious time with. I always thought he was on the make, you know? A bit of a social climber.'

'Really, that is interesting,' Blonnay said. 'And was his social climbing successful?'

'I don't think so. None of my lot were fooled. You can only tell real breeding when you have pedigree yourself.'

Blonnay was enjoying himself immensely. What a peculiar thing to say, he thought, in fact, what a peculiar thing to think. He returned to the subject of Rusty.

'Do you know if he had any close friends or acquaintances?'

'No, as I say, he wasn't really my type. There is one person I believe he skied with quite often though.'

'Oh?'

'The chap everyone calls Gluey Hughey, you know him?'

'I have heard him mentioned.'

Charles decided he had been questioned enough on police matters for one flight and decided to attempt to change the subject.

'Shall I give you a brief introduction to the game of polo?'

'That would be great,' Blonnay, a sponge for all new knowledge, replied earnestly.

By the time they were taxiing to the stand at Geneva airport Blonnay had a good grasp of the fundamentals of the game and was floating on a cloud of new terminology: neckshots, nearsides, hired assassins, knock-ins, hooks, bells, hooters and chukkas.

As they waited for their bags Blonnay thanked Charles for having imparted so much wisdom and said he looked forward to a similar lecture on cricket. He then saw his bag roll onto the conveyor belt, grabbed for it and, seeing he had just ten minutes to catch the next train to Savigny, bid his travelling companion farewell.

Blonnay was somewhat thick-skinned but he was also a detective: he had noticed a bag with Charles's name on it go round three times without Charles even glancing at it. Realising that Charles was prepared to leave his bag going round and round indefinitely and wait an hour for the next train in order to avoid their travelling together any further, Blonnay decided to let him. Besides, it would give Blonnay a chance to write down all his new vocabulary on the train. He carefully chose a different carriage to the one containing that very rowdy crowd of young people heading to Grondère for New Year's Eve.

Whilst Blonnay had been living his English Christmas dream, the festive period for Lucy and her friends in Grondère had been the usual round of rushed gatherings squeezed in between looking after holidaymakers. Lucy and Alain spent Christmas Eve with Anne and her partner, Jacques and then had a Christmas Day meal with Tommy, Sally, Poppy and Jodie, their singer friend who was studying voice in Lausanne.

Not a fan of the New Year's Eve mayhem in Grondère, Lucy decided that she was not going to join the heaving, sweaty mass of humanity in Grondère's Grande Place at midnight.

'How say,' she asked her friends one evening, 'we do it differently? We could take the last cable car up the mountain and ski down to the Cabane Mont Grondère, have a fondue and then skin up a bit and watch the fireworks from the safe altitude of 2,400 metres?'

'I haven't done that for years,' Johnny said. 'Count me in.'

'Me too,' seconded Poppy.

'I know you didn't enjoy the mayhem of the Grande Place last year,' Tommy laughed, 'but isn't this taking it to the other extreme?'

Alain and the others all thought it was a great plan and so Lucy persuaded the Cabane to take one last-minute booking for eight in the hope that Eddie and Émilie would be back from Andorra by then.

A huge fire was crackling away in the Cabane when Lucy and her friends arrived, and the staff had laid the tables with festive baskets with winter leaves, berries and candles.

Gluey Hughey was already sitting at the table with Lucy's name card on it and greeted them with a big smile as if he were the host.

They all grinned and accepted their interloper with good humour while the manager of the Cabane pulled a face at Lucy and hastily added another place setting.

'After all,' Lucy whispered to Poppy and Sally in the ladies, 'it is an honour, that of all the New Year parties going on tonight, ours is the one that Gluey Hughey has selected to gatecrash.'

Perched on a rocky outcrop in the shadow of Mont Froid and facing the Bec Interdit, the Cabane Mont Grondère was a solid, stone-built refuge constructed to withstand the harsh weather conditions of the high mountain. But it was also a pretty building, with a traditional sloping roof and large stone sundial embedded above the front door. It had decorative wooden shutters bearing the old emblems of the canton of Valais and even the wooden fire ladders attached to the outside wall added to its quaintness. Inside, candles and oil lamps gave a warm glow to the cosy interior and the wooden clad walls, small, latticed windows and gingham curtains provided the traditional charm that tourists loved. But that night the Cabane was full of locals only and, between them, Lucy and her friends knew almost everyone in the tightly packed restaurant. They sat on benches at their long wooden table, greeting everyone across the room. It was a cheerful evening for sharing huge *caquelons* of fondue and a few bottles of white wine.

Whilst Lucy and the others were just tolerating Hughey's presence, Alain was delighted to see him: the *Police judiciaire* had failed to find an address for him the previous day and, despite contacts at the highest level, the staff from the Grondère Population Bureau who had access to the files of all foreign residents, had firmly refused to return from their various holiday locations for something that, as far as they could see, could clearly wait until the new year. Alain, as he had admitted defeat and conceded that they would indeed have to wait until the New Year to find Hughey, had pointed out to his team that the *Police judiciaire* appeared to wield greater influence with the incomers than the locals.

Knowing Hughey could be a slippery customer, Alain decided to bide his time, but Lucy spotted that he was being very generous with the wine, making sure that Hughey's glass of wine was never empty: she looked at him quizzically. Alain just shook his head and winked at her and Lucy, concluding that Alain must have his reasons, looked the other away.

Eddie and Émilie had made it back from Andorra in time and over supper they presented Sally with Émilie's silver medal from the race.

'I can't accept this, Émilie,' Sally protested. 'It's your first silver.'

'Yes, you can, Sally,' Émilie insisted. 'Without you Eddie wouldn't have been there and made me that huge bowl of porridge that morning. I'm convinced that's what made the difference.'

'Got to be porridge,' Tommy agreed, taking the medal to the cheers of the whole restaurant, who were thrilled to see Émilie amongst them. 'Thanks, Émilie,' he said, putting the medal around Sally's neck. 'You do us a great honour and so, as Sally doesn't realise that, I'll accept it on behalf of the team: Eddie didn't have a clue how to make porridge properly, I taught him that.'

After dinner, they ordered a *café de l'amitié* and the large wooden bowl with lid and numerous individual spouts was duly brought to the table. With the steam escaping from the spouts, they passed it around. Initially a few of them coughed as the vapour from the strong, spicy mix of coffee, alcohol and spices caught on the back of their throats, but they soon got the taste for it and passed it round and round, trying to remember which was their spout and arguing over the one with a distinctive chip, until it was completely drained. After a while, no one cared which spout they drank from: between the *café de l'amitié* and the fondue, they had all shared whatever germs they had anyway. After that Lucy made everyone tell a story of a past New Year's Eve, it could be true or false and everyone had to guess afterwards. Poppy told a ghost story that was so far-fetched it had to be false and Johnny told such a dirty tale, it had to be true. Gluey Hughey, normally not a great conversationalist, told them of a New Year's Eve when he had supped with royalty and snuck the aristocrats into a ski bum's after-party through the toilet window, without anyone knowing who they were boogying or snogging with. He bragged that he had carried a drunken princess back to her chalet and handed her over to a rather irate bodyguard.

'True!' they all shouted. 'It has to be true.'

Hughey nodded, happy with the success of his tale, and having been able, for once, to boast without invention.

At half past ten they put their ski gear back on and stepped out into the night for the skin up to the chosen viewpoint for midnight. They were aiming for a high point which would give them a view over Grondère on one side and down the Rhône Valley on the other.

It was a clear night, with an almost full moon on the wane which cast a ghostly shine on the snow and rocks that it touched but a dark shadow everywhere else. With bright headlamps they skied as far as they could down into a deep hollow and then took out their skins and attached them to the undersides of their skis. A little worse for wear for the wine and liqueur in the café, some of them huffed and puffed a bit to begin with and got a good teasing from those who had consumed more modestly, but eventually everyone got into a rhythm, the laughter gave way to effort and the only sound was the click-clack of boots against bindings as they tacked their way upwards.

Alain waited patiently for the right moment and, when he saw that everyone else was distracted, he fell into step beside Hughey and made him hang back. Hughey looked at him suspiciously.

'I was just wondering, Hughey, if you knew Jordan Russell at all?'

The question was loaded and Hughey knew it. He hesitated: if the detective had asked him the question it was because he knew something.

'I knew Rusty, yes.'

'We're struggling to put together a picture of the man. Anything you can tell me that might help me understand what he was like, who he socialised with, who he skied with, would be greatly appreciated. All off the record, of course.'

'I used to ski with Rusty, about twice a week. But all we talked about was skiing: I don't know much about him.'

'When did you meet him?'

'Oh, about four years ago, just after he settled here. We got talking in The Pub and I was telling him about the runs I'd done that day and he asked if I would take him with me. I took him once to make sure he was good enough to ski with me. He wasn't my standard but he was a good enough level, and of course, he improved a lot skiing with me these past few seasons. After that we had a sort of standing arrangement, every Wednesday and Friday: if one of us wasn't at the main station at opening, then no problem, the other went skiing alone. Friday was always a bit on and off but Wednesdays usually worked. But he was away a lot too.'

'Over four years you must have got to know him a little, he must have talked about his family, friends.'

'Not really, we mostly scoped our lines and discussed where we wanted to ski.'

'But everyone chats on the chairlifts and in the gondolas.'

'He was very focused when he was studying for his *patente*, he was so determined to get that qualification and so he talked a lot about that then. After he got it, his main topic of conversation, almost his only topic, was about his plans for the hotel and bar. I was looking forward to the opening party, he had promised it was going to be a fantastic do. I guess that won't be happening now ...' Hughey sighed.

'No,' Alain smiled to himself: that was one party that Hughey would have actually been invited to and now it would never happen. But Alain was not going to let Hughey wriggle out of his questioning that easily.

'Family? Friends?'

'He never mentioned family, except that he visited elderly family members in South Africa when he was there.'

'And yet, we can find no family in South Africa. The police there think most of his family moved to Australia, but we haven't been able to find any.'

'That's odd,' Hughey said spontaneously.

Alain looked at him and waited for more detail.

'I remember now, he said he managed a family business remotely and had to go back there regularly to keep an eye on things in person: that's why he travelled so much.'

'There was no family business.'

'Ah.'

'Did you make your plans by phone?'

'No, I don't have one.'

Alain looked at him askance, he didn't know anyone who didn't have a phone. No wonder Hughey was so hard to track down. But how he got wind of all the free parties without one was a real mystery.

There was silence for a moment as Hughey tried to think of some information that would be harmless to him but get Alain to leave him alone.

'Recently, he told me that he had made a promise to himself that he wouldn't open his bar until he had skinned up Mont Froid and skied down Le Monstre – a sort of milestone. He said, once the bar was open, he wouldn't have the time. He asked me to do it with him, but, to be honest, I liked skiing with him but he was not good at skinning, he was too slow and didn't have the stamina to keep up with me, so I said I didn't fancy it. I certainly wouldn't have gone with him on a day like the one he attempted it – madness!'

'Indeed, and he paid the price.'

'But are you sure it wasn't an accident?'

'No, Hughey. We are not sure of anything.' Alain did not mention that they knew one thing – that Rusty had been with someone else and that person had not come forward. He couldn't rule out the possibility that that person was Hughey, but something told him Hughey was telling the truth. He also didn't mention the diamonds found in Rusty's safe. Not wanting Hughey to feel he was being victimised or harassed in case he disappeared, Alain decided to halt his interrogation. It was, after all, a night for celebration.

'Thank you, Hughey, that has been really helpful. If you think of anything else, even if it's a tiny detail that you think might be relevant, will you let me know?'

'Yes, I will.'

Alain gave him a friendly pat on the back.

'The others have put a bit of distance between us. How about we put on a sprint and catch them up?'

Hughey nodded. Boastful he may have been, but he really was a good athlete and he and Alain caught up with the others in a short space of time.

As they continued their steep climb upwards, the dark south face of Mont Froid, the very mountain that had claimed Rusty's life, flanked their climb on the right. The north face that was known as Le Monstre was on the other side but even the gentler south face seemed to loom over them like a haunting giant. As they gained height they drew level with its higher flanks and it seemed less daunting. When they reached the lower summit they were aiming for, and stood upon its large flat crest that overlooked Grondère on one side, the deep, dark Rhône Valley to the other and the vast ski domain all around them, the sky opened out and the moonlight lit up the landscape. The stars sparkled above and the world below them sparkled too.

There was so much to look at. The lights of the resort shimmered red and gold, giving the impression of steams of volcano lava spreading molten seams along the streets. As they took the skins from their skis and carefully folded them in their backpacks, impromptu fireworks sparked up at irregular intervals far and wide, from the bright centre of Grondère, from the lower-lying ski slopes, from the deep darkness of the mountains and forests surrounding and all the way down the adjoining valleys. Bursts of fire in the blackness of night: it was a stunning sight.

'Great idea, Lucy,' Johnny complimented her.

Alain just wrapped his arms around her and she nestled the back of her head against his chest. He didn't say anything and Lucy didn't need words to know how much he loved her and anyway, putting up with her rowdy friends on New Year's Eve was proof enough.

At midnight they heard a cheer rise above the boom of the electronic drumbeat from the Grande Place and the fireworks went crazy. For the next twenty minutes, private individuals in expensive chalets launched into an annual competition which ensured the local council never had to spend any money at all. From all directions around the resort and in the mountains the sky was filled with glorious technicolour gunpowder and even the smell of it reached the group on the mountain. The slope groomers stopped their work and turned their lights in a salute towards the resort and blew their klaxons loudly.

'I've never heard that before,' wondered Tommy.

'No, because you're usually down there in the thick of it.' Tommy opened a bottle of fake champagne and handed round small beakers as they spun around watching the spectacle below.

'I was never above a firework display before,' Sally said. 'You think they go mega-high but from here they look quite small.'

'Yes, even the high ones only reach a height of 300 metres,' Tommy explained, 'so you should be pretty safe up here, Lucy.'

Lucy grinned: this sort of New Year's Eve was much more to her liking, and the best was yet to come, the moonlight ski back down to Grondère.

The fireworks were still sparking up erratically through the darkness as they set off, slowly snaking in a line down the empty, freshly groomed slopes lit by the moonlight and their headlamps and led by Eddie and Tommy holding fire torches.

As they arrived in the lower altitudes, their headlamps and the fire torches became essential to avoid the ruts in the snow which were now hardening over with the low night temperatures.

A large red firework shot overhead and as it exploded Alain gasped: the huge aerial pattern opened out to form the head of a roaring wolf. He was so surprised he nearly caught an edge.

'Did you see that?' he asked Lucy as she came up behind him.

'Yes, great chrysanthemum!' she exclaimed. 'What a finale!'

She clearly hadn't seen what he had seen. He wondered what it could mean.

Later, as Lucy sank into bed exhausted, all she said to him was, '*That* was my sort of New Year's party!'

He smiled and kissed her forehead; she was already fast asleep.

Six

*Mr Whickham is blessed with such happy manners as
may ensure his making friends – whether he may be
equally capable of retaining them, is less certain.*
Jane Austen, Pride and Prejudice

'Oh Lucy,' Suzie called over to her, in early January.
'Come and meet Rory, he's our ski leader for the next
fortnight.'

Lucy obediently headed over to be introduced to the tall,
handsome man who was holding court at the opposite
corner of the bar in The Pub.

'Oh hello,' he said, as he was introduced to the fresh-
faced, red-headed beauty. Lucy felt she was being
undressed in front of everyone. 'Haven't I seen you
somewhere before?'

Normally this would have been the corniest chat-up line if
there hadn't been the very real possibility that he had seen
Lucy before. She had just featured in Swiss Tourism's
summer marketing campaign and photos of her emerging
half-naked from a mountain lake were on posters and
magazine adverts the world over.

'I don't believe we've met,' she answered quickly, before
he made the connection. 'Lucy Wilson.'

'Ah, and are you a member of our merry band?' he asked.
'I don't remember seeing your name anywhere.'

'I am not,' she replied, 'although, Suzie did invite me to
tag along last week and I had a great time.'

'Well, tag along again, it would be our pleasure to have
you.'

Lucy knew that he meant more than skiing. She looked at
him. There was definitely a physical attraction between
them and his eyes left no doubt. Rory was a predator of the

most charming type. Impressed but not tempted, she smiled and kept the conversation firmly on skiing.

'I'd love to join you all for a ski, thanks.'

She managed to extract herself from Rory's mesmeric charm and returned to her friends at the bar while Suzie stayed and chatted to her ski club friends.

'Ohmigod!' Lucy laughed. 'I think I just met a real-life Mr. Whickham!' referring to the charming villain of Jane Austen's *Pride and Prejudice*.

'That'll be Rory, then,' surmised Johnny. 'That man's a fucking legend.'

'You know him?'

'We all know Rory,' Poppy nodded knowingly. 'He's been coming here for about five years now. He comes a couple of times a season with that exclusive ski club lot. I know what you mean, the man has an irresistible magnetism.'

'So how come I've never heard of him?'

'Last season you had other things to think about.'

'Ah yes,' Lucy had temporarily forgotten that the previous season she had been under a bit of a cloud.

'So, did you resist his "irresistible magnetism"?' Johnny asked with an evil grin.

Lucy grinned back.

'I think I can escape his clutches, thanks Johnny.'

'I wouldn't even try,' sighed Poppy. 'Oh, to be young again!'

'Poppy!' exclaimed Sally. 'Sometimes you really shock me!'

'After all this time you should know I have no regard for your bourgeois morals,' Poppy teased.

'You wouldn't really fall for such an obvious bounder, would you, Popps?'

'Fall for? No!' Poppy replied. 'Sleep with? Absolutely! That man just oozes sex appeal.'

Lucy spat out her beer and nearly choked. Sally nearly split her sides laughing.

'You girls are so old-fashioned,' Poppy continued. 'A man like Rory could never be a mate for life but for a brief bit of mating, he's probably pretty good. Such men turn sex into an art form. I suspect a night with Rory is a very worthwhile experience.'

'Just like me,' added Johnny. 'In my day, I was a real magnet for women.'

'Yes Johnny,' Poppy replied. 'Of course, you were.'

Lucy looked across the room to where Rory was propped against the wall, entertaining his friends but watching everything going on around him. He caught her glance and raised his glass.

Irritated with herself for having been caught showing interest of any kind, even if it was simple curiosity, she smiled back and looked away.

'Oh Lucy, watch out,' Poppy teased. He's got you in his sights.'

'Yes, I feel it.' Lucy agreed. 'There is something strangely compelling about him.'

'Don't worry,' Johnny reassured her. 'He's already worked out you're too much like hard work or he'd already be over here turning on the charm. If he had more time he might enjoy the challenge but he's only here for two weeks and Rory's a fast worker; he won't be alone tonight.'

'Thank you for providing the male perspective, Johnny,' Lucy laughed. 'So according to you, my virtue is only safe from Rory because he can't be bothered, is that right?'

'No, I only pointed out that you don't need to worry about him pursuing you, and why,' Johnny defended himself, asking himself, not for the first time, why women got affronted when you told them how it was.

'Well, Johnny, I am greatly reassured,' she laughed.

'Mind,' he added, with a note of warning in his voice, 'Poppy might shag him but she wouldn't ski with him, would you Popps?'

'No, I bloody well wouldn't,' Poppy affirmed. Looking at Lucy she added, 'You remember I warned you about that group, well he's the main reason!'

'Warning duly noted,' Lucy replied. When experienced skiers like Johnny and Poppy issued a warning like that, she knew to listen.

Johnny was right in his analysis that Rory would be saving his energy for other prey: Lucy saw no more of Rory until the following week when she joined Suzie and the Grondère Diamond Ski Club on a very beautiful morning and 40cm of fresh powder. He smiled when he saw her and was just as charming as on their first meeting, but Lucy felt that his interest in her was peripheral only. While they waited for the higher lifts to open, they skied a few lower slopes, and then, realising the lift company had decided it was too dangerous to open the higher sections of the resort, there was a bit of a discussion at the head of the group after which Rory started to lead them into a traverse across the ridge under the main cable car. Lucy realised they were heading for a corridor that held a particular significance for her and stopped. From that spot, she knew she could still turn back and ski down a safer incline.

'What's up, Lucy?' asked Suzie who was just behind her.

'I'm sorry, I don't feel it, I'm going to ski off the other side.'

'Oh, okay, you sure? We've all done our avalanche training and we're all equipped.'

'It doesn't matter, Suzie, one of my best friends died in an avalanche down The Tube, it's a couloir I can never ski, even if I felt the conditions were safe, which I don't.'

Lucy looked down on the beautiful untouched face below her. The steepness and the powder no longer fazed her: following her day heli-skiing she was confident in her technique, but the snow did not look stable and knowing that Danny had lost his life there was discouragement enough.

Suzie knew better than to try and influence a fellow skier's decision. Rory doubled back to find out what was holding them up.

'Come on, Lucy. Live a little dangerously,' he urged with a mocking smile.

Lucy smiled, remembering Johnny and Poppy's warning and shook her head.

'Sorry Rory, I find the *live* bit of that sentence more appealing than the *dangerously*,' she said firmly.

Rory shrugged, clearly writing her off as a total coward and headed back to his ski club members who were straining at the leash.

'See you in The Pub later?' Suzie asked.

'It's a date, and Suzie …'

'Yes?'

'Stay well to the left and watch out for anyone dropping in above you from the right.'

Suzie nodded and set off to follow the rest of the group. Lucy slid off along the ridge until she found a wide gully she knew would lead her back to the patrolled slopes. As she gently traversed down, Lucy felt a little disappointed in herself. Am I sensible or just a coward? Do I lack Suzie's spirit for adventure and Rory's sense of daring? Somewhere along the way am I missing out on life's great adventure? She didn't have the answer: until she met Suzie and Rory, it wasn't a question she had ever asked herself.

Later Lucy was genuinely relieved to see Suzie in The Pub and hear that it had all gone well and they had had a lovely ski with no mishap.

'But you were right, it wasn't stable,' Suzie admitted. 'I stayed well left as you told me and I sat on a shoulder until I was sure there was no one above or behind me. Rory and the others were heading back to do it again but the patrollers were standing blocking it off and it came down shortly afterwards.'

'Thank goodness you're all safe,' was all that Lucy said. Inside she felt vindicated in her choice not to ski The Tube but she was appalled that Rory could put his ski club followers in such danger.

'You made the right call,' Poppy said when Lucy told her friends about the Diamond Ski Club's close shave. 'Well done, Lucy, sometimes it takes more courage to turn back and not launch yourself down a face you know is likely to turn on you. That's not what skiing's about.'

'I swear that guy has a charmed existence,' said Johnny.

'Rory?'

'Yeah, our Rory could fall in shit and come up smelling of roses,' Johnny grinned.

Poppy agreed. 'He always seems to be right on the edge, but always gets away with it.'

'I have heard,' Jamie began, his voice honeyed with mischief, 'that Rory and Alessandra Rosset have been enjoying each other's company.'

'Noooo,' Sally exclaimed in disbelief.

'Oooh, Lucy, your eyes are as wide as saucers!' Jamie teased.

'That's just so unlikely,' she replied.

Poppy was grinning so much she could hardly speak.

'Hot and steamy,' Jamie confirmed.

'How could you know such a thing?' Sally asked.

'I have my sources,' he winked.

'Hasn't Alessandra taken an apartment in the block above Sammy's restaurant?' Poppy asked.

'Ah,' exclaimed Sally. 'That explains your inside knowledge then, Jamie.'

Jamie just laughed and tapped his nose.

'It must be considerably more comfortable for Rory than the studio provided by the ski club,' Poppy joked.

'They have been witnessed practically undressing one another waiting for the lift,' he disclosed, eyebrows raised suggestively.

They all chuckled at the thought of Rory and one of Switzerland's most successful property magnates together.

'How on earth did they meet?'

'Humphrey is an inactive local member of the Grondère Diamonds, I believe he introduced them.'

'That old devil,' smirked Johnny. 'Not that inactive … He's been up to his mischief again!'

'Personally,' Poppy concluded, 'that woman has rocketed up in my estimation. She, at least, has had the courage to have a bit of fun.'

'She has all my admiration,' Sally laughed.

'And all my gratitude,' Lucy added with a wide grin.

Their conversation turned to other subjects and their current favourite topic: their imminent trip to Leicestershire. The men rolled their eyes as talk turned to outfits, accessories and speculation about the bride's dress. But a large component of any wedding is anticipation. One special day can occupy many more in the careful and considered discussion of all imagined possibilities from the moment the invitation arrives. The same can be said after the event, for then it is not the imagination at work but the memory, dissecting each delectable detail, from the decorations, venue, clothing, guests, food and music, all, of course, with the assistance of numerous photos. A wedding should be savoured for as long as possible and this one was no different except perhaps that few of the Grondère guests would ever have been to one quite like it.

Seven

*When you realise that you want to spend the rest of your
life with someone, you want the rest of your life to begin
as soon as possible.*
        Nora Ephron, When Harry met Sally

A warm light filtered through the colourful stained-glass
windows of Leicester Cathedral. On a cold, bright January
afternoon, the guests for Sebastian, Lord Shilton and
Tonita Shalott's wedding were bathing in this warm glow,
waiting for the bride to arrive. Sebastian, Viscount
Lunstag, Lord Shilton for just a couple of short months,
was already there, standing by the front pew with his best
man, an old university friend.

Lucy looked around the congregation; there was a healthy
contingent from Grondère looking pretty smart out of their
ski clothes and a lot of people who looked even smarter.
Wealthy banker friends of Sebastian from New York and
London, Tonita's contacts from the design and fashion
worlds and a lot of British members of the nobility whose
invitations had been carefully researched and advised by
Mr. Humphries (Sebastian's butler) and Mr. Taylor (his
land agent) to whom Sebastian deferred in all matters of
protocol.

The press had come too: this beautiful young couple who
had joined the British aristocracy from an 'illegitimate'
branch of the family were fast becoming firm favourites
with the media. Sebastian and Tonita had totally
'legitimised' their position by allowing the press shared
media coverage of the ceremony for a generous fee which
was to be donated to local charities. Numerous
photographers awaited Tonita's arrival outside and one
'shared' cameraman and photographer discreetly filmed
the guests in their finery inside the cathedral.

Appearing perfectly relaxed, as he stood chatting happily with his best man and the bishop, Sebastian, a tall redhead with a freckled complexion, looked distinguished in traditional morning dress. Lucy had been able to trace his handsome features in the portraits of his Shilton ancestors hanging on the walls of Lunstag Hall, reinforcing his right to be there despite coming from an illegitimate branch of that great family. Lucy's sharp eyes scanned the cathedral, the guests, the decorations – recording every detail. As the bells rang out, she spotted Tonita's father and his third wife sitting in the front row on the bride's side of the cathedral where Jodie stood composed by the piano waiting for her moment.

A hushed whisper that the bride had arrived started at the door of the cathedral and rippled through the guests in the pews, creating an electrical sense of expectation. The rumour was confirmed by a small altar boy running down the aisle and informing the bishop. The bishop nodded with a smile to Sebastian and walked with purpose to the main entrance to greet Tonita. A hush fell as the double wooden doors opened wide with a loud clank and everyone rose for the bishop to lead in the bridal party. To a special arrangement of The Carpenters' *We've Only Just Begun*, Jodie sang Tonita down the aisle.

Eschewing the need to be 'given away', Tonita glided down the aisle without anyone at her side, looking every inch the lady. Playing on her pseudonym, The Lady of Shalott, she wore a mediæval-style dress in ivory satin with a short train and an oval belt encrusted with pearls just below the hip, cleverly hiding the little bump that only Lucy and a few others knew about. Long, open sleeves and a low, oval neckline were also edged with pearls and Tonita's long, black hair hung in ringlets down her back with only a small gold, net Juliet cap threaded with pearls. Behind her, her young half-sister, Ruby, also wore a little mediæval-style dress, but in a heavier, patterned satin, and her half-brother, Leo, a tunic and hose. Beside them trotted Słowik, the little Italian greyhound that had shared so many adventures with Lucy, clad with a pearl-encrusted collar and looking every inch the aristocrat. The artist in Tonita had created a stunning mediæval pastiche, worthy of the Pre-Raphaelite paintings she so loved, that made everyone present gasp.

Lucy felt the tears of joy well up and dabbed them away before they blinded her completely; she didn't want to miss a single detail. Beside her Poppy and Sally grinned at one another; Lucy always had a good blub when she got emotional. The song wasn't helping either – Lucy knew from Jodie that it had been a favourite of Tonita's mother, who had died from breast cancer when Tonita was still a teenager, and that Jodie, together with the flautist and pianist had adapted the song to create a more classical arrangement to suit Jodie's voice and fit the time required for Tonita to walk down the aisle.

As Tonita reached Sebastian's side, she turned to Jodie and nodded her thanks. Lucy saw it and her shoulders started to shake. Alain gave her a hug and tickled her hand to help her shake off the emotion overload.

The formal part of the ceremony and the readings gave Lucy the chance to pull herself together. She had been asked if she would like to read the Shakespeare but Lucy, knowing she was likely to cry, had said she would rather Poppy did it and she greatly enjoyed Poppy's accomplished reading of the 29th sonnet. It was the one that spoke of love being worth more than the wealth of kings and Lucy understood why Tonita and Sebastian had chosen it, for their love had come late and unexpectedly and she knew that, despite all the wealth that had come their way, they valued this love above all else.

Jodie's second song was a classical piece in German and Lucy, not understanding it, was able to enjoy the beauty of Jodie's voice without the emotion of the more modern piece she had sung on Tonita's entry. It was fortunate for all present because the song was from Schumann's *Woman's Life and Love* cycle and if Lucy could have understood the words she would have sobbed without restraint.

Tonita and Sebastian walked back up the aisle together beaming. In keeping with the unorthodox choice of music, the organ blasted Andrew Lloyd Webber's *Hosanna*. This caused some mystified looks and a few smirks from those informed enough to know that the song came from a requiem mass, but Tonita and Sebastian didn't care – they thought it sounded splendid, and, accompanied by the cathedral bells cast by Taylors of Loughborough with the Leicester Cathedral bell-ringers using every ounce of their skill and energy to celebrate their new local lord and his new wife, it did.

Jodie wriggled through the crowd to join them as they filtered out of the cathedral and they all hugged her and told her how brilliant she was.

Alain looked at Blonnay and Sylvie Jacquier and gave a loud sigh of relief.

'What was that for?' Lucy asked him in astonishment.

Blonnay answered for him.

'We managed to get through that without a murder – remarkable!' he grinned.

Sylvie laughed, 'Congratulations, Lucy, your reputation is ruined.'

'Well, thank goodness for that,' she smiled.

Poppy gave her a hug as they watched the married couple take their time to say hello and pose for the crowd of well-wishers they had attracted. The new Lord and Lady Shilton understood the value of local goodwill.

'I'm glad Tonita didn't overdo her mediæval theme and allowed Sebastian to stick to traditional morning dress.' Poppy joked.

'Oh, I don't know,' Jodie laughed. 'I think he'd look pretty good in a doublet and hose.'

'Wasn't that more Elizabethan? Tunics came before that didn't they? Like what Leo's wearing?'

'I guess but I think you're allowed a bit of licence when you're creating a living tableau.' Sally was the group's acknowledged fashion expert. 'Look, his tie is the exact same fabric as the children's outfits, so she has *tied* it all in nicely.'

They all groaned at Sally's pun and stood enjoying watching the official and unofficial photographers get their fill of Sebastian and Tonita sitting in the Shilton family six-horse driven coach which would take them to the outskirts of the town before shifting to the Range Rover which would take them back to Lunstag Hall for the wedding breakfast.

'It's amazing how the photographers know who to photograph.' Sally commented, slightly peeved that none of the members of the press present had deemed her worthy of their focus.

'It's their job, you daft thing,' Tommy laughed. 'These guys know the *Who's Who* better than its compilers.'

'I guess so. Still I don't wear a dress often, it would be nice if someone recognised the effort.'

'I recognise the effort,' he reassured her, giving her a peck on the cheek and promptly going red – public displays of affection not being his thing. He and Sally were off to visit his family for a few days after the wedding, he was looking forward to introducing his Australian girlfriend to his family.

'You do look stunning, Sally,' smiled Poppy. 'The whole thing was stunning, wasn't it?'

'It was, what a shame poor Carla and her daughter lost their right to be here,' Lucy commented.

'You cannot be feeling sorry for that ghastly pair today of all days. And anyway, think about it: if they hadn't murdered Malcolm then this wedding would never have taken place; secondly, if Carla had got her way, you and I would be in prison instead of her and Genna and thirdly, if Carla had been organising a wedding for her son, we'd definitely never have been invited, let alone staying at Lunstag Hall.'

'I know, I know, but I was thinking what a shame it was for Sebastian and Tonita, neither of them has much of a family, do they?'

'No.' said Poppy looking across at Tony Onion, Tonita's father, who was clearly enjoying working his daughter's new connections.

'Hey! Isn't that the Diamond Ski Club bloke, talking to Tonita's dad?' asked Sally.

'Rory? I do believe you're right, what on earth is he doing here? He must have come with Alessandra Rosset.' They all had a giggle at this idea.

'Oooh, look there's Prince Anwar over there, his wife's so beautiful. They're staying at Lunstag too apparently.'

'They weren't at breakfast.'

'They just flew in to the local airfield this morning, by private jet.' Sally informed them.

'How do you know?'

'I overheard the butler sending a car for them.'

'Crikey,' said Poppy, 'it's another world isn't it?'

Lucy grinned.

'That breakfast buffet was amazing: I couldn't eat breakfast like that every day, I'd be enormous.'

'I could,' said Tommy.

Lucy and her friends had arrived the previous afternoon. Upon arrival they had been greeted by a real-life butler and shown to their rooms by a real-life housekeeper.

'I feel like I'm in *Downton Abbey*,' Sally had whispered as they wandered the long corridors to the guest quarters.

'Well, I don't want any night-time antics in the corridors from you lot,' Poppy warned jokingly.

'Poppy, we all know that if anyone is going to get up to any scandalous bedroom-hopping, it's going to be you!' Sally retorted.

'Which room is Jodie Scott in?' Lucy asked the housekeeper hurriedly to distract her.

'Miss Scott is in rehearsal at the cathedral at the moment,' the housekeeper replied. 'I will let her know you're here when she returns.'

Blonnay and his girlfriend, Jilly, were the only ones amongst them who had visited Lunstag Hall before. It had been during the Reichenbach Falls murder investigation and Jilly Ferguson, a DI from Scotland Yard had accompanied Blonnay to interview the previous Lord Shilton and see if he had any connection with their investigation. Unfortunately for him, he did, but he didn't know it; he had sent them away with as much haste as common courtesy would allow. If he had heeded their warning, he might have still been alive, and they would not be at Lunstag Hall for the second time.

Jilly had studied history at university and had been a bit peeved on her previous visit not to have seen more of the country house as it was one that was not open to the public. This time she was particularly determined to see it properly and this time she was there as a guest of the family. On their arrival, the butler, Mr. Humphries, had nodded and smiled at Blonnay and Jilly to show that he had recognised them and to indicate that he graciously

82

bore them no resentment for failing to prevent the death of his previous employer. After all, he now had Sebastian McDonaghue to look after – a true gentleman and most appreciative.

As each couple had been shown to their room, they were handed an invitation to join Sebastian and Tonita for pre-dinner cocktails at 6 o'clock. Inspectrice Sylvie Jacquier and Sandra Guérin, Sally's co-manager of the vineyard, who had only met for the first time on the flight over, seemed to be getting on well and happily agreed to share a room, despite the housekeeper's offer to find another if necessary.

'I promise you, this is luxury,' Sylvie reassured her, 'we are mountain folk, used to sharing dormitories in refuges.'

'I don't know about mountain folk, but that one's a true lady,' commented the housekeeper approvingly as she shepherded Lucy and Alain to their room.

'Oh, and more,' Lucy told her. 'She's also a life-saver, mountaineer, crack shot, ace skier, the list goes on.'

The housekeeper smiled at her patronisingly.

'You have just described the accomplishments of the *average* English lady to me. What makes a *true lady* is her grace, presence and generosity of spirit.'

Lucy grimaced to Alain as they were handed their invitation and the door closed behind them.

'I guess that rules me out then.'

'Do you want to be thought of as a *true lady*?'

'I'm not sure, let me get back to you on that. Either way, she was making a "true" compliment to Sylvie, and you have to admit Sylvie does have star quality.'

'I do. I'm lucky to have her on my team.'

'This room is something else, isn't it?'

Lucy looked around the spacious room with rich furnishings and en-suite bathroom.

'It is. We obviously got special treatment in room allocation.'

'Thank goodness the housekeeper didn't choose for us: she'd have put Sylvie in here and shoved us in the maids' room.'

As they chuckled there came a knock on the door and Tonita, unable to wait for the pre-dinner cocktails, entered with a beaming smile on her beautiful face.

'Can I take her away, please Alain,' she asked, hugging them tightly. 'I've been dying for her to arrive. Sebastian's in the library kicking his heels, he's asked if you could join him there.'

Alain smiled, 'How could I refuse?'

He headed down to the library to a warm greeting from Sebastian while Tonita dragged Lucy off to show her her dress and tell her all about the plans for the following day.

'You invited your dad, then?'

'For the sake of keeping the peace, yes, and for the kids. I don't want them to know how much I loathe their father.'

'I think it was a wise decision. It's not for long. Is he staying in the house?'

'Christ, no. I couldn't have handled that. I've shoved them in the Dower House, we haven't got a dowager to put in it and it's a good walk away. I'd rather have Ruby and Leo here in the main house but I'll have them with me tomorrow.'

'I take it he's not giving you away then?' Lucy teased.

'Are you kidding? He lost the right to that privilege a long time ago. And thankfully, in this day and age, no one, including him, seems to expect it. I think he's just relieved to be invited.'

'Are the children excited?'

'Totally unfazed. They seem more excited about seeing you and Poppy. They should be here soon, they said they would come over before supper.'

'And how are you adapting to being lady of the manor?'

'Lucy, I cannot lie to you. I love it! Sebastian has a lot to learn about running the estate and all the various businesses but we get loads of time together, and I'm setting up my studio in a converted barn. Oh, and I have news ...' she patted her tummy smugly.

'Oh, that's wonderful! Congratulations!'

'I wanted you to be the first to know.'

'I'm honoured.' Lucy planted a spontaneous kiss on Tonita's cheek. 'You'll make a great mum, Tonita.'

'Do you think so? I've been so selfish for so long, I do worry about being up to it.'

'I think the fact that you worry means you are more than up to it. I'm already looking forward to taking your child hiking in the mountains.' Lucy didn't mention the wolf, she thought it was probably not the right moment.

'Me too. I'm not quite at three months yet. We'll make an announcement after the honeymoon.'

'Which is where?'

'California – we're tying it in with visiting the Shilton vineyards out there. C'mon, let's go and find Poppy. The children should be here soon.'

Dinner on the eve of the wedding had been an informal buffet as there were so many house guests. Blonnay and Jilly had been given a personal tour of the house and grounds by Sebastian's agent, Mr. Taylor, and were full of the architectural wonders and works of art they had seen. Poppy and Lucy enjoyed the cocktail-making talents of Mr. Humphries and Lucy, a former barmaid, was able to share a few recipes of her own with him.

Sally, Tommy and Sandra were now in earnest conversation with Mr. Taylor. Sally and Sandra were running Sebastian's Swiss vineyard and Tommy was going into farming. From the odd parts of the conversation she could overhear, Lucy gathered they were discussing the merits of organic agriculture.

Lucy looked around with such pleasure, it was written all over her face.

'I can see you observing everyone and taking it all in,' Alain grinned.

'Of course. I was also reflecting on the victory of joy and love over evil and cruelty.'

'It isn't often I can follow your thought process but, for once, I totally get where you're coming from.'

They grinned and sipped on their Charlie Chaplins, one of Lucy's favourites.

'Fancy them having sloe gin,' he teased.

'Fancy,' she winked. Lucy had brought a little bottle of her Swiss sloe gin for Sebastian and Tonita. It would probably not see out the evening.

Back at Lunstag Hall, after the wedding ceremony, the wedding breakfast was also a stunning demonstration of Tonita's artistic talents. With no mother of the bride or groom to constrain her choices, her creative flair had produced a scene of breathtaking beauty.

Flowers hung in wreaths from the rafters of the great hall and a small chamber orchestra played from the minstrels' gallery. The white-clothed tables were decked in frothy arrangements of small ivory-coloured roses from which tall, tapered candles rose from silver candelabras. It looked ethereal. Tonita had discovered most of the family silver and porcelain that hadn't seen the light of day for decades stowed away in the cellars of the great house and decided that it should all be used again. The old-fashioned plates, glasses and cutlery had inspired her to create an old-fashioned theme with a modern twist using her own-designed menus and name cards in tiny modern cardholders and favour bags. Lucy and her friends oohed and aahed over every tiny detail while the men and Sally looked at the wine and beverages list with considerable interest. There was one wine in particular that held special significance for all of them: a sparkling white from the Swiss vineyard, Le Cerf sous la Lune, called *La Dame de Shalott.*

When it arrived and everyone rose to greet and toast the entry of the married couple, the party from Grondère group all turned and also toasted Sally and Sandra.

'Congratulations. You did it!' Lucy declared.

Sally and Sandra smiled happily. The wine had originally been Malcolm McDonaghue's concept and had been planned as a surprise for Tonita on their wedding day. The two young women had worked hard to ensure that it was ready and delivered in time and in prime condition for Malcolm's son's wedding.

Sebastian mentioned his father with fondness in his speech and raised a glass to him, whilst also thanking his vineyard team. The two women suddenly found themselves the focus of everyone in the hall, which made Sandra a little uncomfortable but Sally shamelessly lapped up the attention.

After the meal and speeches there was an informal photo session on the lawn, and Tonita, who had insisted that it last no more than half an hour for the sake of her guests, made sure that the official photographer took a picture of her and all the Grondère girls together in the rose garden. In the frosty fading light of the wintry afternoon, the bare tangled stems of last summer's roses, the black latticed frames of their supporting arches and the dark yew hedges made a romantic frame to the shot. More accustomed to ski clothes than their flimsy dresses, they quickly began to feel the cold and hurried into the big marquee on the lawn for the evening party.

The marquee was a very different affair to the great hall, it looked like an 80s disco with mirror balls hanging from the roof and garish lighting. The DJ had received an instruction to play every song requested by the guests and they all had great fun running up and demanding their favourites. They rock and rolled until late when the guests gradually started drifting off to their various homes and hotels.

At one point, Lucy took a pause from the dancing and stepped outside on her own to take the air and look at the stars. She overheard Alessandra Rosset and Rory paying their respects to the bride before leaving for their hotel. Rory and Tonita must have worked out they had a common link with The Netherlands but they clearly had not established any common acquaintances.

'I must be mistaken, it's many years since I lived there,' Tonita said softly, 'my only connections there now are linked to my jewellery business.'

'Oh no, I don't know anyone in the jewellery business, I'm an oil and gas consultant,' she heard Rory saying.

'Strange,' Tonita said pensively, as she spotted Lucy and linked arms with her, leading her for a walk around the formal parterre garden. The house windows were all still ablaze and the freshly formed frost on the low hedges sparkling in their reflected light. 'I'm sure I've seen that man before: I wonder where. He used the word "baguette" when he looked at my ring, unusual for someone outside the business.'

'Trust me, Tonita, if you had *met* Rory, you would remember. He is the sort of person who leaves an impression. I suspect that you have probably caught sight of him in Grondère,' Lucy smiled. 'He is a good-looking chap and he does stand out in a crowd.'

'That must be it,' Tonita agreed, unconvinced.

'As for the jewellery term, that doesn't surprise me a bit. He's a known womaniser: I bet he knows more than I do about jewellery, make-up, fashion … everything!'

Tonita laughed.

'You are funny, Lucy, it wouldn't be hard for anyone to know more than you on those subjects, but yes, you are probably right. Men who love women do seem to gen up on female matters in order to ingratiate themselves. I meet a lot of them in my business. You don't like him?'

'I think he has great charm and magnetism.'

'That's not the same thing.'

'No, it's not the same thing. I wouldn't go so far as to say I didn't like him though, in fact, I have to admit, I find him attractive, maybe that's why he makes me feel uncomfortable. Poppy would give her right arm for a night with Rory.' They both laughed.

'I see what you mean: you prefer a safe man, Lucy.'

Lucy shook her head and grinned, 'I prefer an honest man.'

As daylight dawned, Buck's Fizz and croissants were served to the hardcore partygoers who were still standing. The Grondère crowd, determined not to miss a second of the festivities, munched on their croissants and were the last to bed. After only a few hours' sleep, they were amongst the first to rise and go downstairs for breakfast so that they could have one last chance to observe and admire the guests.

Breakfast was a very quiet affair, with many nursing sore heads. Guests drifted in and out, some grabbed a quick coffee, clearly under time constraints of flights and trains, and others were having a more leisurely breakfast before setting off. Prince Anwar and his wife politely smiled across at the Grondère table but sat with their own friends. Sebastian and Tonita, looking pale but happy, wandered around, greeting people, thanking them for coming and bidding them farewell. It was altogether calmer than the previous day.

Until Sally, surfacing later than her friends, entered the room with Tommy and caught sight of the pile of newspapers on a table in the entrance way. The papers had been arranged to show the pages bearing the press photos and reports of the previous day.

'Ohmigod!' she exclaimed. 'Look at this! We're all over the Mail.'

Lucy, having been convinced that the newspapers would have ignored the bride and groom's less glamorous connections, had ignored the newspapers. But now she headed over to where Sally was gleefully pointing to a report which had taken a slightly different stance to the others. Whilst commenting on the various celebrities and members of the aristocracy present, the paper had also reported on the couple's Swiss links. There was, of course, a story to tell about various plots and murders but, out of respect for the occasion, the paper concentrated on the hotel and vineyard. The photo of Tonita surrounded by all the Grondère girls straddled the centrefold. There was a photo of Jodie – the 'Grondère Nightingale', and a complimentary little paragraph about her singing at the ceremony. More importantly, a photographer had clearly been mingling with the guests as they left the church and there was a large and flattering photo of Sally and Sandra, sub-titled *Miss Sally Collins and Miss Sandra Guérin, the all-female management team of Lord and Lady Shilton's Swiss vineyard, Le Cerf sous la Lune.*

'I am totally made-up,' Sally declared. Tommy and Lucy grinned.

'That'll go down well with the in-laws,' Tommy said, giving her a proud hug.

Sally looked at him shrewdly and, with no attempt to disguise her theft, took the paper, folded it and put it into her handbag.

'I'm suddenly very hungry. Breakfast?' she said, looking around the room with a wide smile.

'Our table is over here,' said Lucy, seeing amused looks being cast in their direction. Realising that any attempt at discretion was useless and too late anyway, Lucy led her buoyant friend to the table where the rest of the group was waiting eagerly to know what all the fuss was about. The paper reappeared to be handed around before Sally firmly retrieved it and placed it securely back in her bag.

Lucy left Sally to tuck into breakfast and took her coffee over to another table where Sylvie Jacquier was sitting chatting to Sandra. Lucy had huge respect for Sylvie, but although Sylvie was always friendly, Lucy felt the young detective was holding something in reserve: probably because Lucy's boyfriend was Sylvie's boss and, of all of Alain's team, Sylvie was the most professional.

'Who would have thought, from the Lesteraarhorn to Leicester Cathedral,' Sylvie joked.

'Indeed, who would have thought it,' Lucy smiled, thinking of the housekeeper's words and still wondering what set Sylvie apart as a true lady.

'And next stop, Poland. Are you ready for next week?'

'I am, although I have to admit that it doesn't come at the best of times. My boss wasn't too happy about giving me more time off after this.'

'No,' Sylvie nodded. 'My boss,' she nodded in Alain's direction, 'wasn't a problem but I really do feel bad leaving the team mid-investigation. But we promised.'

Lucy felt a bit ill at ease going on a city break with Sylvie. Even though they had been through some harrowing moments, the only time they had spent any length of time together was when Sylvie had been her protection officer on the Lesteraarhorn.

This time it would be different: they were booked to fly to Warsaw to respect an important social engagement.

'Yes,' Lucy agreed. 'And a promise is a promise.'

Eight

The intensest form of hatred is that rooted in fear.
George Eliot, Daniel Deronda

One beautiful crisp winter's morning after they had returned from England, Lucy and Poppy went skinning in the forest below the old *bisse* path. They had hit a quiet spell before the half-term peak and were enjoying chatting away, catching up on all the news. Jodie had called to say she had already received some professional bookings as a result of her performance at Sebastian and Tonita's wedding and she could start thinking about renting a decent studio in Lausanne instead of the tiny student room she had been in until then.

'She's on her way,' Poppy was saying, 'just a few television appearances and a recording contract and we'll not be seeing much more of her at all.'

Lucy gasped.

'It's not that terrible,' replied Poppy, until she saw what had caught Lucy's attention.

Ahead of them on the path, standing still as a statue, was a man, his gun pointing at something. As they approached him, he lowered his gun and snarled at them.

'You stupid, loud bitches. You've frightened it off, I won't get another chance like that!'

Poppy was most indignant.

'Do you have a permit for hunting out of season?' she asked priggishly.

'I don't need a permit to kill a wolf, I'm protecting the future of my livestock.'

'A wolf?'

'Yes, don't come bleating to me when it starts killing calves in the summer. Or when it attacks you, you stupid, interfering cows.'

'But aren't wolves a protected species?' Lucy inquired.

He scowled at her and skied further down the path, scanning the snow for wolf tracks. Poppy and Lucy pulled faces at one another and prepared to continue to climb. Suddenly, a large female wolf bounded out from a bush beside them, looked at them quickly and then disappeared into the woodland ahead of them. It was Poppy's turn to gasp.

'Oh my goodness, it was crouching right beside us all the time that man was shouting at us!'

'I can't believe we've just been eye to eye with a wild wolf.'

'No, wow!'

They looked at one another and giggled nervously.

'Well, that confirms the howling at dawn you heard in December. That chap didn't like your protected species line though,' Poppy said as they continued their climb towards Old Folk's Rock.

'He didn't. But we all know you can't just go around shooting the things,' Lucy said. 'I talked to Jean-Marc when I first heard the wolf call in December, and he reckons you can get into real trouble if you get found out.'

'Yes, and it's not even the hunting season. Well, he backed off anyway. Did you see how shifty he looked as he skied off?'

'I did, but I understand it from his perspective too. I'm a bit nervous about walking alone in the forest now I know we have a resident wolf.'

'You shouldn't be, the wolf's not interested in you. But I do think you would be happier if you had a dog with you: you know you want one anyway.'

'I don't think a dog would be able to save me if a wolf wanted to eat me although it might warn me. But you're right: I do miss walking with a dog. I got so used to having Słowik beside me I feel almost selfish walking alone now.'

'What breed would you go for?'

'Oh, I don't mind. Anything from the rescue centre would do. But I do have a bit of a weakness for Welsh border collies. They're so sharp and sparky.'

'That sounds just the right match for you. And I understand they can make good truffle hunters.'

Lucy smiled: Poppy and her truffles.

'But I don't have the time or the room for a dog in winter. I don't even know where I'll be living this time next year. Summer would be fine at Alain's chalet though. Hopefully, if I get enough clients, it could accompany me on my guided walks when I get my diploma, but for now, I must just learn, like the rest of us, to share the mountains with the wolf.'

'I'm on cloud nine. How wonderful, my first wolf!'

Lucy looked at her askance.

'I'm not sure I share your joy.'

'You'll come round. Just wait till we tell the others.'

Carla Sturridge returned to her cell with a smile of vengeful satisfaction. She sat on her bed and thought over what had just happened. Carla didn't get many visitors: usually it was the Swiss police asking more questions or some simpering well-doer from the Red Cross. This visit had come out of the blue and had been most profitable in terms of little luxuries, tradeable goods and information from the outside world, in particular Grondère.

When she had seen that familiar face in the visitor room she had laughed out loud.

'What on earth are you doing here?'

'Information,' came the honest reply.

Her interlocutor had come in search of any useful titbits of knowledge that could potentially damage mutual enemies.

Carla had been happy to oblige; anything that could hurt her ancient foe Poppy or that grasping social climber Tonita, was of interest to her. She wasn't sure that the information she had provided was terribly useful, but her visitor had seemed to think so and had promised to return with more expensive goods once Carla had had time to reflect as to whether she had any further useful information.

She dabbed a little of the expensive perfume she had just received behind her earlobes to overpower the odours of her ghastly prison mates and hid it carefully in her locker before heading off to choir practice. Carla didn't particularly like participating in the choir, she wasn't a choir-sort-of-person, but it was a chance to see her poor daughter, Genna, who was coping badly with prison life. She hid a smaller bottle of perfume in the hem of her jacket for Genna and some packets of cigarettes for trading in her pockets. The guards turned a blind eye to the exchange of goods provided it wasn't too blatant. Carla had another reason for having joined the choir: she enjoyed the company of Letty Braythwaite, the only other Englishwoman in this Swiss jail. It was Letty who had set up the choir. Letty was a woman of her own class and was usually a good source of news of the only part of the outside world Carla cared about. For once, it was Carla who would be able to give Letty news of Grondère.

As Alain had correctly surmised, the surveillance of Rusty's bar and restaurant had indicated no further activity and the *Police judiciaire* were eventually obliged to unseal the property and hand the keys back to the landlord who was keen to get it rented out again as quickly as possible. In order to protect Tommy from anyone who might still be holding out the hope of retrieving the diamonds and find out he had helped build the hiding place for the safe, they also leaked the information that they had located and emptied it.

Both Sammy and Alessandra were outbid for the lease of Rusty's place by a London-based company. No one seemed to know who they were other than that they had a great deal of money and had brought their own people over to run the place – never a popular move in a ski resort where regular employment is a rarity and jobs are fiercely fought over. The new name 'The Palace' drew scorn from the locals for its lack of connection with the resort, but whilst the locals continued to refer to it as Rusty's place, The Palace quickly became popular with Grondère's wealthy visitors: it had clearly gained 'in-place' status. Whilst the residents of Grondère expected a venue to earn its reputation, The Palace had a different strategy: it paid influencers to create one. And it worked. A new sort of visitor began to frequent the resort, the like of which Grondère, until then a hard-core ski resort, had not seen before. Thin, willowy women with big lips, tiny waists and wide hips could be seen pouting and taking selfies in the strangest of places.

'I have just seen one of those Instagrammers posing in front of the ticket queue,' Poppy remarked. 'Why would they do that?'

'Because it's the closest they're going to get to the slopes?' Johnny suggested.

They all laughed.

'I could buy a new car with the price of her outfit,' Poppy complained, 'I'd hate to think that fancy one-piece was never going to see the mountain.'

'I think it made it as far as Cauettes. It's this one, right?' Sally helpfully showed a photograph of the woman concerned, up on the mountain, in a sexy stance, holding her skis suggestively between her legs.

'That's her,' Poppy confirmed. 'Where did you find that?'

'Oh, there's a whole load of sites where they post their images but they tag Grondère.'

'You don't follow that stuff?' Lucy exclaimed.

'Not often, but yes, I like to see the outfits and I think the poses are funny. Look at this one: you'd freeze skiing with your cleavage on display like that.'

Lucy looked at it with horrified fascination.

'You have to admit, there's something very compelling about it. And look at this: she posted it two hours ago and she's already got 5,000 likes. It's almost pornographic.'

'Give that here,' Johnny commanded. Sally handed over her phone to Johnny, who was the only person in the resort who still firmly refused to buy a smartphone, just as he was holding out against wearing a ski helmet. Johnny perused the various images on the site with the discernment of a true connoisseur. 'Lurvely,' he said lecherously, reluctantly relinquishing Sally's phone to Poppy.

'Porn,' Poppy confirmed.

'I saw her skiing,' Tommy said. 'She was out with Benoît.'

Benoît was a ski god, one of the Swiss Ski School's top instructors: he was booked up a year in advance.

They looked at him with curiosity.

'And?'

'Classic beginner stance: snowplough, bottom sticking out, not so sexy.'

Sally laughed.

'Benoît doesn't take beginners! The Palace must have paid for the whole thing. No one taking photos of her skiing then?'

He shook his head.

'It wouldn't make me want to go on a ski trip.'

'It's not aimed at people like you, duffer. It's aimed at people who want to be like her and all the other influencers on that site.'

'Well, it's working,' Lucy said. 'Ski school is busier than ever. I have never had so many beginner skiers. I don't mind it, I think it adds a different, more modern dimension to the place and lots of work for people like me. We can't pretend that the outside world doesn't exist or stop it from coming here.'

'More's the pity,' Poppy said. 'Shame The Palace didn't give work to more people from here,' firmly putting an end to the discussion.

'Hmmm,' Johnny murmured, resolving to finally invest in a smartphone.

Poppy and Lucy went by to console Sammy for not getting Rusty's place. He smiled and offered them a glass of *Petite Arvine*.

'It would have been great,' he shrugged, 'but it's okay, there'll be other opportunities.'

He was busy so they took their drinks away from the bar area and sat sipping them in a quiet corner.

'Oh, Lucy, don't make it obvious but turn round and have a look. Sitting at that table is a glamorous middle-aged blond in a black, fur-collared jacket talking to a distinguished grey-haired chap in a blue blazer.'

Lucy discreetly turned and looked at a sun-tanned couple enjoying an intense conversation.

'So, who are they then?'

'That is Lara Stanley and, talking to her, is Lionel Sturridge.'

'No! Carla's second husband?'

'The very man.'

Lucy grinned and took another look.

'He's not as handsome as Malcolm, but he has something.'

'Pots of money, I think, is his main attraction. He's a banker and a wine trader, or was. I haven't seen him here for years.'

'And her?'

'Oh, I see her from time to time, she is one of the people I told you about, set up the Diamond Ski Club, she still runs it. She and Carla set up the club when Carla was married to Lionel: people used to joke about their names, called them the LaLa-s.'

Lucy grinned, she loved hearing a bit of Grondère history.

'Were they married long? Carla and Lionel?'

'Not long. A couple of years, I think. She hooked up with him after her divorce from Malcolm but he got a knee injury which prevented him from skiing and he didn't want to spend so much time here. Carla didn't want to move to London where she would have been a total nobody when she was already a big fish here, so she chucked him over and agreed to go back and work for Malcolm.'

'Well, I guess his knee's better if he's skiing now.'

'Must be.'

Poppy smiled.

'I don't think I'll bother going over to say hello. He looks pretty engrossed with Lara.'

'She's very glamourous, isn't she?'

'I think she looks like mutton dressed as lamb myself,' Poppy sniffed.

'Are they an item?'

'I have no idea, I doubt it. She's not young enough for him and he's not clever enough for her.'

'Really? What does she do then?'

'She's also in the finance business, tax advisor, accountant, fund manager.'

'Oh,' Lucy knew nothing about any of these. Her eyes glazed over.

'Well, it looks like Suzie will be busy this week. She told me she was on duty for the Diamonds for the next fortnight. Lara likes to be escorted royally on the slopes.'

They grinned at the image. Rich clients often skied with an entourage and great display of wealth. It made for good people-watching from the chairlift.

'Oh look, Milly's just joined them.'

Lucy turned to see Milly, looking very smart, sitting down with Lara Stanley. Lara seemed to be introducing her to Lionel.

'She did say her parents used to ski with the Diamond Ski Club, I guess she knows them from that.'

Milly saw them looking, smiled and waved at them. They waved back and stopped looking: the last thing they wanted was to be invited across to join Milly and her old family friends. But Lucy was curious all the same.

Two days later Suzie did ask Lucy if she'd like to join her, Lara and Lionel for a ski.

'I'm finding them quite heavy-going to be honest, so if you'd rather not, that's fine.'

'Oh, I'll come along,' Lucy said. 'I'm a bit curious, I'll admit.'

'I'd like to do the High Boulevard.' Lara declared. 'Lionel hasn't been there for years and I haven't done it this season yet.'

'Are you sure?' Suzie asked. 'I haven't been there for a couple of weeks and so I have no idea what condition it's in.'

'No one else is heading that way,' Lucy added. 'There's usually a reason.'

Lionel looked at her as if she was dirt.

'I think it is you that has joined our party, not vice versa. If Lara wants the High Boulevard then she shall have it.'

'That's me told then,' Lucy whispered to Suzie as the other two skied on ahead. Suzie grimaced.

'I think you could have a point though. Look at that pristine sheet of whiteness. Why haven't the powder hounds already skied it all off?'

They traversed across the flank of Mont Froid, on the other side to the Bosses Bol where an untouched field of snow glistened below them.

'Fantastic!' declared Lionel and launched himself into it before Suzie and Lucy had the chance to warn him.

The wind had pressed down the surface of the powder, creating a thick crust. As Lionel's skis crunched through the top layer they became wedged below, making it impossible to turn.

On and on he went, like a train stuck in the tracks, unable to turn.

'Bugger!' said Lara.

'Quite,' said Suzie.

'Well, we can't leave him down there on his own, we'd better get on with it,' Lucy added. She launched herself into the slope, keeping her legs as close as possible together and trusting to her speed and the undulations of the mountain to help her make wide turns. She followed close on Lionel's trajectory in case he should need help.

The four skiers laboured their way through the crusty snow until they could turn back onto the main itinerary. It was hard work but they all made it down without twisting a knee or getting totally encrusted.

As they reached a more giving snow, they all burst out laughing with relief.

'That was bloody awful,' Lionel declared. 'Whose idea was that?' He looked pointedly at Lara who held up her arms in surrender.

'My sincere apologies everyone, I owe you all a drink.'

When they reached the sunny terrace of the Vache à Lait they stopped and Lara promptly went inside and came back with a bucket of champagne.

'Next time, Suzie and Lucy, I will listen to your words of caution.'

Lucy looked on smiling. Now the ice was broken she could see that these older skiers still had a great sense of fun and adventure and she enjoyed the light-hearted chat that followed.

'They're not so bad,' she said to Suzie afterwards.

'No,' laughed Suzie, 'they had the good grace to admit they'd got it wrong and they certainly lightened up afterwards.'

Sammy was disappointed not to have won the lease for Rusty's Place and even more disappointed at its rapid success. But he was hearing rumours of another nature that he decided to mention to Tommy.

He popped into the ski shop, Golden Mountain, where Tommy was working his final season to finance his joint farming project. Tommy was intrigued: this was unusual for Sammy, he didn't normally leave his bar much during the high season.

'What's up?' he asked.

'This probably sounds like sour grapes,' Sammy grimaced at his own pun. 'And I am pissed at not getting Rusty's place but the place is starting to get Grondère a bad reputation.'

'That's a mighty accusation.'

He looked at him earnestly.

'I'm not one to rag on a fellow business but they're not really part of the business community and there are rumours of things happening there, bad things, to girls.'

Tommy looked at him and instantly understood his meaning.

'That's awful!'

He nodded his head.

'You want me to spread the word, warn the girls?'

'More than that, I think you should tell Alain. You know him quite well, don't you?'

'I can't go telling tales to Alain, it's just hearsay and I'm not the resident informant.'

'Maybe you could ask Lucy what she thinks then? At least she can warn her friends. I promise, it's not because I didn't get the lease.'

'Okay, okay, I'll talk to Lucy. Jeez!'

Tommy thought about it for a while and then decided it was too important not to talk to Alain directly. Alain called Adjudant Corthay, the head of the local force for a quiet word.

'I have also heard rumours,' he replied.

He had been contacted by a concerned member of the local council. There were rumours circulating that some young female visitors and seasonnaires were suddenly leaving the resort without warning and the date rape drug was believed to be the cause.

'But what can we do? If no one comes forward with a formal complaint, I have nothing to go on but rumours.'

'It is a delicate matter,' Alain agreed. 'But I have a colleague who is perfectly equipped to deal with delicate matters.'

Inspectrice Sylvie Jacquier was livid.

'Here? In my home town? I'm not having that!'

Alain gave her all the information he had, which was more speculation than anything else.

'Can I talk to Lucy about this? She's more in touch with the seasonnaire scene than me.'

'As long as you don't get her into danger. She's not in the police and she's already had more drama than most civilians get in a lifetime.'

———————————

Lucy watched through the porthole of the cabin as the baggage handlers loaded the last bags into the hold. Sylvie Jacquier had kindly given up her window seat, claiming she preferred the aisle seat because of her long legs, but Lucy knew it was out of kindness and she appreciated the gesture: she loved to gaze out of the window during a flight.

'I'm looking forward to a change of scene,' Sylvie said, firmly clicking her seatbelt on.

'Me too, I've never been to Poland. Imagine a raclette restaurant in the heart of Warsaw!'

'Yes, it seems like quite a niche market. I don't know how the Polish will take to melted Swiss cheese and potatoes.'

'Lina seems to have a good business brain. I'm sure she's researched it all thoroughly.'

'Hopefully the presence of the Swiss ambassador will give her a good bit of publicity.'

'The Swiss ambassador, blimey! How did she swing that?'

'She didn't: I did.' Sylvie beamed cheekily. 'I knew that he was a personal friend of M. le Procureur and so I called in a favour.'

'That's brilliant! Well done. Does Lina know?'

'Oh, yes. I had to tell her: receiving an ambassador requires preparation. There are certain rules of protocol that must be observed.'

'I guess. I'd never really thought about it.' Lucy grinned. 'Will we be expected to curtsey?'

Sylvie laughed. 'Oh Lucy, I know you're joking but, even if you weren't, the Swiss don't do curtseying.'

Lucy winked. She was looking forward to seeing Lina again. She had only met her twice, but the three women had formed a common bond during the investigation into the murder of Lina's best friend the previous summer. Lina had since returned to Poland, but not without taking a little bit of Switzerland with her.

'So how do you address an ambassador? I take it we will be allowed to address him, or is it a her?' Lucy pondered.

'Him, and I believe the correct term is *"Votre Excellence"*.'

'Bloody hell, "Your excellency". Really?'

'I guess it depends how important it is to the ambassador that such formalities be observed,'

'You mean, it depends how stuffy he is?'

'Yes.'

During the rest of the fight, they discussed the sites they would like to visit in the short time they had. But the tourism would have to wait for the next day: that evening Lina was expecting them.

'You look fantastic! How wonderful!' Lina rushed to the door to welcome them. Taking them by the hand she thanked them again and again for making the trip to the opening of her raclette restaurant and for coming early so she had time to show them around. She showed off the restaurant, pointing out all the Swiss paraphernalia she had used for 'authenticity', the raclette machines and the kitchen, all the while turning them round so she could admire their Swiss national costumes. Sylvie, being Swiss, had her own and Lucy had borrowed one from some ancient stock Sally had found in a wardrobe in Christophe's farm.

'What a great idea,' Lina laughed. 'You must stand with me and receive the guests.'

It was just as well, for the Swiss ambassador and his wife had been expecting to meet them.

'I had heard of you Frau Jacquier, I am told you are a remarkable police officer. I am delighted to meet you,' the ambassador shook Sylvie's hand warmly.

'And you, Frau Wilson, it is an honour to meet Switzerland's poster girl.'

Lucy smiled gaily; she had decided that when your half-naked body is adorning a major publicity campaign for Switzerland's tourism agency, the only sensible approach was to be brazen. She had taken the money and so she must take the attention. Most people didn't usually recognise her as the 'lady in the lake' but the procureur must have tipped his friend off.

The ambassador posed for photos for the press with the two women in their national dress before moving on to perform his professional duty of working the room: smiling and shaking hands.

Shortly afterwards, as Sylvie and Lucy stood at the entrance greeting Lina's invitees, they wondered how many more people could cram into the space. The presence of the Swiss ambassador (and Lina's efficient use of that information) had ensured a wide attendance by the press, restaurant critics, local VIPs and influencers. Lina was ecstatic but stressed, she kept rushing off to support her staff.

'I did not expect so many people,' she whispered to Sylvie and Lucy. 'It's wonderful, but …'

'What do you need us to do?' Sylvie asked her purposefully.

'If you don't mind helping serve and clear the tables, that would be a huge help, but,' Lina looked across to the raclette machine where her boyfriend was scraping cheese and looking very shiny as he tried to cope with demand, 'what I could really do with, is the second raclette burner being fired up.'

'Leave it with me,' Sylvie said. 'Lucy, you okay to wait tables?'

'I am,' Lucy said firmly. 'Not only am I dressed for it, I have experience.'

'Great.'

Sylvie sidled up to the ambassador who was standing nearby.

'Your Excellency, national pride is at stake, how are you on the raclette machine?'

Lucy looked on astounded as the ambassador raised his eyebrows, looked around, analysing the situation. Sylvie paused before adding, 'an excellent photo opportunity', then waited: she knew better than to hurry a diplomatic decision process.

He nodded determinedly, 'Lead me to it!'

For the next quarter of an hour, M. l'Ambassadeur scraped melting cheese onto plates as his wife added the pickles and potatoes, Sylvie and Lucy served and Lina kept topping up supplies whilst the photographers present seized upon this moment of spontaneity with relish.

The ambassador lapped up the attention and proved most competent with the apparatus, but Sylvie knew not to overplay her hand: after fifteen minutes she relieved the ambassador and Lucy sat him and his wife at a table and made sure they dined as dignitaries should.

Lucy smiled as she observed the happy scene: a noisy, bustling restaurant full of happy people. To her mind, Lina had succeeded: she had not only imported the traditional raclette meal, she had also managed to import the feeling and spirit of that quintessentially Swiss tradition, the enjoying and sharing of food and drink in fun company.

As the evening drew to a close and numbers dwindled, the diplomatic couple, having stayed well beyond the hoped-for time, took their leave, wishing Lina well and promising to return regularly. Lina thanked them profusely for their timely intervention.

The ambassador turned to Sylvie and Lucy and shook their hands.

'It was not quite the evening you expected,' Sylvie smiled. 'Thank you for being such good sports.'

The diplomatic couple laughed and said they had felt much more at home than at many of the functions they attended. Exhausted, Lina, her team, Sylvie and Lucy collapsed into chairs, relaxed and laughed as they finally shared a drink.

The next day Lucy and Sylvie devoted to sightseeing, wandering around the old town and seeking out some of the socialist architecture left over from the Soviet bloc era. At the end of the day they stopped by the restaurant to take their leave of Lina who proudly showed them all the press coverage with the photos of themselves and the Swiss ambassador at the raclette machine and gave them copies to take home with them the following morning.

'I can't believe you did that!' Lucy exclaimed to Sylvie, browsing through the pages of the newspapers at the airport. 'Got the Swiss ambassador slaving over a hot raclette burner.'

'I could see he was up for it, otherwise I'd have just done it myself from the outset.'

'You are certainly a better raclette scraper than a waitress,' Lucy teased her.

'I am a bit heavy-hipped between the tables,' Sylvie shrugged. 'I don't know how you move around like that, you seemed to glide around the room.'

'I really enjoyed it,' Lucy confessed, smiling to realise that the evening had finally broken the ice between them and put them on a footing of solid friendship. She thought of the housekeeper at Lunstag Hall's words 'grace, presence and generosity of spirit' and thought she understood. Sylvie had, with ease, turned a minor crisis into a major success. Staying quietly in the background, she had used her charm and persuasive powers to stage a publicity coup for both the ambassador and Lina. It had been perceptive, effective and very kind. Maybe that's what the housekeeper recognised in Sylvie and caused her to call her a true lady. Lucy was silently agreeing with the housekeeper when she had another thought.

'You know, I just realised, I haven't waited on tables since the night Malcolm was murdered.'

'That seems such a long time ago.'

'Yes, and in fact it's almost exactly a year.'

'And now we have another unsolved murder on our hands. At least you're not involved this time.'

Sylvie did not know how wrong she was.

Nine

*It was important, Dumbledore said, to fight, and fight
again, and keep fighting, for only then could evil be kept
at bay, though never quite eradicated ...*
J.K. Rowling, Harry Potter and the Half-Blood Prince

'I've never been in here' Sylvie told Lucy and Sally who
she had agreed to meet in the bar at The Palace, just to give
her a cover while she checked it out.

'Nor me – too expensive and I'm feeling like a total
peasant in this cosmopolitan crowd,' Sally agreed looking
around at the fashionable young people who had jetted in
from London, Paris and Geneva for the weekend.

Lucy sipped on her cocktail and winked at Sylvie.

'Still, if the drinks are on your expenses, I have no
objection to feasting my eyes on all these beautiful
people.'

'True, it's like being in a page from Vogue,' Sally sighed.
'Look at that woman's sandals, they must have cost a
thousand.'

'Really?' Sylvie was surprised. 'There doesn't seem to be
much to them.'

'I don't think I could actually walk in them,' Lucy shook
her head. 'I haven't worn high heels for years.'

'No, not much opportunity up here,' Sally sighed. She
loved a chance to get dressed up.

'You had some for Tonita's wedding.'

'Yes,' Sally thought fondly of her photo in the British
tabloid that had so impressed Tommy's family.

'I'd rather have a pair of new ski boots,' Lucy sighed. 'I
hope we don't stick out too much as not belonging here,
or that won't help you much, Sylvie.'

'Hey Lucy!' Milly bounced up to them, looking like she had stepped from one of those pages from Vogue Sally had mentioned. 'I haven't seen you in here before.'

'No,' Lucy smiled, 'I'm lucky tonight, I have been invited by my friend Sylvie.'

'That's nice. I haven't seen you around,' Milly looked with curiosity at Sylvie.

'I'm a teacher in Savigny,' Sylvie lied quickly before Lucy or Sally blew her cover. 'I met Lucy when she was a waitress.'

Well, that, at least, was true, Lucy thought, admiring Sylvie's quick thinking. It was a lie designed to deflect attention and it worked. Milly immediately lost interest in Sylvie and was focusing with great interest on Lucy's earrings, a gift from Tonita.

'Ohmigod, are they real?'

Lucy fingered her only designer possession self-consciously. The earrings had been inspired by Malcolm McDonaghue's book on Swiss wines that Lucy had edited. 'Er, yes, they were a gift.'

'Nice friend! Do you realise that that's a special edition pair of Tonita Shalott earrings you're wearing?'

'Well, I know they're Tonita's: she gave them to me. But as for limited edition, that I didn't know.'

'There's a little diamond in one of the grapes, that's the telltale sign. Take one off!'

'Sorry?'

'Take one off, I'll soon tell you.'

Lucy removed one of her earrings and handed it to this fashionista who peered at it with great authority.

'You see, look, there's a tiny number printed in the back. Wow, she must think a lot of you, 001.'

Lucy, Sally and Sylvie shrugged at each other as Lucy hurriedly reattached the item to her ear lobe.

'I shall be even more worried about wearing them now.'

'Oh no,' Milly said firmly. 'You've got it – flaunt it. Especially in here. Anyway, my glass is empty so I must go and get it filled up again. There's always some rich man in here eager to buy you a drink. I just take the champagne and look at them adoringly as if they were gods, it seems to be what they like and then I just go and dance all night: I love the DJ in here.'

Lucy smiled at her warmly, it seemed as if Milly was really starting to find her feet in Grondère.

Milly flitted back to a table and joined a crowd of elegant young people.

'Well, that's made it look like we fit in a bit better, Milly coming over like that,' Sally commented, but Sylvie didn't reply. Lucy looked at her: she had gone rigid.

'I saw that barman pour something in that bottle of champagne that's just gone to that table,' she uttered through clenched teeth.

'Are you sure? Might just have been bitters or something. They all seem to be drinking from the same bottle.' Lucy wondered if Sylvie ever switched off and stopped being a policewoman.

'Just keep an eye,' Sylvie said. 'Hopefully it's nothing.'

They continued to enjoy cocktails and pose for some selfies as Sylvie spied on the barman.

'I'm sure he's done it again,' she said as another bottle of champagne headed to the same table.

Milly seemed to have forgotten the dance floor and be having a wonderful time, giggling and laughing with the young men and their limitless supply of champagne. Then she seemed to be lolling about a bit.

'Do not take your eyes off her,' Sylvie commanded and stepped outside to call Alain and Adjudant Corthay. She returned a few minutes later to find Lucy and Sally looking panicked.

'Where's she gone?' she asked, seeing them looking helplessly about for Milly.

'We're so sorry,' Lucy exclaimed. 'It was as if this guy knew we were watching, he came over and stood in front of us, blocking our view and by the time he moved aside, she was gone. And some of those men too.'

'They can't have left the building, I was by the door. They've taken her to a room.'

'Oh no,' Lucy was distraught to think she had let Milly down.

'These guys?' Sylvie showed them a photo of the people who had been at the table which was now empty. It seemed she hadn't been taking selfies at all but close-ups of everyone at the table.

'Yes, that's the one who blocked us.'

Sylvie marched to the reception desk where the girl on duty was filing her nails.

'Which room are these men in?' she demanded, showing the photo.

'I can't tell you that.'

'Oh yes, you can.' Sylvie whisked out her police ID. 'And give me a pass key immediately, a young woman is in danger.'

Still the receptionist hesitated, looking at them blankly.

'Get a move on,' snarled Sally, 'or I'll make sure every girl in town knows you are a traitor to your sisters. You will not dare to go outside!'

That worked: the girl, in dumb shock, programmed a key card and said, 'Second floor – Golden Suite 201.'

'You two stay here to wait for the back-up and send them up to me,' Sylvie told Lucy and Sally and darted off, up the stairwell.

Lucy and Sally looked at each other and nodded.

'We're expecting the cavalry,' Sally told the receptionist. 'Be sure to send them up as soon as they arrive. And don't you pick up that phone to warn anyone, or I shall personally rip off those perfectly manicured nails one by one – and enjoy every second of it!'

They raced up the two flights of stairs after Sylvie, hoping they weren't too late.

Sylvie opened the door and saw Milly, semi-conscious lying on the bed, with the three men leering over her. Lucy and Sally appeared behind her as she entered the room.

'Well,' said the man who had blocked them from seeing them taking Milly out of the bar. 'Uninvited guests. Come on in girls and join the party.' He moved quickly towards Lucy and pinned her against the wall.

'I fancy this one.'

As one of the others advanced towards Sally she looked at him menacingly.

'Have to drug the girls to get laid, do you? What a big man you are.'

The third young man made towards Sylvie, pulled her away from the door and slammed it shut.

'You're a bit older than I normally like but I like a bit of a fight.'

'That was really not a clever thing to say,' came a muffled remark from Lucy.

This he had already worked out, as he lay bent double on the floor, unable to clutch his wounded genitals, whilst Sylvie smartly handcuffed his hands behind his back.

Lucy's assailant let go of her to go to his friend's assistance but found himself on his back without knowing how he got there.

As he picked himself up and he and the other uncuffed man went for Sylvie she sighed and got out her gun. This made them hesitate.

'You wouldn't dare,' one of them said.

'Oh yes, she would,' Lucy grinned. 'I've seen her in action, and she's the best shot in the Swiss police.'

'Police! Fuck, let's get out of here.'

Both men tried to push their way past Sylvie to the door, but a sharp twist of the arm had one of them on his back again and Sally, not wanting to miss out on the fun, smashed a glass vase over the head of the other.

'Take that, scumbag!'

'I'm out of handcuffs,' shrugged Sylvie.

'I'm a bit surprised that you had any on you at all, fancy carrying such an object to a date night with us, not very flattering,' Lucy joked.

'Will these do?' said Sally, taking some fancy curtain ties off the fancy curtains.

Sylvie nodded and trussed up her groaning casualties with some very tight knots. They winced as she pulled them extra tight.

'Nice!' Sally admired her work. 'Proper sailing knots those.'

There was a knock on the door and Alain called to let them know it was him and Adjudant Corthay. Another local officer was with them. Lucy quickly covered Milly with a blanket.

'We did nothing,' shouted the large man as the officers entered. 'It's our word against theirs!'

'Oh look,' Sally said, holding up her phone with a grin, 'seems I accidentally left my phone on: it's been recording all this time.'

'That's not allowed!' he snarled back.

Alain replied. 'I think you'll find that in a case like this, it is. Thank you Sally.' He made a sign for her to switch it off. He looked at the scene before him.

'Nice work, ladies.'

'Thanks,' Sally replied as if she had done all the work on her own.

'Can you get rid of this trio of *scumbags*?' Sylvie asked the local men, winking at Sally: Laurent Blonnay was not the only one who could purloin a useful new word when he heard it. 'Capitaine Dupertuis and I have a scumbag barman to arrest.'

The municipal police dragged the three miscreants to their feet and took them away.

'Lucy, are you okay? You're shaking,' Alain asked.

'I was fine before but now I'm so angry and upset, I can't stop it.'

'But hon, look at all you've faced before, you've been so brave!' Sally cajoled.

'These men, they're wealthy, privileged, they're supposed to be civilised human beings, I bet they have beautiful girlfriends at home but they get their kicks out of drugging unsuspecting young women. They do this for *pleasure*! I can't believe such viciousness exists.'

'Oh, Lucy, it's out there and we see it all the time.' Alain sighed. 'The worst of it is that that little lot will get some hot-shot lawyer and get themselves sent home.'

'How can you put up with that?'

'The way I put up with it personally, is, if I can see that we have changed things for the better. This lot might get off lightly but firstly, after the public disgrace, they are unlikely to reoffend and secondly, think of all the Millys that won't be having their lives wrecked because we've put a stop to their game. Each little victory has a ripple effect.'

Lucy smiled, 'That's a good way to look at it.'

Milly suddenly let forth a loud snore from the bed.

'Can you and Sally accompany Milly to the hospital? We need to know exactly what she's been given.'

Milly awoke to a white world and Lucy's lovely face looking down at her kindly.

'What happened? Where am I?'

Lucy saw Milly's eyes fill with dread as she started to remember where she had been before she lost consciousness.

'It's okay,' Lucy told her. 'You had the best protection officer in the Swiss police looking after you last night, and I should know, she saved my life last autumn.'

She gave Milly a brief account of what happened.

'So, your teacher friend, she's really a policewoman?'

'Yes, she's not a teacher, that was a little fib to avoid us blowing her cover.'

Milly smiled and dug her head into the pillow.

'Please say thank you from me,' and promptly fell asleep.

Lucy smiled at Sally and shook her head.

What, she thought, am I going to do with Milly?

'Scumbag,' Blonnay repeated with relish, as he listened to Sally's recording of their triumph over evil. 'What a wonderful word.'

'Yes, Sylvie seemed to take a liking to it too,' Alain smiled. 'But I still feel bad that Lucy and Sally were put in such a situation.'

'I get the impression Mademoiselle Collins enjoyed every second of it and Lucy also rose to the occasion.'

'Yes, but she was in shock afterwards: they are civilians, we are supposed to protect them.'

'Alain, you would not have been able to hold them back, Sylvie tried.'

'Yes, thank God for Sylvie.'

'Again.'

'Yes, again.'

Ten

If grass can grow through cement, love can find you at every time in your life.

Cher, The Times, May 1998

The Palace's reputation and popularity evaporated overnight and the company running it retreated to London in disgrace. Alessandra Rosset dropped out of the race to secure the lease and this time Sammy got his wish, his second establishment in Grondère.

Sally and Lucy popped into Sammy's wine bar, La Grappe d'Or de Grondère, to congratulate him on securing the lease on Rusty's place.

'You're turning into a real tycoon, Sammy,' Sally teased. 'Will you still talk to us when you're rich and famous?'

'Never forget my roots, but please enjoy the fruits!' he grinned at them, pouring them each a free glass of champagne.

They laughed.

'What will you call the place?' Lucy asked. 'Rusty didn't seem to have named it, which is odd as he was so long getting it ready.'

Sally agreed, 'And you can't keep "The Palace": apart from being naff, it's got such an awful reputation now.'

'Good question. Rusty did have a name for it actually, but it was really corny: "Le Repaire".'

Sally sniggered.

'That's even worse in light of what was going on there.'

'Point taken,' he grimaced. 'I was thinking of something a bit more local, and a little tribute to Rusty – even if he was an old rogue, he was part of the Grondère community and it was his baby after all: what do you think of the Rusty Grapes – La Grappe Rouillée? It ties in with the name of this place too.'

119

Lucy smiled. Sammy really had found the flair for business. When she had first met him he had a reputation for talking a good business plan but never implementing one. That had all changed now.

'It's a great name, Sammy.'

'Thanks. I won't have time to have an opening party now, I just need to get the place up and running. I thought we could hold a function at the end of the season: a sort of tribute to Rusty.'

'That's a lovely idea, Sammy,' Lucy said approvingly.

Sally held up her glass.

'To Rusty, the old rogue.'

'What are those two looking so smug about?'

Charles Sidforth-Sykes asked Humphrey as they watched Rory and Alessandra canoodling and quaffing champagne in La Grappe d'Or.

'Goodness knows; Rory's certainly spending more time in Grondère since he met the head of our White Snowflake project.'

'Ah.' Charles looked thoughtfully at the couple.

'You're not still brooding over that, are you?'

Charles, being true to his record of poor business judgement, had sold his investment in the consortium at the wrong moment.

'No, no, it'll always rankle of course, but I've calmed down since your nephew's project paid off.'

Having made one bad investment too many, Charles had been on the verge of bankruptcy before an unexpected windfall came his way, thanks to Humphrey.

'You could always buy your way back in to White Snowflake, you know.'

'No, no I think I'll let that one go.'

Charles, thanks to some advice from Humphrey, had now placed his money in some safe, less profitable investments, having first bought back his apartment and re-joined the Grondère Diamond Ski Club, which now always met in La Grappe d'Or.

'No, Humphrey, what I'm missing, is a bit of romance.'

'Really?' Humphrey loved a bit of matchmaking and was feeling buoyant after his successful mating of Rory and Alessandra.

'Yes, I quite fancied my chances with Alessandra but that ski club chappie beat me to it.'

Humphrey smiled: Charles was nothing if not delusional. Humphrey had heard an entertaining report of a very clumsy attempt to seduce Tonita Shalott, now Lady Shilton.

'There are lots of attractive women who come out with the Grondère Diamonds.'

'Yes, but I fear, old chap, that after all of these years as a bachelor, I've quite forgotten how to go about it. That chap over there doesn't seem to have a problem, he seems to grab all of those too.'

'Yes, so I have heard.'

'I thought about that Suzie girl, you know, the guide? She's a smart cookie.'

Charles had been out skiing with Suzie and the other members for social reasons, he did not need guiding round the slopes of Grondère but he did need to meet some new people: his group of friends had dwindled since a few of them had been put in prison by Alain and his team.

Humphrey raised his eyebrows, a less suitable candidate than Suzie he could not imagine, she was far too independent and dynamic for Charles, no wonder Charles wasn't getting anywhere if he was setting his sights on women like Suzie. It looked like Humphrey was going to have to sort out Charles's love life as well as his finances.

'I think Suzie's got a boyfriend back in the UK.'

'Really? Well you and I know how much that counts when people are on holiday.'

'But I thought you were looking for a steady partner, not the sort of love life Rory has.'

'True, true.' Charles looked despondent and Humphrey racked his brains.

'There's Lara Stanley?'

'I was hoping for something a bit younger.'

'And less high-powered?'

'Exactly.'

'I have a young cousin who is coming out in a couple of weeks, she's a bit timid and might like to be escorted around the slopes.'

'That's a cracking idea, is she a looker?'

Humphrey wondered to what extent he could exaggerate the charms of his rather horsey-looking cousin, Jemima.

'I'll be honest with you, Charles: she's no great beauty and she's not the brightest bauble in the box, but she is honest and kind and, after all you have been through, Charles, I think you could use a bit of kindness.'

'Can she ski?'

'Oh yes, she can ski.'

Blonnay stood nervously at the arrivals hall in Geneva airport. He hadn't seen Jilly since Sebastian and Tonita's wedding, although they had spoken almost every day. He had been busy on the Jordan Russell inquiry and she had been working on a complicated financial fraud case. Having successfully resolved her case, she had taken a two-week holiday to come and ski with Blonnay and discover his world. He had rented a small flat in Grondère for the fortnight.

She came through security with a big smile and a very big suitcase.

'Hmm, glad the car has a big boot,' he joked after a hug and a long kiss.

'Tea and marmite supplies,' she teased, knowing he liked neither.

He shrugged and led her to the carpark.

'Unbelievable!' she said five minutes later.

'What?' he asked.

'Under five minutes and we're already on the motorway, how did that happen?'

He resisted the urge to brag about Swiss efficiency and just said, 'Geneva is a small airport: in Zurich it takes longer.'

'How much longer?'

'About ten minutes.'

She laughed.

As they drove past Lausanne and circled Lake Geneva the traffic news came on the radio.

'That was short. What did it say?'

'It said that everything is moving smoothly on the roads in this part of the country.'

'You're kidding?'

'No.'

Jilly burst out laughing.

'I never heard a traffic report like that before.'

Again, Blonnay decided on a tactful approach.

'It is a small country, it is easier to manage the traffic flow. We do get traffic jams. On this road on a Friday evening, all the weekenders head for the mountains which is why I suggested you fly out on a weekday.'

'Good planning' she said.

'Yes,' Blonnay agreed.

An hour later they were climbing the winding road that led from Pattier to Grondère, with Jilly looking excitedly out of the window up at the mountains and the city of wooden chalets looking down into the valley. They went straight to Golden Mountain where Tommy was waiting for them. Jilly had her own boots, and so he found her a good pair of all-mountain skis.

'You're going into ski school, I hear,' he chatted away in his warm West Country accent as he adjusted her bindings.

'For a few days; I think it's a good way to meet people and also Laurent won't feel he has to nursemaid me all the time,' she joked back.

'Very sensible,' he agreed, 'but I feel I need to warn you that Poppy has wangled it so that you're joining her class, so there'll be no slacking.'

As dusk fell, the reunited couple were sitting on their balcony drinking a glass of *Dôle blanche* and admiring the sunset over the Cortey Massif that Lucy and her friends had heli-skied in December. They contentedly watched the lights twinkling throughout the resort, as skiers returned to their chalets and hotels to prepare for the evening's activities. Snatches of music and the throbbing boom of drums reached them from the après-ski bars.

'I am so excited about hitting the slopes tomorrow,' she said happily.

'I'm sorry I can't join you,' he looked a little guilty, 'I have no time off until the weekend.'

'Laurent, we agreed, we are both in the police, we know the score, no reproaches, on either side, remember? Anyway, I don't want you to see me ski until I've had a few days' instruction. How is your investigation going, by the way?'

He had to reluctantly admit that they had very little to go on so far and were currently looking into Rusty's travel patterns which were showing a regular pattern between South Africa, Switzerland and The Netherlands.

She told him a bit more about the complexities of her case for which she now had the long arduous task of preparing for trial.

'It's complicated enough,' she told him, 'but when you add the requirements of English law on top it can be most confusing.'

'Swiss Law isn't too complicated. But that's because we have a proper coded law, you are always dealing with jurisprudence.'

'True, it can get a bit higgledy-piggledy,' she agreed, 'but then, much about my country is higgledy-piggledy.' She smiled and snuggled up to him as she warmed to her subject, 'The Victorian road and rail networks, the London Underground, plumbing, sewers, our health system ... our *pantomimes*. I think there is beauty in both: compare the beauty of a legal system crafted by decisions made by lawyers and judges over hundreds of years to the carefully coded law crafted by human intelligence. It's like comparing the beauty of a natural gorge, carved by the natural elements over centuries to a Norman cathedral, crafted by artisans over decades. Both are beautiful.'

'So you are comparing nature to artifice? English law having evolved naturally and Swiss law having been crafted by man?'

'I suppose I am. Like a wild-flower meadow to a formal parterre garden, or a wild rose to a hybrid-tea. Neither is better than the other but one has a beauty that has occurred naturally and the other's beauty is due to man's intervention.'

'When you come from England, which had its natural countryside redesigned by Capability Brown! And all this to try to reconcile me to your antiquated legal system?'

Jilly laughed and held up her hands in defeat.

'It was worth a try.'

Eleven

*When I go hiking and I get over the hill, that means I am
past the hard part and there is a snack in my future.
That's a good thing as far as I am concerned.*
Ellen DeGeneres

The following morning Jilly joined her class at the main
lift station and they all took the cable car up the mountain
together. It was a lively group of thirty-somethings like
herself, young professionals from all over the UK. She was
a little offended to see one of the young men whispering
to Poppy and looking in her direction.

'What's the issue?' she asked Poppy as they sat together
on the next chairlift.

'Charlie has set himself a target for this week: he wants to
go down the Bosses Bol.'

'Which is Grondère's famous mogul field.'

'Indeed.'

'And he's worried my joining the group might prevent him
from achieving his objective?'

'That's about the size of it. We've been practising bumps
for four days in preparation and I think they're ready. The
thing is we need to do it today because tomorrow's going
to be a bad weather day.'

'Ah.'

'I told him, not to worry, if you weren't up to it, we'd do
it at the end of the day after the lesson has officially ended
and that I was sure you wouldn't mind waiting for us in a
bar.'

'I'm cool with that,' Jilly grinned.

'Why are you laughing?'

'Let's just say, you won't be leaving me in any bar.'

Poppy smiled; this was good news.

They did a few warm-up laps on the freshly groomed slopes and Poppy was pleased to see Jilly keeping up with the rest of the group, but she kept lingering at the back. They were a fun group and Jilly was soon joining in the distinctive banter and teasing so characteristic of ski school. Once Poppy saw that Jilly had found her ski legs again, she took them down a small and short mogul field.

She was pleased to see her students applying the technique she had drummed into them over the past four days, straightening their legs to traverse the bump and then bending energetically to break their speed as they turned round it. It was not particularly elegant but it was careful and controlled and she knew she could trust them to descend the Bosses Bol with the appropriate level of skill and caution for a first time.

Jilly held back until the rest of the class had reached the bottom; Poppy could hear an audible and collective intake of breath from the others as she set off. By the time Jilly joined them they were high-fiving with glee: Jilly had bounced elegantly and easily down the bumps and was clearly better and more experienced than any of them at bump skiing.

Charlie smiled and looked at Poppy.

'I don't think we need to wait till the last run of the day.'

'You're right, we'll do the Bosses Bol straight after lunch,' Poppy nodded.

Over their spaghetti and goulash, the group chattered excitedly in anticipation of the afternoon's adventure.

'I didn't realise you were that good,' Poppy said to Jilly. 'You told the ski school, cautious intermediate.'

'I never really know how to gauge my level, I usually go with the same crowd and we're all about the same standard so I've never measured myself against anyone else. But I know I can handle Grondère's wall, as I usually ski the

Portes du Soleil and le Pas de Chavanette is my favourite descent.'

Poppy laughed, 'You really should be in a higher group.'

'I'm happy with this crowd; they seem like a fun bunch and I'm not here to prove anything. Besides, you said the weather was going to be poor tomorrow so it'll be safer with a group. I'm in the Ski Club of Great Britain so I can meet up with some other members next week and ski hard.'

'That's a good idea.'

After lunch they skied down to the chairlift that would take them up to the Bosses Bol.

Poppy gave them a briefing about following in her tracks at the entrance and what to do if they fell. She asked Jilly to be sweeper.

'Just in case anyone leaves their skis behind them,' she grinned.

As they skied through the saddle of the pass, steep rock rose to their right. Something caught Poppy's eye and she screamed at them all to stop.

'*Bouquetin*!'

She pointed to a rocky outcrop atop of which stood a huge ibex. They all gasped at the beauty of the creature standing stock still, its curved horns silhouetted against the blue sky.

'I never saw that before, a *bouquetin* beside the slopes, wow.'

They stood and watched it for a while until they realised that a traffic jam was forming behind them as skiers arriving behind jostled to get a better view and get their phones out to take pictures.

'Time to go,' Poppy shouted. 'And don't stop to let anyone past, it's their job to avoid you if they want to overtake!'

They followed her down the dip and onto the narrow path that traversed the top of the wide mogul field.

A couple of the class members felt their legs weaken a little and instinctively open into a snowplough to slow themselves but Poppy was ready for them.

'Let your skis run, it's too narrow here for snowploughing. If you feel you're picking up more speed than you want, brake by sliding.'

They bumped nervously along the path as it rose and dipped until Poppy gradually slid off the path and guided them off the track onto the slope below, traversing the larger moguls until she reached a part where the bumps were gentler and more spaced out.

'Turn where I turn,' she said reassuringly. She set off and took three wide turns down the steepest part of the slope and turned to watch them. A few of them were opening their skis a little and reverting to learner techniques such as stepping round their turns but this was a natural and instinctive reaction and she didn't pick them up on it, she knew that they would be able to parallel turn once they had found their confidence.

They grouped together and Poppy pointed above them.

'Well done, you've done the hardest part. Now it's all pure pleasure, choose your line and rendezvous at the bottom of that pillar over there.'

Poppy watched them down with pride; it wasn't the most stylish skiing but for her it was a thing of beauty. Her students had pushed themselves and just taken their skiing up a level. Charlie fell halfway down, but he lifted his legs as she had told him and got himself into a traverse position where he could plant both skis into the snow and bring himself to a halt.

'You okay?' she asked as she skied down to him, as he shook out the snow that had collected in his jacket.

'Oh yes,' he grinned. 'But you know what this means? I've missed a bit so we'll just have to do it again until I get it right.'

His classmates were all eager to repeat the experience and so they did it two more times.

'That's enough now, Poppy said. 'Your legs are tired and that's when accidents happen.'

She knew from her many years on the mountain that it was often that 'just one last run' that landed skiers in the emergency ward of the local hospital.

They looked disappointed.

'Coffee break,' she ordered, 'and then I have something else planned for you.'

It was now well after the time when they should have been heading down but, once she saw they were all rested, she led them home another way.

'Where are we going?' Charlie asked, as they passed through another pass where a sign read 'Good skiers only'. Poppy just smiled and touched her nose.

She led them down a winding path where the mountain rose on one side and the snow was piled up on the other to form a sort of Cresta Run. Full of confidence they crocodiled down the tunnel past waterfalls and rocky outcrops until they arrived at the top of another slope that looked even harder than the Bosses Bol. They looked down it and then up at Poppy in trepidation. Poppy laughed.

'Don't worry, we're not going down there. I want you to keep at least five metres apart and traverse all the way to the end. We're headed for that *col* over there.'

When they reached the appointed spot, Charlie whistled as they looked down upon the sunny bowl of Grondère and, between them and the resort, a huge field of small bumps.

'Just let me at them,' said one of the girls.

'Not quite yet,' Poppy said, looking at her watch and taking off her backpack. 'Our lesson is now officially over and the sun is over the yardarm.'

She took out a bottle of white wine and some small beakers.

'I normally do this on the last day, but I've brought it forward on account of the blizzard due tomorrow and because you lot have just stonked it!'

They cheered and tapped their ski poles above their heads before sitting down on their backpacks, sipping on their white wine and admiring the view as the sun dipped to their right and the shadows lengthened.

I don't think I've ever had a class that's made two weeks' progress in four days before, Poppy thought as she watched them basking in achievement and pure happiness and exhilaration. This was the highlight of being a ski teacher, when you got a group that gelled and excelled. She realised how much she would miss passing on the skills of the sport she loved but retire she must. Poppy was well over retirement age and she was beginning to feel the toll of such a physical job; she had already reduced the number of days she worked, but she loved it so much it was going to be hard to let go, especially at moments like this one.

'Come on you lot,' she smiled. 'Those lovely sun-softened bumps will start to freeze soon. Time to play.'

They bounced down the small mushy bumps, not afraid to fall because the snow was so soft and the slope much gentler than the one they had been doing all afternoon.

'Thank you, Poppy,' they all hugged her when they got back to the main lift station. 'That was a really special day. You coming for a drink?'

'Are you kidding? You lot have worn me out, I need a bath and an early night if I'm to lead you through a blizzard tomorrow.'

'You Jilly?'

'I'm on for quick drink before my boyfriend finishes work,' Jilly replied. They all put their skis on their shoulders and set off for The Pub.

'And carry your skis straight, Mike,' Poppy shouted as she retreated to the calm of her little apartment.

Mike, the culprit, grinned.

'She's been on at me about that all week. Now I do it on purpose just to get a telling off.'

'You warped person!' one of the girls tapped him on the head.

In The Pub they sipped on mulled wine and cold beers and Jilly dodged questions about what she did for a living.

'I'm an archivist,' she said, thinking it wasn't really a lie, her job did involve a lot of report writing and filing and hoping it sounded sufficiently dull to discourage further discussion. It was.

'A Swiss boyfriend,' one of the girls quizzed her, 'that's awesome, you can ski all the time! Is he a ski teacher? Is that why you're so good?'

'Actually, we've never skied together, I wanted to get some practice in first.'

When pushed on his job, she told them he was a civil servant, thinking once again that it wasn't strictly a lie. They soon tired of talking formalities and switched to their day on the slopes and watching themselves on the videos Mike had captured with his GoPro – Charlie's crash on the Bosses Bol proving particularly popular.

The following day, as predicted, it snowed heavily and the group was confined to the main axes of the ski area. Poppy kept them busy at the edges of the slopes, practising powder. There was a lot of falling and laughing but Poppy promised them a sunny final afternoon.

'Also,' she told them, 'you will find that these conditions are the best teacher there is. You cannot see and so you are having to rely completely on your technique. Once the sun comes out again, everything will seem easier.'

On their final afternoon the sun pierced through the clouds but the temperatures, and therefore the snow, stayed fresh and they had a final fling in the powder, with wonderful visibility and definition. Afterwards they headed back to the ski shops to return their gear and hit après-ski for the last time.

Jilly said goodbye to all her new friends cheerfully, but carefully avoided exchanging phone numbers and Facebook addresses, telling them she didn't do social media. She didn't know why, but she didn't want any of them to know her real identity or that she was a police officer. Nobody seemed to notice: they were all too distracted with their plans for a last night out.

Jilly, full of confidence, was ready for a weekend skiing with Laurent.

After another week skiing with various members of the GB Ski Club and a final weekend with Laurent, Jilly did not want to return to London.

'I think it's being so close to the sky, even when it's snowing there seems to be more light; London is so gloomy at this time of year. I just feel so charged,' she told him. 'What is it about the mountains?'

'Oh, once the mountains get you, they never let go,' he joked. 'Look at Poppy, Lucy and all their friends; they came out for a season and never went home. It's like the *Hotel California*!'

'Sorry?'

'*You can check out any time you like but you can never leave.*'

'Well, I don't want to. I don't have much on my plate now. I just need to finish the paperwork for that money laundering case. How about I check back in for Easter?'

Blonnay was so happy, he couldn't believe his ears.

'I will see if I can hire an apartment,' he said, beaming from ear to ear.

The night before Jilly went home, she and Laurent met Alain and Lucy for dinner.

'I'm curious,' Lucy asked Jilly. 'How would you compare the two experiences? Ski school versus the ski club?'

'Both worthwhile,' she replied. 'Ski school was great for getting my ski legs back, getting to know the ski area and having a ready-made group of people my own age to socialise with, but skiing-wise, I'm at a stage now where I just need to clock up mileage on my skis and for that I was better off with the ski club. I met this nice girl too, Jemima: if I get back at Easter we can hopefully ski together again.'

'Your own ski buddy, that's great!'

'Yes, although she's found *luuurve* while she's been here so I'm not sure how much I'll get to see her.'

'Really, a local?'

'Local ex-pat, her cousin lives here and introduced her to some chap called Charles, a bit older apparently, but he's been wining and dining her and he's got a nice pad too.'

'Hang on a minute, we're not talking about Charles Sidforth-Sykes here, are we?'

Jilly suddenly found herself the focus of concentrated stares from all three of them.

'I don't know his surname. What is this?'

'What's her cousin's name?' Laurent asked.

'Humphrey. Dunno his surname either.'

'Oh but we do.'

'That's hilarious,' Lucy grinned.

'Why?'

'Humphrey loves playing matchmaker. I'm surprised though, he has introduced a member of his own family to Charles: he's a bit of a duffer.'

'I don't think Jemima's used to getting a lot of male attention. She reckons Charles didn't fancy her much at first, until they skied together; she beat him down Le Monstre and he was smitten.'

'But I thought Charles skied with the Grondère Diamonds these days?'

'He does, but Jemima isn't actually a member: she says it costs too much and she prefers the SCGB anyway. She says the Diamonds is all a bit competitive for her, not skiing-wise, but socially.'

'I can relate to that,' Lucy said.

'And the leaders: she likes Suzie but she says Rory terrifies her.'

'I can relate to that too.'

They all chuckled over their dishes at the thought of Charles in love.

'You're quiet,' Lucy said, as she and Alain walked back to Anne's after dinner. It was easier to head back to her apartment as it was more central, she had a spare room and Alain refused to share Lucy's single bed in the little chalet when he was in Grondère overnight. He had his own place in Savigny which he was using less and less.

He stopped and, for a moment, looked dazed and stared through her. Lucy stood still and waited. Twice before Alain had had strange glimpses into the future: at first, they had both been disturbed by the experience, but on both occasions the strange information provided had been an invaluable warning and they had learned to accept and try to understand them when they came. It was a cold, starless night, Lucy reflected as she waited, a depression was moving in: snow was on the way.

'Most bizarre,' he declared as he shook himself out of his trance.

'Scary?'

'No, not this time.'

'Sense of foreboding?'

'No, just mysterious. I saw a woman, dressed in floaty garments; she was dancing on a mound and laughing and then she turned and looked straight at me and …'

'And?'

Alain laughed and shook his head.

'You're not going to believe this but she had the face of a wolf.'

'That is bizarre!'

'It must just be all this talk of wolves.'

'Possibly. But we can't ignore it completely.'

They entered the building behind La Grande Cour where Anne lived as quietly as they could so as to not annoy the neighbours.

'A woman with a wolf's face,' Lucy whispered, as they cuddled up to sleep, 'what on earth can that mean?'

Twelve

It is always our treasure that the lightning strikes.
Harriet Beecher Stowe,(1857), in Annie Fields, ed., Life and
Letters of Harriet Beecher Stowe (1898)

It was February half-term and Grondère was packed with families of almost every nationality. Sebastian and Tonita had flown out with Ruby and Leo to give them some solid skiing time. Neither Sebastian nor Tonita had the intention of skiing much themselves during this busy time: the slopes would be packed and the queues horrendous. Sebastian would be busy checking out the Swiss components of his business empire and Tonita was planning to do very little except look after herself and her now visible bump. Their honeymoon in California had felt more like a business trip, visiting the Shilton vineyards there and being wined, dined and entertained by all the people they felt they needed to keep happy. It had been wonderful but tiring.

Tonita, looking forward to a rest, had booked Lucy for the entire week to take the children skiing and Ruby and Leo were excited to know they would have Lucy's undivided attention.

On their first afternoon, while the children and Lucy were in the mountains, exploring more distant ski areas together in an attempt to avoid the crowds, Sebastian was surprised to spot Prince Anwar standing at the reception desk. He stepped outside the office he shared with Anya to greet him, with Anya following closely behind. She knew that Prince Anwar was not booked in.

'Anwar, I had no idea you were coming, what a great surprise!'

One look at the Prince's serious face stopped him in his tracks.

'Actually, I'm not booked in, I need to speak to you, and more importantly, Tonita, on a matter of the most serious nature.'

'Meeting room three is empty,' Anya suggested. 'I will go and find Tonita, I think she's sketching in the upstairs bar.'

Sebastian nodded at her in gratitude for her efficiency and led Prince Anwar up a flight of stairs to the comfortable meeting room they used for private dinners. Within moments a waiter was with them, bringing soft drinks and a few minutes later, Tonita entered, looking puzzled.

'Anwar, what a wonderful surprise.'

He looked at her sadly.

'Tonita, please sit down, what I have to tell you is painful and unpleasant,' he looked at her little bump and seemed even more uncomfortable.

Tonita sat quietly and waited for the blow.

'Have you heard from your father recently, Tonita?'

'Actually, no,' she replied. 'I have been trying to contact him because he's late with the children's school fees, but I can't get hold of him. I've had to pay them myself to avoid the children being exposed to any embarrassment at school. It's very irritating, I can't believe he's short of cash.'

Prince Anwar sighed.

'Your father has disappeared, Tonita, and he cannot be short of cash as he has taken $50 million of my government's money with him.'

'What?' Tonita's face was as black as thunder. As the news sank in, she murmured under her breath.

'50 million!'

'It is a small portion of the transaction that your father was managing. We have discovered that your father has been in the habit of "borrowing" some of the money entrusted to him to undertake certain confidential transactions on our behalf, to do his own short-term profitable deals at the same time, always making sure that the money was in the right place when required for our purposes. On this occasion, neither he nor the "borrowed" money has reappeared which is how we uncovered what he was up to.'

'How dare he? How dare he do that to them?' It was clear Tonita was not thinking of Prince Anwar's defrauded country but of her half-siblings. 'And his wife?'

'She is helping us with our enquiries and will remain in the country until this matter is resolved and our money has been returned. But it seems he has abandoned her.'

'This is just awful,' exclaimed Sebastian.

'It is a most unsatisfactory turn of events,' the prince agreed.

Tonita sat in stunned and angry silence.

'You have no idea, Tonita, where your father might be hiding? If he hasn't paid his children's school fees then I'm assuming he hasn't deposited any large amounts with you.'

She shook her head.

'I know you were estranged from your father, but I thought when I saw him at your wedding, maybe you were on better terms these days.'

Tonita shook her head again.

'He was only invited for the children's sake and I can assure you, Anwar, if I knew where he was, I would tell you, and leave him to take the consequences. It would probably be better for him, for if I find him, I may very well kill him.'

There could be no doubt as to the strength and sincerity of her words. Her father had always let her down but to hurt his other children too was the final unforgiveable act of betrayal.

Sebastian looked at her tenderly.

'It'll be okay, Tonita, we'll get through this together.'

'I have,' added Prince Anwar, 'explained to my fellow government ministers, that there is no love lost between you and your father. It is fortunate that you explained the situation to me last autumn. It has enabled me to ensure that you will be left alone. All I ask is, that in return, if you hear anything, if your father tries to contact you or his other children, you will inform me.'

Sebastian and Tonita looked at him horrified.

'That sounds awfully like a threat,' Sebastian said softly.

'Please understand, I have personally vouched for you and made sure you and the children are not used in any way to force your father out of hiding, all I ask is that you return my faith in you.'

Tonita nodded her agreement.

'My absolute priorities are my sister and brother and my unborn child. I will not flinch from any act in order to protect them.'

'Thank you, Tonita, I knew I could count on you.'

With this, the Prince took his leave.

'You will not stay?' Sebastian asked him as he accompanied him to the door.

'No, I will return to Geneva directly and fly to the Cayman Islands tomorrow.'

'Is that where you think he's hiding out?'

'We have uncovered some offshore accounts and interests there. He seems to have favoured the place as a hub for his unofficial transactions but it is a small place and we have many sets of eyes there. I doubt he would choose to live there. If I'm honest, his behaviour is puzzling, he could have carried on for years without ever being found out. The only supporting evidence we can find is that we have discovered he rents a large property in the Caymans and that a young woman lives there, very comfortably, on his financial support.'

'A mistress.'

'Almost certainly.'

'How awful!' exclaimed Tonita when Sebastian gave her this additional damning piece of information. 'He never could stay faithful for long. And he's left that poor woman in the hands of the authorities he's defrauded. This time he's reached new heights of despicability.'

'But still, would you really shop him to a foreign power?' Tonita looked at her morally upright husband and laughed. 'I have no idea. I said what I had to say to get Anwar off our backs. Let's hope my scruples on the subject never get tested, for I fear I would shock you.'

Sebastian laughed at her pragmatism.

'The more pressing dilemma,' she frowned, 'is what on earth to say to Ruby and Leo.'

The following evening, Sebastian and Tonita had invited Alain and Lucy for dinner at La Grande Cour. They had discussed it beforehand and agreed that Alain should be told about Tony Onion's disappearance. Alain was someone Sebastian trusted implicitly and he felt it was better the *Police judiciaire* knew, just in case Tonita's father should turn up, looking for refuge.

'It's a good job you mentioned it. I just saw today, there's an Interpol warrant out for his arrest. Lucy told me Tonita's father was a bad lot but this is on another level.'

'It is.'

'What about the children?'

'They don't know anything at the moment, I'm afraid we've invented a story about a Caribbean holiday until we can think of something else. That way, they don't get distressed trying to call their mother.'

'What a mess,' Alain commented.

'Indeed,' Tonita forced a smile. 'Oh, dear, I should have known it was all going too well! But we're not going to let it spoil our week together before we head back to the Murky Midlands.'

Sebastian grinned: Tonita had picked up that phrase from the staff at Lunstag Hall and they had quickly understood its significance. They had been glad to be able to leave the winter fog and gloom behind them for a week of Alpine sunshine.

'Quite right,' he agreed, raising his glass, 'here's to families!'

'At least,' Lucy added, 'this time Grondère is your retreat from trouble and not the location of it.'

Alain looked at her and smiled to disguise the sinking feeling her words had triggered. He didn't know why but he knew she was wrong.

When young, Alain's mother had never had a problem sleeping, but now, Anne inevitably found herself awake for a couple of hours around 3 or 4 o'clock in the morning. It was not something that troubled her, it was something she accepted with serenity, as part of the ageing process. It had become part of her routine to get up, make a warm drink, go back to bed and then switch on the radio, leave it on and let it lull her back to sleep. She never turned the lights on or tried to read, if she did that she might as well admit defeat and start her day early. The streetlamps outside provided enough light for her to feel her way around the kitchen.

That night though, when Anne woke in the early hours, and went into her kitchen to make herself a herbal infusion, she closed the door behind her as gently as she could so as not to wake Alain and Lucy who were enjoying the sound sleep of youth in the spare room, having rolled in around midnight following their dinner with Sebastian

142

and Tonita. Their overnights at her conveniently placed flat were becoming more and more frequent and Anne was beginning to wonder if she would have to move out. They needed a place of their own but she didn't really want to vacate hers. She was rather hoping that when he retired, her partner Jacques Aulnay would move in with her.

While she waited for the water to boil she looked out of the window from where she had a view of the rear façade of La Grande Cour. It had been snowing heavily for a few hours and it made for a pretty scene. In the snow everything was unclear and hazy and the streetlamps threw funnelled spotlights on the torrent of falling snowflakes.

Anne smiled as she thought of how it all began at La Grande Cour for her son and Lucy: the strangest of beginnings. To her right, further away, something caught her eye, small lights, torches or something, were floating around the White Snowflake building site. It looked quite pretty. They hovered for a while and then were suddenly gone. She watched on for a bit longer but they didn't reappear. She presumed it to have been some drunks leaving the nearby nightclub. The snow kept falling thicker and thicker: great news for the resort, there would be a deep enough base to take it right through to the Easter holidays and beyond.

That morning, Lucy opened the shutters of Anne's spare room to a world of complete whiteness. It was still snowing: giant snowflakes landed on her face and she had to brush them away to see anything. She reluctantly closed the window so she could admire the deep layer of snow atop the chalet roofs. Parked cars had been transformed into huge white lumps and the hedges and plants of the chalet gardens had assumed a variety of shapes: triangles, humps, columns: it was a total transformation. Alain stirred and turned over and so she grabbed her coat and headed into the kitchen, made herself a cup of tea and took it out onto the balcony: from this side of the building she was protected from the wind and she could see the main part of the resort and its thoroughfares. The streetlamps projected large warm globes of light through the blizzard. The snowploughs had been clinking and clunking away since 5 o'clock in the morning but, despite their best efforts, the roads were still white. A few early risers, on their way to work, were wading their way through the deep snow on the footpaths, occasionally daring to step out into the road, slipping about precariously until the oncoming terror of some large piece of snow-clearing machinery chased them back onto the path.

This was the day of the snowplough. The drivers, perched in their high cabins, like kings on thrones, thrived on conditions like these, it was what they were trained for and nobody was left in any doubt as to who was in charge in Grondère today. Long ridges of snow were piled along the roadsides waiting for the clearance crews with their huge lorries and giant snowblowers but, as yet, they had not been able to make any real impact, so great was the volume that had fallen in so short a time. The piles just kept growing and the snowploughs continued to pass.

It would be hours before the snowploughs made it up to Lucy's chalet on the Colline, she would have to go straight to work from Anne's. She hoped she had the low visibility visor of her goggles in her locker, it would be a total white-out up on the mountain; it was already a white-out in the village.

Anne joined her to watch the scene, which was getting quite lively as the delivery trucks began to attempt the climb up to their clients' establishments. She brought out a cover for Lucy and a coffee for herself.

'Surely your clients will cancel this morning.'

'Not a chance – Ruby and Leo, it'll take more than a blizzard to put them off.'

'Ah. They'll be raring to go then and already enjoying a hot bowl of sweet porridge at the hotel. Do you have time for breakfast?'

'Oh yes, slope patrol won't be opening until all the slopes are secured. I'll text Tonita to delay our start.'

'In fact,' Lucy laughed as they set the table for breakfast, 'today's conditions are exactly what Ruby and Leo need to improve their technique. They're both still a bit too upright: skiing in poor visibility will make them bend their knees more and feel the undulations of the snow rather than relying on their eyes.'

Anne smiled at Lucy, thinking what a good teacher she must be. She herself had taught all her life and believed that a good teacher always looks for different ways to help the learning process. Lucy had obviously been thinking hard about how to help Ruby and Leo progress.

Alain appeared, looking slightly dishevelled and well-rested.

'Look at that!' he remarked. 'Must have snowed at least 60cm.'

'Yes, and it's still coming down.'

'Driving down to Savigny's going to be interesting,' he laughed.

'You Swiss think nothing of driving in the snow, I still find it scary.'

'It's just practice, I rather enjoy it, makes a change to all that boring tarmac.'

'I think the snowploughs started at 5 o'clock,' Anne commented. 'Thank goodness it doesn't snow like that every night.'

'It didn't seem to disturb Alain,' Lucy laughed. 'He slept through the whole thing.'

As Lucy and Alain kissed goodbye and went off in their different directions, Lucy to pick the children up from the hotel and Alain for the police headquarters, he said thoughtfully, 'It must be strange for you, being in the centre of the resort, I'm not sure you like it that much.'

'Your mum's place is certainly very convenient, and I'm very grateful to her for putting us up all the time, but you're right, however much easier it is to be in the centre, I missed being up on my balcony this morning, looking down at the snowy scene in the peace and quiet.'

'We must find our own place for next winter.'

'Something will come up: my dad always says that "things have a way of working out".'

'Let's hope he's right. But I'm not sure it's a theory that can be applied to my job.'

'Drive safely,' she said and headed across to La Grande Cour thinking how much fun she, Ruby and Leo would have working their way up to the main lift station through snow now over knee-deep high. She would turn it into a game.

When Lucy picked up the children, Tonita asked her to be careful what to say around Ruby and Leo and to ask Poppy to join them for afternoon tea after skiing.

Thirteen

*A genuine coincidence always means bad luck for me;
it's my only superstition.*
Marjorie Allingham, Police at the Funeral

After tea, once the children were out of hearing, Tonita told Poppy of Tony Onion's disappearance.

'Where do you think he is?'

'No idea. Anwar told Sebastian they're starting their search in the Cayman Islands, that's where he's been shipping the money around for his dodgy transactions. They've found a luxury residence there, oh, and with a mistress in it. But it's too small a place for him to hide out; I think the States is a more likely hiding place, or Italy, he often spends the summer there, so he knows his way around. I didn't bother mentioning that to Anwar. He can do his own hunting.'

'Maybe he's not in hiding, maybe he's had an accident and is lying in a ditch somewhere,' Lucy suggested weakly, 'that would explain why he changed his modus operandi.'

'Oh Lucy,' groaned Poppy, 'Tonita's just had a visit from a government official, even you can't seriously defend the man.'

'If it's true, he's even wickeder than you led us to believe, Tonita,' Lucy said softly.

Tonita nodded.

'Now you know where I get it from,' she tried to joke.

'On the contrary: it shows, Tonita,' Poppy said, 'that you are *not* like him. Your decision to agree to become your siblings' guardian, so that you could look out for them, seems almost prescient.'

'Sadly, yes.'

'It also looks like your father is about to pay for his previous misdemeanours.'

Tonita looked at Poppy shrewdly.

'What are you getting at, Poppy?'

'Justice is looming, Tonita. Can't you feel it? I can. In my experience, what goes around comes around … eventually, even though it can take an awfully long time. I have a feeling your dad is about to reap the harvest of his precious bane.'

'Well, I hope he gets his just desserts without dragging me and the children into it.'

'He's not likely to show up here or in the UK, is he?' Lucy asked. 'Would the Swiss or the Brits extradite him?'

'No idea. You're not likely to offer him sanctuary, are you, Tonita?' Poppy asked guardedly.

'No, I'm more likely to hang, draw and quarter him myself.' Tonia replied with a ferocity that made Poppy and Lucy wonder how far from the truth her statement actually was.

The holidays ran their course, the resort was bustling because of the fortuitous fresh snowfall. Lucy called every morning to collect Ruby and Leo and brought them back exhausted and happy at the end of the afternoon. They would then all spend some time in the hotel pool before Lucy left them for baths and supper.

One evening, with Ruby and Leo in bed, Sebastian ensconced with Anya in her office, Tonita was enjoying a quiet drink at the hotel bar. It had been a lovely day, Lucy had taught the children in the morning and she and Sebastian had had their first ever ski together. They had taken it gently as she was now four months pregnant and, as an older mother, she knew not to take any risks. They cruised the groomed slopes and just enjoyed the mountains and sunshine. Lucy and the children had joined them for lunch in a mountain restaurant as Ruby and Leo excitedly told them how they had been down their first itinerary and 'skied powder and moguls'.

'Crikey,' Tonita said, looking impressed. 'Should you be going down such challenging runs already?'

'It was easy!' boasted Leo. 'I'm a natural, Lucy says so.'

'Well, if Lucy says so, then that must be right.'

'Exactly,' said Leo, tucking into his huge serving of macaroni.

'This afternoon, Lucy has promised us we can do the ski cross track!' Ruby added.

Tonita looked at their sparkling eyes and rosy cheeks and thought back to her own introduction to skiing, in the happy days when her parents were still together. She remembered how she had been nervous to keep up with all the other children in her ski class and the joy of discovering she was just as good, if not better. She had never been particularly sporty but skiing just clicked naturally.

'Thank you,' she smiled at Lucy. 'You clearly have given them a love of the sport.'

'They're a joy to teach,' Lucy smiled. 'I just have to explain once, and they can do it. But, by the way,' she whispered, 'just in case you're worried: they weren't moguls, just beautifully formed little bumps on the fresh snow.'

'Oh, don't tempt me,' laughed Tonita, 'I love bumps but my love of this little bump will have to take precedence this winter,' she patted her tummy and they all laughed.

'Yes, no bumps for you, my Lady Shalott or is it Shilton?' Sebastian joked.

'I like both titles,' Tonita replied. 'Can I have two? You have two, Viscount and Lord.'

'That poem's just too sad,' Ruby said. 'Why would you want to be sad like the Lady of Shalott?'

'Goodness,' said Tonita, 'where did you get that from?'

'We read it at school: I didn't like it much: it doesn't have a happy ending.'

Tonita smiled wistfully. Life didn't always have happy endings, but she didn't want Ruby to know that just yet. Her father's desertion would hit the child hard, as it had her all those years ago, but she would protect her from it for as long as possible.

'Sometimes there can be great beauty in sadness, Ruby. A lot of artists, writers and composers find inspiration in disappointed love, lost battles, death even. When we're back in the UK, how about we visit some galleries together and I'll show you how artists use sad things to create beautiful ones.'

'That would be cool!' Ruby smiled and turned back to tackling her sausage and chips.

Sebastian looked at his wife adoringly, she really was unexpectedly good with children. Tonita, it seems, had surprised herself.

'I could use a drink,' she laughed.

'I'll have one for you,' he teased. 'Lucy?'

'Thanks, just a little more,' Lucy grinned. 'I don't usually drink when I'm teaching and I'll need all my reactions about me if we're racing this afternoon.'

And so, as she was sitting quietly, thinking back on her happy day, Tonita's guard was slightly down when Alessandra Rosset crept up on her.

'Tonita, what a lovely surprise!'

Tonita knew it was no surprise for Alessandra and it was certainly not lovely for Tonita. But she knew she could not snub the chairwoman of the company that was making her so much money.

'Alessandra, please come and join me. What will you have?'

'I'll have a glass of red, thanks. Your house *Pinot* will be fine,' she condescendingly told the waiter who ran across to take her order.

'A Bloody Mary, Tonita?' Alessandra raised her eyebrows.

'Tomato juice only, I'm afraid. I don't normally like tomato juice but my taste buds are all awry.'

'Ah yes, I had heard. Congratulations. Motherhood can be a wonderful experience, I'm told.'

'Thank you,' smiled Tonita, sensing the cynicism and total lack of empathy in Alessandra's voice. She reflected that one year earlier, when she was engaged to Malcolm and full of ambition and material greed herself, her attitude would have been much the same, viewing motherhood as a weakness, as an opportunity to be exploited, the chance to seize someone's place and advance at their expense.

Ah, she thought, inwardly jolting, *that's* what this is about … and suddenly the old Tonita was back, ready to do battle.

'In fact,' started Alessandra, 'I was wondering if, now you've got so much on, with the baby coming, becoming a lady, the success of your jewellery brand, you still want to be bothered with our little consortium?'

Tonita was amused at Alessandra's transparent approach. She decided to play with her a little.

'What did you have in mind, Alessandra?'

Hoping she had caught Tonita at a mellow moment, Alessandra thought she would start the bidding low.

'For your shareholding, I'm prepared to offer 20 million Swiss francs.'

Tonita smiled sweetly. She and Sebastian had, just the previous week, gone through all their combined assets to set up a holding company for their first UK tax return. He had valued her interest at 40 million Swiss francs, but that of course, was just on paper, you had to find someone to pay that and it certainly was not the figure they would be giving the Inland Revenue or the IRS in the States.

'We both know it's worth a lot more than that.'

'30, that's a good offer.'

Tonita inclined her head: it probably was, but she had no intention of relinquishing her shares. It had been Malcolm's project and she felt he would have wanted her to keep an eye on it for him.'

Seeing her hesitate, Alessandra mistakenly thought it was her cue to apply some pressure.

'Come on Tonita. Get out while you can. Concentrate on making babies and pretty jewels.'

Tonita's eyes flashed but she just said she needed time to think about it.

Thinking she was making headway Alessandra added, 'I understand, you need to talk to your husband about it. While you're at it, maybe you could ask him to reconsider my offer for La Grande Cour. I'm also interested in the vineyard.'

Tonita laughed out loud.

'Goodness, what next? Do you want my husband too?'

Alessandra was taken aback, humour was not her strong suit.

'Your lives are in England now, you have an estate to manage, three children to bring up.'

It was Tonita's turn to be shocked, how could Alessandra know that? As far as she knew, only the authorities in the countries concerned knew about her father's disappearance. Alessandra didn't seem to realise she had said anything wrong.

'Holdings in Switzerland don't fit into the Shilton portfolio, you don't want to be tied to Grondère.'

Tonita decided it was time to put an end to the discussion. She decided to do so gently, she didn't, after all, want to fall out with an important business partner.

'I will think about your offer, Alessandra, and I will talk to Sebastian, but I have to tell you, I think it is unlikely that we will be selling any of our Swiss assets. We were just saying the other day how complementary we thought they were to our other interests, we see La Grande Cour as the perfect platform for showcasing our wines from Valais and the New World and I'm planning to diversify my design business to tie in with the estate and the wine businesses to create a whole range of merchandising.'

'I see.' Alessandra knew a *no* when she heard one.

Tonita continued.

'Since Sebastian left his Wall Street job and I have based my design studio in Leicestershire, he is applying all his know-how to building and consolidating our interests so you see, it was living in New York that didn't fit in with our business activities, not Switzerland.'

'I see,' scowled Alessandra.

'And, with you doing such a great job at the helm of White Snowflake, I do not feel the need to be too active in the business end of the consortium. Unless, of course … you would like me to be more involved?'

She smiled wickedly at her adversary. Alessandra grimaced.

'No, that's okay, I prefer to exercise full control over our day-to-day activities.'

'Ah, then I shall leave you in peace,' Tonita smiled, leaving the unsaid 'for now' hanging in the air.

Later, as they were getting ready for bed, she recounted the evening's encounter to Sebastian. He congratulated her on not allowing Alessandra to rile her and managing to show her mettle whilst remaining polite.

'Beautifully handled, but why didn't you send for me to join you?' he asked.

'I can handle her,' Tonita smiled 'and besides …' she winked as she hopped into bed and held out her arms for a hug, 'I was enjoying myself far too much.'

Fourteen

Nothing is seen so new and green
As the new young green of Beech.
                        Cicely Mary Barker, The Beech Tree Fairy

The Jordan Russell murder investigation had ground to a halt. Rusty had grown up in South Africa but Alain and his team could find no family who claimed anything but a distant (and involuntary) connection with him. It seemed that as soon as he had finished compulsory education, he had completely disappeared off all official radars. There was some evidence of working for a diamond mining company and an unfinished business degree at a rogue business school in England. After that, they pieced together that he had worked as a barman in a French ski resort where he had developed a passion for skiing. He had lots of friends but no one he was close to. He never seemed to have legally officialised his residence anywhere until he arrived in Switzerland. He had managed to obtain a European passport through a French grandparent and had started building his credentials in Grondère by taking intensive French lessons and acquiring his *patente*. The strange thing was, he didn't seem to have any obvious source of funds and yet he had found enough money to finance leasing and renovating a rather large hotel.

'He is loaded,' Alain concluded. 'He must have made a lot of money illegally and have a bank account elsewhere. But why can't we find transfers of that money into his Swiss account?'

'Cash,' Sylvie said. 'Who knows what he brought with him or how. He's always had a healthy sum in his Swiss account.'

'Lucy said people couldn't work out how he could afford to delay opening his hotel. A few people thought he might have been into drug dealing.'

'Well, it's a possibility. But I think we'd have got wind of it if someone was dealing large volume in Grondère. Whatever he was up to, if he was working on the dark web and in virtual currencies, we're going to have a hard time proving it.'

'No paperwork. Not even in the safe. And nothing on his computer. If he held all his details in his head he must have been a genius.'

'Risky filing system.'

'This guy seems to have lived risky since he left school.'

'And yet, he seems to have been trying to build some kind of stable existence here.'

'Maybe, but although lots of people knew him, nobody seems to have known anything about him. And he clearly didn't trust anyone – look at that elaborate safe.'

'If the decoration of that bar is anything to go by, he liked *elaborate*,' Sylvie smiled.

'Where better than a ski resort to establish your new identity?' Blonnay added. 'The population is so transitory, nobody asks any real questions about where you come from, what you have done in the past. All they care about is how well you can ski and if you can pull a pint.'

'That's so true,' Sylvie agreed. 'It's a great place to hide. Nobody really cares about your past here and I think that's not all bad. I know at least two ex-cons living in Pattier who have built a good life here and are now pillars of the community.'

'You're making it sound like a last-chance saloon.'

'I think for some people it is a second-chance bolthole.'

'So, are we saying Rusty was some repentant baddie trying to go legit?'

'He does seem to have been building some veneer of respectability. Maybe that was his long-term plan and someone didn't agree with it.'

'Perhaps. I think it's more likely he had stolen those diamonds and someone from his past did find him.'

'Or someone else knew about the diamonds and wanted to steal them.'

'But who? Let's face it: we're no closer to the truth now than we were in December.'

'I'd hate to fail on this one.'

'Me too, but for the time being, all we can do is keep digging and hope for a lucky break.'

During half-term Lucy and Sally managed to find time to join the Mardi Gras festivities. This February event passed mostly unnoticed by visitors in the resort: the majority of the festivities, such as the parades, took place down in Pattier, away from the main tourist area. The most visitors got to see of this ancient tradition was when the carnival band made an occasional appearance on the slopes, playing their unique brand of carnival music to intrigued foreigners. But Mardi Gras was of great importance to the locals, and incomers like Lucy and Sally had grown to look forward to it almost as much as those who had grown up in Grondère. Jodie had kept her diary clear so that she could join her friends for the masked ball in Pattier and the girls had, following Lucy's inspiration, made dresses in the style of Cicely Barker's tree fairies; they had little tunics and green tights with balloon skirts covered in leaves of the trees that Lucy had decided best reflected their identity. Jodie was a tall, graceful willow tree, Sally a eucalyptus in tribute to her native Australia and Lucy's skirt was covered in the glossy, transparent spring leaves of the beech tree she so loved. She was enchanted with it and kept wafting around to make the leaves flutter. They all had green woollen shawls to protect them from the cold and Lucy had asked a local girl who knitted beanies to make them each a beanie as a surprise present for her dear friends. Jodie had a close-fitting cap with edges shaped like the end of willow leaves that contrasted with her dark brown ringlets, Sally's beanie was shaped like an upside-down gum nut sitting neatly on her long, straight blond hair and Lucy's glorious dark red hair was crowned with a little brown beech nut. Lucy had also attached some miniature koalas to Sally's skirt.

Since Milly's 'very bad night' (as it was now referred to) Lucy and Sally had been keeping her close to make sure she stayed out of trouble: they had decided she should join the outing and so they had to make her a dress in haste. It was decided for her that she should be a sycamore because it had big leaves and they could cut those out of the remaining fabric more quickly. It was too late to have a beanie knitted so Lucy found her a pretty green one from her collection and they pinned some cardboard winged samaras on it. Milly, illustrating that she too could be enterprising, even managed to find some sycamore samara earrings from a local jewellery maker.

'It's amazing, isn't it, how many craftspeople there are in this place!' Sally said as they were getting ready. 'People with proper, old-fashioned skills, who can knit, sew, crochet and make pottery and jewellery.'

'And woodwork,' Lucy added, thinking of Gluey Hughey.

'Yes, and then there are all those photographers and a plethora of painters. I think there is a disproportionate number of creative people here compared to anywhere else I've ever lived.'

Lucy thought about it.

'I think you have a point. I wonder why it is. Do you think mountains draw creative people to them as well as sporty ones like us?'

'But you're creative too.'

'Me?' This had not occurred to Lucy.

'Yes, look at all those things you make with the plants you dry. Teas, soaps, creams, flower mixes for salads plus all those dried herbs, that's artistic too.'

'I hadn't seen it that way,' Lucy laughed, 'but yes, okay, so what's your grand theory?'

Milly was watching on fascinated as Sally tried to work out what her grand theory was.

'I think that mountains kindle creation: whether someone was actively creative already or had a creative side sleeping inside them, like you.'

'So, mountains draw it out of you? By magic or inspiration?'

'Oh, I don't know, I'm beginning to wish I hadn't started this.'

'No, it's good,' Lucy said, 'come on, let's develop it.'

'It could just be a life-style thing,' Jodie offered. 'People who choose to live here have a more holistic approach to life – and more time to develop their creative interests. Or maybe it's economic?'

'That's far too logical,' Sally grimaced. 'But valid. Even the people who grew up here make their own jams and pickles. Is that by creative desire or economic necessity?'

'Or just tradition?' Jodie added.

'No, I think you were on the right track before,' Lucy said. 'I don't know whether it's the magic of the mountains or whether they just inspire, but they definitely are a factor: even if I only dry a few flowers, it's definitely to immerse myself more in the hills, as if when I'm not there physically, I still have a part of the mountains with me. And look at the painters and writers they inspired: Turner,

Twain … And you, Jodie, you can't put it down to pure logic and economy – you found your voice again here.'

Jodie smiled: Lucy had, as usual, found the winning argument.

'Okay, it's official: we attribute the exceptionally high number of creative people in Grondère to the magical powers of the mountains!'

'Exactly,' Sally beamed. 'Are we ready?'

As they walked up to the main lift station, hugging their woolen shawls to them for warmth, Milly asked Sally, 'Do you lot always banter on like that? It was a bit like being back in philosophy class.'

'I didn't used to,' Sally admitted. 'I blame Lucy,' she said loudly so Lucy could hear her. 'She draws it out of you. Watch out, it's catching.'

Lucy just grinned.

'I like it,' Milly said. 'But I will have to sharpen my mind a bit before I can join in.'

Poppy was waiting for them to take their photos before they took the gondola.

'Enjoy yourselves, you lovely tree fairies!' she shouted as they rushed to catch the last gondola down to Pattier to party the night away. Poppy had long ceased partying all night and she had decided to spend the night sorting through her photos from last year's ball.

Tommy and his farming partner, Christophe, were waiting for them at the bar with the first round of drinks. Lucy was not sure this was a good idea: Christophe had been showing a bit of interest in Jodie and she knew that that was his main motivation for attending. She was not sure that there was any interest on Jodie's side, but that was for Jodie to decide, not her.

'Your outfits aren't very imaginative,' Sally teased. The young men had come as lumberjacks in checked shirts and trapper hats. 'Apart from the hats, you're pretty much in your working clothes.'

'That's enough cheek from you trees,' warned Tommy exaggerating his West Country accent and raising an inflatable axe menacingly. 'Any more of that and we shall be chopping your trunks.' He looked down at Sally's shapely legs in their green tights. 'And that would be such a shame.'

'You duffer!' she said lovingly.

Lucy laughed but she was also looking out to see how Jodie and Christophe greeted each other. As she watched, the most extraordinary thing happened. Christophe nervously turned to greet Jodie, unsure of his reception, and she quickly gave him the ritual three kisses on alternate cheeks and then introduced him to Milly. Christophe looked visibly thunderstruck. He hesitated, composed himself and presented his cheeks to Milly. He couldn't take his eyes of this grinning, sweet-faced woman with blonde curls poking out from under her green beanie, and, unlike with Jodie, he was immediately at ease with Milly who smiled at him and led him to the dance floor.

Jodie went to stand with Lucy who was looking dumbfounded.

'I do believe I just saw love at first sight … at first sight!'

'Yes, and much more suitable,' Jodie agreed.

'I wasn't sure if you were keen on him or not.'

'Well, he can't have been that keen on me, I seem to have been instantly forgotten.'

'You don't mind then?'

'Not at all. Relieved. Nice guy and, in other circumstances I might have gone for it. But the truth is, I'm not going to be around to look after the chickens.'

'Are you leaving us already?'

'At the end of my year in Lausanne, yes. Since Sebastian and Tonita's wedding I have had a lot of interest. Sarah

Pring has become my mentor and she says she's already speaking to the main opera houses across the world about me.'

'That's wonderful, Jodie.'

'Do you know who Sarah is?'

'Yes, I do actually.'

'Crikey, most people have only heard of The Three Tenors, Kiri Te Kanawa and Katherine Jenkins and that's about it.'

'That's about it for me too, but I accidentally caught some of that TV show she does about being able to teach anyone to sing,' Lucy added jokingly, 'I wondered if there was any hope for me.'

'Oh Lucy, I don't mean to be mean, but that's just television you know, it's not true. You can only teach *anyon*e to sing provided they actually have some basic musical ability. For the truly tone deaf, there is nothing even Sarah Pring can do.'

'Whatever,' Lucy shrugged laughing. 'If she helps you to get half as well-known as any of those big stars you mentioned, I promise to love her forever.'

Jodie smiled, 'If I can just make a living at it, Lucy, it'll be a dream come true. But imagine, treading the boards of La Scala or Covent Garden.'

'Doesn't that frighten you?'

Jodie looked bemused.

'Are you kidding? Lead to me to it!'

'I am so happy for you, but I will miss you.'

'I will always return to Grondère: I will always need my fix of the mountains to charge my batteries.'

'You see?' Lucy grinned. 'It is the magical pull of the mountains.'

'Yes, yes, you win the argument. But I will always come back for you guys too. You also have your magical pull.'

'That's good to hear. Never forget us, will you?'

Jodie shook her head and looked over at Milly and Christophe jiving like they were the only people on earth. 'Do you think she will?'

'What? Forget you? Yes, probably.'

'No, feed the chickens?'

'Oh yes, no problem – farmer's daughter.'

The happy band danced all night and Sally, Lucy and Milly headed back uphill in the cram-packed morning post bus. Tommy and Christophe took Jodie down to Savigny to catch the train back to Lausanne and future stardom.

'You and Christophe seemed to hit it off,' Sally couldn't resist teasing Milly a little.

'Yes, he seems a really nice boy,' Milly said. 'Oh god, I sound just like my mother. Why is it that as soon as you take a guy home and your mother says "he seems like a nice boy" you go off him?'

'I know exactly what you mean. And why are the wicked boys always so much more attractive? More sexy?'

'Dunno, but after my "very bad night" I've been thinking back to some of those nice boys I wouldn't look at before and realising that some of them were real gems.'

'Good men – that what our mothers want for us. They know, as we know now, that the wicked men are the ones that betray us and break our hearts.'

Lucy looked at Sally, she knew the story of her friend's broken heart. Milly did not know the story, but she understood that Sally was talking about herself.

'And then you meet a Tommy, don't you, Sally?'

'Yes Milly, and you know how to really appreciate him because of the shits you met along the way.'

Milly's phone buzzed and she smiled as she tapped in a quick reply.

'I'm betting that was Christophe wishing you goodnight.'

'Yes, it was and yes, I'm ready for a good man,' Milly admitted, snuggling up to Lucy and resting her head on her shoulder, preparing to go to sleep.

'Can I just point out?' Lucy said, amused. 'That you two just did that all by yourselves. Without any help from me, you have just conducted a rambling philosophical banter, and in full hearing of a busload of drunken ski bums.'

Sally smirked.

'You see, Milly, I warned you – it's catching.'

Fifteen

Do you not know, my friend, that each one of us is a dark mystery, a maze of conflicting passions and desires and aptitudes?
Agatha Christie, Lord Edgware Dies

Now that he had found free, and very comfortable, lodgings in Grondère, Rory was in town much more often than his contract with the Diamond Ski Club required. During the day his blond locks could be seen heading off in the direction of all the secret off-piste runs and the evenings saw him and Alessandra flaunting their relationship in the expensive bars and clubs. There were even rumours that they might marry.

'No,' said Johnny, 'that would just ruin it.'

'Playboys do settle down eventually,' Poppy laughed.

'Like who?'

Poppy tried to think of a famous playboy who had settled down: she went through the list in her head but could not think of one who had made a successful, stable marriage.

'See!' said Johnny. It wasn't often he won a point over Poppy.

'Okay,' she said. 'It's doomed. But she's having a good time now.'

Alessandra was having a good time. Not only was she passionately in love with Rory but they were to become business partners. He had put her in touch with some wealthy investors who were interested in joining the White Snowflake consortium.

They had appointed Rory a director of the company with the specific mandate of coordinating their White Snowflake investment.

Rory was clearly very pleased with himself and his rise in fortune: he was practically swaggering around the resort.

Humphrey watched over all these proceedings with glee: as a member of the White Snowflake consortium, he stood to benefit from the financial results of this relationship, but this was not the main source of his pleasure – Humphrey loved nothing more than watching someone putting on a show and Rory and Alessandra were putting on an almighty show. They were fast becoming the hottest couple in town. Everyone wanted them at their table and Rory and Alessandra were more than happy to grace all the various functions and dinners they were invited to.

'Mark my word, there will be fireworks,' Humphrey told Johnny as they were watching the rugby at The Pub. 'It is the sort of fire that will eventually blow itself out with one final mighty explosion.'

Johnny, who freely acknowledged Humphrey's superior understanding and knowledge in such matters, nodded.

'Is that why you introduced them then? To watch the fireworks?'

'Indeed,' Humphrey grinned mischievously. 'But I never imagined they would be such dynamite. This is the stuff of Anthony and Cleopatra, Taylor and Burton, Depp and Paradis.'

'Aren't you overdramatising it a bit?'

Humphrey tapped his nose.

'Mark my words, high drama is exactly what we're in for, and,' he rubbed his hands with glee, 'this time, stick with me for the front row seats.'

'So, Alessandra,' Tonita, as principal shareholder, asked, 'do we know who is actually behind this company, Ruaidrí Investments Cayman LLC?'

She had flown out for the AGM of White Snowflake to discover some surprise items on the agenda.

'It's a group of British and South African hedge fund owners who place their excess private capital in a diverse range of solid investments across the world to give them global financial security.'

'And avoid paying tax …'

'Possibly.'

'So, we haven't done due diligence on any of the individuals, where their money comes from? We don't even know their names?'

'We don't need to, 40 million Swiss francs is already sitting on deposit at the bank awaiting our acceptance.'

Alessandra looked around the room smugly; the other board members were impressed. Humphrey, the only person to whom Tonita could have looked for a bit of support, had rushed off to be at the birth of his latest grandchild, forgetting to give anyone his proxy vote.

'I don't need to tell you that 40 million Swiss francs will totally cover all our anticipated construction costs and enable us to purchase more rundown sites for development.' Alessandra pushed home her advantage.

Various members murmured their approval: those with minor holdings, reassured that their investment was secure with such financial backing, and those with major shareholdings already mentally calculating the dividends to be reaped from expansion. This Alessandra Rosset really was in another league. They congratulated her on her catch and approved the new investor.

After the meeting she looked smugly at Tonita.

'Your money is multiplying nicely thanks to me. Why do you try and block me?'

'I am not trying to block you, Alessandra, I am just asking the questions any responsible shareholder should ask.'

'Advised by Sebastian of course.'

Tonita looked at her sharply.

'Sebastian has swum in the deep, shark-infested waters of Wall Street, Alessandra. I consider his advice to be of immense value, as should you.'

'And his advice on this was?'

'He didn't say we should refuse the investment. Just do proper due diligence on anything coming out of the Cayman Islands, make sure not only that the money was there, but that it was clean. Unfortunately, I have been outvoted, greed seems to have won the day.'

'Aren't you greedy, Tonita? Don't you like being rich.'

'Of course, but not to the point of losing my principles.'

'Principles don't make money, Tonita.'

'Please just make sure, Alessandra, that in your disregard of principles, you do not also disregard the law. That can be very costly.'

Alessandra looked affronted.

'Tonita, I am offended.'

'I am also offended, Alessandra. I have asked you to do a thorough background check on a new investor and you have manipulated the board to deny me. You are sailing too close to the wind. Watch it. I will not allow you to sail us into murky waters.'

Feeling rather pleased with her metaphor, Tonita flounced out of the meeting room as only Tonita could flounce. Alessandra had to be impressed. She was ruthless but not ungenerous: she could admire Tonita's strength of character and intelligence. From that moment on, she considered Tonita a much more worthy member of the consortium than she had previously.

'Ah, Tonita, glad I caught you.'

'Rory, isn't it?'

Rory had clearly been loitering in the lobby of La Grande Cour with the clear intention of waylaying her. Tonita sighed. She had a late afternoon flight and her taxi would be arriving any minute.

'I'm actually on my way back to the UK, Rory. Is it urgent?'

'No, of course not, we can talk by phone if you want. I wondered if you could give me your number, now that we're fellow board members and equal partners.'

Tonita hesitated: she didn't really want to give her phone number to this pushy man, but at the same time, he had a point: as the representative director of Ruairdí Investments, he did have the right to be able to contact the other main shareholder in the White Snowflake consortium.

Her hesitation did not go unnoticed.

'I could, of course, ask Alessandra for it, but I prefer to deal directly with my co-investors.'

Tonita scribbled down her number on a scrap of paper from the front desk.

'Here,' she said, 'but I don't really have much to do with the day-to-day operations of the consortium, Alessandra is better placed to answer any questions you might have.'

Rory leered at her as he carefully folded the paper and ostentatiously placed it in his top jacket pocket.

'Of course, and very wise too. But I think it's important to develop a more personal relationship with my business partners.'

'Oh.' Tonita didn't really know what to say to this: apart from Humphrey she hardly knew any of the other shareholders and she had no intention of developing her personal relationship with Alessandra or Rory.

'Alessandra and I are concerned that you want to put the brakes on the Colline development.'

'Why should I want to do that?'

'It's where your friend Lucy Wilson lives, isn't it?'

Tonita bit her lip: she didn't want to admit that it hadn't occurred to her that Lucy's chalet was one of the properties affected by the new project. She was surprised that Lucy hadn't mentioned it, but she was more upset at herself for not having been a good enough friend to be aware of Lucy's situation. She brought her thoughts back to her own current predicament – Rory.

'Have I shown any signs of wanting to halt the project?'

'Alessandra mentioned that you were reluctant to accept our Ruairdí Investment ...'

'That was nothing to do with sentimentality,' Tonita sighed, wishing she had given the emotional aspect more consideration. 'I just wanted her to do more thorough due diligence on your company.'

'Nothing personal, I hope?' he winked.

Tonita was getting bored. She looked at Rory directly in the eyes.

'What exactly is your point, Mr Gordon?'

'I just wanted to establish a good working relationship and assure myself of your commitment to our mutual interests.'

He is really beginning to get on my nerves now, Tonita thought to herself, wishing her car would arrive.

'As I said already, I try not to interfere in the day-to-day operations of the consortium.'

Rory seemed not to notice his charm was, for once, not working its magic, and persevered.

'I thought maybe, we could have dinner next time you're in Grondère, get to know each other a little better?'

Tonita looked at him in amazement, was this slimy individual actually flirting with her?

Rory's tone became more velvety and suggestive as he sidled closer.

'Yes, who knows what avenues we might find to explore together …'

Tonita nearly choked with indignation.

'Mr Gordon, I don't know what sort of business relationships you are used to conducting but please let me make myself very clear: if you ever consider using my phone number for anything other than a purely business-related matter you will find yourself very unpleasantly surprised.'

Relieved, she saw her car drive up; the porter, smirking with pleasure at her rebuffal of Rory, marched up and seized her bag as Tonita nodded goodbye to the staff at the front desk and flounced out without another word to Rory. The lady does protest too much, methinks, Rory grinned to himself as he walked back to Alessandra's place, sure that he was on course for another conquest.

What a cheek! Tonita said to herself, as her driver headed down the mountain in the direction of Geneva Airport.

Livid, she called Lucy to have a therapeutic rant.

Sixteen

Nothing in life is to be feared, it is only to be understood.
Now is the time to understand more,
so that we may fear less.

Marie Curie

Lucy and Sally were having a ski day together a few days after Lucy's weekend in Warsaw. They were playfully skiing over the bumps that led down to Grondère's famous 'wall', Bosses Bol, when Rory steamed past them, followed by Suzie and a group from the Diamond Ski Club, easily identifiable by their fur collars and skin-tight designer outfits with shiny buckles. They all stopped at the crest where the path narrowed into a one-ski track.

'You girls joining us? We're off to ski Le Bol du Diable,' Rory asked.

'No thanks,' Lucy replied, 'we're just sticking to itineraries now, it's a bit late in the day to be going down a west-facing slope.'

'You really aren't very daring, are you?' he mocked, as his followers looked on adoringly.

'No,' Lucy replied. 'I can enjoy my skiing more if I feel safe.'

Suzie grinned and mouthed 'too much testosterone' at Lucy from behind Rory's back.

'You could take the Petit Bol with Suzie,' he taunted, 'she's taking the scaredy-cats that way down.'

'I thought, Rory,' Suzie corrected him, 'we had agreed on the term "cautious".'

'Ah yes, so we did,' he said maliciously. 'Well, come along, *adventurous* ones, follow your leader. See you at the bottom, *cautious* ones.'

Sally grinned as he skied off, his golden locks flying behind.

'That guy really is too much, does he ever wear a helmet?'
'No,' Suzie said. 'I have skied with him in blizzards and never seen him in one. He seems to be impervious to the cold.'
'And fear,' added Sally.
'Yes, that too,' Suzie agreed. 'Coming?'
'No thanks, I am straining at the leash to get at that beautiful field of perfectly formed bumps below me.'
Lucy agreed.
'I have been so looking forward to skiing the Bosses Bol, I don't get to do it with my clients.'
Suzie smiled understandingly.
'See you at the bottom then?'
The friends nodded and watched Suzie lead 'the cautious ones' towards the Petit Bol.
'I like her,' Sally said. 'She seems really sound.'
'Yes, I like her too. She just gets on with her own thing and doesn't let anything faze her.'
'Or anybody.'
'Or anybody. Enough interruptions. Shall we hit those bumps?'
Sally launched herself down the mogul field and bumped her way down with gusto. Lucy followed, a little slower but with equal enthusiasm, weaving her way from one gully to the other to make it last as long as possible. They didn't stop until they reached the bottom where Sally looked back up and declared, 'I so want to do that again.'
With short queues and few skiers, they were able to get another two runs in before feeling the need for coffee. They stopped at the canteen at the foot of the valley where Rory, Suzie and company had just sat down for a late lunch. They smiled politely but declined the invitation to join the Diamonds: Lucy could see that Rory's club members that day (mostly female) were not as keen as Rory and Suzie to have additional competition: it also

looked as if lunch would be a little beyond Lucy and Sally's budget.

'I wonder which one he's going to choose tonight?' Sally joked as they retired to an outside table with their coffees and chocolate bars.

'I thought he was with Alessandra Rosset.'

'He is. Amongst others. From what I hear, he's performing quite a juggling act.'

'Really? Where d'you hear that?'

'Anya. The Ski Club apartment is just beside La Grande Cour and Anya says she's lost count of the number of expensively dressed women she's seen entering and leaving it.'

'Well, Anya's not a gossip so that must be true.'

'She says she doesn't know any of them so they must be tourists.'

'Meaning Diamond Club members.'

'Probably.'

'Unbelievable! Most of them are married. Where does he find the energy? He skies all day, every day and he's often at après-ski.'

'You know what Johnny calls him …'

'Fucking legend.'

'Exactly, literally.'

The girls giggled and headed off to a different sector where more glorious bumps awaited them, leaving Rory to hold court and Suzie to try and keep some semblance of order.

That Friday, Alain and Lucy met at Anne's flat for an *apéro* before Anne headed down to Savigny to spend the weekend with Jacques. Alain and Lucy were now spending all their weekends at her flat and she kindly moved out to allow them a little privacy. It was not an ideal

174

arrangement for any of them but they knew it was temporary and they all enjoyed the weekly drink and catch-up.

Lucy described her night at the Mardi Gras ball and Milly and Christophe's 'love-at-first-sight' meeting. She then had Alain and Anne laughing out loud as she described the handsome young ski guide who had all the Diamond Ski Club women fawning over him. She described with humour, his daring skiing antics and his reputation for sexual encounters.

'He sounds like a real, old-fashioned Casanova,' Anne joked.

'Absolutely, he has a wicked charm that seems irresistible to women.'

'I hope, not to you,' Alain said, half-teasingly.

'Already tried and resisted,' Lucy laughed. 'And he clearly finds me far too "proper" and a "scaredy cat". But I'll tell you who has taken a real dislike to him – Tonita!'

'Really? What on earth can she have to do with such a person?'

'Well, he was at her wedding, remember? With Alessandra?'

'Ah yes, I remember.'

'But it's this company he represents, Rooardi … or something like that … Anyway, apparently, it's become a shareholder in White Snowflake, and he's been driving Tonita nuts, starting to flex his muscles and lording it over her.'

'Yes, I can see that that's not a strategy to win Tonita's heart.'

'No,' Lucy giggled. 'When she was over for the last board meeting he actually tried it on with her. She was furious! She called me from the taxi just after she'd left and she was still fuming. Hang on a minute, let me try and remember her exact words, ah yes, she called him "that irritating, jumped-up little sex toy of Alessandra's"!'

'Oh,' Anne said admiringly, 'not a fan then.'

'Definitely not.' Lucy laughed. 'Tonita certainly doesn't mince her words when she dislikes someone.'

Seventeen

No coward soul is mine
No trembler in the world's storm-troubled sphere
                    Emily Brontë, Poem, Last Lines

The chalet had emptied early and Lucy, who had no clients booked, had a day to herself until she met Poppy to watch the rugby in The Pub. She couldn't face the busy slopes but the skies were clear and inviting so she decided to go for a quiet skin through the forest.

As she gently climbed the lane it was so beautiful it took her breath away. There had been a fresh snowfall overnight and, as she entered the deep shade of the forest, the snow was banked steeply on either side of the path. She found she was the first to make tracks along the old *bisse* path. As she clicked along, the path gradually narrowed on either side and all around her were undulating mounds of uneven snow. The snow-laden branches of the towering pines and larch trees drooped heavily towards the ground trying to shed the weight, the lower ones touching the piled-up snow beneath. It was like walking through a long, deep tunnel with thick, impenetrable curtains of deep green, festooned with white. Shafts of sunlight filtered through the canopy creating alternating pockets of light and shade. Lucy was so absorbed in admiring the silent winter wonderland that it took her a while to realise she had company. An inner instinct told her she was being watched and she turned her head upwards to see a large wolf standing on the banked-up snow above her. Lucy took a sharp intake of breath.

What do I do now? she asked herself. She looked around her in a panic and quickly analysed her options. She could not ski away: it would show fear. Her skins would slow her down anyway and the wolf would be too quick for that.

She could not climb a tree, she would need to release her bindings for that and the moment she stepped into the deep snow, she would sink. No, her only option was to stand her ground, show no fear and, if necessary – fight. She clutched her poles and prepared for the encounter. The wolf hesitated and looked at Lucy with curiosity.

Lucy used the stand-off to release her helmet from her backpack and put it on, reasoning that if her head was encased in a big plastic bubble it would reduce the area the wolf could bite and maybe also offer some protection to her throat.

Still the wolf stood still and bided its time.

Lucy wrapped a spare fleece around her neck and then, not knowing what else to do, she took her phone from her pocket. She would not call Alain, he would not be able to helicopter her out of trouble this time, so instead, she did the strangest thing: she started to take photos of the wolf.

At least this way, she thought, they'll be able to identify my aggressor. She was fairly sure it was the same female she had seen with Poppy early in the season. It was a beautiful specimen with a thick coat of grey fur tinged with light brown, cream underparts and bright yellow eyes. It was clearly feeding well.

The wolf seemed puzzled, mildly offended even, then turned and vanished.

Lucy, having lost all appetite to continue her expedition, also turned and returned the way she had come, turning constantly to look behind her. As soon as she reached the main path she ripped off her skins, not bothering to fold and pack them away she held on to them and raced down the mountain with them flying from her hands. She reached the chalet trembling and ran herself a hot bath in which she then sat drinking a hot chocolate and crying with the relief and the shock.

'Must have decided there wasn't enough meat on you,' Poppy joked as Lucy related her encounter in The Pub.

Johnny swiped through the photos on Lucy's phone in disbelief.

'Bloody hell, girl,' he said. 'You're looking death in the gob and you start taking photos of it?'

Humphrey, who only came into The Pub for the rugby, was glad he hadn't missed seeing Lucy's photos.

'In all my time here, I've never seen a wolf. What a stunning specimen.'

'Don't tell everyone, will you.' Lucy suddenly realised the spotlight would be on her again, and she did not want to get caught up in the middle of the wolf debate.

'Of course not, if you don't want us to,' Poppy said. 'But you will show the photos to the authorities, won't you?'

'Yes, good point, I'll just pop out and send them to Jean-Marc, he'll see the sighting is recorded without making a fuss.'

Lucy went outside to call her friendly nature warden.

Lucy reappeared with a big smile, Humphrey handed her a big beer to match it and they settled down to enjoy the match.

'Now the danger is on the pitch, wearing a green jersey,' Humphrey said.

'I know you were frightened out of your wits, Lucy,' 'Poppy said to her at half time, 'but I don't think you were in danger. The animal was probably just curious, I expect you disturbed it.'

'Maybe. I was having to work hard trampling down that load of fresh snow.'

'You know, Man has lived alongside wild animals since the beginning of human existence: men and wolves used to hunt together, that's how the relationship between men and dogs started.'

'I know you're right, Popps, but when you come face to face with an animal that could consider you as prey, that could attack and kill you, that you can't give orders to or reason with, it's not the rational human inside you that surfaces but your animalistic survival instinct.'

'I understand, but don't give in to this visceral fear that you find in so many places. Be vigilant, keep out of its way, yes, and make sure the animal never feels threatened but *DO NOT LET* it spoil the mountains for you, it's folklore!'

'Yes, Poppy,' Lucy said with resignation: it wasn't that easy.

'That animal has as much right to be there as you,' Poppy continued, 'and I think you were very privileged to see it. Thank goodness you had the presence of mind to take some photos.'

'They are pretty special.'

'Yes, I'm quite jealous.' Poppy grinned. 'The first time we saw it, I was not quick enough.'

March was a glorious month for skiing. The weather was warmer, the snow conditions were excellent and the children were back at school which freed up the slopes for those who weren't limited to school holidays. It was a time when groups of young people came on holiday together, some young professionals discovering a new sport for the first time, and many were groups of friends on their annual pilgrimage to the mountains. There were also groups of middle-aged friends and corporate outings. All the après-ski venues were packed to the brim. Grondère was buzzing with people having a good time and the mood was festive. Lucy and Sally took some time to go to après-ski and ski for themselves, determined to enjoy living in a ski resort and not leave all the fun to the visitors. They often took Milly with them and Tommy and Christophe joined them when they could. Lucy realised that, although the group of friends had changed slightly, they were still a close-knit band, just different. Jodie and Eddie would always belong, but she knew she would see less and less of them as they took their different paths.

Émilie's success on the World Cup circuit had continued. Whenever she was racing the whole village was abuzz. The instructors working on the hill would make sure their lessons ended at a time and place where they could get to a TV screen and her result was the first topic of discussion. Lucy couldn't watch all of her races but Eddie made sure everyone was updated with text messages and photos. Eddie, of course, never missed a race. If it was in Europe he was there, if it was Canada or the States he was planted in front of a screen. She had a few near misses with two *médailles de chocolat* and then, at last, in March, the news they had all been waiting for – a first-place finish in the downhill in France. The news spread round the resort like wildfire and lifted the mood of the entire place onto another plain. It reminded Lucy of when the local football team won in her northern town. People walked around with wider smiles and had an extra bounce in their step. Émilie's place in the Swiss ski team was now secure: as long as she could stay injury-free she had a good few years of travelling the globe ahead of her.

There was one week in March in the Grondère calendar that Lucy looked forward to with great anticipation: the week that Ski4All Wales was in town. Lucy had become good friends with the family and volunteers that ran the adaptive ski charity and, when she had been going through tough times the previous March, suspected of murder and suspended from work, she had found great comfort in their company and in doing something for others, rather than sitting home feeling sorry for herself. This March she had cleared her diary so that she could be a volunteer for the entire week.

Lucy and Alain had last seen Bethan, Dave, Jo and Mia the previous September in Wales at their festival fundraiser, *The Big Cwtch*. So much had happened since then, she had much to tell them. The night they arrived she met them at their hotel, helped them unload and generally got in the way as everyone collected their keys and found their rooms. It was a massive undertaking with adaptive skiers and their carers, some visiting Grondère for the first time, taking all the attention, as was correct. Lucy stayed for dinner with them and, once all the skiers were settled, the volunteers all gathered in the hotel bar for a good catch-up.

Great lovers of Grondère, they lapped up all the information Lucy had to give them about the changes in the resort, her own adventures and of course, the latest news. The murder of Rusty ranked a lowly second, as far as the Welsh were concerned, to her encounter with the wolf.

'Wow,' said Mia, 'how cool is that!'

'I don't think it's cool,' Jo replied. 'I'd be terrified if I came face to face with a wolf.'

'Unlikely in the deepest, darkest, bowels of Wales,' Bethan teased, with big wide eyes.

'Thank goodness for that,' Jo said.

'Well, I'd love to see one.'

'Mia, the poor wolf would be terrified if it came face to face with you,' Dave remarked.

'True,' they all nodded earnestly. Mia was tiny but scared of nothing and no one. If anyone could face down a wolf, it was definitely Mia.

'But don't go looking for it, will you Mia, there's a good girl,' Bethan added.

The week continued in glorious sunshine, the adaptive skiers, used to skiing on an artificial slope, enjoyed the sensations of skiing (and falling) on snow. The happy band made everyone in Grondère smile as they moved sitskis and wheelchairs around the resort and loaded them on and off the ski lifts. Lucy was all in wonder as some of the lifties she knew as being normally grumpy went through a personality transformation as soon as they were needed to help and advise. Other skiers too, used to queue-barging, pushing and shoving, happily stood back and waited patiently while the Welsh jumped the queues and the lifties slowed down the chairlifts to enable them to load their sitskis. It brought out the best in people, Lucy observed, to put others before themselves and you could see that skiers were pleased to see their sport being shared and many also fascinated by the technology that facilitated this.

'I think it's time,' Bethan told her, 'that Grondère had its own adaptive skiing charity.'

They were sitting on a chairlift together following Dave, his skier in a sitski and buddy who were on the chair in front.

'I think you are right,' Lucy agreed, 'it would be wonderful to see this being an everyday thing.'

Bethan then explained that she had already spoken to some local people who were interested and they were planning to set up their own charity.

'You'd make a great pilot, Lucy, why not do an adaptive course? Another string to your bow.'

Lucy grinned. Bethan was so good at seeing how to make the best use of the available resources.

'I'll think about it,' she said, knowing that to Bethan, that was as good as a yes, and she was now committed. She was right.

'Great, I'll give them your number.' Bethan smiled.

Lucy realised that Bethan was now mentally ticking it off her 'to-do' list. You had to have a special talent to not only run a charity, but to inspire and motivate others to join you on the journey: Bethan was a natural. But Lucy didn't mind being 'steered' towards adaptive skiing, she had been thinking about it anyway and just needed a little push. Bethan, of course, had already worked that out.

For a week, the small group from the Ski4All Wales Wednesday Ski Club enjoyed all the fun and spills of a normal ski trip.

His case not progressing at all, Alain joined them for an afternoon on the slopes and he and Lucy had a go at piloting the sitskis when they were empty.

'This is amazing,' he said. 'What a piece of equipment!'

Lucy spotted Bethan watching on with interest.

'Watch out, or Bethan'll have you signed up before you know what's hit you.'

'Do you know what?' he smiled, 'I don't mind if she does. Do you think the skiers might object to being driven by a policeman?'

'I think they'd bloody love it!' Bethan answered as she sidled up to him. 'Have you got any fellow officers who we could entice to join you?'

Alain grinned, 'I can think of one or two.'

Dave came over to see if Alain wanted to try loading the sitski onto the skilift and Alain enthusiastically accepted the offer. Lucy watched as they skied off towards the chairlift and Dave showed Alain how to unblock the rig for loading: she felt a big surge of affection.

'Well, I didn't expect that,' she said, almost to herself.

Bethan grinned widely.

Lucy grinned back, 'And don't tell me you did either, because I just won't believe you.'

'No, I didn't, but if there's one thing I've learnt in this charity game, it's that people so often surprise you. I'm so lucky, I get to see the best side of people. And what a result, two new pilots recruited in one week.'

'And so what's the new charity going to be called?'

'Grondère4All, d'you like it?'

'I do, it rings well and it echoes your charity's name too.'

'We're going to do wonders, my lovely. Everyone should have the right to be up here with us, in these beautiful gnarly mountains, don't you think?'

Lucy looked around her. They were standing at the bottom of a sunny bowl composed of gentle red and blue slopes. To their left was the steep, forbidding wall of rock that was the Bec Interdit, behind them the pyramid of Mont Froid and to their right, the park where the acrobats flipped and did tricks to the delight of all. It was a bright sunny day and the panorama opposite presented a line of uninterrupted peaks stretching as far as the eye could see. The visibility was so clear it made the Massif du Cortey, standing proud directly in front, seem close enough to touch. Its folded layers of snow and ice, overflowing and overhanging one another, shone in the sunshine like spring snow. And at the heart of all this, sitting in the sunshine, lapping it all up, a group of happy adaptive skiers from Wales.

'Yes,' she smiled. 'I never tire of the beauty of this place. Everyone should get the chance to be here.'

Eighteen

Storms make trees take deeper roots.
Dolly Parton

'Charles doesn't seem to like your boyfriend very much,' Jemima remarked on the chairlift.

Shortly before Easter, Jilly had returned to Grondère and she and Blonnay had taken up quarters in an apartment with an even better view than the previous one. He continued to work and she skied with the SCGB or with Jemima, if Jemima wasn't skiing with Charles. Jilly had not concealed her true profession from Jemima, Charles's acquaintance with Laurent would have made it impossible to hide.

'Really? Why do you say that?'

'I suggested we meet for a drink and he gave me a hundred reasons why he wouldn't have time, and yet he has plenty.'

'Did you ask him why?'

'Yes.' Jemima laughed. 'He mumbled something about rude Swiss policemen and underhand questioning practices.'

'I'm afraid Laurent would probably take that as a compliment. Still, that's a shame. I would like to meet him.'

'Maybe in the future, if we are still together.'

'Do you think you will be?'

'I hope so. It's not a great passion, you know, for either of us. But he's very attentive and kind and, I have to admit, with my plain face and at my age, I had quite reconciled myself to staying single.'

'Still, you shouldn't compromise on love. There must be some feeling.'

'Do you think so? I'm not so sure. Sometimes passion can blind us to a person's faults. Many arranged marriages work out just as well as love matches.'

Jilly laughed.

'It seems a very business-like approach.'

'I think I can make him happy and be happy with him.'

'Well – looking at the divorce rate – you could have the right strategy. I don't think I've ever heard though, of someone arranging their own marriage.'

'Charlotte Lucas, in *Pride and Prejudice*!'

'You're right, that's so funny. And we sound just like Elizabeth Bennet and Charlotte discussing pragmatic love. So, is Charles your Mr Collins?'

'He certainly can be as pompous. But he also has a heart of gold. I try to see him as more of a Colonel Brandon.'

Jilly laughed in reply as they hopped off the chair at the arrival station.

'Mind,' Jemima added, 'Charles did say one nice thing about your Laurent.'

'What was that?'

'He said he was the only French-speaker he had ever met who could pronounce his surname correctly.'

The Easter holidays arrived and with them hordes of visitors from all around the world. Tonita and Sebastian were back in town for two weeks and looking forward to having some happy time with Ruby and Leo before breaking the news to them about their father.

They had booked Lucy to ski with the children for the entire two weeks but Sebastian had also promised to ski with them on Lucy's days off and Ruby and Leo were eager to show him how good they were.

Poppy had also been recruited to take the siblings to the massive climbing wall in the sports centre for an initiation into the world of climbing. They all met the afternoon the family arrived for a happy reunion and to work out their schedule. Sebastian had much business to see to with the hotel and the vineyard and so, before he set up his meetings, he wanted to know when the children would be free for him to ski with. Tonita's baby bump was now quite large and she declared that she would be mostly drawing and resting during the day. She was designing the artwork for the vineyard's first catalogue.

'Still no word on your father?' Poppy asked when the children had been sent to go and organise their ski kit together for the following morning.

'Not a word,' Tonita replied. 'Fortunately, he never called them much at school, so they haven't noticed his absence. I talked to Anwar and managed to negotiate weekly calls with their mother on the strict condition that she didn't tell them about their father's absence.'

'That's something.'

'Yes, but I don't know how much longer we can keep up the charade. They normally fly home for Easter but fortunately they love their skiing and this place so much, persuading them to come to Grondère was not difficult.'

'So, you have bought time until the summer holidays.'

'Exactly. At that point we'll have to come clean and tell them the truth. I am not looking forward to that.'

'You are convinced he's disappeared for good.'

'Yes. I can't see him digging his way out of this one. He must have planned his disappearance meticulously, maybe he's even had cosmetic surgery.'

'*No!*' Lucy exclaimed. 'Really?'

'No. He was always so vain about his good looks, I can't see him parting with them.'

The three women laughed.

'To be honest,' Tonita added, 'if it was just up to me, I'd be happy never to see him again. I hope he never resurfaces.'

There was a buzz in the resort on those first days of the holidays. Early each morning a regular stream of ski instructors in their red jackets headed enthusiastically towards the main lift station to prepare for a busy day on the slopes whilst Lucy went to the hotel to join Ruby, Leo and Tonita for breakfast and then take the children skiing. After a day on the slopes she took them back, joined them for afternoon tea and a swim in the hotel pool.

'You're getting to be a regular feature!' Anya, the hotel manager commented one evening.

'I'm making the most of ski instructor perks!' Lucy admitted.

'Quite right too!'

'Actually, I was wondering if I could come and see you sometime. I have a business idea I'd like to put to you: to do with my summer walks.'

'Sure. Let me get the Easter rush over and then I'll have more time.'

Towards the end of the Easter holidays the mood in the resort gradually changed: tiredness was setting in. After nearly two weeks of non-stop teaching and catering for visitors, all the resort workers knew there were just a few days of intensive work remaining before they could start to relax and enjoy the wind-down to the end of the season. As Johnny and Louie headed out for their early morning walk, the area around the main lift station was littered with ski teachers chatting, drinking steaming cups of coffee, darting in and out of the breakfast bars and kitting out for the day ahead. Johnny exchanged a few words of encouragement with the instructors he knew and then, to avoid the Easter holidaymakers who would be soon heading uphill for the slopes and the parents who would be dropping off their children at ski school, the pair walked downhill towards the outskirts of the village. Johnny nodded at the doorman of La Grande Cour as they went past. It was a clear, fresh morning: steam rose from their hot breath. Johnny savoured the moment, drinking in the scenery and taking deep breaths of the cold air. He relished this quiet moment of the day: just him and Louie, before going into his office, leaving Louie at home for his morning nap.

The melted snow from the previous warm day had frozen and Johnny trod carefully: he was getting too old for spills now. They reached the building site of the White Snowflake complex, ghost-like in its winter standstill, with frozen scaffolding and snow-shrouded building materials. Johnny started to turn back when Louie disappeared in amongst the snowy mounds of piled-up earth and rubble.

'Come on Louie, you know the routine. Your long walk is at lunchtime; you'll make me late for work.'

But Louie's highly powerful sensory nose had detected something delightfully smelly, and he was not willing to abandon it to another dog. Louie was excited, this pungent scent was attacking his senses like nothing he had ever known, he was really onto something and so he ignored Johnny's increasingly urgent calls in order to concentrate on locating and digging it up before Johnny got there and spoilt his fun.

Johnny arrived just as Louie had uncovered a rotting human hand. Louie looked up at Johnny with the smuggest expression a dog could make.

'Fuck,' said Johnny. 'Now I really am going to be late for work.'

He actually had his mobile phone with him for once, it was a new smartphone and the only function he hadn't quite got the hang of was the phone. Eventually he found the right buttons to push and called the police emergency number 117.

'Leave that,' he ordered Louie, who was continuing to scuffle around the burial site while they waited for the police to arrive. 'You've had your fun and proved what a fucking superstar you are again, but let's not spoil the police's fun by buggering up their murder scene.'

There was no doubt in Johnny's mind that he was looking at a murder scene. While he had been on the phone, Louie had scraped away at the corpse and the blood that had seeped out and discoloured the snow around it before freezing solid, clearly came from a hole in the man's chest.

Capitaine Dupertuis received the call as he was preparing to head down to Savigny. He kissed Lucy goodbye and quickly arrived on the scene, closely followed by Inspectrice Sylvie Jacquier.

'Thanks Johnny, I'll let you get off to work. I'll send someone to get your statement later.'

Louie looked at Alain and barked.

'Thank you, Louie,' Alain said.

But Alain's gratitude did not seem to be what Louie was waiting for: he barked again and pointed his nose down another hole he had been making a couple of yards from the corpse. Alain understood, went over to look down the hole and saw enough of the dark object lying there to know it was a gun.

'Well Louie, your powers of detection are becoming invaluable. I may have to recruit you soon.'

Louie turned and trotted off with Johnny quite happily, now he knew that he could leave his discoveries with someone who appreciated their importance.

While Alain and Sylvie waited for the pathologist, the spring morning sun began to warm, melting the thin covering of ice from the dead man's face. The two police officers stood and stared, in astonished recognition.

'Call Blonnay and tell him his holiday just got cancelled, Jilly too,' Alain said. 'We're going to be needing some British help. And make sure the British press do not get hold of this!'

'Where are you off to?' she asked as he turned towards the village.

'I'm going to La Grande Cour to talk to Tonita, I don't want her or the children to hear from anyone else that their father's body is lying rotting on the White Snowflake building site.'

'How long has he been lying there?' asked the procureur, highly irritated at having spent his day with the police press office making sure the press did not get hold of Tony Onion's name.

'The lab people haven't confirmed it yet, but they reckon maybe a month or even more.'

'I have been going back through the weather reports,' Blonnay looked up from his computer. 'The body was under a good 60cm layer of snow and the last time we had that much snow was at the beginning of the half-term holidays. Remember, we had a good metre over a few days?'

'I remember,' Alain said. 'It was just after Sebastian and Tonita arrived, we had dinner with them the night it started, the kids were so excited that they could ski in some powder with Lucy.'

'Well, that's a pretty good alibi,' grimaced Sylvie. 'Lady Shilton will be needing one.'

Blonnay looked over her shoulder and whistled.

'That's not good.'

'What is it?' Alain asked, joining them. They all stared at the screen in disbelief.

'She will have to be interviewed.'

'Well I'm not doing it,' protested Blonnay.

'Nor me, I don't believe she's involved for a second.'

'We were all at her wedding and I'm her alibi,' Alain grimaced.

'That leaves you, M. le Procureur.'

Nineteen

Sorrow has its rewards.
It never leaves us where it found us.
                                        Mary Baker Eddy

'Thank you for coming, Lady Shilton,' the procureur began, indicating that Tonita should take a seat.

'Am I a suspect for my father's murder?'

'There are questions that must be asked, Lady Shilton. Since the discovery of your father's body yesterday, new information has come to light.'

'Where are Alain, Laurent and Sylvie?'

'All three of my investigating officers were at your wedding and all three have refused to interview you because they know you personally. One of them may even be your alibi: it would appear Capitaine Dupertuis had dinner with you on the evening we believe the crime was committed.'

'That's comforting and worrying at the same time,' she replied, thinking her position must be more serious than she realised. Her reaction on learning of her father's death had surprised her: she had been truly upset and was now feeling deeply sad.

'Shall we begin?'

'Yes, let's get it over with.'

'You have a gun, Lady Shilton.'

'No.'

'That wasn't a question: it was a statement. You have a gun licensed in your name. A Sig Sauer pistol.'

'I *had* a small handgun but I got rid of it a year ago. It is only now you mention it that I realise I forgot to cancel the registration.'

'How did you "get rid of it"?'

'I gave it back to the person who gave it to me – my father. Oh …' Tonita paused as it dawned upon her why the question had been asked. 'He was shot? With my gun?'

'Yes.'

'That's why I'm here.'

'Yes.'

Tonita was quiet for a few moments as she digested the fact that she was now a suspect in her own father's murder. 'But you told me yourself: I have an alibi.'

'Yes, and a most excellent one, but alibis can be broken and errors can be made on the timing of a crime, especially when the body has lain undiscovered for some time.'

'Ugh,' Tonita shivered at the idea of her father lying under that pile of rubble and snow for over a month, with people passing to and fro, just metres away.

'Can you explain how you came by the gun and how you returned it to your father? It seems a strange gift for a father to give to his daughter.'

'It's a *horrible* gift to give anyone!' Tonita exclaimed. 'My father and I have been at odds for many years. He arranged for me to receive the gun and shooting lessons for my birthday a good few years ago. I had started travelling regularly to the States and his message was, that as I wouldn't see him, he could at least send me some protection. I was pretty offended but I took the lessons (I had already done some rifle shooting at school; I actually was a pretty good shot), but I found owning a gun more of an annoyance than anything else, always having to declare it, make sure I stored it securely. I hated carrying the thing and eventually, when I finally agreed to meet him in Bern last year, we argued and I gave it back, telling him in the process that it had poisoned my existence like he had poisoned my life. I was so glad to be rid of the thing.'

The procureur looked at her, appalled.

Tonita stared back at him unrepentantly.

'But you failed to register the transfer of ownership …'

'Yes. Not clever of me, but my fiancé was murdered shortly afterwards and d'you know what? I clean forgot about it.'

'You don't seem to understand, Lady Shilton, this is most serious.'

'Oh, I understand all right, M. le Procureur, but I didn't kill my father. Firstly, it's not my style and secondly, as much as I hated my father, I do love my half-brother and sister and would never have deprived Ruby and Leo of their father.'

'Unless you wanted to take his place: I understand you are their guardian.'

'I do not need to go about stealing children, you may not have noticed, but I am making one of my own!'

The procureur had noticed and bit his lip for having made such a tactless remark.

'Your father was wanted by another state in connection with embezzlement of government money.'

'Downright theft, more like.'

'Yes. Have you any more information on that?'

'No. I said I would inform the Swiss police if I heard anything from my father and I would have done so. And if the disgruntled Arabs had disposed of him, they wouldn't have used my gun: I'm sure they have more up-market killing equipment and anyway, they wouldn't even have known about it.'

'Who else did know of the existence of the gun?'

'That is a very good question. Malcolm, of course, but he's dead. I may have mentioned it to a few other people.'

'Your husband?'

'No, I don't think I've ever mentioned it to Sebastian. His mother knew, of course.'

'Mme Sturridge?'

'Yes. I was so mad when I returned from seeing my father in Bern. I walked straight into the hotel bar for a stiff gin and had a bit of a rant to Malcolm. I think she was present. But she has no reason to hate my father.'

'You?'

'Yes, she probably hates me. We always made out we got along but she was a thorn in my side and I probably was for her.'

'And you married her son who has, I believe, disowned her.'

'And I married her son who has disowned her.'

Tonita frowned. She hadn't given Carla another thought since the trial, she had just wanted to forget and move on, but she could see how Carla might resent her having become Lady Shilton.

'But she's in prison so she can't have done it, and anyway, how would she have got hold of the gun? No, it doesn't make sense.'

'Are you putting yourself forward as a more likely murderer?'

Tonita smiled grimly. 'From your perspective I can see that I am a more likely candidate, I have motive, opportunity and a weapon. But it's not me. Don't you have anything better to go on?'

'We are exploring several leads but you will understand why we cannot dismiss your potential involvement, however much we would like to.'

'I do. And I know your team, they will sort it all out.'

'I sincerely hope so.'

With this he asked her to keep Alain and his team informed of her movements, wished her a good day and left. He didn't think she had anything to do with her father's death, if for no other reason than she was not stupid enough to leave her gun at a murder scene. But he needed more than supposition.

Sebastian was waiting for Tonita outside the police headquarters in Savigny and they drove home in silence. Lucy had stayed with the children after skiing, playing in the pool and telling them stories to try and help take their minds off the death of their father.

'I've just sent them up for showers,' she told Tonita when she came in. 'They were fine while we were on the mountain, but they're fretting about their mother, they don't understand why they can't see her.'

'I don't think she'll be allowed to leave Dubai until the government has got its money back,' sighed Sebastian. 'I wonder where he stashed it! Let's hope Anwar's people can track it down and we can get this swept under the carpet before the press find out: they've only just calmed down after the murder of the previous Lord Shilton.'

'What I don't understand,' Tonita said, 'is why, when I had no love left for my father, none at all, I feel so sad.'

'Regret?' Lucy offered. 'Things left unsaid?'

'Maybe. Though what I could have resolved or said to such a lousy father I do not know. Maybe just regret that I couldn't love him.'

'You certainly didn't get lucky when they were handing out fathers,' Lucy said, whose own father could not have been more different to Tonita's.

'No,' agreed Sebastian, thinking of his own father who he still missed every day, but then he remembered his mother whose evil knew no bounds. 'And however reassuring it may be to know that I am not the only member of the family with a criminal parent, I hope Alain and his crew get to the bottom of it quickly.'

'There's one thing I forgot to mention to the procureur, Lucy.' Tonita added. 'Alessandra Rosset knew that my father had vanished when no one else had that information and before the body was found.'

'That's odd.'

'I thought so at the time. Will you mention it to Alain?'

'I will.'

Anya came over and looked at the gloomy trio.

'You three look like you would benefit from the restorative qualities of champagne. I think you can allow yourself half a glass, Tonita,' she winked and opened a bottle before they had a chance to reply.

That Friday evening, when Lucy and Alain met at Anne's for what had become their weekly *apéro*, the talk was inevitably the discovery of the body and another murder in Grondère. Anne had clearly heard that a body had been found and knew that Alain was working on the case but she had not heard much more.

'Hang on a moment,' Anne exclaimed as Alain and Lucy revealed the identity of the body and the fact it had been lying there for so long. 'The White Snowflake building site you say? Don't say anything, give me a moment.'

She went to the window and scrunched up her face, trying to recall the facts.

'I may have seen something. On the night you had dinner at La Grande Cour, I saw lights, torchlights, moving around over there.'

Alain got up and stood beside her. She pointed in the direction of the site. Through the various chalets and buildings there was a clear view, directly to the spot where Tony Onion's body had been found.

He asked his mother a few more questions but it was clear that once again, her window-watching had provided his investigation with crucial information. They now had supporting evidence of the exact date of and a probable time for Tony Onion's murder: the trouble was, it now meant that Tonita did not have such a strong alibi. Now, only her husband could vouch for her.

Over the weekend Alain spent a lot of time on the phone talking to his team. They started focusing on any camera footage available for the time and area concerned and going door to door to see if anyone living in that area could back up Anne's sighting. A few light sleepers in that neighbourhood confirmed having seen the torches and one householder even claimed to have heard a loud noise that he had dismissed as a bit of falling scaffolding at the time but that could, in hindsight, have been a gunshot. Alain felt that they were beginning to get somewhere.

On Saturday, the day they were due to leave, Tonita called Lucy to tell her that she didn't want to leave Grondère while under suspicion, even if the police hadn't asked her to stay, and so, she had decided to stay in town for a few weeks and see how things developed. She had hastily enrolled the children in the local international school.

'I can't send them back to boarding school with this hanging over them. Also, it'll hopefully prevent them letting anything slip to any schoolfriends with big ears and nosey parents.'

Lucy and Poppy both agreed this was a sensible plan.

On Sunday morning Poppy had taken Ruby and Leo to the climbing wall to try and take their minds off being sad. It was Lucy's day off and she had been hoping to ski with Alain but, as he was too busy, Lucy called Suzie and joined up with her to ski the south-facing sector above the forest. It was a quieter sector due to the rickety old gondola that serviced it and, when it was snowing, a good bad weather option. Conditions were still excellent with good snow cover for that late in the season: they had already done a few runs and were just scoping their next line when they ran into Rory.

'Hello,' said Suzie. 'Didn't know you were still around?'

'Staying with Alessandra,' he winked slyly. 'I've finished with the Diamonds for this year. Skiing for myself from now on.'

He looked at Lucy challengingly.

'I thought I'd just dip into the forest over there, do a bit of weaving in and out between the trees. Fancy joining me?'

'That area is out of bounds to protect the animals,' she commented.

'You really are Miss Goody Two-Shoes, aren't you?' he replied scornfully. 'I hope you're not a telltale too.'

She shook her head sorrowfully as Rory skied off and she and Suzie watched as he slid off the track and launched himself into the dark cover of the forest.

'He's right, of course,' Lucy said. 'I sounded like a school prefect.'

'Maybe,' Suzie said. 'But not very nice for the animals: there aren't many areas where they can rest undisturbed and the breeding season has begun. It's interesting that he's staying with that property tycoon. I wonder if that's who he was staying with in December, I didn't think he met her until January.'

'He didn't, but what did you say? He was here in December?'

'Yes, most of the month, I think. He said he was between contracts. I was too busy moving in and finding work to ski with him.'

'Do you know who he did ski with?'

'No idea. Local members I expect.'

'Was Rusty a member of the Diamonds?'

'He was a local member, like Charles. Lucy, you don't think Rory had anything to do with that? I know he's a rogue but he's not a killer.'

'I'm sure you're right.'

But Lucy did wonder.

They carried on their way, finding some safe corridors where the snow, even several days after the last snowfall, was untouched, if a little heavy. It was a different technique as they couldn't force their turns but had to take wide turns using the natural contours of the hill.

'We would have had an easier time of it in the forest,' sighed Lucy as they sat in the chairlift. 'I hope you don't regret coming with me instead of Rory.'

'Stop beating yourself up over that,' Suzie said. 'I don't agree with ripping through nature reserves either.'

'I'm glad.'

'Look over there,' Suzie pointed at the lifting snow clouds: the sun's rays pierced through, forming an even arc of light shafts falling on the distant massifs. 'How beautiful is that?'

They sat back, admiring the view, oblivious to the fact that they would not have had an easier time of it in the forest.

Rory stared at the wolf; the wolf stared at Rory.

The wolf bared its teeth, Rory started sweating. He had skied over the wolf's tail and woken it from its slumbers. In a flash it had jumped up and blocked his trajectory. The creature was in considerable pain and understandably angry.

Panicked, Rory looked around him; he thought he could pick out a different line through the trees, change direction and make a dash for it. As the wolf crouched, poised to pounce, Rory launched downhill and skied as he had never skied before – for his life.

Twenty

Words are nets through which all truth escapes.
Paula Fox, News from the World

'You know that Rory bloke?'

'The Ski Club Don Juan?'

'The very man.'

'What about him?'

'Well, I don't know if it's relevant?'

Lucy hesitated, the word 'telltale' still ringing in her ears.

'Go on.' Alain was interested, Lucy's instincts were often accurate, and she was clearly bothered about something.

He poured her a glass of red wine to help her deliberations. Lucy sipped unconsciously until the rich tones worked their magic and the questions she had been asking herself all day took shape. Was she allowing her own reservations about Rory influence her? She decided to let Alain decide.

'I could be completely off-piste but Suzie told me today that he was here in December. I know that Rusty was a member of the Diamond Ski Club and if there's one skier around who's capable of skinning up Mont Froid in a blizzard, it's Rory.'

'That is interesting. Could he also have slid down again covering his tracks?'

'Oh easily, he's got great technique and the man knows no fear.'

'Do you know anything else about him.'

'Not really, even Suzie doesn't know what he does. He just says "consultant" when he's asked.'

'If ever a word covered a multitude of sins, it is the word "consultant",' Alain said. 'It's right up there with "export/import".'

'But the other thing is … I'm sure I remember him saying to Tonita he spent a lot of time in The Netherlands, and that's the hub of the diamond trade, isn't it?'

'Indeed.'

'I don't want to get him into trouble or anything, I could be totally mistaken.'

'But you have a feeling?'

'Yes.'

'I'll have Blonnay and Jilly check him out. Don't worry, if he checks out okay he'll never know.'

'Thanks.'

'Now, stop worrying about it.' He kissed her. 'What else is bothering you?'

'He called me "Goody Two-Shoes",' she pouted.

'He did? And you're worried he's right?'

Lucy nodded.

Alain went to his mother's kitchen wall and removed a framed poster of Lucy emerging half-naked from a mountain lake – the same image that had been used by the Swiss tourism agency for their recent marketing campaign. He held it up and shook his head.

'Is this the image of a saint?'

She grinned as she shook hers.

'Nope.'

'Let me just call Blonnay and ask him and Jilly to look into Rory Gordon first thing and then you can prove how *good* you are,' he grinned.

_____

The following morning Jilly and Laurent were in police headquarters early to follow up on Lucy's hunch. Jilly laughed as she pulled out her computer to log in to her secure link with Scotland Yard.

'He sounds like a charming rogue, doesn't he? A bit of a modern-day Raffles.'

Blonnay smiled, 'I like the word rogue, it verges on the criminal, without being violent.'

Jilly, whose love of vocabulary almost equalled that of her Swiss boyfriend added, 'It does, in Jane Austen's day he would have been called a rapscallion or a rake; I wonder which category he falls into.'

'Tell me the difference.'

'A rapscallion or rascal is someone naughty, mischievous, without regard for the consequences of his actions but without malice. A rake is much more sinister, will let nothing and no one stand in the way of his pleasures, seems to enjoy causing pain and destruction and it usually leads to the total ruin of himself and those around him. We're talking Dorian Gray or … look at this.'

She had called up Hogarth's series of prints *The Rake's Progress* illustrating the fall to ruin of a dissolute young man which had two hundred years later inspired an opera of the same name.

'Oh, that's *La carrière du libertin*!' Blonnay made the connection with the French name.

'You could use libertine in English too or cad, bounder, scoundrel although they're all a bit dated, like rake and rapscallion. You're more likely to hear rogue nowadays.'

'I was beginning to think they all started with "r".'

'Like Rory?'

'Yes. What sort of name is Rory then?'

'I think it's Scottish, let's do a search.'

Jilly did a search on the name.

'How weird is that,' she exclaimed. 'Listen to this. Rory, a name of Irish origin, meaning Red King of which the Scottish Gaelic version is Ruairidh from the word "ruadh" meaning red-haired or … rusty. And look, written beside it is Russell, Rusty's surname which has a similar meaning but with Norman roots.'

'What are you two so engrossed in?' Alain asked as he hung up his jacket and switched on his computer.

'Just a quirky coincidence but we discovered Rusty and Rory's names mean the same thing.' Blonnay looked a little shamefaced at having been found investigating the the source of a name rather than its bearer.

Alain casually looked over Jilly's shoulder at the computer screen. Then he looked more carefully.

'That is very interesting.'

'Really?' Blonnay was not used to Alain taking an interest into his frolics into vocabulary.

'I think you're onto something. That word is ringing an almighty bell,' Alain said, pointing at the Gaelic version of the name – *Ruairidh.*

Alain picked up his phone and called Lucy.

'Why does the word Ruairidh sound familiar?' He spelled it out as none of them were quite sure how to pronounce it.

'It sounds a bit like the name of that company Tonita was complaining about. I thought it was a strange name at the time.'

'That's it! The company that Alessandra Rosset's lover-boy Rory represents!'

'Yes, I think so. But I couldn't swear to it.'

'Can you check with Tonita – get me the exact name, urgently?'

Minutes later Lucy called back.

'Ruaidrí Investments Cayman LLC is the exact name of the company.'

Alain made her spell it out, wrote it down and handed it to Blonnay who could not help but note that Ruaidrí was the Old Irish version. Rory, Rusty, Ruaidrí – all different versions of the same name.

'But Alain,' Lucy continued, 'Tonita's very worried as to why you're asking. She says she was against taking money from this company but the other shareholders outvoted her.'

'Just tell her we can't say anything yet and to keep it quiet. But it could just put her in the clear – of the murder anyway.'

He ended his call with Lucy. Jilly and Blonnay were already hitting their computer keys in a frenzy. Sylvie arrived for work and Alain updated her on their latest line of enquiry.

'Can you go through the ski pass information for the day of Rusty's death again?' Alain asked her. Sylvie ploughed through the information from TéléGrondère but could find nothing to show Rory had skied that day.

'I'll go through the photos again,' she said. 'We couldn't find any photos of Rusty but maybe the cameras caught this other guy. Trouble is, with everyone wearing helmets these days, it's hard to even identify gender. Any clues as to what he looks like?'

'Lucy says he has long blond locks and never wears anything on his head.'

'Well, that should help.'

While Sylvie was still trudging through the grainy photos from the lift operator, it wasn't long before Jilly's search through her British connections threw up a partial company registration for Ruaidrí Investments in the Cayman Islands. The full list of names of the executive board was not available but one of the founding directors was named as Jordan Russell and the other as Rory Gordon.

'Breakthrough!' commented Alain. 'Great work team!'

Blonnay happily allowed Alain to congratulate them for their cleverness, even though it had been an accidental find rather than careful investigative research – sometimes, after all, police work required an element of luck.

'Mind, if Rory is behind that company, it's pretty brazen to invest in a project part-owned by your victim's daughter,' Sylvie commented. 'I have found a photo that could be him. I'll just send it to Lucy.'

A few minutes later, Lucy confirmed that the man in the picture was Rory.

'Jackpot,' Alain said cheerfully. 'Now we have him on the slopes on the day concerned and a direct connection to the victim. Find out for me,' Alain told his team, 'just exactly who this opaque Rory Gordon is. Jilly, we are going to need you to work your contacts.'

Jilly turned into a very serious DI Ferguson and started taking a closer look at Rory's financial dealings. She contacted her colleagues in Scotland Yard to do a thorough background check. As the afternoon turned into early evening they had a pretty good picture of Rory's true occupation and were able to send out some further queries to contacts in The Netherlands and beyond, before turning their thoughts to dinner. Blonnay and Jilly headed back up to Grondère and decided that, to make up for Jilly's lost holiday and ski time, they would treat themselves to a meal at a traditional restaurant.

'It has been a very fruitful day,' Blonnay said contentedly as he watched Jilly plunge her fork into her fondue like a native.

'Yes, it's amazing that Rory Gordon has slipped under the radar for so many years. He's been constantly travelling the ski resorts of the world with no visible signs of revenue but a very healthy bank account. His tax declarations must be complete fiction.'

'If he even makes any. We still have no link to Tony Onion,' he sighed.

'Perhaps not, but we do know that Rory spoke to Tony at Sebastian and Tonita's wedding. Maybe they already knew each other.'

'Yes, and we can at least connect Rory and Rusty. To think it all started with our investigation into the word "rogue" which goes to prove what a profitable study language is and …' Blonnay patted the bulging notebook in his jacket pocket, 'I have so many new words I could yodel for joy.'

Jilly shot him a warning look.

'But I won't,' he reassured her.

The following morning, their overnight searches had thrown up some very interesting travel patterns, indicating some form of smuggling.

'In light of what we know – probably diamonds,' Blonnay surmised.

'Yes, have you noticed how Rory and Rusty always travel with their ski kit, even when toing and froing between the same ski resort? I bet they stashed the diamonds in skis or boots. I'd love to have a look at Rory's gear to work out how he's been escaping detection,' Sylvie said.

'But there's more.' Jilly wrinkled up her nose, trying to work out Rory's dealings. 'He receives regular payments from another account in the Caymans but I can't identify that one.'

'So you think he's working for someone else?' Sylvie asked.

'Yes, Rusty too.'

'I think,' Alain decided, 'that we have enough to pull in Rory Gordon for questioning, at least relating to the death of Jordan "Rusty" Russell.'

Two days later, however, Rory was proving difficult to find. He was not at Alessandra Rosset's apartment: the police had put it under surveillance as they were unsure about the extent of Alessandra's involvement but, although she came and went, a check by a cooperative member of the hotel staff in her absence confirmed he was not hiding there. The murder investigation team sat discussing what to do next over their morning coffees.

'I wonder where on earth he's got to!' Alain exclaimed.

'He could be anywhere by now,' Sylvie replied.

'You'd think Interpol would have had some sighting if he's left Switzerland, an airport, port, train, something.'

'Borders are so porous these days, we'd probably only hear if he changed continent. He may even have other passports. But surely the recognition cameras would have picked him up, he's a pretty striking bloke.'

'Maybe we should tap Alessandra's phone.'

Blonnay took an internal call and Alain sighed, trying to work out their next course of action: Rory's elusive movements were a real setback. They really needed to get their hands on him. If, as they suspected, Rory was Rusty's murderer, he was probably also Tony Onion's.

Blonnay put down his phone with a huge grin.

'What?'

'That was the missing persons department. Rory Gordon is awaiting collection in Sion hospital.'

'Nooo! I didn't expect that!'

'No ID card on him, of course. Took a while to connect him to our search as he was in a pretty bad way when they brought him in and the hospital had a struggle to work out even what nationality he was. It was only when they initiated a police search procedure that the missing persons department made the connection. I've got a number for someone at the hospital.'

Seconds later, Blonnay, still beaming, confirmed they had definitely found their man.

'The doctor says although they've set his broken bones, they can't do anything with his head: apparently he's not making much sense.'

Minutes later, Blonnay and Jilly were racing down the Rhône Valley with the blue lights flashing, leaving Alain and Sylvie in the office to call off the Interpol search.

'It's all beginning to unravel, Sylvie,' Alain commented as he paced the floor, in between calls.

An hour later, Blonnay called to update them.

'He's a gibbering wreck! You're not going to believe this: he claims he was chased over a cliff by a ferocious wolf and fell down a ravine. According to the rescue services, a dog walker spotted him from afar and called mountain rescue but he seems literally to have been frightened out of his wits.'

'Have you managed to get anything useful out of him?'

'Yes. It's hard going, but, in between him telling her how attractive she is and propositioning her, Jilly's been getting the essential facts out of him and piecing it together like a jigsaw. From what we can gather, Rusty's death was actually an accident.'

'An accident! So why didn't he just come forward?'

'He didn't want us asking him questions and looking into his affairs. As far as we can work it out, he and Rusty were doing to Tony Onion, what Onion was doing to his employer. Of the $50 million Onion "borrowed" for his side deal, Rusty and Rory somehow managed to filter off $10 million's worth to do their own sideline in illegal diamonds. Having brought the diamonds across from Africa in his ski equipment, Rusty had them in his safe. Rory would then deliver the diamonds, hidden in his ski equipment, to their end destination – probably The

Netherlands. The chain broke the day they skinned up Mont Froid to ski Le Monstre: Rory was irritated that Rusty was so slow, so he suggested they take a shortcut but, in the fog, they totally misjudged it, the ridge was too steep, Rusty's skins lost hold and he fell. Rory realised he was in trouble and needed to get the diamonds out of Rusty's safe but he didn't know where it was or how to get into it, so he covered up their tracks to try and win time.'

'But, thanks to Tommy, we got there first.'

'Well, so far that all sounds plausible, even if Rory doesn't.'

'But listen to this, he says he did not kill Tony Onion!'

'What?'

'He just goes silly at that point and says Tony was angry and wanted his money back. Then he starts chanting "I know, I know. Not telling, not telling," – like a five-year-old. I tell you, the guy's totally barmy. Jilly is still trying to question him but the doctor wants to put him into a psychiatric unit.'

'Oh no, if they do that we won't be able to question him.'

'I know, so what do you think?'

'Give Jilly another half an hour to see if she can get any more out of him and then get back here and let's put our heads together. I'll get the procureur in.'

Later, all five of them sat around a table and drew together everything they knew.

'It doesn't make sense,' Alain said. 'Tony Onion would have been able to find $10 million from somewhere to make up the shortfall. He'd just done his own side deal, he must have been rolling in it.'

'I agree,' said the procureur. 'Let's just work slowly through the scenario. With his dodgy contacts Onion could even have borrowed that much. It would have needed a bigger amount to force him into hiding.'

'Like the entire $50 million he'd sidelined?'

'Like the entire $50 million,' agreed the procureur. 'Now that does sound like a more likely scenario.'

'So, the rest of the money was sitting in a money laundering account and whoever was in control of that account decided to keep the lot? We'll have a problem getting that information through the proper channels,' Alain assessed.

'And lose time, so we have to find another way to find that missing link,' Blonnay agreed.

Jilly, having a hard time following as the team had slipped back into speaking French, asked where they had got to in their deliberations.

'There might be another way, I think I have an idea,' she said. 'You said the Dubai government had been doing their own research in the Caymans, do you think they would share their findings? They're not normally very open but this is in their interest.'

Alain called Sebastian and asked him for Prince Anwar's number. Within a very short time, an anonymous fax appeared with some names and addresses.

'He wasn't hopeful,' Alain told them, 'I got the impression that his lot came up against a system almost as opaque as their own.'

'I can work with this,' Jilly laughed. 'I think I can see a weak link in the chain.'

She returned to her computer and then her phone. Blonnay explained to the procureur that Jilly's speciality was money laundering. She had just spent months unravelling a very complex case.

Half an hour later there was a loud 'Eureka!' from the Englishwoman.

'Tony Onion's mistress is a local girl. Prince Anwar's lot had her name and the address of the villa but not much else. She has recently had to relocate due to a fall in income.'

'How did you find that out?'

'As you say, you have to look for another way, the banks won't talk but real estate agents are a chatty bunch. I built up some good relationships with them during my last case. The luxury rental villa recently vacated by Tony Onion's girlfriend is now fetching a fraction of the price Tony Onion was paying. He was paying well over the market rate.'

'And to whom was he paying all these high amounts?'

'A company called Adamantem Clava Investments Cayman LLC!'

'No! Really?' Blonnay was impressed.

'Yup.'

'That can't be a coincidence.'

'Nope? In fact it looks like someone's poor attempt at a joke that may just have backfired on them.'

The others were lost: Blonnay shook his head sadly at his illiterate colleagues.

'Never underestimate the value of a classical education. *Adamantem Clava* is Latin for Diamond Club,' Blonnay told them, as if nothing could be more obvious.

The penny dropped.

'So, the connection has to be this Grondère Diamond Ski Club, there's a lot of money floating around in there and Rory and Rusty were both allowed in, despite not being part of that set. Presumably because they were useful errand boys,' Sylvie said.

'That's a big assumption,' the procureur said. 'We have to be careful casting aspersions like that on our foreign guests, and from what I can see there's no connection between the Grondère Diamond Ski Club and Tony Onion, other than an overseas rental.'

'So, who is the link? Who knew everyone? Lady Shilton?'

'Tonita didn't know Rusty. I think she only met Rory at her wedding when he accompanied Alessandra Rosset?'

'Mme Rosset?'

'We don't know if she knew Rusty, and her acquaintance with Rory seems recent. We know she's desperate to get hold of La Grande Cour and Lady Shilton's shares in the White Snowflake project. Lucy tells me there is no love lost between Mme Rosset and Tonita. But I don't think she has any connection with Tony Onion, although she let on to Tonita that she knew he'd disappeared before we had even found his body and when we did, she knew whose body we had found. She knows something.'

'We'll have to question her but I can't see her laundering money and smuggling diamonds. It doesn't fit her profile.'

'Lucy, of course,' admitted Alain, 'knew all the parties.'

'You're not suggesting your own girlfriend is involved in diamond smuggling and money laundering?'

'No,' laughed Alain, 'but she may hold the key.'

He called Lucy who was just setting off for a ski with Sally and Tommy and put his phone on speaker.

'Humphrey Watson knows everyone you have mentioned and he's a member of the Diamond Ski Club,' Lucy said. 'But then Humphrey knows everyone. Now I think about it, Poppy knew them all too, but neither of them could have had more than a fleeting acquaintance with Tonita's dad. I think you need to talk to Suzie,' Lucy said. 'She knows everyone in that club. She never talks about them but if anyone can give you the inside track on that lot, it's her.'

'Okay, can you find her?'

'Suzie will already be on the mountain and she never picks up her phone when she's skiing.'

'Call her anyway and keep calling her until she picks up, we need to talk to her now. You are *not* to let her know why, for all we know she could be or be with the murderer. Just find out where she is and let us know.'

'Christ!'

'Yes, whatever you do – don't be alone with her, especially not on the mountain.'

Lucy didn't reply; this was ridiculous, she knew that Suzie was no murderer, but then the thought that she could be skiing with one sent a shiver up her spine. Especially when she remembered who Suzie had said she was skiing with that day.

'Alain?'

'Yes?'

'I remembered something: Suzie is ski leading for the Diamonds today. She's guiding Lionel Sturridge and Lara Stanley cross-country, planning to overnight in Italy.'

Alain paused. One of those names rang a very loud bell.

'Could the link be Carla Sturridge? Lionel is her ex-husband.'

'Lionel Sturridge visited Carla in prison a few months back, I remember seeing the records and thinking how decent it was of an ex-husband to bother with a murderous ex-wife,' Sylvie noted.

'He clearly had another reason,' the procureur said.

Lucy remembered something else Poppy had told her.

'Carla and Lara were friends many years back when Lara lived here. They founded the Grondère Diamond Ski Club.'

'Which links them both to Rusty and Rory,' Sylvie said.

'And Carla knew all about Tony Onion through Tonita.'

Blonnay concluded, 'That completes the loop.'

Alain nodded, 'It's thin but it is a glimmer of light; we need to play for time, I don't want them leaving the country while we follow this line of enquiry, let's reel them in.' The procureur nodded his agreement and Alain continued, his tone now decisive.

'Lucy, change of plan, *don't* call Suzie. If you see her, try and separate her off from the others, but otherwise stay out of it.'

'Rory might be with them too.'

'Oh no he won't be, we know where he is; Rory won't be skiing Grondère or anywhere else again for a long, long time.'

He turned to Sylvie, 'Call your mates at TéléGrondère and tell them to track the ski passes of Suzie Vaill, Lionel Sturridge and Lara Stanley, they can't have got far yet, even if they were on the first lift, the lift system has only just opened. If they're heading off-sector we need to know where they leave it, so we can work out where they're headed. We need to stop them before they get to Italy, because if they find out about Rory, they won't come back. Then get your gun and your skis and call the helicopter.'

He turned to Blonnay and Jilly.

'We're doing this on a bit of a hunch. By the time we get back I need you two to have some hard proof of the link between the Diamonds, the Rusts and the defunct.'

He left the room leaving the young couple looking at one another, their eyes wide open.

'My last case took me six months and your lot want me to unravel this in a few hours?'

Blonnay nodded. Jilly looked at her computer.

'What I need,' she told him, 'is a non-stop supply of coffee and chocolate.'

'I'm on it.'

Twenty-One

My dad always told me there's three things you need to have in the boot of your car: a blanket, a shovel and a flask. And he's right – because whenever I've killed a man, I'm parched.

Sarah Millican

By the time the helicopter buzzed over the slopes of Grondère, Alain and Sylvie knew that Suzie and her clients had worked their way to the far edge of the Grondère domain and the last cable car they had taken was up Mont Grondère only 15 minutes earlier. This meant they were heading backside and then probably planning to skin further cross-country towards the Italian border.

'They should be easy to find,' Sylvie said grimly. 'There's just one problem.'

'What's that?'

'We don't know what they look like in their ski gear. What colours they're wearing, look at how many parties of three there are.'

'You're right. But we know who that lot are. That's Lucy down there.'

A helicopter, not an everyday sight in other circumstances, is a common sight in the mountains and so Suzie and her party thought nothing of it when the helicopter buzzed overhead, but Lucy and her friends were surprised to have one land so close to them.

'In!' Alain commanded. 'We need your eyes.'

The three friends threw their skis into the rack and obediently jumped in. The helicopter flew over the route once more. It was a matter of minutes before Lucy shouted over the hum of the rotors.

'There's Suzie.'

'Sure?'

'Yes, orange jacket, purple trousers, and white helmet, that's definitely Suzie. I recognise Lara's sky-blue ski pants too.'

A party of three could be seen skinning across the plateau, heading south, away from Mont Grondère.

'Look at that skin-tight outfit with the fur trims and gold bling,' added Sally. 'Only a member of the Grondère Diamond Ski Club would be seen dead wearing such an outfit!'

Alan ordered the pilot to set down at a point where they would have an uphill advantage and be able to catch up with Suzie's party easily. He and Sylvie jumped out, closely followed by Lucy and the other two.

'Where do you think you're going?' Alain asked them. 'Wait with the helicopter! You can't come with us.'

'We don't want to go with you,' Sally answered.

'Free heli-ski drop in the back country,' shrugged Tommy. 'You'll excuse us? Not an opportunity to be squandered.'

Alain watched stupefied as the trio started planning their lines.

'You'll be needing the space in the helicopter to transport your baddies anyway,' Lucy told him, planting a soggy kiss on his cheek. 'I'm not worried: you've got Sylvie with you.'

And off they skied.

Sylvie laughed, 'At least it looks like an illicit heli-ski drop-off now. If Suzie and her mates were suspicious, they won't be now.'

Alain and Sylvie eyed their quarry with more solemnity.

'We can cut them off at the next pass, before they cross the border,' Sylvie said. She knew Grondère by heart and could have skied it in her sleep. Alain nodded and off they set, hoping that they would catch their suspects unawares and that they didn't have any guns in their backpacks. Their advantage, they hoped, was that none of them knew that Rory was in police custody and so a visit from the *Police judiciaire* was the last thing they were expecting on their ski day.

Lucy and her friends had a great time skiing down a beautiful, gentle bowl of powder. It was not an official helicopter drop-off and so there wasn't a single track upon it. They bounced gleefully, throwing up snow over their heads. Lucy was now so much more confident in her technique that she picked up speed and allowed herself to play with the natural lines and folds of the landscape.

'You really have got powder skiing now, haven't you?' Sally complimented her as they joined the more familiar off-piste track that led back to the resort.

Lucy smiled with pleasure, she felt she had finally left that infernal 'good skier' plateau on which she had been stranded for so long and finally crossed over into the 'excellent skier' category.

She looked up at the backside of Mont Grondère and thought how the previous spring they had scattered Danny's ashes in the same spot. It was a beautiful, wild spot and she was happy to think Danny was floating around there with them.

As they played around the bumps and dips in the lower part of the bowl she glanced back from time to time to make sure she could still see Sylvie and Alain above them heading towards the pass to Italy on skier's right.

'Here should be good,' said Tommy as he halted ahead of her, pointing to a big flat rock, baking in the morning spring sunshine. They all took off their skis and clambered onto the rock. Lucy got out her flask of tea, Tommy got out some flapjacks and Sally, a bottle of white.

'Binoculars?' asked Sally. Tommy handed her his pair and Lucy got hers out.

They sat munching on their biscuits and sipping their tea, staying alert and ready to watch the action.

Just as sound carries over water, sound can carry a long way in a snow-clad valley reserved for off-piste skiing. There are fewer skiers and no machinery, but Alain and Sylvie made no sound as they sped to cut off Suzie's party at the pass. They, however, could hear the whoops of glee from Lucy, Tommy and Sally and almost every word uttered by Suzie's group and so they knew that the party had no idea that they were being pursued.

Suzie's keen eyes had spotted the helicopter drop-off, seen the party of three head in the other direction and picked out the two skiers heading their way.

'I wonder who they are?' Alain heard Suzie pointing them out to Lionel and Lara and looking up to see the darkly-clad skiers descending expertly in between the rocks towards them.

'They're clearly professional skiers,' commented Lionel. 'Look at the woman, she just straight-lined that cliff.'

'Must be heading for Italy too. At that speed they'll get there well before us,' Suzie smiled. Lionel and Lara were not fit and the climb was taking much longer than it should with frequent stops for them to gasp for breath.

'Next time we must get a helicopter to drop us off and avoid this climb,' Lara panted.

'I don't know how they wangled landing there,' Suzie commented. 'Lionel's probably right, they must be pros.'

They reached the pass and began to remove their skins for the ski down to Italy. Suzie whipped hers off in no time and turned to help Lara with hers when they realised Alain and Sylvie were standing watching them.

'Hello,' said Lara, looking at the handsome stranger who was about to spoil her day.

'Mme Stanley?'

'How do you know my name?'

Suzie, who had recognised Alain, was dumbfounded. He looked at her in a way that made it clear she should say nothing.

Alain introduced himself and Sylvie.

'I apologise for interrupting your ski day, Mme Stanley, but I must ask you to accompany me and my colleague back to Savigny. We would like to talk to you about your connection with Rory Gordon.'

'Rory, what on earth for? I am not going anywhere but Italy today, Officer. I will be happy to talk to you about that young rascal on my return.'

'I am afraid it cannot wait, Mme Stanley: we are investigating a murder and we believe you have information that could be of great interest to us.'

Suzie's eyes opened so wide, Sylvie almost laughed.

'Murder? Who has been murdered? Whatever Rory has done, it's nothing to do with me.'

'I'm sorry but I must insist.'

While Alain was talking, Sylvie gestured to Suzie to put her skis back on and slide away from Lionel and Lara.

Lionel became most indignant.

'Look, Officer, we are British citizens and you have no jurisdiction over us, especially as we are on the Italian border.'

Lionel turned round, looking for Suzie to back him up. He was a little surprised to see her standing some five metres away.

'Technically the Italian border starts at the foot of the pass, not here on the shoulder,' Suzie said unhelpfully.

Lionel looked down the steep incline leading to Italy. Having seen how the Swiss police officers had skied the face above them, he knew he had no chance of outskiing them, besides Swiss police officers often carried guns. His only chance was to try and convince them to let them go.

'Look here, Capitaine, we're not here very often, we're old birds and I'm not sure I'll ever get the chance to ski this route again: why don't we just come into the station when we're back from Italy? It's not as if we're fly-by-nights, we're honest folk, you can count on us to show up. We obviously want to cooperate with your investigation, it's in our interest to protect our reputations. We'll only be a few days, then we can tell you all we know about Rory, although I'm afraid I can't help you much. I hardly know him, other than as an excellent ski leader.'

The two police officers looked completely unmoved by his fervent reassurances.

'Look here, Officer,' Lara tried another approach. 'I'm not taking this! If you want us to change our plans, you will have to arrest us.'

'Okay, Mme Stanley and M. Sturridge, I am arresting you in connection with the murder of Tony Onion. Will that do?'

'This is utterly ridiculous! I insist on my rights, I will not talk to any foreign police officers without the presence of a British lawyer. I want to speak to the British ambassador.'

'As you like.'

Still protesting loudly, the couple were escorted to the helicopter which was now waiting for them on a flat a little lower down the slope.

Suzie skied down at a little distance behind them and looked at Alain, peeved.

'I've been so looking forward to that trip. I can't ski the route on my own, I guess I'll have to ski back down to Grondère.'

'I'm sorry we messed up your plans, Suzie. I'd offer you a ride, but we're heading straight for Savigny and I think you'll find that down there …' he pointed to the hollow where Lucy and her friends were picnicking, 'is a little reception committee eager to hear every word that has been uttered here.'

Suzie grinned: life was certainly not dull in Grondère.

'You're not going to swear me to secrecy, are you? That would be mean.'

Alain grinned, 'Just tell them to keep it to themselves.'

Suzie nodded and skied off in the indicated direction, gliding through the narrow passages between rocks and bouncing over the tricky hollows and wind lips.

'She's pretty good,' commented Sylvie.

'Indeed, by all accounts she's quite an extraordinary woman.'

'I look forward to meeting her properly another time.'

Suzie sprayed Lucy and friends in a triumphant arch of snow as she ostentatiously hockey-stopped in front of them. She was handed a small glass of *Fendant* as she started relating her tale to an avid audience.

Back in Savigny, Blonnay and Jilly had been working hard. With her British colleagues, Jilly had been investigating the financial dealings and business activities of Lionel Sturridge and Lara Stanley. She had also had the idea of calling upon many of the contacts she had recently made across the globe to hunt down any movements leaving the Caymans from the suspicious accounts. Apart from some very complicated tax dodging devices, Lionel's affairs seemed legitimate. Lara had a complicated web of business interests, trust funds and investment portfolios all over the world. Her travel history showed regular visits to the Cayman Islands.

'Her business is complex but legitimate, at least by the standards of the laws of the countries she operates in. She seems to have set up a central trust fund in the Cayman Islands as her main declared business,' Jilly said. 'That's where she lodges her accounts and pays the little tax she pays, but I can't establish a link to Tony Onion or to Ruaidrí Investments, so where is it?'

'We need to find it quickly or we'll have nothing to charge them with and we'll be in trouble.'

They kept looking and their breakthrough finally came in the form of a phone call from London.

'Gotcha!' exclaimed Jilly.

Blonnay looked at her.

'Is that good English?' he asked.

'Informal,' she replied, wondering if it was an appropriate time to explain the vernacular of tabloid newspapers, particularly during the Falklands War in the early 1980s. She decided to save that discussion for later.

'I won't go into how they've done it but it's not actually a very complicated chain. It's a lot easier when you know where to look. They have been able to track some movements between The Rust account and a bank in Switzerland. A transfer of 40 million Swiss francs was recently made to a bank here in Grondère and then to The White Snowflake project.'

'*No!*'

'Yup.'

'That's brilliant.'

'On the basis of that, I can also trace a movement for the same amount on the same date from the Diamond account to the Rust account. I can also see several incoming payments totalling $50 million in December but I can't yet identify the source; I'm guessing that's Tony Onion's original transfer.'

'Genius! So now we have a direct money trail from Tony Onion to Lara Stanley and then to Rusty and Rory.'

'Yes,' she smiled. 'I think so. If we go by current exchange rates, if we add the value of the diamonds found in Rusty's safe, we're about on the money.'

She looked at the depleted chocolate supply beside her computer.

'I'm feeling a bit sick.'

Twenty-Two

Do you want to confess or shall I tell you how you did it?
Kerry Greenwood, Cocaine Blues

'So, after all that, the stolen money is sitting here in Grondère?' Alain was astounded.

Blonnay looked at his girlfriend with pride.

'Well, most of it, if you add the value of the investment in White Snowflake to the diamonds sitting in Bern, I think we have the full amount. The White Snowflake consortium was obviously too eager for fresh cash to check out where it came from,' Jilly explained. 'Having done his side deal, Onion was holding his money in a money launderer's account in The Cayman Islands but the account holder, either Lara or Lionel, or both, filtered off $10 million's worth to finance Rory and Rusty's sideline in illegal diamonds.'

'That doesn't look good for Tonita, – her dad, his "borrowed" money.'

'It looks worse for Alessandra Rosset – her lover, his company, Tonita's dad's "stolen" money,' Sylvie pointed out with her eyebrows at full tilt.

'True,' grimaced Alain.

The procureur burst out laughing. They looked at him bemused.

'This place and the way all the intricate strands of its web connect together is a constant source of amazement to me. Here's another strand: I have been invited to a dinner reception tonight. Alessandra Rosset is the guest speaker. *Real Estate – The New Swiss Eldorado.* I'm not going to be able to keep a straight face.'

'Does she know her lover's in a padded cell in Sion?'

'We haven't told anyone and we confiscated his shattered phone: there are a lot of missed calls, she's clearly wondering where he is. I wonder why she didn't report it.'
'Let's leave her for now, she has no idea who I am, I'll see if I can find anything out tonight. In the meantime, I'll leave you all to untangle this mess and interview your well-to-do detainees.'
And off he went, still chuckling.

'Well, well,' Alain said. 'It is strange the way things turn out. Okay, we'll need to split you two up so we have the financial stuff right. Jilly, you come with me, we'll tackle Lara Stanley. Blonnay and Sylvie, you can have Lionel Sturridge.'
He grinned at Blonnay, 'Should be a vocab-fest for you.'
Blonnay nodded with glee, 'I am looking forward to it.'

Lara Stanley sat in stony silence as the British officer explained why she had been brought in for questioning.
'I will not speak without my lawyer being here.'
'That is, of course, your right' Alain said. 'But it is a Swiss lawyer you need, not an English one.'
She was permitted to call her lawyer in London who said he would get a Swiss lawyer to her as quickly as possible. At which point she clammed up completely and was taken away.

'That went well,' Alain smiled as they left the interview room. He didn't mind; he was used to waiting and he was sure they were finally getting to the crux of the case.
'Let's check up on their hotel bookings while we wait, people like that are creatures of habit, they must always go to the same hotels.'
He called Lucy, who was in The Pub with the whole gang and she spoke to Suzie who was able to confirm that both

Lara and Lionel always stayed in the Chalet des Sommets, a traditional four-star hotel in the centre of Grondère. The hotel records showed that both visitors had been in resort on the night of the murder during the half-term break. Alain wrote this down on a note to be passed on in the other interview room.

'I wonder how Blonnay and Sylvie are getting on,' he asked Jilly as they headed out to a local restaurant for dinner.

Blonnay was having a wonderful time. Lionel Sturridge, believing the Swiss police to be vastly inferior to the British police, thought he could bluster his way out of his current situation.

'You've got it all wrong, Officer. Do you know who I am?'

Blonnay was puzzled.

'Yes, of course I know who you are: that is why I arrested you.'

'What I mean is, I am a successful businessman with interests and influential contacts all over the world.'

'Oh, I see.'

Blonnay was silent.

'So?'

'I don't understand,' Blonnay played dumb. 'You want me to dismiss you from our investigation because you are an important businessman and you know important people?'

'I am above suspicion!' Lionel stuttered, 'My record is unimpeachable.'

That was the first word Blonnay noted down. What a lovely word, he thought, it must be the opposite of what people keep trying to do to American presidents. He would enjoy researching that later. In the meantime, he replied thoughtfully.

'Throughout history, many important men, previously believed to be un-im-peach-able, have been found to be otherwise. Do you have any interest in the Cayman Island investment companies, Ruaidrí or Adamantem Clava?'

'I thought this was a murder inquiry, my financial interests cannot be of interest to you.'

'On the contrary, murder and money are often connected and, in this case, we are very interested in a large investment made by Ruaidrí Investments in a Swiss property consortium.'

Lionel began to look more uncomfortable.

'I have no financial interest in that company, never heard of it.'

'But you do have an interest in Adamantem Clava Investments Cayman LLC?'

'I have interests in lots of small offshore companies.'

'To avoid paying your taxes?'

'That's not your business, I am not a Swiss tax payer.'

'You are right. But fraud and money laundering in Switzerland are my business.'

'I told you, I have no interest in that Ruuuardi company.'

'No, but you do have a shareholding in Adamantem Clava Investments Cayman LLC which made a transfer of 40 million Swiss francs to Ruaidrí Investments which then purchased a stake in White Snowflake.'

Lionel turned white.

'Even if that is true, which I'm not saying it is, you cannot have obtained that information legally.'

'True, but, if the money transferred was obtained illegally, the Cayman authorities will eventually send us the information we require, especially as the money seems to have been illegally diverted from another sovereign state.'

Lionel looked completely confused.

'But that money's clean.'

'Ah, so you do know about the investment?'

'Err, I knew that one of the companies in which I have a small shareholding has made an investment in White Snowflake through a shell company but that's legitimate.'

'So you don't know where the money for that investment came from?'

'Well, no, these are umbrella companies with multiple shareholders which just facilitate investments.'

'In our world it's called money laundering,' Sylvie said quietly. Blonnay smothered a smirk as Lionel started to look even more uncomfortable.

'And this particular investment turns out, not only to be laundered, but stolen from a very angry Arab state.'

At this point, Lionel looked as if he was about to burst into tears.

'This can't be right,' he blustered, 'I would never dabble in anything illegal.'

'But you might turn a blind eye?'

'No. Never! I am no criminal.'

'Well someone is …' Blonnay left the suggestion hanging. There comes a point in an interview, he thought to himself, when the internal debate occurring within the person being questioned is almost physically visible. Lionel was at that point at that moment. The calculations of self-interest versus self-preservation, and the weighing up of the comparative sins of disloyalty to an old friend against being caught on the wrong side of the law, were practically written all over Lionel's face. As Lionel's deliberations seemed to stagnate, Blonnay decided to help the process along.

'Do you have a gun, M. Sturridge? Something like this one?'

Blonnay showed him a photo of the little handgun that had killed Tony Onion. The tactic was almost too effective – Lionel looked as if he might faint. Sylvie held out an arm to prevent him falling forwards and knocking himself out on the table.

'You have seen this gun before?'

Lionel shook his head.

'But you know something about it?'

He nodded: the full implications of what he was involved with had finally dawned upon him. Murder was not something he was prepared to take the blame for.

'My ex-wife told me about it. She said it had belonged to Lady Shilton and Lady Shilton had given it back to her father. She thought it would be a great way of getting Tonita into trouble.'

'And to whom did you pass on this information?'

'To Lara.'

'And what did she do with this information?'

'I honestly do not know. It was just meant to be a bit of fun.'

'That blind eye again?'

'Perhaps.'

Realising their detainee was completely drained and probably not going to be able to tell them much more, they got him to identify the companies owned by Lara in which he had an interest, then they ended the interview. A very unhappy Lionel was taken down to a cell for the night.

'Good evening, Mme Rosset, that was a fascinating speech.'

'Thank you.' Alessandra eyed the procureur suspiciously. He realised that she knew exactly who he was despite his constant endeavours to avoid the public spotlight.

'Shall we talk?' He led her to a quiet corner where they could not be overheard.

'Rory Gordon: I believe he is a *friend* of yours?'

'Rory?' She looked honestly concerned. 'Yes, it's obviously no secret from you that we are in a relationship, but I am actually worried. I haven't seen him for a few days.'

'Did you not think to contact the police?'

'I did, but Rory is a bit of a free agent and …' she tapered off.

'He has disappeared before.'

She gave the nod of a woman who knows her lover is unfaithful but chooses to ignore it. The procureur felt momentarily sorry for her: here was a woman in love.

'I can tell you that M. Gordon is safe, but he is not well and he is in police custody.'

She looked at him askance.

'Rory's a bit of a scoundrel but he hasn't done anything seriously wrong, has he?'

'I cannot tell you any more. Would you be willing to be formally interviewed?'

'Of course,' she replied, knowing she had no choice. 'But you said he was unwell?'

'He is in safe hands, do not worry about that. Can I just ask you one thing? Do you know if he possessed a gun?'

She gasped.

'I saw a small gun in his bag once. He said it wasn't his, he was just looking after it. You don't think he killed Tony Onion?'

'How do you know about that? We have not released his name to the press.'

'It is my building site, M. le Procureur.'

'Ah yes.'

She looked completely broken. The procureur decided not to mention she was sitting on 40 million Swiss francs of stolen money for now, he would leave that to his team.

He escorted her, in a state of shock, to a waiting police car which would take her to Savigny.

234

In Savigny, Sylvie interviewed Alessandra Rosset and quickly established that she knew nothing about Rory's activities. She genuinely had believed that Ruairdí Investments was a valid company and had suspected nothing more serious than tax evasion. It was Rory who had told her that Tony Onion's children had become Tonita's responsibility but she had only seized on the information as a useful negotiation tool, she hadn't asked herself how he knew because she hadn't known it was a secret.

This was plausible but it didn't explain how she had known whose body had been found on her building site.

'Oh, I found that out very quickly,' she said. 'As soon as there was police activity on the site, I had someone listening in. When I found out, I also thought it could be useful information for negotiating the purchase of Tonita's shareholding.'

She realised how these statements must make her appear – ruthless and without scruples – but she didn't care: she had nothing to hide and that was how you survived in business. What she did care about was what had become of Rory and where he had got the money.

'I have an idea,' Alain said to Blonnay as they watched the interview. 'How about you and Jilly take Mme Rosset, if she'll agree, to see Rory? I'm sure the doctors will allow him to have a visit from his girlfriend and it will, of course, have to be under police supervision.'

'Do you think she'll agree?'

'She's sitting on 40 million francs of stolen money, remind her that it's in her interest to cooperate.'

'She'll agree. I think she's really in love with him.'

'Poor woman, she's in for a shock.'

Twenty-Three

I'd rather have roses on my table than diamonds on my neck.

Emma Goldman

Rory was sitting up in bed, loudly singing *Who's Afraid of the Big Bad Wolf* when the delegation from the *Police judiciaire* arrived. The two officers handed Alessandra a hand recorder and stayed at the half-open door to listen in.

'Hello Lissy,' Rory greeted his shocked lover, 'have you come to play with your handsome piggy wig?'

She slowly and incredulously moved towards the side of his bed and gently took his hand.

'The grub here's awful,' he pouted, 'and they won't let me have any champagne, it's not fair!'

'No,' she answered, 'you must get better soon so you can come home.'

'Yes! Home Baby!'

'Rory, darling, all that money, the 40 million Swiss francs, whose money is it? Is it yours?' she pressed.

'Yes, mine now,' he smiled, looking pleased with himself.

'Where did it come from? The investors you told me about, do they really exist?'

'Ooh, sorry Lissy, told you a little fib. You don't mind awfully, do you?'

She shook her head. 'No, of course not, Rory. So is it really your money?'

Blonnay was impressed: Alessandra was a good interrogator.

The truth was that Alessandra could hear Tonita's damning criticism and warning ringing loudly in her ears and she desperately wanted to know whose money it was. She was praying that the money really was Rory's but she had a sinking feeling Tonita was about to be proved right.

'Well, not officially,' he said, tapping the side of his nose. 'But it's naughty money, and I don't think anyone will say anything if we keep it,' he added confidingly.

She shook her head, exasperated as he winked at her.

Laurent looked at Jilly knowingly, they knew where Rory's money came from, the Diamond Club company in the Cayman Islands, but was it from Lionel, Lara or both?

'Darling,' Alessandra said, 'I'm not very good at this guessing game, could you give me a clue. Who gave you the money?'

'Okay, I'll give you a clue.'

Rory began to hum a tune, Alessandra only vaguely recognised but both Blonnay and Jilly recognised it instantly as the theme to the film *Doctor Zhivago – Lara's Theme* and as Alessandra looked despairingly in their direction mouthed the name 'Lara'.

'Lara!' she exclaimed, as if it was a quiz.

'Clever girl!' he exclaimed. 'Got it in one.'

'Not Lionel?'

'No, he's too square and way too stupid. But don't tell anyone, it's our secret.'

The two officers held their breath. So, Lara was the mastermind behind the whole thing. She was Tony Onion's money launderer.

But Alessandra was puzzled.

'But Lara is a highly reputable businesswoman, Rory. Why did she hide behind you? Why do you think she won't say anything if you keep the money?'

'Can't say, Lissy.' He whispered in her ear, 'Never bite the hand that feeds you, bad manners.'

He then burst into chuckles. Alessandra looked despairingly toward the door from where Blonnay mimed at her to ask about the gun.

Alessandra took a deep breath: she had just found out that her lover was a complete fraud. Now she could only hope that he wasn't also a murderer.

'Rory, darling, tell me, you had a gun, didn't you?'

'Ah yes,' he said, 'not my gun.'

'That gun killed a man, Rory. The police think you might have done it. Whose gun was it?'

'Lara's gun!' he cried. 'She did it, I saw her! Shhhh!' He added looking towards the door. 'I think we're being spied on. Don't tell a soul and we'll get away with it. We're going to be rich, Lissy! You can go to work every day, I know you like that. But I'm just going to go skiing. No more travelling: Rusty was right – time to go legit.'

Alessandra smiled at him and patted his hand fondly. She sighed: the worst was over. She took a few seconds to gather herself and then stood up sadly and went to the door where Jilly and Blonnay were preparing to leave. She handed them their recorder. What they had heard was totally inadmissible in court but they knew what line to take in their questioning.

'What will happen to him now?' Alessandra asked, holding the door ajar.

'Oh, he'll be sent back to the UK where they can pay for his medical expenses; we can't prosecute him in that state and we're pretty sure he's not our murderer.'

'Is it okay if I stay with him for a while?'

Blonnay nodded as she turned sorrowfully and went back into the room.

'Poor woman, she really did love him,' Jilly remarked.

'Yes, sad. And I wouldn't be in a hurry to get back to Grondère if I was her either, she's got a lot of music to face.'

'Indeed.'

As they walked back to the car, Blonnay started singing

'*Qui craint le grand méchant loup, méchant loup, grand loup noir?*'
And they laughed all the way back to Savigny.

Sylvie was waiting for Blonnay and Jilly back at headquarters. Whilst they had been with Rory and Alessandra, help had walked into the station in a rather unexpected shape.

'We have a visitor, Capitaine Dupertuis is with him now.'

Blonnay walked into a meeting room to see Alain serving coffee to an uncomfortable-looking Charles Sidforth-Sykes. Alain grinned inwardly, he knew how much Charles disliked Blonnay but also how much Blonnay appreciated Charles's range of vocabulary.

'M. Sidforth-Sykes is here at the suggestion of his girlfriend.'

'Ah,' Blonnay looked at Charles hopefully.

'We heard you had taken Lara in for questioning and Jemima remembered me telling her something that might be of use to you. I told her it was poppycock but she said I should tell you anyway and let you decide.'

'She sounds like a very sensible young woman,' Blonnay encouraged him, thinking that, however much sense Jemima Watson may have, it had not manifested itself in her choice of lover.

'Jemima? Yes, smart gel, not sure what she's doing with an old duffer like me.'

Neither detective contradicted this statement, confirming his belief that they were against him.

'I don't want to get dragged into this,' he began. 'I've nothing to do with any of these people, you realise that?'

'Your name has not yet come up in our investigations,' Blonnay offered unreassuringly.

'Now look here,' Charles blustered, 'I have come here of my own accord to try and offer you my assistance, I don't want it backfiring on me.'

'If you have nothing to do with the murder of Tony Onion, then you can have nothing to fear.' Alain tried to calm him down.

'Tony Onion? Is that who it was? The body on the building site? Tonita's father. Christ!'

Alain and Blonnay looked at each other, mystified. If Charles hadn't known the identity of the victim on the building site, how could he have any useful information to give them.

'So, what was it you came to tell us?' Alain asked gently.

'Oh, early on, when I started courting Jemima, I walked her back to Humphrey's one night. We stayed up late, having a nightcap with Humphrey and then I walked home. It was snowing heavily, the night of that big dump, you know?'

'Yes?' Alain replied, disguising a sense of rising excitement.

'I saw Lara Stanley. I just thought she must have been out somewhere for the night and I offered to escort her back to her hotel but she said she was fine. I got the impression she was waiting for someone, and then I saw there was a man hanging around in the shadows so I left her to it, I was clearly in the way.'

'Did you see who he was, the man?'

'No, I thought it was that popinjay, Rory Gordon, but it was just an impression, I didn't see him properly.'

'Popinjay!' Blonnay was unable to retain his excitement, not at the evidence, but this wonderful word. Charles looked at him confused.

'Yes, you know, a coxcomb, peacock, in fact I think it means parrot.'

'Of course!' exclaimed the detective, surprised at Charles's etymological knowledge, ' "papagaya", how fantastic!'

Alain uh-hemmed to bring them back to the matter in hand. Blonnay scribbled the word down while Charles looked at him curiously and Alain returned to the interrogation.

'And where was this?'

'There, just by the White Snowflake site.'

'And Miss Watson can confirm that you told her of this encounter?'

'Yes, I had quite forgotten about it until Jemima reminded me.'

'Think very carefully, M. Sidforth-Sykes, as you were walking away, did you hear anything?'

Charles thought very carefully.

'No, nothing. Do you think that was him lurking in the shadows? Tony Onion? Not that whippersnapper, Gordon? Do you think she did it? Christ, I'm maybe the last person who saw him alive? Apart from her? This is awful. But why would Lara do that? No, it must be a mistake.'

They watched as Charles realised and came to terms with the enormity of what he might have witnessed.

'I'm sorry, I can't remember anything else.'

'That's okay. Monsieur, your statement is already a great help to us: your having seen Mme Stanley is key. You are sure?'

'Oh yes. Of that I'm sure.'

'Thank you, M. Sidforth-Sykes, for coming forward, we really appreciate it.'

Charles looked delighted at this remark. For the first time since he had encountered them, he found himself in the novel position of being in favour with the *Police judiciaire*. With a promise to keep his information to himself and to ask Jemima to come in the following day to make a statement, he went off with a spring in his step.

Alain turned to Blonnay.

'How many did you get?'

Blonnay looked at the page in his new notebook.

'Seven,' he said happily: 'poppycock, duffer, gel, whippersnapper, courting – I knew that one, of course, but I didn't think it was in current usage, I need to ask Jilly. But oh, the glorious "coxcomb" and "popinjay". I swear, of all our English-speaking connections, Charles Sidforth-Sykes is by far the finest supplier of exotic vocabulary. I love that man.'

'I'm not sure it's mutual.' Alain chuckled.

'Oh, I'm sure it's not,' his colleague replied nonchalantly. Alain shook his head as he watched his nerdy colleague hurry off for an in-depth discussion on vocabulary with Jilly.

Sylvie had meanwhile returned from Grondère where she had had the interesting task of rifling through Lara Stanley's belongings.

'You should see her jewellery collection!' she told Jilly. 'I never saw so much bling in my life. It's all very showy, except she has some of those lovely Tonita earrings like Lucy, and a pendant to match.'

Jilly was all attention.

'Really?'

'Yes, you've seen them, those pretty gold grape things? I only know because Milly made a big deal of them when she saw Lucy wearing them.'

'I haven't, but something's ringing a bell, in those papers that Prince Anwar's people sent through.'

'You mean, the information received anonymously?' Alain corrected her. He was also paying attention to anything that might help them connect Lara Stanley to the murder.

Jilly was rummaging through the papers on her desk. The Swiss officers shook their heads and looked at each other despairingly. Jilly Ferguson might be a good police officer but she clearly had not benefitted from the tidy, organisational skills imparted by the Swiss education system.

'Here,' she cried, waving a paper at them. 'It's in the transcripts of Tony Onion's text message to his wife before they lost trace of him. Listen: *My darling Angelica I have to disappear for a while and you may hear some bad things about me. Please believe me when I say this is not what I intended and I will do everything in my power to sort things out. I carry with me the limited edition earrings and pendant that I promised you from Tonita's collection. I hope to be with you soon and see you wearing them.*'

'I wonder if they have a number on the back?' Sylvie said as she opened the bag and brought out the Tiffany's box containing Lara's earrings and pendant.

'What?' asked Alain; wondering how women knew such things.

'075. Jackpot!'

Alain and Blonnay looked on blankly.

'They're one of a limited edition,' Sylvie explained. 'If these are the ones Tony Onion bought for his wife, we've got her.'

'It'll take us ages to get that information out of Tiffany's.'

'But not Lady Shilton.'

Alain called Tonita and one hour later they had her personal list of purchasers of her Grapes limited edition. Tony Onion had purchased number 075 in Milan in February, just before he went missing. It was time to interview Lara Stanley again.

Surrounded by an English lawyer and a Swiss lawyer that Alain had only ever seen on the television before, he and Sylvie sat down to interview Lara Stanley. They had no proof: they would eventually be able to obtain hard evidence of the financial transactions but murder would be harder to prove. They had managed to keep Rory's insanity quiet and so bluff was all they had.

'Do you recognise this gun, Mme Stanley?'

'No.'

'And yet, Rory Gordon tells us he saw you use it against Tony Onion.'

'Rubbish, the man's a fool.'

'And yet you entrusted him with 40 million francs.'

She looked at him askance.

'I don't recall doing anything of the kind.'

'Then the money invested in the White Snowflake project belongs to him?'

She didn't reply.

'Where were you at 3am the morning Tony Onion was murdered?'

'I have no idea, what was the date?'

Sylvie gave her the exact date.

'I'm pretty sure I was in Grondère then but I can't remember the exact day.'

'It was the night we had the first big snowfall.'

'Oh, then yes, I remember, I was safely tucked up in bed so I could ski the powder the following morning.'

'Can anyone verify that?'

'No, I sleep alone, Officer.'

'But we have a witness who puts you at the murder scene.'

'It's Rory's word against mine. I put it to you that he is your murderer and is trying to pin it on me.'

'We have a second witness who also saw you close to the murder scene that night.'

Lara hesitated and bit her lip. That idiot Charles must have told them he saw her.

'Even if I did go out that night for a walk, being seen near the site of your crime is not an eye-witness to the crime.'

'How long have you known Tony Onion?'

'I don't believe I ever met Tony Onion.'

'Really?'

She looked at him cagily wondering how much he knew. She was about to find out.

'And yet he has been renting a villa from you in the Grand Cayman for five years.'

'My agent deals with all rentals, I have nothing to do with the administration.'

'And you have been facilitating his financial transactions for the same period.'

She looked at Alain and realised he had nothing and was just trying to draw her out.

'This is all supposition. I demand to be released immediately.'

'I'm afraid I cannot do that; you might leave the country.'

'I most certainly would: you have no reason to keep me here. This is unacceptable.'

Sylvie decided to try the jewellery link.

'You have, in your possession, a pair of Tonita Shalott earrings and a pendant.'

'What if I do? I have a lot of jewellery.' She sensed a trap.

'They're not in keeping with the rest of your pieces. How did you come by them?'

'I can't remember, I think I was given them.'

'You can't remember?'

'I can't say. They are just trinkets, I have many more valuable pieces.'

'Did you know they were part of a limited edition? A numbered limited edition? And that we know who purchased them?'

The realisation was almost visible on her face as it dawned on her that the earrings connected her to Tony Onion. She looked at them slyly.

'Ah, I remember,' she said. 'Rory gave them to me, shortly after the date you mentioned.'

'Rory gave them to you? Why would he give them to you rather than Alessandra Rosset?'

'I remember now. He asked me to look after them for him, as he didn't have access to a safe.'

Alain sighed: she was sharp and was going to be tough to break. And yet he was convinced she was guilty.

They ended the interview and left Lara to be escorted back to her cell. They knew they couldn't hold her much longer under arrest without solid proof.

Twenty-Four

There is always a pleasure in unravelling a mystery, in catching at the gossamer clue which will guide to certainty.
Elizabeth Gaskell, Mary Barton

Alain and his team were under pressure. They had been obliged to release Lionel Sturridge who was almost certain to flee Switzerland to the security of Britain, but this didn't concern them. They were sure he couldn't advance their murder enquiry any further and they had some useful contacts in the UK police who could be relied upon to pick up Lionel should they need him back. Soon they would also have to release Lara Stanley and cancel the murder charge: apart from the eye-witness account of a madman and Charles Sidforth Sykes having seen her close to the scene of the murder, they did not have enough actual proof to convict her and they could not crack her under interview. She would be much more difficult to keep track of if she left the country and headed for the Cayman Islands and they were convinced she was responsible for Tony Onion's murder.

As the Grondère murder team were labouring to find some concrete proof to connect Lara to Tony Onion's murder, Tonita was settling into a quiet routine in La Grande Cour. Sebastian had headed back to the UK to look after affairs at home and Ruby and Leo were enjoying the local international school where the teaching style seemed a little more relaxed and sports lessons were skiing. She had resigned herself to the fact that she would never get their boarding school fees reimbursed but she realised that, whatever happened, they would probably be leaving that school anyway. She was quite enjoying getting in some practice at playing at mum, picking the children up from school and doing their homework with them. Lucy and Poppy stopped by regularly to keep her spirits up and also to entertain and distract the children.

I am lucky, she thought, to have such friends.

But in the late evenings as she sat in the restaurant or the bar on her own, she realised how much she missed Sebastian and felt strangely uneasy: as if someone was out there, wishing her ill.

The end of the season was now in sight and the resort was slowly winding down. Easter had been early and so there was still plenty of snow on the hill and good skiing to be had but the weather was much warmer. It was a time when the residents could take some time to go skiing for themselves and have long lunches on sunny terraces.

But still there were signs of spring, Lucy could detect the scent of the rising sap of pine and juniper in the breeze and the odd early bee had started nosing around the woodwork as she sat on the balcony of the little chalet having her morning cup of tea. Every morning she sat out there now she felt a little sad to know that the day was approaching when she would have to move out forever. She needed to start sorting through her belongings and doing a clear-out. She hadn't seen Alain for days, he hadn't even had time to chat much on the phone so she knew he must be reaching the end of his case. She could also tell he was stressed.

Rumours were circulating round town about Rory, Lara and Lionel being under arrest, confirming Alain's assessment that it was impossible to keep anything a secret for long in Grondère. She wondered how on earth people found such things out, she knew none of her crowd had leaked the news. Then, as she thought about it, it was clear: the hotel staff would have been questioned, the hotel searched, Rory had disappeared and Sammy had told her that Alessandra Rosset was mooching around the apartment block where she lived, and where Sammy had his bar, looking shell-shocked.

Suddenly Lucy detected movement around her chalet. She kept perfectly still and held her breath. A wolf? A deer? No, it was Gluey Hughey. How on earth did he know where to find her? She supposed it must be the same way he always knew when there was a party going on.

He put his finger to his lips and made signs to ask if he could come up.

'What's up, Hughey?'

'I want to show you something.'

From his backpack he took out a beautifully carved she-wolf.

'It's stunning, Hughey, I think it's the most beautiful carving I've seen of yours so far.'

'Thank you,' he smiled looking at it with pride. He sat there quietly.

'Would you like a cup of tea or coffee,' she asked, remembering her manners, although it was a bit bizarre to be sitting on her balcony with Hughey at daybreak. He shook his head. She wondered what was so urgent that he had needed to show her his work at such an unsociable hour.

'The photographer in town has offered to sell my pieces in his gallery,' he said.

'That's great!'

He jolted backwards and made the whispering sign again. He clearly didn't want to wake her housemates.

'You have seen her too,' he said.

'Yes, twice,' she replied. 'I was pretty scared the second time, I was on my own.'

'She means no harm, she's just passing through,' he told her. 'She lets me sculpt her, I don't get too close.'

'You're braver than me, Hughey, a brief encounter was quite enough.'

'I needed longer to get her right. This is my prototype, after that I can do others.'

Lucy smiled; she supposed Hughey just wanted to share his love of the wolf and his experience of carving her with someone. She didn't know how wrong she was.

'There is another she-wolf on the mountain, Lucy.'

'Sorry?'

'Another she-wolf. She only comes out in wolf-weather.'

Lucy knew from her chats with Jean-Marc that this meant during times of poor visibility, when it was foggy or snowing.

'What do you mean, Hughey, why are you talking in riddles?'

'Because Lucy, we are not having this conversation but you need to know.'

Lucy was baffled.

'Up there,' he nodded his head towards Alain's summer chalet, higher up the hillside. 'There is a small chalet, higher than Alain's, towards the waterfall at the end of the old *bisse*. She lives there.'

Lucy knew the one he meant. It was a sweet little sixties-built holiday cabin.

'You must go.'

'Hughey, nobody lives up there in winter, it's too remote and even now, with spring on the way the snow is still pretty deep.'

She stood up and went to the end of the balcony: the chalet he was referring to could not be seen from there, but she could detect a thin trail of rising smoke, as if, somewhere up there, someone had a log fire burning.

'You can ski down to it or get there by quad or snowshoes on good days. Today is a good day.'

Lucy looked at him dubiously.

'You want me to go there?'

He nodded.

'Now?'

He nodded again.

'But why? Even if there is someone up there, it's a bit odd but it's not a crime.'

'I have seen her at night. She stalks around La Grande Cour.'

Lucy began to understand and her heart filled with dread.

'You think Tonita is in danger?'

'And the children. I have a bad feeling about her, I think she has got a taste for killing.'

'Christ, Hughey! How can you think that and not go to the police? You know that Alain would believe you!'

'No. This cannot come from me, I have no proof, it's just a feeling. You have to promise me, my name mustn't come into it.'

'But who are you afraid of? Her?'

'Please, Lucy.'

Lucy realised that Hughey had finished. Once Hughey had decided to clam up there was no way of getting any more out of him. He had already said a great deal by his standards. She would just have to do as Hughey asked. He was clearly very uncomfortable about being identified as an informant.

'Okay, Hughey. What do you want me to do?'

An hour later, Lucy was waiting for the first lift for the south-facing sector of Grondère. The same rickety old gondolas that she had taken just a few days earlier when she and Suzie had seen Rory as he launched upon his forest ski. She did not then know that Rory had run into the wolf – that was one piece of information the police had managed to keep to themselves, largely because the helicopter crew that picked Rory up had come from a different valley.

Contrary to Hughey's insistence that she go alone so she wouldn't be seen, Lucy had asked Sally to go with her but Sally had an important meeting, Poppy was teaching and so Lucy, without any expectation, had sent a text to Milly asking her to meet her at the top station immediately.

When she reached the top station, however, Milly wasn't there and Lucy could see she hadn't even opened her message. She shrugged, put on her skis and traversed downwards and towards the forest edge – alone. Probably better, she thought as she followed Hughey's instructions, skiing down the forest path, he said the wolf woman has sharp eyes.

'The real wolf sleeps between the second and third bends, on the right-hand side above the old *bisse*,' Hughey had told her, 'so you won't disturb her.'

That would explain, thought Lucy as she skied down, counting the bends, carefully keeping an eye out for any movement, why the wolf was watching me along the *bisse* path: I was close to her hiding place.

At the fifth bend, Hughey had told her to leave the path, walk to the left and conceal herself in the bushes in a position from which she could observe the chalet door.

This is ridiculous, she thought, clicking out of her bindings and leaving her skis under a convenient bush, why wouldn't Hughey just let me call Alain? The police could be here by now and find out whoever this 'she-wolf' is. Maybe I should just call them anyway, but then on what grounds do I send them on what might be a wild goose chase when they're in a middle of a difficult case?

Mumbling these thoughts to herself, she scrambled along behind the wall of snow lining the path, sinking into the odd hole in her ski boots, thinking how unsuited she was to subterfuge and half-convinced someone was watching her in amusement. If Hughey hadn't been such an oddball she would have suspected a set-up job.

When she thought she was level with the chalet, she settled down in a ditch, with a plastic cushion under her knees to keep the damp from the snow seeping in and raised her head just high enough to have a view of the front entrance. Apart from the smoke coming from the chimney, there was no sign of life in the ramshackle little chalet. The shutters were open, but the chalet seemed dark inside and grey net curtains hung at grimy windows. It was hard to believe it was inhabited. Lucy had often looked at it as she walked past but had never seen anyone in it.

After about ten minutes, she heard the chug of a quad and then saw Hughey drive up and park outside the chalet. He didn't even look to see if she was there, he was clearly determined that no one could link her presence back to him.

He heaved a couple of boxes of wood onto the porch, opened them and neatly added them to the stack against the wall.

He then unloaded a couple of shopping bags from the quad and left them in front of the door and drove off.

It wasn't long before the door opened and a woman appeared, had a quick look around, picked up the bags and lifted them inside. She came back to the door and took a long, puzzled look in Lucy's direction. Lucy resisted the urge to duck down, she figured any movement would be detected, so she stayed perfectly still and held her breath which wasn't easy as she was shocked by what she saw. The woman looked around some more, a little squirrel darted from behind Lucy and ran out onto the path, then scrambled up a tree five metres away. The woman's eyes followed the little creature without emotion then closed the door.

Thanks, fellow redhead, for the distraction, Lucy thought before ducking out of sight and scrambling back to the path. As she was clicking into her bindings, wondering how to ski past the chalet without being noticed, two skiers conveniently appeared and so she tucked in behind them to make it seem she was part of their group and skied past the little cabin taking care not to glance at it.

As soon as she was out of earshot, she dropped back from the skiers, halted in a place she was sure she could not be seen from the chalet and phoned Alain. It was understood between them that she would never call him at work unless it was important and so he picked up immediately.

Out of breath she explained what she had seen.

'This changes everything,' he said. 'Thanks, we'll take it from here.'

He looked at his mystified team.

'We've been looking at this all wrong,' he said.

Twenty-Five

*You don't love someone because they're perfect, you love
them in spite of the fact that they're not.*
Jodi Picoult, My Sister's Keeper

The next few hours were spent in very specific background
searches until they had enough to call Lara Stanley back
for interview.

'You must release my client or charge her,' her lawyer
started. 'Admit it, you have no proof.'

'You are right,' Alain nodded, 'new information has come
to light and we no longer believe that your client shot Tony
Onion.'

Lara and her lawyer looked startled.

'But,' Alain added, looking Lara directly in the eyes, 'we
do believe she is shielding the murderer.'

Lara went white and he knew they had finally cracked the
case.

'You have a sister, Mme Stanley.'

Lara closed her eyes in pain and nodded.

'Your younger half-sister disappeared a long time ago to
marry an older man. The marriage was short-lived and
when you saw your sister again, she was going through a
mental breakdown. This part, I admit, is supposition – am
I right?'

Lara nodded but stayed silent.

'That man was Tony Onion, wasn't he?'

Again, she nodded, sadly.

'Since then your sister has been in and out of institutions,
at your expense, and she is currently hiding in a remote
chalet above Grondère, also at your expense – please don't
deny it: we have discovered that the chalet is being rented
by a company of which you are the sole shareholder and
director.'

'Your sister, Orfilia, was Tony Onion's second wife, and it was her that Rory saw shoot him, wasn't it? We are sending a team to the chalet now to pick her up.'

'No,' she cried, 'I shot him. She didn't do it, you can't arrest her, she'll freak out. You have to let me go with them.'

Alain lost no time in pressing home his advantage.

'We're wasting time. When you have told us the truth, Mme Stanley, only then will you be allowed to accompany us to arrest your sister. But I suggest you start talking quickly! She may realise she has been seen and disappear again. She does that, doesn't she?'

Lara now had tears in her eyes.

'And, however noble your gesture of trying to take the blame,' added Jilly, 'if you go to prison in her stead, you won't be able to look after her anymore, will you?'

The look in Lara's eyes showed that they were right: it was time to tell the truth.

She nodded and began.

'My beautiful younger sister came to me when our mother died, I did my best but she was always mentally fragile. I was so wrapped up in my career that I didn't notice she was starting to enjoy male attention. She had a nice job working as an air stewardess and that's how she met that awful man. He left his wife and convinced Orfilia to marry him almost immediately without telling her family and friends and she went off to Dubai to live with him, sending me just a postcard to say how much in love she was, that I should be happy for her. She promised to come back to visit but she never did and I was so hurt, I didn't make the effort to go to see her.

'The next time I heard from her was just under two years later, I got a call from a hospital in Dubai to go and get her. When I got there, she was almost unrecognisable, she had had two unpleasant miscarriages, the last, in the desert when he had been too busy driving jeeps in the dunes with his business pals, to take her to hospital.

'He had clearly quickly realised that she wasn't mentally stable and instead of helping her, he'd pretty much abandoned her to her own devices. I'm not even sure the last child was his.

'After that it was one expensive institution after another, I couldn't keep her with me, she'd run away all the time. Eventually, I placed her in one in Montreux, she seemed okay there and they managed to keep her there.'

'Until February?'

'Until February. She knew I was in Grondère, she found me here and begged to have a holiday and stay with me. It was the worst possible timing, just as everything was coming to a head.'

'Your plans for Tony Onion?'

'Yes.'

'Which were?'

'I didn't mean for him to die: my plan was to ruin him, and ruin his life. As he had ruined hers. I have been building up a relationship with him for years – remotely – I couldn't afford for us to meet, he would have spotted the strong resemblance between me and Orfilia.'

'So you started laundering his illicit transactions for him?'

'Yes, it took me a while to work out how he operated and then I began by building his trust. I started by renting him a property to house his various mistresses – he went through them quite quickly. And then I began offering him my bank accounts to move money around. I was waiting until he wanted me to move an amount so large that he wouldn't be able to bridge it and then I would hold on to it. I knew that it would blow his little game with his employer and I just had to wait and let his employer do the rest and destroy him.

Then Rusty went and fell off a mountain: it wasn't a big deal, I could have covered the value of the diamonds but Rory wasn't in on my plans for Tony Onion and he was starting to panic about paying him back. He'd met Tony Onion at Lord Shilton's wedding and I was worried he'd tell him who I was.'

She looked exhausted and took the glass of water that Laurent offered her. She took a deep breath and continued. 'The gun was meant to muddy the waters. It was Carla's idea – a bit of fun, she said to Lionel. I had Rory purchase it from Tony for me, and my plan was to leave it in Rusty's place to create a link between Rusty and Tonita and throw suspicion on her. In late January, once I had the gun, I put my plan, to ruin Tony Onion, into action and didn't execute the agreed repayment. Tony was furious when he found out and he had no idea where to find me, I had made sure he never knew who I really was. He couldn't go to his employer and say that he had "lost" $50 million and so he had to go into hiding to wait to be reimbursed in the hope of at least being able to get his family out of Dubai. After that I didn't think any more about the gun, the opportunity to plant it never materialised.'

'But Orfilia found it,' Alain said softly.

'Orfilia found it. On the night I finally agreed to meet Tony so I could confront him and tell him who I really was, that he would never be getting his dirty money back and that he could rot in hell to pay for what he had done to her, Orfilia must have followed me and Rory. I left and she must have confronted him and shot him afterwards. I didn't see her there but Rory did.'

'No wonder Rory was confused.'

'Yes. Poor Rory. He didn't know about Orfilia. Not many people do. I knew something had gone wrong when I spotted her wearing those bloody earrings. I took them away from her but I had no idea where she'd got them. I only really understood later on, when Rory told me that a body had been found on Alessandra's building site and that I could trust him not to say anything. A cloaked bribe of course. I should have pulled the plug on the plan when Rusty died. I should have realised things were going wrong.'

'So what was Rusty and Rory's role?'

'They worked for me. They fronted deals so that I could hide my identity and I let them do their own little side deals in return, mostly smuggling illegal diamonds. But I always limited the amount they could get their hands on – a greedy pair. I set up Ruaidrí Investments as a bit of joke, so they could move money around easily but also so I could keep tabs on them. I'd never let them play with such a large amount before. When Rusty fell off Le Monstre without having told Rory where he had stashed their latest consignment, I could have pushed Rory off Le Monstre too. But it wasn't about the money for me: I decided to put the rest of it into Ruaidrí Investments and see if Rory could make it grow via the White Snowflake consortium. When Tony Onion's body was found Rory made it clear that I would not be getting the money back.'

The picture was clear. Alain pushed back his chair and nodded at his colleagues.

'Thank you, Madame Stanley, my team will now take you with them to pick up your sister.'

She sighed and let herself be led away by Sylvie and Jilly. Laurent and Alain stayed behind to start following up on all the various communications and administration that followed a resolved case.

'Well done,' Alain said to Laurent. 'Tidy work.'

'Thanks to Lucy spotting Orfilia Frank in the chalet. I wonder how she knew …'

The police quads raced uphill to the chalet where Lara's sister had been hiding only to find it empty. Lara, already in a state of some distress, became completely distraught.

'She's gone to look for me, she must be wondering why she hasn't heard from me for two days. She normally doesn't leave the chalet during the day.'

'Think,' asked Jilly. 'Where would she go? Where do you normally meet?'

'The hotel, it's the only place I can think of. She can't get far, I keep her passport and I make sure she has no cash.'

Sylvie looked at Jilly, 'We'll try the hotel and if she's not there I'll call for a helicopter.'

As the officers and their back-up headed back towards their quads Sylvie stopped to take a panicked call from Alain. Then they sped off again with renewed urgency.

———————————

Back at her chalet, Lucy was sorting through her vast collection of beanies in anticipation of moving out. It was not an easy task: each beanie had its own unique story to tell. One had been bought with her first pay packet as a ski instructor, another was a gift from Sally, another she had worn when she visited Bern, another had been with her when she had been hiding on the Lesteraarhorn, another was a hand-me-down from Danny. It was just too difficult to part with any of them. She didn't notice the front door quietly opening.

'What have you done with my sister?' the voice said.

Lucy looked up with a start. Just a few metres away stood a ghost-like Lara Stanley, but it wasn't Lara, it was the woman in the chalet and she was clutching a long kitchen knife.

'You were spying on me,' the woman insisted. 'Did my step-daughter send you? I have seen you with her. She never liked me.'

The woman kept moving forward: Lucy fought her instinct to run onto the balcony and jump off and tried to stay calm. She looked at her phone; it was sitting on a chest of drawers behind the woman. The woman saw the direction of Lucy's glance and laughed softly.

'That won't help you now. You've already used it to tell them where to find me, haven't you?'

Lucy was wracking her brains trying to work out how to call for help. The occupants in the nearby chalets wouldn't hear her, even if they were at home – the balcony really did seem the only option. She decided she needed to stall while she thought.

'I don't know who you are,' she stammered, 'but I think you look like Lara, are you her sister?'

'Hah!' spat the stranger. 'You spy on me and say you don't know who I am, well I don't believe you. I'm sure my step-daughter has told you all about me: nothing good of course. She never did accept me, always refused to meet me. I blame her for her father turning against me.'

'I'm sorry but I don't know your step-daughter.'

'Oh don't lie to me, I have seen you, kowtowing to her and his other children, the ones I should have had!'

Lucy taught a lot of children and kowtowed to a lot of parents: she was completely mystified – and scared. This woman was clearly unstable and very dangerous.

'And you have her earrings, the same ones he bought for that other woman! They should have been mine.'

Lucy suddenly made the connection.

'You mean Tonita? You're, you're Tony Onion's second wife!'

The stranger was surprised to realise that Lucy genuinely didn't know.

'I just wanted him to come back to me, to love me like he did before,' she whined pathetically. 'He didn't even recognise me at first and then, when he did, he just looked at me with hate in his eyes. "I should have known you were behind all this!" he said. To me, the woman he once loved. He accused *me* of messing up *his* life!'

'And so you shot him?'

'I didn't mean to, I was just so hurt, the gun sort of went off.'

'That's really sad,' Lucy sympathised. 'But what does that have to do with me? Why are you here?'

'Because you have told them where I'm hiding and they'll lock me away again and I just want to stay with Lara. *And* you will tell Tonita and I'm not having that. She never acknowledged me and she must or, or …'

'Or what?' Lucy asked gently. 'You're not really a bad person, are you? You don't really want to hurt anyone else.'

The woman began to cry.

'I just want Lara. What have you done with her?'

Lucy was almost crying herself when Milly breezed in.

'Hello Orfilia!' she said brightly. 'What on earth are you doing here?'

'Who are you?' Orfilia said, staggering backwards, holding her knife out towards both women.

'Don't you remember me? I suppose I was just a kid last time you saw me. I'm Rupert and Caroline Stanford's little girl, Milly. You used to play with me and my Barbies when you and Lara came round to our farm for Sunday lunch. You were so kind to me.'

Milly chatted on about common acquaintances and places as if it was perfectly normal for them both to be standing, uninvited, in Lucy's chalet with Orfilia holding a large knife. Milly seemed almost manic the way she kept talking and talking until suddenly Lara Stanley appeared at the door.

'It's okay, darling, it's all right now, I'm here.'

She went over to her sister, took the knife from her and hugged her tightly. Milly quickly took the knife from Lara and Lucy nearly fainted with relief.

Jilly and Sylvie came in and gently led the two sisters away while Lucy and Milly collapsed on the sofa in a huge hug.

'I think, Milly, we can call it quits now.'

'Yup! Good thing I totally misread your message. I saw you wanted to go for a ski immediately and then when you weren't at the lift station I read it again and saw that you'd sent it first thing. Silly me, so as I was there anyway I skied down and thought I'd stop in to apologise for being such an airhead. But I saw her arrive just before me and I thought she was behaving a bit fishy, also she looked oddly familiar; so I listened in before I knocked.'

'Well, thank goodness you did.'

'I didn't realise who she was until you started playing for time and got her to talk. Then I made the connection and recognised her voice. The police told me to stay outside and I did until you seemed to be running out of wind, then I thought I'd better come and give you a hand. I knew they were on their way.'

'Well it was very brave of you, thanks.'

'Poor Orfilia, she was always a bit loopy. "Delicate", they used to say. We were always told to be nice to her before they came round. My parents lost touch with Lara a bit when she started travelling the world for her business and Orfilia completely dropped out of the picture. I heard she'd got married and it hadn't worked out. What a tragedy.'

'Yes, it seems like Tony Onion did a lot of damage to those who loved him.'

'Can I be part of the gang now, Lucy? I seem to be almost as good as you are for attracting trouble.'

'Oh Milly, you're already part of the gang.'

Lucy's phone buzzed.

'Alain's on his way.'

'Oh good,' Milly laughed, 'I'll put the kettle on, let's have a cup of tea before we have to give our statements.'

Lucy grinned.

'I've just had a thought … Wait till Tonita hears what her family have been up to now!'

Twenty-Six

*Death cancels our engagements, but it does not affect the
consequences of our acts in life.*
Katherine Anne Porter, 1932, Letters of Katherine Anne Porter
edited by Isabel Bayley 1990

Once Lucy and Milly had given their statements to
Blonnay and Alain, Lucy asked Alain if she could be the
one to break the unexpected resolution of her father's
murder to Tonita.

'I would love to see her face,' Lucy admitted.

'I'm afraid that's a police task and I think Blonnay was
also rather looking forward to it.'

'Oh okay.'

'I think it might be a good thing if you do come with me,
Lucy,' Laurent offered generously. 'Tonita may need a bit
of support as Sebastian's in Leicestershire. But you must
just be there as a friend, you must let us do the talking.'

When they arrived at La Grande Cour, Tonita was waiting
for them in the lobby and she showed Laurent, Jilly and
Lucy into Anya's office.

As she listened to the sad tale unfolding Tonita's
expression spoke volumes: she was appalled.

'Let me get this straight,' she said, once the bare bones of
her father's case had been put before her. 'Lara Stanley is
my father's ex-wife's sister?'

'Half-sister,' Jilly corrected, 'that's why we didn't spot the
connection, different surnames.'

Tonita paused, taking it all in.

'And Lara plotted to ruin him to punish him for what he
did to Orfilia, but Orfilia followed her to the big
confrontation, stayed behind to confront him herself and
then shot him, with my gun that Carla told them about and
Rory bought from my father so that they could frame me
for Rusty's murder which was actually an accident?'

265

'That's a pretty succinct summary,' Laurent surmised. 'We are sorry, Lady Shilton, that you should once again have been subjected to disagreeable events in Switzerland.'

'Oh, Laurent, for goodness sake, stop being so formal. You are a good friend, please don't stop calling me Tonita.'

Laurent smiled with delight. Tonita continued pensively.

'I really had forgotten that woman ever existed. I had even forgotten her name. I never knew her, or her sad story. Poor creature: meeting my father was certainly the beginning of her descent into hell. And as for him, I knew he was bad but his treatment of her is truly disgusting … I wonder, if I had agreed to meet her, accepted her, been nicer to her, things might have turned out differently.'

Seeing Tonita heading towards self-blame Lucy felt it was permissible for her to speak out.

'Tonita, don't you start punishing yourself, you do not have even the tiniest part of the blame in this. You were in your teens, looking after your mum, trying to get your career going. And history shows that your father never, ever did anything but please himself with complete disregard for the happiness of others.'

Tonita smiled her thanks at her friend's vehement defence. 'You are kinder to me, Lucy, than I deserve. Once my mother was gone, I also single-mindedly disregarded the feelings of others, as you know all too well.'

Lucy dismissed her objections with an impatient wave of her hand.

'And,' Lucy added, 'Lara and Milly both say Orfilia was mentally unstable all her life.'

'Do you have any other forgotten family members we ought to be looking out for, Tonita?' Laurent asked.

'No, Laurent, I really think that's it now.'

Blonnay and Jilly stood and took their leave.

'And so to conclude our discussion,' Laurent said to Jilly as they walked back to the police car to head back to Savigny. 'Rory was a rascal and Tony Onion a rake.'

'Yup, I concur,' Jilly smiled at him happily: he really was the cutest word-nerd.

Watching the two officers leave the hotel, Tonita smiled.

'You know what I'm thinking, Lucy?'

'No, Tonita, mind-reading is not one of my skills.'

'And yet, back there, I would have thought it was,' she said teasingly.

'Back there I could read your face.'

'Well, if I say "Poppy's prediction", does that take you any closer?'

'Ah yes … justice!'

'Justice. She said this was leading towards my father finally getting his come-uppance and she was so right: his past sins finally caught up with him. But oh, that poor woman!'

'She'll be okay, she won't go to prison, Alain says she'll probably just go back to one of those luxury "secure homes" that Lara pays for and Lara will probably get off lightly too.'

'I guess so. And now I have to work out how to get $40 million back to Anwar's people without too much fuss.'

'I think you know the right person to help you sort that out.'

Tonita smiled.

'I'd better call Sebastian. Wait till he hears about this one.'

Lucy gave her a hug and left Tonita to call her husband. She headed over to Anne's where she knew Alain was waiting for her.

'Please don't ask me,' she said later as Alain enquired how she just happened to see Orfilia Frank in her chalet hideaway, 'you would be turning me into a bad person: either I have to lie to you or break a promise to someone else.'

'I won't insist,' he said, 'but it was a lucky break, you just happening to pass by the woman's door as she opened it.'

Lucy squirmed and changed the subject.

'How sad,' she said, 'all this caused by that horrible man.'

'And a vengeful sister, don't forget. If Lara Stanley had concentrated on looking after her sister instead of being her avenging angel, everyone would still be alive and well.'

'Except for Rusty.'

'Except for Rusty.'

Poppy, Johnny and Humphrey were having a drink in Le Bar des Deux Moines and their conversation had naturally turned into a post-case review.

'Interesting, isn't it?' Poppy remarked. 'Lucy, confronted by the wolf, dons her helmet, prepares for battle and takes a photo for posterity. Rory, who I seem to remember, accused Lucy of being a scaredy-cat, finding himself in the same situation, runs for it and falls off a cliff.'

'So,' asked Johnny, 'what's your point?'

'I'm not sure,' she grinned.

'I know,' said Humphrey. 'What you mean is that true courage is not actively seeking out danger but how you react when danger comes looking for you.'

'EX-ACT-LY,' Poppy beamed at Humphrey.

Humphrey beamed at himself.

Johnny groaned.

'You knew it was going to cause sparks when you introduced Rory and Alessandra? But even you can't have foreseen this. You should be ashamed of yourself!' Johnny teased Humphrey.

'It is true,' Humphrey chuckled, 'that that particular piece of matchmaking delivered well beyond my expectations! But I am not the slightest bit ashamed. On the contrary I thought Alessandra could do with a bit of fun and she certainly had that. My actions didn't lead to anyone getting hurt or murdered.'

'Only just,' Johnny wagged a finger at him. 'The collateral damage isn't minor. Madness and a broken heart.'

'Oh rubbish, Rory was barking already and Alessandra will soon get over it.'

'I agree. Personally, I'm a bit jealous: I would have done exactly the same as Alessandra if I'd had the chance,' Poppy exclaimed.

'Really?' asked Humphrey.

'Really.'

Johnny nodded. 'Poppy's convinced our Grondère Casanova had special powers in the bedroom.'

'I suspect she's right,' Humphrey laughed.

Poppy, unrepentant, grinned.

'Ah well, I can only speculate. Men like Rory don't enter my sphere often. I will miss him.'

'Yes, we all will,' agreed Humphrey.

Johnny nodded and raised his glass, 'To Rory,' he said. 'Fucking legend.'

Twenty-Seven

I refuse to believe that you cannot be both compassionate and strong.

Jacinda Ardern

Tonita called an extraordinary board meeting. Sebastian flew over to attend in an advisory capacity but it was Tonita who, reminding her co-board members of her majority interest, took the chair. She did not fail to remind them in her opening remarks that it was she who had advised caution on the involvement of Ruaidrí Investments Cayman LLC and that this time she would not be ignored.

There were calls for the immediate dismissal of Alessandra Rosset. Tonita let them rumble on for a few minutes and then called them back to order.

'Ladies and gentlemen,' she said firmly.

Humphrey sat in the front row with a huge grin on his face. He was relishing every second of the chaos. Tonita looked at him, raised her eyebrows and carried on. She was not going to let Humphrey distract her.

'Mme Rosset has made a serious error of judgement and has put us on the wrong side of the law but the situation is not irreversible: we can reimburse the bad money and we can still pursue the Colline development although I think we must either delay or partially scale it back.'

There were murmurs of agreement.

'However,' Tonita continued, 'despite Mme Rosset's error she is not a criminal and I believe that she continues to be the right person to take the White Snowflake consortium forward. No doubt if this were a public company, she would have to go but we are not a public company and I think she will be more cautious in the future.'

There were noises of incredulity and resistance. Sebastian spoke.

'I am not a shareholder, but my father did set up this project and I am convinced Tonita is right. If you curb Mme Rosset's absolute authority, establish a committee to do due diligence on all incoming investors and review all major expenditure, then I also think she is still the best person for the job.'

Between them Tonita and Sebastian eventually convinced the board to let Alessandra keep her job. Sebastian sweetened them further by proposing fresh investment from Shilton Holdings.

'As long as it's made clear to her that if she oversteps the mark again, she's out,' the shareholders eventually agreed.

'Oh, I think you can rely on Lady Shilton to convey the message,' Sebastian said, smiling at Tonita as he did so.

'Count on me,' she assured her board.

As the board members drifted out of the meeting room, with Humphrey making an elaborate bow in her direction, Sebastian whispered to her, 'Try not to enjoy it too much.' Tonita grinned back.

'Can't promise you that.'

Alessandra was waiting for Tonita in a smaller meeting room.

'Are you my executioner?' she asked as Tonita entered.

Tonita poured herself a glass of water before replying.

'There is a stay of execution, Alessandra. If you would like to remain as chairperson of White Snowflake and, if you will agree to certain changes in the decision-making process and a few other small conditions, then we would like you to stay.'

'To stay?' This was unexpected. While she had been sitting waiting, Alessandra had been working out a damage-limitation strategy to confront the media fallout which would necessarily result from the loss of such a prestigious and visible position.

Tonita outlined the conditions agreed upon by the board which Alessandra had no problem agreeing to. She even admitted that it would be good for her personally to have some formal due diligence and compliance procedures in place.

'But how did this come about? I thought the board members wanted my head.'

'They did. Sebastian and I spent a lot of time reminding them how profitable the consortium had been since you took the helm and that, apart from this hiccup, we have all had considerably little to do for our returns.' She grinned. 'I also pointed out that, if we did ask you to leave, our personal workloads would increase considerably until we had found someone to replace you, and that I personally had no idea who that person could possibly be.'

'You are a good negotiator, Tonita. But why would you and Sebastian do that for me? You do not like me.'

'True, I don't much like you, Alessandra. But I do respect your abilities and maybe, over time, we can learn to like one another. After all,' she hesitated, thinking how she herself had changed and how Lucy and Poppy had grown to like her, 'everyone deserves a second chance, don't you think?'

Alessandra nodded, astounded at this unexpected reversal of fortune. Tonita then issued her final ultimatum.

'But, before you agree, I have some conditions of my own.'

Ah, thought Alessandra, so there is a catch. But as Tonita named her terms, she was puzzled.

'Is that it?'

'That is it.'

'I can do that.'

'Good.'

Tonita stood to leave and said the words Sebastian had advised her to say, even though it went against her nature. 'Let's try and stay in better touch, Alessandra, be better partners.'

They shook hands and Tonita stood to leave, but it was stronger than her, she couldn't deny herself a parting shot, 'I hope he was worth it.'

She smiled and left Alessandra to ponder as to whether her fling with Rory had been worth the humiliation of having to yield to Tonita's will.

Humphrey had arranged to meet Poppy in Sammy's wine bar, La Grappe d'Or. She was intrigued to know the reason for her summons: she and Humphrey normally only met by chance.

'There's someone I understand you wish to meet, Poppy,' he began. He did not need to continue for at that moment Alessandra Rosset appeared, straight from her meeting with Tonita as he had requested. She was looking decidedly drained and bad-tempered. She looked at Poppy with undisguised disappointment.

'I thought you said you were buying me a drink over a debriefing, Humphrey, you didn't mention anyone else.'

'Oh, I am buying both of you a drink,' Humphrey said gesturing to the bucket of champagne on the table. 'I don't need a debriefing, I was at the board meeting. I don't believe you have ever met Poppy. She's a bit of a fan of yours.'

'Really?' Alessandra looked cynical but shook hands with Poppy reluctantly and sank into the nearest chair.

'If it's for another moral lecture, I've already had one, thanks, and it was quite enough.'

'Oh, I don't think Poppy's one to preach morality, quite the contrary, I think you will find in her a bit of a kindred spirit. I'll leave you ladies to it, Sammy has been told to keep the champagne coming.' Humphrey winked and left.

'Aren't you a friend of Tonita's? I remember, you did the reading at the wedding,' Alessandra asked suspiciously.

Alessandra was puzzled. How could she and this older woman possibly have anything in common? They clearly didn't move in the same circles.

'I am a friend of Tonita's,' Poppy confirmed, 'I'm not quite sure what Humphrey is expecting me to say to you, but I am not as strait-laced as my younger friends, in fact I'm rather jealous.'

'Jealous?'

'If I had been younger and capable of attracting Rory I would not have hesitated.'

Alessandra wrinkled her brow and then laughed.

'You must be the only person in town.'

'Now, maybe. But then people are quick to change their views with hindsight.'

Alessandra took a gulp of champagne and shrewdly assessed the woman opposite her.

'You do not think me a bad judge of character?'

'No, I think you probably knew Rory was a bad lot, we all did, maybe not as bad as he turned out. But I don't think you were really concerned about his character, I think you were looking for excitement and were attracted to that dangerous side in him.'

Alessandra looked at Poppy appraisingly. Poppy's eyes sparkled with mischief and Alessandra realised that she was in the company of a woman who understood the pleasure of giving into temptation. She saw she could trust

Poppy: after all, Humphrey's last introduction had proved worthwhile.

'You are probably right, but it nearly cost me very dear.'

'I'm sure.'

'It will be difficult to find someone to match Rory,' she avowed.

They made for an odd pair: one of Grondère's most materialistic residents, sitting and laughing with its one of its least. Alessandra told Poppy of the good things about her affair with Rory and Poppy found the words to console her whilst enjoying every detail. After two bottles of champagne, Poppy felt she had been right about Rory, and Alessandra felt completely vindicated about having loved him.

'Thank you, Poppy,' she said, shaking her hand heartily as they bid one another good night. 'I was feeling foolish and wicked and now I just feel wicked, which is much better.'

'My pleasure,' replied Poppy. 'I hope we meet again.'

'I hope so too,' said Alessandra, and she meant it, it was as if Poppy had miraculously lifted a guilty load from her shoulders.

Sammy came to clear the glasses away as Poppy was gathering her belongings.

'Looks like you two got on like a house on fire. What on earth did you find to talk about with her?'

'Just girl talk, Sammy, just girl talk.'

With this, Poppy waltzed off, leaving him scratching his head.

Alessandra took the lift up to her apartment feeling much happier and less battered and bruised than when she had left Tonita a few hours earlier. Now she started to look forward. She began to cheer up at the idea that the price Tonita had exacted for keeping her position in the consortium was not that high considering the pleasure she had obtained in risking it. Oh Humphrey, you old rogue, she thought, you knew exactly what you were doing introducing me to Rory and now Poppy.

Suddenly, she knew she had the answer to Tonita's question. Yes, she thought, with a broad smile on her face; Rory had definitely been worth it.

Prince Anwar returned to Grondère to meet with Tonita. She greeted him warmly on his arrival and took him into the same meeting room in La Grande Cour in which she had recently dealt with such alacrity with Alessandra Rosset. He thanked her for having organised the speedy return of his government's money.

'I hope we can remain friends,' she said.

'I am relieved you feel that way,' he replied.

'I thought you were very fair in the circumstances, I'm just so sorry that it was my father who caused all of this.'

'You are blameless, Tonita. I was worried you would resent my putting you under the pressure, but I had to make sure he didn't use you and the children to escape justice.'

'Well, he certainly didn't do that.'

'No.'

'And the children's mother?'

'She will be free to leave our country, in fact we desire it. She has been well treated but she has undergone a big shock, she is not well, I fear. But she doesn't seem to have any family or friends to go to.'

'She can come to us, for the children's sake, and mine – I have grown used to having them with me. I have discussed it with Sebastian and, with the only claimant to the position of dowager being in prison, we will put her in the Dower house. I cannot have her living with me.'

'I understand. It is very good of you and Sebastian. Being with her children will heal her.'

'I hope so. I'm taking them out of boarding school, the local day school is excellent and then she will have something to occupy her every day rather than spending money in your shiny shopping centres.'

He grinned at her.

'If I may, I'd like to return to the issue of the missing money …'

'Ah yes, the missing 10 million. I'm sorry, I don't have the rest of your money.'

Prince Anwar took a pouch from his pocket and emptied hundreds of diamonds onto the dark polished surface of the meeting room table.

'These have been restored to me by the Swiss authorities.'

Tonita gasped. There was a mix of cut and uncut diamonds of the highest quality. She held some of them up to the light and admired their beauty.

'I was wondering,' he continued, 'if you could help me with these. I cannot be seen to be trading illegal diamonds. Can you use them?'

'Oh, I can't use unsourced diamonds either, it's more than my reputation is worth. Especially if this story gets out.'

The Swiss police had done an outstanding job of keeping her name out of the press and, more importantly, away from the British tabloids.

'But, from your time in Amsterdam, you must know who will.' He looked at her astutely.

She hesitated. 'I do but I would not wish to be seen dealing with them either.' She gasped: she had suddenly remembered where she had come across Rory in the past. He had been pointed out to her at a jewellery conference in Amsterdam as someone useful if you were looking for cheap gems. She had at the time dismissed the information as it was a dangerous path to tread and she did not want to risk jeopardising her promising career. No wonder the man had given her the creeps. Still, the memory came too late now, to be useful to anyone.

'You must know someone who could conduct such a transaction on our behalf,' Anwar continued. Tonita was puzzled.

'Our behalf?'

'My government has authorised me to leave the money here in Switzerland to be used for charitable purposes and I am hoping that you can also help me set up a foundation.'

'That's very decent of your government. In that case, I know a couple of rough diamonds who might be up for it.'

Twenty-Eight

Weep if you must, Parting is Hell
But life goes on, So sing as well.
                    Joyce Grenfell, If I Should Go

'Poppy, I need your opinion on something.'
Tonita caught Poppy's arm when she brought the children
back from climbing and dragged her into a meeting room.
On the table sat a large plastic urn, standard issue from the
Savigny funeral parlour.
'Ah,' said Poppy.
'Quite! The *Police judiciaire* haven't let me off that
lightly, they decided it was more convenient to deliver my
father's remains here than work out where they belong.'
'Which is where?'
'Frankly, if it weren't for Ruby and Leo, I would flush him
down the loo. I'm not prepared to do all the paperwork to
transport them back to the UK and, to be honest, I don't
want them there anyway. I just want rid of them quickly, I
also don't want it becoming a big issue with his wife
expecting to have her say. She's in no state anyway
apparently. So what on earth do I do?'
'So to summarise, we're looking for a quick, clean
solution where you pay him the appropriate but minimum
level of respect with the least possible inconvenience to
yourself?'
'Exactly.' Tonita smiled: she loved being able to just be
herself with Poppy without faking emotions she didn't
possess.
'We could just take them up into the mountains and scatter
them to the four winds?'
'I thought of that, but I don't think he deserves that honour
and I don't like the idea of him floating around on the ether

279

in a place that the children and I will be constantly skiing and wandering around in.'

'Yes, I agree, the mountains are too special for your father. How about just paying for a spot in the remembrance garden at the church in Pattier. I'm sure they'd be happy for a donation to the church roof.'

'I don't want any official physical signs or documents that link him back to me. The press might go snooping around and jumping to false conclusions.'

'Or correct ones.'

'Or correct ones. But I do want the children, and, eventually their mother, to have a place they can go to feel close to him if they need to.'

'Then I think you should ask them.'

'I'm not sure they're ready for that.'

'I think you underestimate them. They're much more savvy than you realise. And he's their father too, remember. They might resent you for making that decision for them.'

Tonita went and brought the children in.

Ruby and Leo looked at the little urn with great curiosity.

'Is he really in there? All of him?' Leo asked.

'Yes, I think so,' Tonita replied.

'Can I lift it?'

'Yes.'

'It's very heavy.'

'I think most of the coffin is in there too.'

'Ah,' the little boy nodded.

'Was our dad very wicked?' Ruby asked.

'Yes, very.'

'As wicked as Marmion?'

'Marmion! Honestly Ruby, first Tennyson, now Sir Walter Scott, how *old* is your English teacher?'

Ruby looked at Poppy as a point of comparison.

'I reckon Miss Hunter must be a hundred. Her hair's the same colour as Poppy's and Poppy is at least 70 – she told me. But Miss Hunter has more wrinkles and, no way could she go up a climbing wall, so she must be much older.'

'Thanks Ruby,' Poppy stuck her tongue out at her. 'But as I am now fully retired and your Miss Hunter is clearly still endeavouring to educate the youth of Britain, I can only surmise that she is a little younger than me, but thank you for the compliment,'

Ruby stuck her tongue out too and then turned back to Tonita.

'You didn't answer my question.'

Tonita shrugged; Poppy had said she should be honest with the children, so she would give it a go.

'I was a bit surprised by your question, Ruby, but yes, the more I think about it, the more I think the comparison is a good one. Our father was ambitious and greedy and hurt other people to get what he wanted.'

Ruby seemed to appreciate the truth and nodded.

'Like your mum and the wolf lady.'

'Yes, especially the wolf lady.'

'Will the wolf lady go to prison?' Leo asked.

'No, she will go to a safe home where people will be kind to her but never let her out again.'

'And our dad got what he deserved, just like Marmion?'

'Indeed.'

Tonita hadn't realised how many questions they had; Poppy had been right. But she realised she needed to be honest in every respect, positive as well as negative.

'But however wicked our father was, I want you both to know that he really did love you and your mum. The police told me that, while he was hiding, he did everything he could to try and sort things out so you could all be together again.'

She looked at the children to make sure this information had gone in. It had. They looked at her earnestly and she knew it was important to them.

'The police also brought me back these.' She held up the gold grape earrings and pendant that Orfilia had taken from Tony Onion's pocket on the night she killed him. 'He bought my jewellery for your mother but the wolf lady stole them. I thought, when your mother arrives in England, you could deliver them for him.'

The children agreed.

'That means he loved you too, doesn't it, Tonita? He wanted Mum to wear something of you.'

'I hadn't thought of it that way, but yes, thank you. I think you're right.'

Tonita suddenly realised why she had felt so sad at her father's death. Ruby had provided her with the answer, she had resented him so much for his treatment of her mother that she had rejected all his attempts, however weak, to build some sort of relationship. Suddenly the gloom lifted. However wicked he was, like Ruby and Leo she had still needed to know he loved her and, in his own warped way, she saw that he had.

Leo brought her back to the matter in hand.

'Dad didn't really belong anywhere, did he? Can't we just put him back where they found him?'

'I like your practicality, Leo, but no, I think we might draw comment if we buried his ashes under the White Snowflake carpark.'

Leo grinned.

'What did they do with Marmion, Ruby?' Poppy asked. 'It's a long time since I read Marmion.'

'He got muddled up with someone else who got the big fancy tomb and he was buried where he fell, in a nameless grave, on a hill by a little stream.'

Ruby turned to Tonita with a big grin.

'That's it! We know a little stream on a hill, where no one but us will ever know he's there.'

Tonita beamed back.

'The vineyard! Ruby, that's brilliant!'

The next day, after school, Tonita and the children went down to the vineyard with Poppy and Lucy and buried Tony Onion's ashes in a little plot Sally and Sandra had prepared in the vineyard's Japanese garden. It was a beautiful shady spot with a waterfall and a deep green pool surrounded with Japanese maples. To mark the spot, they laid a large stone on which Tonita had painted a mediæval helmet, a shield adorned with a small onion and, written below, Marmion's motto, *Who checks at me, to death is dight*.

Once again it had been Ruby's idea.

'What does it mean?' Leo had asked.

'Miss Hunter said it means *Get in my way and you're dead!*' Ruby replied promptly.

'It's great!' Leo had grinned. 'Can we have that?'

'I am developing great respect for your Miss Hunter,' Tonita had smiled.

What better tribute to a man who, however wicked, had played such a big role in their lives.

'Well done,' Poppy said to her later. 'You came through that with flying colours!'

'Thanks, Poppy. You were right, they are amazing little human beings, aren't they? Who'd have thought they'd come out with all that stuff?'

'In all my years of teaching children to ski, if I have learnt one thing, it's that children always have something to teach you back.'

'Well, now that you have helped me resolve that little difficulty, there is another matter I need your help on.'

'Ah yes?' Poppy was intrigued. What Tonita was about to ask of her next was even more unexpected.

'By the way, what happened to Rusty's body?' Lucy asked Alain that evening.

'What little family we could contact didn't seem interested. Alessandra Rosset has offered to pay for his ashes to be placed in the memorial garden at the church in Pattier,' he replied.

'That's very decent of her.'

'I guess.'

'Why would she do that? She didn't ever meet him and she didn't have anything to do with his death.'

'No, but Rory did. He didn't push Rusty off the mountain but he did indirectly cause his death by taking him up a route beyond his ability.'

'I see. But that still doesn't really explain it.'

'No. I agree.'

'I'll ask Poppy.'

'Poppy?'

'Yes. She and Alessandra are new bezzies.'

'You are kidding.'

'Well, overstating it perhaps, but apparently Humphrey introduced them.'

'Oh dear. Humphrey and his "introductions": there should be a law against them.'

'I don't think it would be fair to stop Humphrey causing mischief, he's so terribly good at it. Anyway, apparently he has scored again. Alessandra is going to support Poppy with this new charity. Give her office space and equipment in the White Snowflake complex.'

'I look forward to hearing how that pans out,' Alain grinned. 'Especially as I hear Johnny is also on the committee.'

Lucy just smiled.

'What are you thinking now?'

'You might scoff but I am very grateful to Poppy and Johnny for warning me not to let Rory lead me into trouble on the mountain.'

'They did that?'

'Yes. I get what they were trying to tell me now: skiing is not about seeking adventure, it is an adventure in itself. Skiing is not about taking calculated risks, it's about calculating and not taking risks.'

'That pair have their own unique brand of wisdom.'

'Don't they just.'

The following day Tonita and the children left for Leicestershire. Tonita, missing Sebastian, wanted to be at Lunstag Hall to prepare for the birth of her first child and Angelica, Ruby and Leo's mother, was due to arrive from Dubai.

'I don't know how that's going to work out,' Tonita had joked. 'My father's wife appears to have relied entirely on her beauty to see her through life. Before all this happened, she spent her days wafting around climatised shopping centres and visiting beauty parlours. I'm not sure how she's going to take to being a single mum in the Murky Midlands.'

'A single mum in a dower house. Come on, how hard can that be? Let's hope she realises how lucky she is to have such a kind step-daughter,' Lucy laughed.

Tonita rolled her eyes.

'We all know, that if it weren't for the children I would have left her to the wolves.'

'No you wouldn't!' Poppy protested.

'I'm sorry to disappoint you but I'm not that reformed a character: *Yes. I. Would.*'

Lucy and Poppy laughed and hugged Tonita tightly as the children appeared, laden with various games and activities for the journey.

'Good luck with the baby,' Lucy smiled. 'Make sure Sebastian sends a message as soon as he can.'

'I promise,' she smiled. 'Thank goodness Alain and his team wrapped this all up before my due date. I can't imagine the Shilton heir being born in Grondère instead of Leicestershire.'

'Nothing would surprise me after this past year,' Poppy joked.

'Really, Poppy?' Tonita raised her eyebrows. 'I'm willing to make a wager that, even at your grand old age, you are about to be surprised,' she said cryptically.

Poppy looked at Ruby and Leo but they just shrugged their shoulders. Leo twisted his forefinger against his forehead. 'She's going a bit crazy lately. We reckon it's the baby coming.'

'We'd better hurry home quickly then,' Tonita joked, 'before I go totally loco.'

The trio bundled into the car and waved goodbye.

'What a lovely family they've become. Next time we see them, there'll be one more for you to teach to ski,' Poppy said fondly.

'It is incredible though, when you think back to when we first knew Tonita, she was so aloof and cold. Now look at her.'

'Yes, surrounded by little ones and happy as a lark.'

'So, in a roundabout way, her dad did eventually bring her happiness.'

'I guess you could look at it like that. I personally think a lot of the credit should go to you and me. I'll tell you something else.'

'What's that?'

'That woman is up to something. Mark my words.'

As she sat in the car and watched Grondère recede into the background Tonita smiled and shook her head. Good old Grondère, she thought to herself, always seems to deliver a little bit more than the average ski trip.

Later that same day Lucy had an appointment with her friend Anya, the manager of La Grande Cour hotel. In her final year of studying for her mid-mountain guide diploma she wanted to pitch an idea for drumming up custom. Her idea was a hike called 'secluded glades and hidden treasures – a forest trail' that she had designed herself the previous summer, which would take visiting walkers off the beaten track and show them some lesser-known places and rarer plants. The wealthy clients staying at the hotel would also enjoy a luxury picnic and go home with some of Lucy's dried Alpine herbs and sloe gin.

Lucy had studied marketing at university and so her presentation was slick and professional. Anya loved the idea and said that if Lucy got some cards printed and a little flyer about the walk, she would be happy to promote it to the hotel's clients.

But the meeting gave Anya another idea. She asked Lucy to wait, went into another room and called Sebastian McDonaghue.

'It was a really good presentation,' she told him. 'Lucy has some fresh ideas and creativity. It got me thinking. We still haven't found anyone to replace Sandy Jennings.'

Sebastian remembered the previous marketing manager who had defected to work for Alessandra Rosset, only to be fired by Alessandra for failing to damage the reputation of La Grande Cour.

'Yes, by all means, ask her if you think she's up to it, but do you think Lucy would want such a job? She seems so much of a free spirit to me.'

'I don't know. Most seasonnaires dream of a stable job. She only need work 50 per cent. That would leave her plenty of time to wander the mountains and still teach skiing if she wants.'

Lucy couldn't quite believe her luck when Anya asked her. 'Are you sure? I mean, I have no actual experience, just theory.'

'I had no experience when I took over the hotel, remember? And, at the moment, *I'm* doing the marketing which I never studied at all: you did, and it wasn't so long ago, a quick bit of revision and you'll be up to date.'

Lucy remembered how Anya had only been the spa manager when Malcolm, Sebastian's father, had been murdered, leaving a vacancy.

'And what about working with friends? I'd hate to fall out with you, or Sebastian and Tonita.'

'As for working with friends, I have to leave you to think about that but let me make it clear, you would be working for me, not Sebastian – I am the manager here. He and I are very clear on that. He is my sounding board but as long as things are running smoothly, which of course they always are,' she added with that classic brand of Swedish honesty which scorns false modesty, 'I'm in sole charge. But Lucy, Grondère is a small place, it's hard not to work with friends here.'

Lucy had to admit that was true; Milly worked in the same ski school as her and she was also pretty friendly with her boss, Melanie.

'Think about it,' Anya said, 'I only need you to work 50 per cent. and you don't need to be in the office unless you have meetings, you can do most of it from home. That gives you flexi time and leaves you loads of time to guide in the summer and teach skiing in the winter if you want to.'

'Anya, I don't need to think about it, it's a dream come true for any ski bum. A stable year-round income with time to ski.'

'Well, let's give it a try. I can wait until the end of May, if you start in June then you can settle in during the slow season and I will have time to do a proper handover.'

Lucy left La Grande Cour skipping. She called Alain and then stopped by at Anne Dupertuis's flat which was just round the corner to tell her the good news. Her next action was to buy a bottle of Swiss fake champagne to take home to her housemates.

Champagne, Tommy had once told her, was 'not just for celebrations, but also the appropriate treatment for depression, emotional shock and exhaustion.'

Well tonight, she told herself, we're in celebration mode!

As Tommy was about to launch into his new life of full-time farming he wanted to introduce all his friends to his new world. One morning, Christophe, his partner, drove up to Grondère in the farm pick-up and Lucy, Milly (for whom this was also a new experience), Eddie, Poppy and Sally all piled onto some hay bales in the open back of the truck. Tommy rode up front with Christophe.

'Is this legal?' Milly asked as they all let their hair fly in the wind and sipped on bottles of beer as they slid around the hairpin bends down the hill to Pattier.

'Probably not but fortunately Switzerland isn't yet in the stranglehold of health and safety ridiculousness you find in other countries. They'd have a problem applying it in Valais anyway,' Poppy shouted.

'Cheers to that! A country that still lets us decide for ourselves,' agreed Sally, whose Australian dislike of authority was not dissimilar to that of her adopted home.

The local municipal police confirmed Poppy's words by beaming at the rowdy group in the back of the pick-up and waving them towards the parking field without the slightest sign of disapproval. As they parked, Lucy could see why: it was a world so different to the international community of Grondère. The trucks and farm vehicles already in the field were parked in between trees, under which stood groups of black cows enjoying the shade. Local people milled about, chatting to one another, admiring the cows, tapping the hinds of the animals with one hand and holding a bottle of beer or, in some cases, a bottle of wine, in the other. It was perfectly ordered without anyone giving orders: everyone knew their place and no policeman would have dared enter this sacred world of Swiss farmers and their cows.

The friends also wandered around admiring the cows and dodging their pats whose diarrhoeal nature indicated that the animals were as nervous and excited as their proud owners. As Christophe went from group to group, dragging Tommy with him to be introduced and looked over, much in the same way as a fine Herens cow, the locals scratched their heads in puzzled wonderment. They were used to foreigners coming to the cow fights, they were used to wealthy foreigners buying prize cows too and paying them to look after them, but none of them had ever come across an Englishman who had actually joined their ranks. However, as they all knew – for there were no secrets in the long, narrow valley of Grondère – that Tommy was joining forces with Christophe who would otherwise have been obliged to sell his family farm like too many of the old families, they were willing to give the young fella a chance and greeted him with kindness, wry smiles and a little scepticism.

Below the cow and vehicle parking field, a huge auditorium, making use of the natural incline of the steep slope, had been carved into the hillside with stepped rows of wooden seating. The party found a spot high up so that they could watch not only the cows in the ring but all the surrounding activity and colour. They spread out over two rows so that they could easily share the conversation and refreshments. Hosts Tommy and Christophe had thought of everything and served up wine, beer, local cheeses and dried meats and they all sat together, selecting their cows and betting amongst themselves. Selecting your cow was not an easy task: muscle alone was no guide. It depended, like any contest of strength, on stamina, courage and determination. The character of the cow was decisive but, apart from Christophe, none of the friends had a clue. Lucy went by numbers that had a significance for her, Sally by appearance and Poppy tried to judge their attitude as the cows entered the ring. Milly was getting inside information from Christophe but was sneakily cross-referencing their names in the pamphlet and picking the most appealing name.

Tommy shook his head in despair.

'It's as good a method as any,' Poppy said. 'For all the years I've been coming to the cow fights, I have never known anyone pick the winner.'

'It's true,' Christophe backed her up. 'Even the experts get it wrong. You just cannot measure that element of stubbornness that makes a real *reine*.'

'No cows in the competition this year, Christophe?' Poppy asked.

'Not this year, I have had too many other things on my mind,' he answered, 'but maybe, next year, we could start with a *génisse*, n'est-ce pas, Tommy?'

'*Absolument*!' Tommy said with conviction. 'We need to show all those old guys we just met that I am not the lightweight they think. They reckon I don't know that the real contest is up on the mountains, but that's where we'll show them we mean business.'

Sally and Lucy smiled knowingly at one another. Tommy was happy which made them happy.

'Is a *génisse* a heifer?' Milly asked.

'Yes,' Tommy said. 'The youngsters fought yesterday. These are the *reines*.'

They all watched on as the glossy black Herens cows were brought together, locked horns and dug in their hind quarters to see which was the strongest. In the early stages of the contest the combats could be over in seconds but, as they weeded out the cows that didn't have the strength (or, as was sometimes the case, the heart) for the fight, the combats began to take longer, with the two cows sometimes immobile for long periods. Lucy looked around at her friends: Christophe was also looking happy – Milly had slid her hand into his and he was gently squeezing it and grinning from ear to ear.

How wonderful, Lucy thought, suddenly feeling a bit left out and wishing that Alain was with her. She wasn't quite sure why he wasn't. He had been behaving oddly recently; even when they were together she sensed he was thinking of something (or someone) else. That morning he had made some lame excuse about having some work to do. As his case was over, and he was such an awful liar, she knew it wasn't true. She hoped it wasn't her friends he was avoiding, or worse, her. They were supposed to be moving in together in a few days and, if he was having doubts, she would rather know before their lives were too entangled.

But Lucy was not one to let any sadness or doubts clouding her mind ruin everyone's day. She shrugged off her fears, smiled and joined in the fun, just in time to cheer her cow chasing Sally's out of the ring.

Twenty-Nine

You're never safe from being surprised until you're dead.
        L.M. Montgomery, Anne of Avonlea

It was the last day of April, the rental contract for the little chalet on the Colline had come to an end and it was time for the friends to move out of the little chalet they had grown so fond of. Tommy and Sally had moved out the previous week with the predictable amount of noise and emotion. Eddie had moved out the day before to set up a base with Émilie and her family. They wouldn't be there much: Émilie and Eddie would be away most of the following winter, he had given up his job to become her agent/secretary and 'mobile support unit' as he jokingly called it. Lucy realised that she wouldn't see much of them for the next few years, but that, once Émilie's ski career was over, they would probably return to Grondère and take over her parents' business.

And so it was that Lucy would be the last to leave their little home.

That morning she sat on her cases waiting for Alain to come and get her in his car. She was still a little worried but he had shown no signs of wanting to change their plans so she hoped that whatever had been bothering him had been resolved. She looked around gloomily: the place seemed bigger without her housemates. They had been told not to bother cleaning as the place would soon be bulldozed, but they had anyway, of course: Tommy had insisted they leave it in a Swiss standard of spotlessness. Out of the window she looked at the neighbouring chalets, all of a similar style and period, a bit ramshackle and worn out, but remnants of a quieter, humbler world. She sighed and went out onto the balcony for one last look. Alain's car pulled up in the parking space at the top of the steep steps. She waved as he ambled down them.

What a fool I am, she told herself, look forward, not back, Lucy.

Entering the chalet, however, Alain seemed in no hurry to leave.

In fact, he had brought an electronic measuring device with him and he started measuring the inside walls and noting them down on his phone.

'What on earth are you doing?' she asked, thinking he had gone slightly mad.

'If I am to start renovations, I need to start ordering materials,' he replied blithely.

'Renovations?'

'Yes, my little *rossignol*, if we are to move in next winter, we have a lot of work to do.'

She now looked at him in a state of wonderment. He laughed.

'I'll stop teasing you. It's ours, Lucy, forever.'

'But I don't understand. What about White Snowflake?'

'After the "Rory" incident, Tonita decided to flex her muscles as principal shareholder. In return for Alessandra Rosset retaining her position as chairman of the consortium, Tonita imposed certain conditions.'

'I'm still lost.'

'Apparently Rory said something to Tonita that made her have a closer look at the plans and she didn't like them. The Colline development has been redesigned to remain more in keeping with its original character: there will be fewer chalets on larger plots and, whilst they'll be luxurious, they will be smaller, traditional and less ostentatious. This chalet has been carved out of the development and will be sold to you and to me on extremely favourable terms, provided that we renovate the building in keeping with the architecture of the new development, which, having seen it, will not be a problem. I hope you don't mind me having taken such a major and presumptive step without consulting you, but Tonita was adamant it was to be a complete surprise.'

'It's certainly that. But, but … how am I ever going to be able to afford it?'

'Oh, I forgot to mention that the chalet's purchase price seems remarkably closer to the one it must have fetched in the nineteen sixties than the value of the land at today's prices.'

He grinned. 'I'm sure your share of the mortgage will be perfectly affordable for you on your new salary at the hotel. Besides, I have spoken to M. Darbellay, the best bank manager in the world, and he has told me it will.'

Lucy was absolutely lost for words. Overcome by a wave of happiness she burst into tears. Familiar with Lucy's reaction to excess joy, Alain hugged her until she stopped gasping for breath and could find the words, in between kisses, to assure him of her complete approval of his secret transactions.

'So that's what you've been up to, you wonderful man. I wondered what all the subterfuge was for. But is it legal?' she asked. 'How can the consortium sell us the land at a price below its true value?'

'Apparently all the board members and investors have cleared it. It seems that when Tonita decides she wants something she is a force to be reckoned with. Oh, and she has purchased the next-door chalet herself so that she and Sebastian no longer have to squat rooms in the hotel when they are here. So we'll be neighbours. And I have strict instructions to build you a window seat.'

Lucy gasped.

'Fancy her remembering that!'

The previous autumn, when they had all been in hiding at the top of the Lesteraarhorn, they had discussed what they would buy if they were rich. Lucy had said she would like her own home in the mountains with a window seat.

And so, instead of loading Lucy's belongings into the car, they unloaded a couple of suitcases Alain had brought containing his belongings. They would stay in the little chalet together until the late snow had melted and the conditions around Alain's place were more favourable.

As they settled into the room Tommy and Sally had been sharing she had another thought.

'Isn't it a bit greedy,' she asked, 'having two homes on the same mountain?'

'I don't think so,' Alain replied. 'We're just carrying on the traditional mountain practice of transhumance. Besides,' he added, 'Tonita has asked if, once I have converted the place as beautifully as I did the Nid des Rossignols, she can rent it in the summer for her step-mother, Ruby and Leo. She has an aversion, it would seem, to having Angelica under the same roof.'

'Yes, she does. Oh that's a great idea, but we couldn't take her money.'

'So I told her.'

'Good.' She went silent and Alain knew she was thinking of something else.

'Now what?' he asked.

'I was just remembering when we were on the Lesteraarhorn and we were all saying what we would buy if we were rich. I mentioned the home and the window seat and Poppy said what she would buy if she could afford it. I wonder if Tonita has also remembered that.'

———————————————

At the same time that Lucy had been sitting in her chalet, waiting for Alain, Poppy's doorbell had rung. She wasn't expecting anyone and she wasn't keen on unannounced visitors. The last time someone had turned up uninvited it had been the previous spring, when the Swiss police came to inform her they were re-opening the Genna Hobbs-Davison case.

Surely they can't have found any more bodies, she thought, apprehensively opening the door.

'Hello,' said a sweet-faced young man. 'I'm Daniel Yeomans.'

'Yes, now that you mention it, I recognise you,' Poppy replied. She was so flabbergasted to see the young artist that she followed on social media in the flesh that she forgot her manners and kept him standing on the threshold.

'I have been commissioned by Lady Shilton to paint a landscape of your favourite view,' he explained.

Fiercely independent, Poppy did not like charity, but she did like Daniel's work and she was torn between indignation and pleasure. She looked into the young artist's earnest, enthusiastic face and chose pleasure.

'Where are my manners!' she exclaimed. 'I'm sorry, please come in. I'm just so shocked.'

'I hope it is a nice shock,' he said hesitantly. 'It is to be a retirement present.'

Trust Tonita, Poppy thought, to find a clever excuse for doing what she had every intention of doing anyway.

'It's a wonderful surprise,' she replied truthfully. 'Can I get you anything? Tea? Coffee?'

'No thanks,' he laughed. 'I don't drink coffee or tea and I'm being put up at La Grande Cour: I feel like I've been fattened up for Christmas, I never stayed anywhere like that in my life and I can promise you, I used up every available bit of body space at breakfast.'

Poppy laughed, 'I can believe it.'

'So if it's all right with you, I'd like to get going as soon as possible so I can get in a full day on the mountain.'

Poppy knew, from Daniel's social media posts, that he preferred to paint his landscapes *in situ* and so, having shown him some photos of her favourite viewpoint in summer, they set off together armed with touring skis, skins and Daniel's painting equipment.

They took the cable car up to the closest point and then skinned to the spot. Daniel looked most strange with a huge canvas loaded on his back but he promised her that he normally carried three and that he was so used to it he didn't even notice they were there.

'I can see why you don't have any winter shots of it,' Daniel laughed as she outlined her favourite view, still sitting very much in the centre of a big snowfield just below one of the main ski areas. The spot was set in a deceptively steep hollow: the local skiers knew not to venture there but any visiting tourist thinking they had found some untouched snow, would soon find out why the snow was untouched, and have plenty of time to regret their mistake as they pole-pushed the long uphill climb out of it. But in summer, it was on Poppy's favourite walk – halfway up the trail to morning coffee at the Cabane Mont Grondère.

'But the lifts close today,' Poppy said. 'How are you going to get up here every day?'

'Oh, don't you worry about that. I have a bespoke bike. I can fit all my painting gear on that and then skin the rest of the way.'

'Electric I hope, for your sake.'

'I can fit a bit of assistance on the front wheel if I need it, yeah.'

He grinned cheerfully. It was clear that nothing could stop him when it came to painting mountains. Poppy watched him set up rapidly and start sketching the scene. It was amazing how quickly it became something recognisable as 'her view'.

Having agreed he could leave his equipment overnight at her flat, Poppy left him to it. He was clearly very self-sufficient. She phoned Tonita to give her a stern telling-off. Tonita just laughed, she could tell Poppy was delighted.

Tonita quickly changed the subject and updated Poppy on their return home, the installation of Angelica, Ruby and Leo in the dower house and reported that the children were looking forward to starting their new school.

'And they might actually get to study some poetry from this century!' she joked before asking Poppy to send her love to everyone.

For the next few days Daniel cycled up the mountain and often didn't return until dark. The evening light, he told her, was too beautiful to miss – it would be a 'close of day' painting, he told her before taking it back to his studio to make the final touches.

'Very appropriate,' she said. 'For a retirement gift.'

Thirty

Go out into the woods, go out. If you don't go out in the woods nothing will ever happen and your life will never begin.
Clarissa Pinkola Estés, *Women Who Run With the Wolves: Myths and Stories of the Wild Woman Archetype*

A few days later, Poppy and Johnny found themselves sitting on a train on an all-expenses-paid trip to The Netherlands, armed with a letter from the Swiss authorities should they be stopped. They also discovered they had been provided with two burly shadows who they assumed to be representing Prince Anwar's government.

'D'you think they've got guns?' Johnny whispered as they pulled out of Bern station with their valuable cargo hidden in an uncomfortable money belt around Johnny's waist.

'Yes,' Poppy answered. 'Diplomatic security staff are allowed to carry firearms under licence.'

'How do you know that?'

'I stumbled across it once when I was searching the internet for information about Geneva Airport. Did you know there is a whole floor of the carpark just for diplomatic staff?'

'No, but it doesn't surprise me – there are so many of them, someone from Geneva once told me according to the locals, the CD on all those number plates in their town stands for "Can't Drive". Are you sure you don't want me to come to the tulip place with you?'

Once their mission was over, Poppy was planning a trip to Keukenhof: it was prime tulip blooming time and it was a place she had always wanted to go.

'Yes, I am sure I don't want you to come with me.'

'That's a bit blunt.'

'You can handle it. Look, Johnny, I am going to be on the first train there and the last train back. I want to fully immerse myself in tulipmania, I want to wander, exalt, talk to strangers, question the producers. You know you don't really want to go and the last thing I want is you tagging along, dragging your heels and making me feel I have to cut it short.'

'Good!' he grinned, knowing that Poppy could also handle 'blunt'. He was happy that he had acquitted himself of an offer he felt obliged to make but not inclined to discharge. 'I will just wander the streets and visit coffee shops.'

Poppy smiled. They had known each other such a long time there was no need for pretence: Amsterdam also had attractions for Johnny that she could not share.

As soon as they arrived, they located the address given to them by Tonita and entered. They found they were expected. Following Tonita's instructions, they made the expert inspect the diamonds in front of them – rather a shock to both of them as neither of them had seen the beautiful gems until that moment.

The gentleman made some phone calls and some other people entered the room.

'I am surprised,' the dealer said. 'This is the consignment I was expecting in January. Where has it been all this time?'

Poppy and Johnny looked at each other, not knowing quite how to respond. Johnny thought quickly.

'Ah yes, it got held up.'

'You are not the courier I was expecting.'

'Ah no, he got held up too.'

'Where is Mr Gordon? I have been trying to contact him. He has been ignoring my calls.'

'Well, the truth is, he lost the combination to the safe.'

'He lost the combination to the safe?' The dealer looked at Johnny in disbelief.

'To be precise, he lost the person who had the combination to the safe.'

'And now this person and the combination have been found?'

'No, the safe had to be cracked.'

'Ah. But why so long, and why does Mr Gordon not bring them to me himself?'

Johnny was having to think fast.

'Mr Gordon is not well.'

'Not well?'

'No.' Here Johnny hesitated and took his time to work out how best to reply. He wondered how Reggie Kray would have reacted in this situation and suddenly inspiration struck.

'You see, Rory's careless ways got him into trouble, and now he's in a bad way.'

'How bad?'

'Very bad.'

'He is alive?'

'He is alive but you won't be seeing him again.'

The dealer looked truly perturbed.

'And so will you be my contact from now on?'

'Nah, this isn't my usual line of business, as you can probably tell. Mrs Smythe and I are just here to make sure that the deal finally gets done and that the people at the top get a fair price for their investment. I'm sure you'll be contacted by someone else in time.'

'I see. Mr Gordon doesn't usually travel with security officers.'

'Sorry?'

The dealer showed them a security camera display with the two protection officers outside the front door. Poppy was relieved and Johnny saw it as an occasion to apply a bit of pressure.

'The people at the top just want to make sure there are no more cock-ups.'

'And you know the value of the goods?'

'Oh yes. I have my instructions.'

The bidding opened at $13 million and they agreed on $15 million – the midway value consented to by Prince Anwar. They then sat in the room for a very uncomfortably long time until they received a phone call from Tonita to say that M. Darbellay, the best bank manager in the world, had confirmed receipt in the new Foundation's account.

They shook hands with the dealer and his companions and left as quickly as they could, trying not to show how eager they were to get away.

Outside the door they found that their two silent shadows had disappeared but a taxi was waiting with a sign in the window bearing the name MRS SMYTHE.

From that moment on, their all-expenses trip was notched up a level. They were booked into a five-star hotel with an unlimited wining and dining budget. Prince Anwar was clearly very relieved to be rid of Rusty and Rory's illegal purchase.

'Johnny, you were amazing!' Poppy collapsed onto the sofa in her room with a huge sigh of relief as Johnny rang room service and ordered two large gin and tonics.

'Thanks,' he said. 'I had to think on my feet a bit there.'

'You did really well, I was totally flummoxed when they said they had been waiting for those particular stones.'

'I didn't tell a single lie. I hope you noticed.'

'Yes, now that I'm out of there, I can laugh about it. You just presented the truth in a way that sounded really sinister.' Poppy imitated Johnny's cockney accent, 'Ees in a bad way: yer won't be seein 'im again.'

They both laughed.

'Although, you did invent that bit at the end about them being contacted by someone else.'

'No, I didn't. Someone else will contact them. There'll always be someone.'

'I swear, Johnny, you have inborn criminal instincts. Imagine, Rusty and Rory would have made a $5 million profit on those diamonds: are you sure you're not tempted to take over their business?'

'Nah,' he shook his head, opening the door for room service. 'I was shitting myself.'

Poppy had her moment of tulip heaven the very next day and the following they returned home, this time travelling first class.

'You're going to enjoy running this Foundation, Popps,' Johnny remarked.

'I hope I'm not doing all the work, you also have responsibilities,' she reminded him tartly.

'Nah, I'm not getting paid, I just get to choose who we dish out the dosh to.'

Johnny had been named applications assessor to the Foundation whose purpose was to distribute the money to Grondère's various associations and charities. Johnny was already contemplating with relish the corruptive benefits such a position would give him.

Prince Anwar was the patron of the Foundation and Tonita was the president but, in reality, Poppy, a salaried secretary and treasurer would be doing most of the daily administration. She was very grateful for the job, she had been worrying about being bored in retirement and the little salary would top up her monthly pension nicely. She smiled contentedly and picked up the menu.

'I could get used to this first class business. Shall we order lunch?'

Lucy was looking after Louie for Johnny while he was in The Netherlands. The temperatures were still low and the snow cover still as good as in the high season. She hoped that the melt would begin soon as she and Alain were now eager to move back into the Nid des Rossignols and Alain was keen to start the renovation work on the lower chalet while he had no major investigation on.

Lucy wondered if the secret Japanese-Alpine garden she had designed and planted around the chalet the previous summer and autumn had survived being buried for six months under its snowy winter blanket.

She decided to go and have a look and so, with Louie at her side, she walked up towards the chalet to check out if the snow had melted enough to allow access. When she finally reached the snow line on the old *bisse* path, she put on her skis and skinned up into the forest. It was a glorious day; a slight mountain mist hung in the folds and hollows of the hillside, but it would soon evaporate in the heat of the sun. The birds were singing noisily and, despite the snow still covering everything, Lucy felt things were moving underneath.

She reached the chalet in no time but it and the garden were still hiding under the snow so there wasn't much to investigate. She didn't feel she'd had enough exercise and so she decided to keep going further up. Past the wolf woman's chalet, now all boarded up and abandoned, and into the forest.

As she clicked her way uphill, delighting in all the spring sounds and smells, Louie started to growl. A horrible deep growl which transmitted real terror. On the path, 50 metres ahead of them, stood a large wolf watching them. Lucy's heart stopped.

I had forgotten about you, she thought.

Louie, shackles up and fur rigid, stood in front of Lucy ready to defend her. It would never be said of Louie that he ran from the enemy.

The wolf looked at Louie with disdain, then at Lucy. Her yellow eyes met Lucy's green eyes whereupon she nodded at Lucy and pointed her nose towards the valley beyond. Lucy felt something strange pass between her and the creature: it was as if they understood each other. She did not know how but Lucy knew the wolf was bidding her farewell, as a friend would. Poppy was right, she had never been in danger from this animal, it even seemed to like her. 'Goodbye,' she whispered.

Instinctively she knew that that was what the wolf had been waiting for: it turned and silently vanished into the undergrowth.

Lucy stood still for a long time and eventually realised she was crying. Relieved and sad in equal measure, she knew she would never see that particular wolf again and this time, she knew she could continue her tour and that she was in no danger.

Slowly continuing her climb she asked herself which type of wolf was more dangerous? Predators like Rory? Those awful men with their spiked champagne? Or the real thing? Which, if she had to see either again and could choose, would she pick? She concluded that, on the whole, she was in no more danger in the mountains amongst the wild animals than in the world of men below and would rather take her chances with the real wolf.

Suddenly she realised she was striding out with confidence. Her fears had evaporated with the morning mist and she knew that she would never again feel afraid roaming the mountains she loved.

Lucy looked down at Louie strutting proudly at her side.

'And *you* are a complete hero, Louie!'

He barked in confirmation.

She bent down and gave him a big cuddle and scratch. He knew he was a complete superstar – gun locator, body discoverer and now … wolf scarer. What other titles could he add to his long list of achievements?

Lucy realised how much she longed for her own hairy companion to share the mountains with. The yearning for a dog can be felt by another dog and Louie understood her wish.

It'll have to be fit for this one, he thought, I like a long walk but she does tend to overdo it.

That week, Sammy kept his promise to hold a small party so that everyone could pay their last respects to Rusty.

On the afternoon of the party, a small memorial service was held in the church in Pattier. Everyone who had known Rusty made the effort to attend and Lucy and Alain were there together with Blonnay and Sylvie.

It was short but touching, with Sammy giving the main address in his own honest style.

'None of us knew Rusty well and it turns out he was a bit dodgy,' he said. 'But he was part of our community – and quite a lot of us here are a bit dodgy – and we loved the old rogue, so here we are. Rusty has now entered the Grondère book of legends for falling off Le Monstre in a blizzard and accidentally endowing our community with a generous trust fund which will help all our local charities do their stuff. And so, wherever you are, Rusty, we won't forget you, mate.'

As they watched the committal of Rusty's ashes in the garden of remembrance, Lucy told the others that she had found out from Sammy why Alessandra Rosset had paid for the church service and the cremation.

'Apparently, before he was shipped back to the UK, Rory asked her to look after Rusty for him. The only person she knew who knew Rusty was Sammy so she asked him what she should do.'

'Love,' Alain said. 'That was the reason. She had it bad.'

'Well, she honours her promises, even if it means eating a little humble pie, so that's in her favour,' Blonnay commented.

'A little humbling,' Sylvie said, 'won't do her any harm.'

'It may even improve her image with the locals,' Lucy added. 'She was an object of terror before.'

'I have to admit though: it's going to take me a while to get used to thinking of Alessandra Rosset as a philanthropist.' Alain laughed.

'She'll soon bounce back, she's built of steel that woman,' Sylvie said astutely.

The party at the Rusty Grapes was attended by everyone who had known Rusty; Gluey Hughey was, of course, there with a big smile on his face and Lucy headed over to reassure him that she had kept his name out of it all. He pointed out to her that Sammy had commissioned a large portrait of Rusty by one of the local artists, it was surrounded by a beautiful wooden frame, with vines and grapes, dusted with a rusty finish. It was beautifully carved and could only have been Hughey's work: his own tribute to his old ski buddy. It hung on the wall by the large mirror that everyone in Grondère now knew had concealed the safe containing the diamonds, the proceeds of which would be financing all the local associations for years to come.

'How do they find out all this stuff?' Alain wondered out loud.

'Don't look at me,' Lucy asked, 'I'm often the last to know.'

'Ah, that Grondère grapevine,' Blonnay laughed. 'It is the most mysterious and effective disseminator of information I have ever come across.'

'Yes,' grimaced Alain. 'It is certainly a law unto itself.'

Carla Sturridge left her cell to go to choir practice for the last time. That day the choir was to perform for the prison officials as Letty Braythwaite, the choir's initiator and leader, would shortly be released. This was a depressing thought for Carla who had appreciated having someone from a respectable background and with cultured tastes to talk to. Although the choir would carry on – Letty had been most insistent about her legacy being continued – Carla did not think she would bother, as the new choirmaster was being brought in from the outside, and everything would be in French.

Carla's daughter, Genna, would also miss the choir. It had given her a chance to shine and had helped to somewhat revive her lagging spirits. Carla sighed. She still felt no regret about orchestrating her ex-husband's murder – just getting caught.

Carla had received two visits the previous day. The first was from that ghastly female police officer asking her to confirm that she had told her ex-husband about Tonita's gun. The officer had only given her the briefest of information about the gun falling into the wrong hands and being used to kill Tony Onion.

Carla had lied to the officer when asked if she knew how Lara had planned to use the gun. She omitted to mention that she had suggested to Lionel that it would be great if it could be used in some way to cause trouble for Tonita.

It was the second visit, from her ex-husband Lionel, that had provided her with more information and she had been sorry to hear how it had turned to tragedy for Lara's poor little misused sister.

But what really galled Carla was learning that Lucy Wilson had, once again, been instrumental in the undoing of her friend, Lara. That even little Milly Stanford had been corrupted by Poppy and her gang and betrayed the Grondère Diamonds. This was all too much to bear and she lost no time in telling Letty all about it. Letty had her own reasons for disliking Lucy and Poppy and listened in stony silence.

'This is a sorry tale, Carla. How tragic for Lara and her poor, poor sister.'

'If Orfilia killed Tonita's father, she was driven to it by his cruelty. No wonder that his daughter is so greedy and mercenary, look at the stock she comes from. No breeding!'

'Indeed.'

Neither Carla nor Letty were from the sort of backgrounds they liked to pretend but the irony of their words would never have occurred to them.

'That conniving little Lucy Wilson is leading her Swiss policeman boyfriend by the nose.'

'That's certainly the impression I got,' Letty agreed.

'And that awful Tonita has got her claws into my son and turned him against me.'

'I'm sure you're right: it isn't natural for a son to disown his mother. It's amazing how the most intelligent of men can be fooled by a cunning woman.' Again, Letty spoke with no sense of irony.

'And look at that Jodie girl, who stole your place: she sang at their wedding and got all the glory that should have been yours.'

Carla's words hit their target – Letty's shattered dreams and wounded pride.

'Look, Carla, I'm not hanging around when I get out of here. As soon as I can, I'm getting out of the country. I will be leading a very quiet existence back in the UK but, if I get the chance to make life uncomfortable for any of our mutual enemies, I promise you, I will.'

'Well, I shall be stuck in here, praying that you get that chance!'

'And if I can offer you some advice: don't give up the choir. You never know who it may lead into your path who may prove useful.'

It was mid-May when Daniel finished Poppy's painting. He delivered and hung it himself and he and Poppy stood back to admire it.

'It's stunning. Thank you.'

'Yes,' he replied without any attempt at false modesty, 'it's a good one.'

Poppy held up a bottle of wine. 'Now do you have time for a drink?'

'I do,' he laughed.

Epilogue

En ma Fin gît mon Commencement
In my End is my Beginning.

Mary, Queen of Scots' motto

Lucy and Alain were now installed in their summer chalet, high up near the entrance to the forest. May was always an unpredictable month in Grondère: if the previous spring had seen Grondère shrouded in mist and fog, this May it had seemed as if winter would never end. Long after the lift system had closed, regular snowfalls had kept the mountains white for much longer than usual. The residents of Grondère had continued skinning up the mountains and skiing down the ungroomed, empty slopes for weeks after the last visitors had departed, smugly congratulating one another on being the lucky ones, living in the mountains and being able to enjoy a private, extended ski season. But eventually, even the most hardened skier longs for a little summer warmth and colour and, by the time the big melt finally arrived, the novelty of living in a world of never-ending winter was wearing thin.

Spring arrived almost overnight towards the end of the month: a wide belt of high pressure settled in over the Alps and now the receding snow line could almost visibly be seen moving up the hillside.

The sudden rise in temperatures had led to many snow slides and avalanches and it had become too dangerous to go ski-touring. It was time for Lucy to put away her ski boots and to dust off her walking boots.

A few days remained before Lucy took up her new job at La Grande Cour and she didn't want to waste a moment. That Saturday morning, Alain had vanished early on the quad looking guilty. Lucy, smiling to herself at his inability to dissemble when he was plotting to surprise her, was planning to visit Poppy to see her painting. But, before she did, she wanted to head higher and have another, longer look at the little chalet in which Orfilia Frank had spent her winter.

The mountains were a sheath of shimmering silver as the sunlight sparkled upon the melting snow rushing downhill as if the water was in a hurry to make up for lost time. Water gushed out of every available aperture in rock and mountain pasture and filtered like tiny veins through the bare ground, trickling into brimming streams, rivers and waterfalls. From a distance it looked like Rivendell, Tolkien's Elven outpost, but close up the ground was saturated and the paths, sodden and muddy.

Lucy could smell burgeoning life in the air as she entered the deep shade of the forest. Fungal dampness had given way to a fresh, sappy odour of emerging leaves, juicy fungi and new bark. Small pink cone flowers from the overhanging larch trees were scattered on the ground like tiny jewels. It made her think of Tonita whose baby was now only a few weeks away: she knew how sometimes Tonita found inspiration for her jewellery in nature's patterns, so she stopped to take some pictures of the intricate detail to send to her.

The *bisse* had not yet been cleared and put into operation but it was full of warm, melted water and smelled like fresh compost. Happy and confident, Lucy strode out towards the empty little chalet. As she approached it, she felt a surge of pity and sadness for Orfilia and the misguided love for Tony Onion that had destroyed her fragile mind. It was the stuff, she thought, of classic love tales, like one of those operas that Jodie would be singing. Lucy wandered up to the small, wooden chalet expecting the shutters to be closed and the chalet to seem forlorn and unloved. To her immense surprise the shutters were open, the grey net curtains had been taken down, washed and were hanging to dry on the balcony railings. The balcony deck had been mopped and scrubbed and the windows were grimy no more but gleaming in the sunlight. Far from the aura of forlorn romanticism that Lucy had conjured up in her imaginings, the place sang out with unrestrained jollity.

Someone had placed some plant pots around the base of the chalet walls and there was a case of red pelargoniums ready to be planted up. On a nearby quad several sacks of soil were clearly destined for that purpose. What was really strange was that she recognised the quad – it was Alain's.

Just then a young woman appeared from the other side of the chalet and unloaded a large sack of soil from the quad, obviously about to start potting the flowers.

'Milly!'

'Lucy. Oh no, you've spoiled the surprise!' Milly pouted.

'Oh no I haven't, I promise you, Milly, I could not be more staggered!'

'I wanted to get the place all smartened up before finding an excuse to entice you up here for tea but, if you're surprised now, I suppose that's good.'

Lucy was laughing so much she had to sit on the chalet steps. 'Explain!' she commanded.

'Well, I needed a cheap place if I wanted to stay in Grondère for the summer and I had some inside knowledge that this place had recently been hastily vacated. I thought there might be a chance that Lara had already paid the rent for the summer and had not asked for a refund: I was right. The estate agent said they had offered a partial refund but she had told them to keep the money.'

'So they let you have it for nothing?'

'Almost. I just have to pay the bills and get the place spick and span again. Honestly, Lucy, it was in a disgusting state. Poor Orfilia had obviously never picked up a cleaning cloth in her life!'

Lucy, still astounded, just shook her head.

'Well Milly. You certainly have learned the ropes in one season.'

'Thanks to you. I figured if I was up here, I could keep an eye on you, in case you attract any more trouble and … you can keep an eye on me too and …'

'And?'

'Keep an eye on the place when I'm down at the farm.'

'Ah ha?'

'Early days. I don't want to rush it. In fact, I'm quite enjoying Christophe's old-fashioned courtship technique.'

'That's lovely news. I'm very happy for you.'

'I should have known I'd end up with a farmer. But this is better.'

'Because it's a farm in the Alps.'

Milly gave her the widest grin. 'The best of both worlds.'

'You said it.'

Leaving the wolf woman's chalet in a very different mood to the melancholic, reflective one she had been in on approaching it, Lucy headed downwards. The path downhill along the old *bisse* was slippery and boggy but the bright yellow button heads of coltsfoot had emerged from the mud and were lighting up the bare ground and earthy banks.

Lucy walked back past her own and Alain's chalet again and smiled at the empty parking space where the quad was usually parked. She had known Alain was up to something again this morning and this time she had caught him out in his subterfuge in helping Milly with her surprise. But she knew now that when he was being cagey it was only because he was preparing good surprises for her. Never again would she doubt him. She might, however, enjoy springing the surprise on him that she had discovered what Milly was up to. With sunshine on her face and in her heart, she bounced downhill towards Grondère.

As she reached the lower altitudes it seemed to her as if the natural world was competing in yellowness. Golden flowers of all shapes and sizes were heralding the arrival of summer and the ascendency of Helios. Damp paths and shady spots sported tufts of marsh marigolds and yellow archangels and, sprinkled across the pastures, were little sunbursts of buttercups, primroses, cowslips, bird's foot trefoil and daisies. Lucy knew all their names now, their properties and habitats and, however humble the plant, she loved each and every one of them. She drank in deep breaths of the mountain air and felt herself filled with its warmth and energy. Every season brings new joy, she said to herself, I wonder what this summer holds in store.

'It is stunning,' she sighed, admiring Poppy's painting with a mug of tea in her hand.

'Yes. When I can no longer make it up there, I will always be able to imagine I'm there. Tonita has been very kind to us.' Poppy said. 'But she didn't need to do all this. I feel a bit embarrassed if I'm honest. I could never offer her a gift of the same magnitude.'

'I was a bit uncomfortable about the house to start with, but it's not like she's playing the Lady Bountiful, she's just used her position and money to make our dreams come true. And isn't making dreams come true what any friend would do, if they could?'

'Yes, I would definitely buy you the world if I could. You're right, we must allow Tonita to share her good fortune.'

'And, you said yourself, that part of her happiness was down to us. I know you were joking but I bet she does think that. It's her way of saying thank you for being there.'

'Oh Lucy, you are wise beyond your years. But I hope it's a one-off, and she doesn't start making a habit of it. I don't want to feel patronised.'

'I think she knows when to leave off. And it's a beautiful painting, I could live with that on my wall.'

'Well, whatever you do, don't say that to Tonita.'

'No fear!'

Later that afternoon, Alain rang Lucy to say he was already home and was cooking up a feast. She raced home to find he was already at the chalet putting nibbles out on the bar.

'Are we expecting visitors?'

'Tommy told me he and Sally were in town so I asked them up for a drink.

Lucy smiled, she needn't have worried on account of her friends, he was clearly beginning to be so comfortable with them, he was inviting them over without asking her.

He grinned mischievously and nodded towards the table. A beautiful carved female wolf sat in its centre: she was sleeping peacefully, curled up under an overhanging, upturned tree stump. There could be no doubt as to whose work it was.

'She's beautiful!' she gasped. 'But Hughey's work is selling for a couple of hundred in the gallery! That's a very generous gift.'

'Maybe it's a grateful thank you for keeping your informant's name a secret?' he suggested.

Lucy blushed: she was not a proficient liar.

'I'm not saying anything,' she said.

'You don't have to, I worked it out ages ago,' he laughed.

'You knew all along?'

'I am a detective, you know. I have other resources, other than you and your army of informants, useful as you all are. I just had to find out who had access to a quad and had regularly been making weekly purchases of wood and groceries at the local supermarket.'

'But that could be any chalet host!'

'On Lara Stanley's account?'

'Oh, that's not very clever of them.'

'No, but then, Lara didn't actually plan for things to work out the way they did and so had no reason to suppose we would look into her grocery bill. We wouldn't have done if I hadn't wanted to just reassure myself. Don't worry, your secret's safe with me. Although how Gluey Hughey managed to end up working for that lot does puzzle me. He must be the only person in Grondère, other than Lara, to have known about Orfilia. Thank goodness he has a soft spot for you.'

'You don't think he was involved with their diamond smuggling, do you?'

'No, I don't. I'm guessing Rusty introduced him to Lara as someone who could run errands for her. His subsequent actions show that he didn't want to help conceal a criminal.'

'I think he's fundamentally good.'

'You think everyone's fundamentally good.'

'I wonder then why he was so scared of being found out.'

'I can answer that one for you.'

'Go on then.'

'Firstly she was paying him on the black, secondly Hughey's papers are not in order. He doesn't officially have the right to live here.'

Lucy looked concerned.

'Don't worry, the guy from the Population Office is going to help him sort that out. I think we owe Hughey a bit of leeway. Without him, we might not have found out about Orfilia and I don't think he meant to put you in danger. I believe that Hughey would never let anyone hurt you and so it's probably a good idea to keep him around.'

'Funny, isn't it? We all complain about his freeloading, but Grondère wouldn't be the same without him.'

'I'll take your word for that. And it's a very beautiful piece. He really is a craftsman of talent. We'll leave Hughey alone, I don't need to dig any deeper for my case and your Grondère grapevine is far too valuable to me to disturb its natural balance.'

Lucy grinned.

'Let's hope we never need it again.'

'Fingers crossed.'

'And I have also found you out today, Mr Detective!'

'You have?' He looked disappointed.

'Yes. I have discovered what your latest bit of subterfuge was about. Most kind of you to lend your quad to our new neighbour …'

'Ah.'

'Yes. Ah.' Lucy looked at him smugly. He looked back her with a similar expression on his face.

'Well, you clever little *fouine,* that's actually Milly's subterfuge, not mine.'

'Oh,' Lucy was taken aback.

'No, you haven't yet detected my secret, or should I say secrets.'

He just looked at her and smiled. But Alain could no longer wait to spring his latest surprise. He led her downstairs to the basement room where she stored all her foraged goods over the winter and slowly opened the door. In the centre of the floor sat a large cardboard box with holes in. It was moving and making little yelping noises.

'Nooooo!' she exclaimed in disbelief. He just smiled and nodded. She approached the box cautiously and lifted the lid. Inside, not one but two little bundles of black and white fur: two Welsh border collie puppies. It was love at first sight. She knelt down and lifted them out, placing them carefully on her knees but they clambered up her chest and licked her face enthusiastically, especially the little salty tears that were inevitably streaming down her cheeks. Alain sat on the floor and joined in the mutual love-in. The puppies crawled over them, widdling in the process but it didn't matter, nothing could dim the joy.

'Shall we go into the light?' Alain suggested after a while. They each gathered up a puppy and headed back to the lounge. The little creatures showed their natural intelligence and curiosity by gambolling about sniffing everything in their new home and returning every few seconds for a reassuring cuddle.

'How did you know? How did you know which breed?'

'I checked with Poppy. She said it was your dream dog, so I had the animal rescue people looking out for an opportunity. Then, just on the morning of the cow fights I got a call. The breeder had a heart attack and these two hadn't been placed. I had to get in quickly.'

'Oh. So you didn't get an unfair advantage then?'

'I may have had a bit of inside information, but I promise you I paid a fair price and the family, understandably distressed for other reasons, was very glad to be relieved of one problem. Nobody else seemed to be interested and if I can't occasionally get the odd perk in this job, that would be a shame.'

She smiled, 'What a lovely perk, rescuing puppies.'

'Apparently, they can be trained to hunt for truffles which I understand from Poppy is a priority.'

'Yes, whenever we mention dogs, Poppy says it's a condition for her dog-sitting. She'll have to take them somewhere else for truffles though: she won't have much success here.'

'Quite expensive training equipment too.'

'Oh, Poppy knows someone who truffle hunts.'

'I should have known. Ah well, as long as Poppy's happy.'

'I'm happy,' Lucy said, looking at him knowing that she had right there in that little chalet and, in her beloved Grondère, in the beautiful canton of Valais in the Swiss Alps, everything she could ever wish for. 'In fact, my heart feels like it's about to burst with happiness.'

'We don't want that,' came Poppy's voice as she entered the chalet, followed by Johnny, Louie, Tommy, Sally, Eddie and Émilie.

Their arrival was accompanied by the noise of an approaching quad and Alain looked up and winked at Lucy.

'Ah, that'll be my quad being returned.'

Lucy returned the wink as Milly joined the fray and they all crowded round taking turns to get a look at the new arrivals. Louie was there first and had a good sniff of the two newcomers. The little pups jumped up at him and he gave their ears a couple of friendly nips to make sure they understood who was leader of the pack: a message that was clearly understood and accepted with docility. Louie looked up at Alain with whom he had a special understanding and woofed his approval. These young lads will be able to keep up with Lucy and look out for her on the mountain, he seemed to say. As usual, Alain was the only person who seemed to understand. Alain thanked him with a scratch and a very meaty bone which Louie then took into the garden to chew on in private. Giving his approval was one thing, but he did not feel the occasion warranted sharing a bone.

The pups didn't seem interested anyway, they were busy being passed around, stroked and cuddled.

'What are they called?' Milly asked.

'I hadn't got that far,' Lucy replied. 'In fact, I haven't even worked out if they're boys or girls.

Poppy picked them up and examined their underparts.

'Both boys,' she told them. 'How about Bill and Ben?'

'Like the flowerpot men!' Tommy laughed.

'It's a bit dull, isn't it, surely we can come up with something better than that,' Sally said.

The next fifteen minutes were spent throwing names around but however clever or imaginative they were, they kept coming back to Poppy's initial throw-away suggestion.

'It's no good,' Lucy sighed. 'It's stuck. There's nothing we can do about it. How about it, pups? Are those your names? Bill and Ben?'

The two puppies, currently chewing at Tommy's socks, looked at her curiously and then ambled over to her.

'Bill and Ben, it is,' Alain smiled. 'Poppy's names win the popular vote. Would you all like to go into the garden?'

And they all moved outside, into the May sunshine, and admired the bright green valley below while Poppy and Milly negotiated first rights on dog-sitting duties. Somewhere inside a cork popped and, as the little dogs curled up exhausted and fell asleep on Lucy's lap, a clink of glasses was heard and Alain uttered the only word that can end any self-respecting Swiss whodunnit.

'*Apéro*?'

I felt my lungs inflate with the onrush of scenery – air, mountains, trees, people. I thought, 'This is what it is to be happy'.

Sylvia Plath, The Bell Jar

Acknowledgements

Thank you to everyone who helped me put this book together: Nicky Christie for the early edit, my fabulous review committee, Richard Adams, Moira Davison, Sarah Francis-Clarke, Lindsay Reuss and Christine Small. My reviewers are now starting to come up with their own plot suggestions: thank you Moira for the idea of planting a body under the White Snowflake building site. My brother, Richard, can't get enough of Blonnay and so I keep growing this character for him. The character list and glossary come to you courtesy of a request for clarity from Nicky Christie.

A huge thank you to Kirstie Swinnerton, who, I don't know how, interprets my stick drawings to produce lovely book covers exactly as I imagined them.

Proofreading is not only an acquired skill: it is an art. Without Nicky Christie and Tanya Freeman, I would have been humiliated more than once by mortifying typos that, fortunately, only they know about.

There really is a M. Darbellay working in a bank in Switzerland and I call him 'the best bank manager in the world' because he was instrumental in helping our local adaptive ski charity secure its first major donation.

Thank you also to the Police cantonale valaisanne and Police municipale de Bagnes for continuing to allow me to fabricate their actions without prosecution.

I have now lived in Switzerland for twenty years and it has been very good to me. Its beauty and the character and quirks of its inhabitants are a constant source of inspiration. I have found my place in the mountains and I am forever grateful to the wonderful resort of Verbier and the people who live there. Their lives, stories and personalities provide me with endless material for my tales.

Dotting the 'i's

I started this book during the first Coronavirus lockdown of March 2020. I had a long discussion with myself as to whether the world of Grondère should reflect this new reality: I decided it should not. We all need a place we can go to and escape reality and I decided to keep Grondère in this place. We were, after all, able to continue skiing in Switzerland during the second lockdown and this was a godsend in those difficult times, although we missed our overseas visitors.

The theme of wolves came to me from nowhere, or so I thought initially. Looking back, it was perhaps subconsciously inspired by a beautiful fiction-documentary called *The Snow Wolf: A Winter's Tale* by Fred Fougea. Shortly after I began writing, a wolf was sighted in the Val de Bagnes, the inspiration for the home municipality of Grondère. It also coincided with a vote on proposed revisions to the hunting law which would have altered the protected status of the wolf in Switzerland. These strange coincidences, of which life is so full, provided me with real time examples of the debates and arguments that this emotive issue evokes. Like Lucy, I do not know where I stand on this issue but I understand both sides of the debate and I believe this is a reflection of the uneasy relationship we humans will always have with creatures we fear.

Glossary of French / Swiss Words

Abricotine *A clear brandy made from apricots.*

Apéro *Also in the English dictionary. Early evening drink: essential part of Swiss / French life.*

Bisse *A narrow man-made ditch built in C17th to channel water, by force of gravity, to agricultural areas subject to drought. Often the subject of violent disputes between different parishes.*

Bol *Bowl.*

Bosse *Bump / mogul.*

Bouquetin *Ibex or mountain goat.*

Cabane *A mountain refuge / restaurant.*

Café de l'amitié *A wooden bowl with multiple drinking spouts filled with steaming, spicy and very alcoholic coffee served at the end of a meal.*

Caquelon *Heavy metal fondue pan.*

Col *A mountain pass.*

Canton *A member state of the Swiss Confederation.*

Colline *Hill.*

Commune *A local municipality.*

Désalpe *When the cows are brought down from the mountain pastures in autumn.*

Dôle Blanche *A light rosé wine made in Valais.*

Fendant *A white wine made in Valais with the Chasselas grape.*

Fouine *A stone-marten, common in Switzerland they live in roofs, chew on cables and make a racket. They are synonymous with nosiness.*

Génisse *Heifer: the young cows have their own cow fight category.*

Grappe *A bunch (usually of grapes).*

Hameau *Hamlet.*

Herens *Black cows indigenous to Valais. They naturally lock horns and fight to establish the hierarchy (the 'queen') of the herd – giving rise to the traditional cow fighting competition.*

Inalpe *When the cows return to the mountain pastures in spring.*

Kriminalpolizei *Swiss German equivalent of Police judiciaire.*

M. *Abbreviation for 'monsieur'.*

Mme *Abbreviation for 'madame'.*

Patente *Diploma required to run a business in the hospitality industry. Exams on accountancy, relevant legislation, and* employment rights and salaries. *A good standard of French is necessary to acquire this qualification.*

Petite Arvine *A white wine made with a grape indigenous to Valais.*

Police judiciaire *The police department responsible for investigating serious crime, including murder.*

Procureur *The public officer who heads an initial criminal investigation and determines when a prosecution can be made.*

Qui craint le grand méchant loup? *Who's afraid of the big, bad wolf?*

Raclette *A semi-hard cheese from Valais, traditionally melted under a burner and served on hot potatoes.*

Repaire *A hide / retreat.*

Reine *Queen, the title awarded to a cow that wins cow fights. All the participants in the big competitions are 'reines' in their own right, having already won 'heats' in other competitions or on the mountain. Sometimes the term is used globally to refer to all Herens cows.*

Rösti *Roasted pancake of grated potato.*

Rossignol *Nightingale.*

Médaille de chocolat *Fourth place (chocolate medal).*

Seasonnaire *Seasonal worker. This is a bastardisation of the French word 'saisonnier' and is not yet in many English dictionaries. As there is no official spelling, I favour the double 'n' as it is closer to the French.*

Sommet *Summit.*

Valais *The real Swiss canton in which the fictional Grondère is situated. Valais is home to many ski resorts and perhaps the most independent-minded and individualistic people of the Swiss Confederation.*